PRAISE FO

The Late-Night Witches

"Magical mayhem, heart, and humor, Auralee Wallace's *The Late-Night Witches* is filled to the brim with authentic family dynamics, self-discovery, and an unforgettable Halloween showdown. You'll fall deeply in love with this enchanting and cozy book, so much so that you'll want to return to it every fall just to experience it again!"

—Breanne Randall, *New York Times* bestselling author of *The Unfortunate Side Effects of Heartbreak and Magic*

"A spellbinding adventure of real heart and humor, *The Late-Night Witches* is packed with fun nostalgia, a picturesque autumn setting, and lovable characters that I was rooting for from the very first jack-o'-lantern. I loved spending Halloween with the Beckett witches!"

—Lucy Jane Wood, author of *Rewitched*

"Wallace (*In the Company of Witches*) infuses humor, magic, and surprise into this well-crafted suburban fantasy . . . Wallace's wonderfully realized characters overcome the exasperation of child-rearing, embrace the bonds of family and friendship, and chuckle through their madcap adventures. Readers are sure to be entertained."

—*Publishers Weekly*

"This fantasy novel has its scares but is ultimately very cozy—the kind of fun, exciting fantasy that warms readers' hearts."

—*Booklist*

"Wallace's wild romp of a Halloween broom ride combines painful family legacies and found sisterhoods with the lost legacies of Hazel Beck's Witchlore series and Andrea Jo DeWerd's *What We Sacrifice for Magic*, plus *Buffy the Vampire Slayer*. Recommended for fans of any of the above or of the recent spate of contemporary witchy novels."

—*Library Journal*

"I picked this for readers who love witchy suburban fantasies with laugh-out-loud mom-power moments; Wallace's blend of snack-fueled magic and family camaraderie made me giggle, cheer, and feel like I could conquer any Halloween monster—especially if I had juice boxes on hand." —BiblioLifestyle

"This book is great! Witches, vampires, magical cats, and humor all rolled into one. A great end-of-the-summer book."

—Red Carpet Crash

TITLES BY AURALEE WALLACE

EVENFALL WITCHES B&B MYSTERIES

In the Company of Witches

When the Crow's Away

The Late-Night Witches

The Haunted Librarian

The Haunted Librarian

Auralee Wallace

Ace
New York

ACE
Published by Berkley
An imprint of Penguin Random House LLC
1745 Broadway, New York, NY 10019
penguinrandomhouse.com

Book design by Ashley Tucker
Interior illustrations by Vikki Chu

Library of Congress Cataloging-in-Publication Data

Names: Wallace, Auralee author
Title: The haunted librarian / Auralee Wallace.
Description: First edition. | New York : Ace, 2026.
Identifiers: LCCN 2026008746 (print) | LCCN 2026008747 (ebook) |
ISBN 9780593818572 trade paperback | ISBN 9780593818589 ebook
Subjects: LCGFT: Paranormal fiction | Novels
Classification: LCC PR9199.4.W3423 H38 2026 (print) | LCC PR9199.4.W3423 (ebook)
LC record available at https://lccn.loc.gov/2026008746
LC ebook record available at https://lccn.loc.gov/2026008747

First Edition: October 2026

Printed in the United States of America
1st Printing

The authorized representative in the EU for product safety and compliance is Penguin Random House Ireland, Morrison Chambers, 32 Nassau Street, Dublin D02 YH68, Ireland, https://eu-contact.penguin.ie.

For all those who like books more than people . . .
but try hard to make exceptions

THE HAUNTED LIBRARIAN

1

The only thing that you absolutely have to know
is the location of the library.
—Albert Einstein, attributed

FOR AS LONG AS AMELIA BATES COULD REMEMBER, she wanted only one thing from life: to be a librarian.

Libraries had always been her natural habitat. Aside from being surrounded by the intoxicating vanilla scent of decomposing lignin and the whispers of long-dead authors, Amelia relished knowing that contained within those bookish walls were so many lives to be lived! Lives filled with romance, excitement, and adventure. The thought alone was thrilling, especially for someone like her, who would never be fortunate enough to experience much of anything due to an extremely rare condition that made her, well, not *normal.*

But she had come to terms with all that a long time ago.

In light of this love, it perhaps wasn't all that surprising that by the time Amelia was eleven, she had read all of Jane Austen and Murasaki Shikibu; the complete works of the Brontës by twelve; and most of Mirza Ghalib and Charles Dickens by thirteen. Despite her best efforts, *Bleak House* had stretched into her fourteenth year.

After that, her pace really picked up.

What did she need from the rest of the world when there were entire universes waiting for her in libraries? No, forget acquiring possessions or piling up great achievements. Never mind traveling or learning new hobbies. All Amelia Bates needed to achieve her happily ever after was a quiet life wandering through dusty shelves laden with books.

Given all this, it was actually quite mind-boggling that she was about to be late for an unexpected, though very welcome, job interview at her dream library.

A chilling blast of wind hit Amelia as she rushed down the steps of her new apartment above the fish shop on the outskirts of a small village not too far from Cavendish, Prince Edward Island. The early warm fall weather had hung on for as long as it could, but now the cold, dark end of autumn had them in its grip. She grunted lowly with disgust. Amelia did not like fall—early or late. One could even say she hated it. Somehow its presence always seemed to be laughing at her. Like right now, as she was peering down at her watch, struggling to see its face in the deepening gloom, she could almost hear *autumn* cackling gleefully at the seconds ticking past.

She had to hurry.

Clutching the hood of her jacket to her throat, Amelia rushed for the boardwalk on the other side of the shop only to be greeted by the sight of giant bruising clouds tumbling over a dark ruffled sea. *No!* Those clouds weren't supposed to be there! Amelia checked herself over as though she might find an umbrella hidden on her person as another gust of wind spattered raindrops over the lenses of her glasses. The forecast had said it would be clear!

Silly meteorologists, they clearly hadn't factored Amelia's job interview into their predictions. Of course there would be a sudden storm. Actually, no. There was no escaping it. She was going to be late, and she had no one to blame but herself.

Inconceivable.

Amelia had never wanted so badly to be on time for anything in her life, and she knew exactly how long it took to get to the library because she had practiced the route seven times. But as was the case with all well-laid plans, things had gone awry. Her wardrobe, in this instance. She had intended to leave ten minutes early, and had in fact been all ready to go, but just as she was about to depart, she realized the perfect outfit she'd selected suddenly didn't seem so perfect. Three times she had changed from her twill skirt to herringbone pants, then back again, and she still wasn't sure if she'd made the right choice. How quickly those ten minutes had disappeared, and now with the wind, she'd be lucky if she made it on time for her interview, because with every step she took forward, the storm was pushing her back by half.

Suddenly, the sole of her boot slipped over the slick wood of the boardwalk. Amelia jerked to remain upright, barely managing to stay on her feet. Once she had her balance, she placed her hand on her chest. That had been close, but thankfully no harm had been—

Snap!

Metal slapped painfully against the nape of Amelia's neck. *Her hair clip!* The sudden jerk had caused it to explode. Masses of curls swelled inside the hood of her jacket, allowing the wind to catch hold and push it back. Amelia's hair swirled as she struggled to yank the hood down over her head once more. This was terrible. Wild and wind-tossed was not the professional look she was going for, and things were only going to get worse the longer she was out here. Maybe if she stayed extra light on her feet, she could run . . . except she couldn't run because there was somebody in her way.

Two somebodies, actually, glowing in the dim light.

Amelia squinted through her rain-spattered glasses, making

out the iridescent couple holding hands up ahead as yet another blast of wind shook her balance. Of course they'd be here. They traversed the boardwalk every night as far as Amelia could tell, always wearing cloaks, always carrying lanterns. *Always* looking so in love.

This was the last thing Amelia needed. She was in a hurry, and they were gliding along in front of her without a care in the world. And it wasn't as though she could go around them. If she did, they'd notice, and she couldn't risk stirring up that kind of trouble.

She had to remember the rules.

Amelia switched from her light hurried steps to determined slapping footfalls on the boardwalk, hoping the couple would hear her gaining on them and clear a path. As she approached, she caught the woman's voice carried on the wind. "It is another beautiful night, my love."

Beautiful? Amelia scoffed internally.

"Not nearly as beautiful as you," the man replied, and kissed his partner's hand. "But can you feel it?"

The woman nodded, and they both looked off to the sleepy fishing village glinting dully in the storm.

"It is a most disturbing sensation," she said. "I fear for those who fall within its grasp."

Disturbing sensation? Fearful grasp? The village looked perfectly fine. What were they talking about? And more importantly, why weren't they getting out of her way?

There was no other choice. Amelia was just going to have to walk right through them. She had to . . . but she hated doing that! Maybe if she could get their attention, they'd move. Amelia coughed, then quickly averted her gaze. *Rule one: Don't look at them.* Out of the corner of her vision, Amelia caught the man's head turn.

"Ah! The storm has routed the pumpkin-haired fish wench."

Amelia's eyes widened. Thankfully, her head was still turned. *Pumpkin-haired fish wench?!* Admittedly, her hair was red, and yes, she did now live in an apartment above a fish shop, but—

Keep calm and carry on, Amelia.

The rational side of her brain—which she referred to as Rational Amelia—was right. She didn't have time for this.

The pair slowed, broke hands, and stepped to either side of the path. Amelia turned her best blank stare forward and kept on at her steady pace. At least they were getting out of the way, but as she reached the point between the two, her boot slipped again, sending her knee crashing to the boardwalk and her foot sliding into the woman's cloak. A deep cold ran up Amelia's calf.

The woman gasped. "Heavens, girl, are you sound?"

Rule two: Do not listen to them.

If only she had been following that rule when the *pumpkin-haired fish wench* comment had occurred. But rule number two had always been of the easier-said-than-done variety. And *was* she all right? Amelia was moving to push herself up when she saw the damage that had been done through her tangled masses of hair. *NO!* Her woolen tights. The woolen tights that she'd bought solely for this job interview because they looked so *librarian*! Now a brown spiderweb covered her knee. The fates had spoken. She should have worn the pants.

The man chuckled. "She is well, my tender heart. Not a drop of blood."

She was not well! Did he not see her tights?

"I fear her stockings are ruined," the woman observed.

Thank you!

"And her hair is lovely," she added.

Also thank you.

"By God, there's enough of it," the man replied. "An entire ship could be lost in those tresses."

What?! What did that even mean? It didn't matter. *They* did not matter. Amelia pushed herself up to her feet, found her balance, yanked her hood back down, and lurched onward in quick steps.

"You are terrible, my dear," she heard the woman say behind her. "She's a fine-looking young thing. Quite lovely."

"Ah, but I see only you," the man answered. "For your beauty bewitched me the moment . . ."

Mercifully, the rest of the statement was swept away in the bitter wind.

Amelia picked up her pace once again to a light but still dangerous jog. What was the worst that could happen? She wrecked the other knee? Just then her step faltered. *Why?* Why did she have to put that sort of thing out into the universe?

Thankfully, she was almost there.

Amelia spotted the branch in the boardwalk that led to the village's main street. She made the turn, snatching blurry glimpses of the hamlet in the dim light. By day, the collection of turquoise, pink, and yellow cottages felt quaint, cheerful, but now that night had fallen, the atmosphere had shifted. The street's potted chrysanthemums appeared gray and spiky in the gloom and the ornamental fishing nets draped over the salt-worn buildings greedy and grasping, as though ready to ensnare anyone who dare pass by. Most unsettling, though, was the season's final scarecrow affixed to a streetlamp. Ordinarily it was quite welcoming, but in the murky shadows of the sudden storm, its warm smile had curved into a sly grin.

Focus, Amelia.

A gust of wind shook her balance. Yes, focus. Here she was getting swept up in silly flights of fancy when she should be using this walk to mentally rehearse her answers for her job interview.

Amelia raced down the sidewalk that led to the far end of the village and the access road that would take her up to her destination atop the small seaside cliff. When she made it to the foot of the cobblestone drive, she peered up the slope, and her heart jumped at the sight of the building towering against the near-black sky.

The library.

The building was constructed in 1873—as was indicated on the engraved copper plaque beside the door—and had originally been a courthouse, replete with jail cells, but it had served many purposes since that time. It was a beautiful three-story redbrick structure with a mansard roof that was lined with black iron railings that poked up at the clouds. Over the last few days, Amelia had relished the sight of the library on more than a few occasions, but tonight, seeing its roman arched windows glowing with buttery light, she couldn't help but think it had never looked more welcoming.

Unfortunately, the building also had a clock right beneath its central cupola.

Its hands nearly made a straight line from the twelve to the six. *Nearly.* She was five minutes late. It was such a small parcel of time, but she could practically hear a death knell, clanging away any hope she had of getting this job.

When the email from the library had arrived in her inbox, she couldn't have been more surprised. Yes, she had recently graduated with an MLS degree, and she had given her contact information to the alumni association, but she had never expected to receive a nighttime job posting with a personalized invitation to apply. Not from this library. Amelia had grown up in Charlottetown, but it was famous province-wide. In total, Prince Edward Island had twenty-five public library branches, a university library, a few legislative and specialized research centers, and, of course, a multitude of school libraries, but this wondrous place had evolved outside all those clear delineations. It was the kind of library librarians dreamed about—large, historic, and completely unexpected in a small village. It was also rumored to hold a trove of uncatalogued diaries, wartime letters, maps, newspapers, and rare books of untold historical value.

Amelia could only hope there weren't too many applicants. While the library was large, the location was remote. That certainly hadn't discouraged her though. The night the posting arrived, she booked the room above the fish shop online, sight unseen. The host insisted on a month, which was more than Amelia wanted, given she did not yet in fact have the job and it would require all her meager savings, but there weren't many listings, and the price was incredibly reasonable, so she had gone ahead. Once she arrived, she realized the reasonable price was likely a reflection of the very unreasonable smell.

Amelia sped past the small parking lot toward the steps of the front entrance. As she neared, a voice called out, "You don't want to go in there, ducky."

Seriously? More gho—

Don't even think the word.

Yes, even the word put Amelia in a bad mood.

Out of the corner of her eye, she spotted a man in a fisherman's cap and heavy overcoat standing by a gnarled oak tree. His face floated aglow in the smoke of his pipe, its spicy scent threading the wind. Amelia strode past, keeping her pace.

And he was wrong. She very much did want to go in.

"I'm warning ya. Something foul has been churned up from deep inside those walls."

Amelia rolled her eyes inwardly. Why did *they* always speak to people when they knew an answer would never come? Boredom probably. The sound of rainwater rushing through the drainpipe anchored to the building greeted Amelia as she navigated over the last of the slippery cobblestones. She grabbed the railing of the front steps and then climbed her way up to the heavy wooden door. When she lifted her head, all she could see was the sign.

CLOSED.

Don't panic. The sign had to be for the general public, not for her, a prospective employee. She really wasn't that late.

Amelia almost reached for the door handle, but then stopped, smoothing her hair back from her face with her palms and then grabbing the bulk of it with both hands. As she arched, she felt her hair clip slide underneath her sweater and travel down her back, between her shoulder blades, until it caught on her bra. *Marvelous.* Now her hair would not only be pumpkin colored but pumpkin shaped. She yanked her hood roughly over her head again. Maybe she could leave her jacket on for the interview . . . because that wouldn't be the least bit strange.

There was no time for this.

Amelia grasped the door handle and pressed down with her thumb. *Locked!* Is this what happened? Five minutes late and you're fired? Or not hired? No, it couldn't be. The email she had received from the library's manager, Rosalinda, had been so friendly. She knocked on the door as strongly as she could with her cold, aching knuckles, but the heavy wood swallowed the sound.

Nothing.

She then rapped on one of the thin glass windows running down either side of the door.

"The hatches 'ave been battened," the sea captain by the tree shouted. "Best be on your way."

No, she would not be on her way. She had a job interview!

Amelia knocked on the glass again.

"Go home, lass!"

He was not helping. And she really wanted to tell him that. But then she would be breaking rule number three. *Do not speak to them.* That was the most important rule of all.

This could not be happening.

What if Rosalinda had already gone home?

What was she supposed to do?

What *could* she do? She'd missed her chance. Amelia's shoulders slumped as she turned to leave . . . just as the door opened, pouring warm yellow light out in the darkness. "Ms. Bates?"

Amelia spun around. "I am so terribly sorry I'm late."

"Don't be silly," a woman said, her voice ripened by age. She shuffled back, making a path for Amelia to come inside. "You're right on time."

2

"Do you want an adventure now . . . or
would you like to have your tea first?"
—J. M. Barrie, *Peter and Wendy*

THANK YOU. THANK YOU. THANK YOU.

Amelia didn't know exactly who she was thanking—her prospective boss probably, for her less-than-rigorous attention to time—but regardless, she was overcome with gratitude.

After enduring the autumnal hellscape outside, the sudden warmth of the library sent a rush of chills racing over Amelia's body, forcing her to close her eyes. Then she remembered she wasn't alone. She blinked. Unfortunately, Amelia couldn't see anything through her fogged lenses.

"You poor thing, you must be chilled to the bone."

"Not at all," Amelia replied, quickly rubbing her glasses on her sleeve. "I'm fine." She suppressed another shiver.

"One never knows how the weather will be this time of year," the woman said. "I'm Rosalinda, the library's manager. It is delightful to meet you."

Amelia forced a smile. *Delightful* felt like a lot of pressure.

Rosalinda had to be in her seventies, maybe even eighties, but her eyes had the enthusiastic glint of a child's, and her movements, though small, were spry. She wore a burgundy shirtwaist dress on her small frame, a cozy cardigan, and a strand of pearls with matching earrings.

"Oh my, what happened to your knee?"

Amelia looked down at her destroyed tights. "It's a little slippery out there."

"You poor, poor dear," she said. "Let me take that wet coat of yours."

Amelia could just hug this woman—*figuratively*, she was not a hugger—but that didn't mean she wanted to hand over her jacket. She realized she couldn't drip her way through the library, but . . .

Amelia pulled down her hood, and Rosalinda's eyes widened.

. . . her hair.

"My curls don't always behave when it's damp."

"And why should they?" Rosalinda remarked, reaching her fingertips out to touch the cloud before thinking better of it. She probably didn't want her hand to be lost alongside the ship in there. "They were made to turn heads."

Yes, and, unfortunately, they often did. It was a cruel irony, given that attention was the last thing life had taught Amelia to want.

Just accept the compliment.

"I— Thank you," she said, shimmying out of the jacket.

"Let me hang this up." The older woman scurried over to a coatrack near the door, placed the jacket over a hook, and then hurried back to give Amelia's elbow a squeeze. "You're so cold. Would you like some tea?" She continued before Amelia could answer. "To be honest, I love this time of year. There's something about that first kiss of icy air that's so exciting, almost mischievous." Her eyes shone with delight as she led Amelia through the foyer. "Don't you think?"

"Yes, I—yes."

The words had sounded about as genuine as they felt. Amelia didn't enjoy lying, but given who she was and what she could do, it was a necessity. Besides, how could she say otherwise? Rosalinda clearly was an autumn lover, and the walls of the library's front entry were literally covered with black cats, witches, vampires, Frankenstein monsters . . .

Amelia eyed a blob-shaped white construction paper cutout with two black eyes and a gaping black mouth.

Ugh. Those too.

Maybe if she were some other Amelia living a different life, she would have been able to enjoy the crunch of leaves beneath her boots or the scent of woodsmoke and overripe apples. She could theoretically see how it might be nice to ride a bike over the island's red-dirt roads lined by golden cornfields or maybe sit beneath a blanket by a campfire at night. It was even possible that *that* Amelia was the type to *want* to carve pumpkins, give out candy, and bob for apples—if people still did that sort of thing—but the point was, she was not that Amelia.

Rosalinda didn't need to know about any of that though. In fact, she could not know about any of that because, if she did, well, it might lead to questions, and questions would lead to lies and flimsy excuses, and that might lead to all this being over, which absolutely could not happen because . . .

Amelia lost her train of thought as she followed Rosalinda into the great, cavernous body of the building.

Because this library was now her favorite place in all the world.

The sensation of being enveloped by thousands of books forced a sigh from Amelia's lips.

"So let me tell you a little bit about the job," Rosalinda said. "The nighttime position includes checking out books and helping visitors find resources in the last hours we're open, but, really, there are only ever a few people who drop by in the evening. Then once the library is closed, there's reshelving returns, tagging new books, and updating the catalogue. That sort of thing. After that, if it's not too late, upstairs, there's boxes filled with donated books, maps, and genealogy documents that need to be—"

"Yes," Amelia said before she could stop herself.

Rosalinda raised her brow.

"Yes. Those are things I would enjoy." And they were, with perhaps the small exception of helping visitors. Interacting with people wasn't a strength of Amelia's *per se*, but Rosalinda had said it herself. There would only be a *few* people. That was why this nighttime position was so perfect for her.

"Well," the older woman said with a magnificent smile, "that's wonderful."

"Yes." And that had sounded strange. A tingle of heat touched Amelia's cheeks. Her lack of social experience was already seeping through. "I'm sure you have many applicants who feel the same way." And why did she say that? Why was she helping the other candidates? Amelia forced a smile.

"Oh, there are no other applicants," Rosalinda answered. "We didn't think it was necessary."

What?! Why? How could that be? Before Amelia could formulate any of those questions into actual speech, Rosalinda said, "Would you mind waiting here for just a moment, dear? I need to . . ." She looked around and wandered away.

The only applicant?

A swell of excitement filled Amelia's chest, a swell she quickly squashed. Just because she was the only applicant didn't mean she had the job.

Once Rosalinda disappeared into the stacks, Amelia took quiet steps to the nautical-compass inlay in the center of the marble floor so that she could take in the shelves from every direction. Books, books, and more books. Two sweeping curved staircases, one on either side of the room, raced up to the second-floor mezzanine, where there were more books still. Just as there should be.

Amelia wanted this so badly, to be here, in this space, living this life. This was where she wanted to be. And now that she knew she was the only applicant . . .

Don't get ahead of yourself, Amelia.

True. She couldn't get carried away, but it was so difficult!

And there was so much she wanted to explore!

Like the study corner in the reference section. Each table there had a lamp with a green-glass shade. She could practically feel the *click* of their beaded chains. Amelia stepped in another quarter turn. And there, by the far wall. She could only catch a glimpse of the cozy nook through the stacks, but there were old leather armchairs by windows with a view of the sea. The perfect place to read away an hour or two. Just then the wind roared, shaking the glass of the old windows. *Marvelous. Simply marvelous.* Amelia turned again, her gaze falling on the children's area. All the little tables with the even littler chairs were adorable—and the carpet beside them divided up into squares with each letter of the alphabet? Inspired. That had to be where children gathered for story time. It was all so perfect.

Maybe too perfect.

Here Amelia had been allowing herself to be entranced by library magic when she should have been doing reconnaissance. Not being surprised was half the battle. Amelia scanned the passageways between the shelves. *Clear.* She looked up again to the second floor. Also clear as far as she could see. She glanced around the room once more. Rosalinda was still nowhere to be seen, so Amelia slowly bent at the knees until she was resting on the backs of her heels. She scanned the spaces underneath the furniture and shelves. Nothing. Her shoulders relaxed, and she rose. This was good. If the library hadn't been clear, she would have handled it, of course. It wouldn't have been the first time. But it was clear, perfectly clear. Actually, the library itself was perfect. Full stop. There was not a single thing she could think of that would make the library any more—

Movement from a dimly lit room off to the side of the circulation desk caught Amelia's eye. Inside was a tall, handsomely proportioned man with glasses and tousled sandy-colored hair leaning over a table. His shirt sleeves had been rolled up his well-toned forearms, and he had a pencil clenched between his teeth, causing small striations of muscle to appear at the corner of his jaw.

Perfect.

Amelia took a few cautious steps to get a better look, her heart picking up a new thudding beat.

Who is that?

And what was he doing? She couldn't be certain, but he appeared to be attending to a book. Not writing, but scraping something from a page with . . . a scalpel?

"You've found him."

Amelia jolted as Rosalinda came to her side.

"I should have known he'd still be working." Affection filled her tone. "When he isn't keeping the library together, he restores old books. Cookie?" Rosalinda held out a tin filled with baked goods.

"He?" It came out as a whisper. "Cookie?"

"Simon, our head librarian," Rosalinda answered. "And oatmeal raisin."

Amelia took a cookie, but suddenly her mouth felt quite dry.

The man straightened, eyes still on the table, brow still furrowed in concentration, pencil still clenched between his teeth. He reached for the tome before him, and Amelia tensed. A person's handling of books said a great deal about their character. She didn't think she could work with someone who was, say, a casual breaker of spines.

Simon lifted the large book from the table, carefully cradling its back in his hand. He then brought the opened pages up to his sight line, searching for some imperfection Amelia certainly could not see. Once satisfied, he lowered the book again to chest height and brushed the pages lightly but briskly with his fingertips When he was through, he rested it gingerly back on the table, then pressed the pages on the left against the front cover with his palm so that he could fold the lot over with minimal force. Once closed, he slid his hand free.

Such care. Such attention. It was *masterful.*

"Yoo-hoo! Simon!" Rosalinda called out. The man didn't react, making her scoff. "He gets so focused sometimes."

Amelia nodded dumbly.

"Simon!"

This time the man's head turned until his gaze found Amelia's. For a second, he froze, eyes widening behind his glasses . . . then the pencil snapped in his mouth. He quickly brushed the splinters from his lips, then came around the table, smiling sheepishly. "I'm so sorry," he called out, giving Rosalinda a questioning look. "I didn't realize anyone was still here." He walked through the doorway but got tangled in a Halloween garland dangling across the head of the entryway. He swatted at the string, but that only served to further tangle its hold. Finally, he stopped and pulled the lot from his neck before unceremoniously throwing it into a small garbage pail.

Amelia had never related to a man more deeply.

Simon then brightened his smile and carried on toward them.

As he neared, the strangest sensation came over Amelia, one she had never experienced before. The only thing she could compare it to was stumbling into a rabbit hole much like Alice on her way to Wonderland. Except she hadn't really stumbled. The man's kind, intelligent amber-green eyes had knocked her in.

You can't know he's intelligent or kind by his eyes.

Rational Amelia was right. She couldn't know that. Regardless, the lines of his face were also quite mesmerizing. Both strong and welcoming. Dedicated-looking too. She could only imagine they were born of forceful concentrated effort devoted to . . . she did not know yet, but he seemed like a man of passions.

You can't know that either.

True. And yet down, down she went.

Amelia noted his tousled hair was certainly unruly but not like hers. No, his loose waves were windswept like he had just returned from a cold morning horse ride on the beach. A fairer-haired Mr. Rochester to her Jane Eyre!

Mr. Rochester? Jane . . . a horse?!

She was getting carried away, ridiculously so, but as the man neared, Amelia realized he was taller than she had first thought. Broad too. And really that was more than she could take because now that she could see him up close, Amelia realized something about herself. There was literally nothing more attractive to her than a tall, broad man with tousled hair wearing glasses with tortoiseshell rims.

Thud!

Amelia had hit the bottom of the rabbit hole, but unlike Alice, who landed unhurt in a pile of leaves and sticks, Amelia was fairly certain she was dead. Except she was still standing, and an all-too-familiar hot tingle was running up her neck to her cheeks.

No! Please! Not now.

It was too late. Once a blush had begun, there was no stopping it. It had been so long, years, since Amelia had felt this amount of blood surge to her cheeks, and she didn't need a mirror to prove it. She could feel the heat radiating from her face.

Maybe no one would notice.

Amelia looked up just in time to see Simon blink.

Of course he blinked. His eyes probably stung, because did anything burn brighter than a blazing-cheeked redhead? He dropped his gaze, probably to spare her further embarrassment, but unfortunately it landed on her torn-up knee.

No! The injustice of it all! Why would the universe give her this opportunity only to throw a godly librarian roadblock in her way? There was no possible way Amelia could get through an interview with this man. She could barely form a coherent thought.

"Simon, meet Amelia," Rosalinda said sweetly, "our new night-time librarian."

Except perhaps she didn't have to interview.

She already had the job.

3

"And, when you want something, all the universe conspires in helping you to achieve it."
—Paulo Coelho, *The Alchemist*

SHARP TAPS OF RAIN HIT THE LIBRARY'S WINDOWS AS the wind squealed and shrieked through the building's eaves.

Otherwise, the space was silent. Completely, awkwardly silent.

Amelia looked from Simon to Rosalinda, then back to Simon again, trying to parse their expressions. Was that horror? Yes, faint horror had touched Simon's eyes, but the moment he caught Amelia watching him, he smiled—*by all the books in the library, he had a dimple!* He then cleared his throat and asked Rosalinda, "I'm sorry? Did you say our new nighttime librarian?" There was a tightness to his tone.

"I did, yes," Rosalinda replied happily.

He gave Amelia another embarrassed smile before turning back to the older woman. "Could I speak to you in the other room?"

"I don't think that's necessary," she answered, still sounding cheerful but also resolved. She did, however, hold out the tin filled with oatmeal-raisin cookies. "Have you eaten?" She leaned closer to Amelia and whispered, "Simon gets hangry when he forgets to eat."

"I am not hang—hungry." He squeezed his eyes shut. "It's just that we've discussed this and—" His gaze slid back over to Amelia. "I think there's been some sort of misunderstanding."

"No. No," Rosalinda said. "No misunderstanding. You're always saying, 'Do what you think is best,' so I did."

Simon rubbed his neck roughly, inadvertently flexing his forearm in a painfully enthralling gesture.

"We both know you've been working too much," Rosalinda continued. "And the only way you're going to have a life outside of this library is if you have help."

"I don't want a life." Simon squeezed his eyes shut again. "That's not exactly what I meant. I mean, I already have a life and—this warrants further discussion. Amelia, I'm sorry, but would you excuse us?" He glared even more pointedly at Rosalinda, then waved a hand for her to follow him.

"Oh, all right," she muttered.

As they walked to the workroom beside the circulation desk, Rosalinda offered Simon the tin again. This time he grabbed a cookie, but he didn't look pleased.

Once they retreated into the enclosed space, Amelia felt all her big, fluffy dreams harden to coal and clatter to the marble floor. She never should have gotten her hopes up. Simon—big, beautiful, hangry librarian Simon—was going to put a stop to this act of charity the fates had thrown her way. She should have known it was all too good to be true.

After one last glance, Amelia turned away from the workroom. She didn't want to appear to be eavesdropping, but that didn't mean that all the tiny hairs in her ears weren't strained to attention.

". . . discussed this." That was Simon. "With everything happening with the library, now isn't the right time."

"I have it on good authority that now is exactly the right time," Rosalinda replied.

He groaned. "Don't start. Please."

"Simon, I know you don't believe . . ." Rosalinda's words dropped to below hearing.

Believe in what? Sharing in your glorious librarian duties?

Her voice rose again just enough for Amelia to hear "The library chose her."

What? Amelia clenched her fists to stop herself from looking over. *The library chose her?* What did that mean? How had the library chosen her? Libraries didn't make choices.

"Really?" Simon asked, evidently straining to keep hold of his skepticism. "And how exactly did the library do that?"

Thank you.

"Well," Rosalinda said with more mischievous delight, "I received so many names from the schools, too many really, so I wrote them all out on slips of paper and put them in a bowl. I then asked this charming young boy to take it up to the second floor and . . ."

And what? Rosalinda's voice faded again but soon came back into hearing. ". . . the pieces came fluttering down, but her name was the only one that landed on the circulation desk."

What?! That's why she was the only contender?

A long pause followed, then, "I have no words."

"Simon, first, life is far too short not to have fun, and second, we need a nighttime librarian," Rosalinda said. "I can't work the hours I used to, and you can't work every shift. Not now. Not with everything that's going on with the building."

Amelia looked around. Everything seemed perfect to her.

"Besides, wouldn't it be nice to have another librarian who could make it up to the second floor?"

"You know I don't mind taking care of the second floor myself, but we do need that funding for an elevator. The ramp is not accessible enough and—" He cut himself off with a sigh. "Rosalinda, you know how much you mean to me, yes?"

Well, that was very sweet.

"We both know I would be lost without you, but—"

"Simon," Rosalinda said, "look at her."

"I'm sorry?" Simon sounded as confused as Amelia felt.

"Really look at her."

Amelia froze, head averted, willing herself to look natural, which probably ensured she appeared anything but.

"Now, you tell me she doesn't . . ."

Doesn't what? Unfortunately, the rest of the conversation was lost to imperceptible whispers. Then Amelia caught movement from the corner of her eye. She turned to face the two coming toward her. They both looked quite serious, which had to mean Simon had won. She was going to be shown the door.

"So," Rosalinda said firmly, "we've discussed it."

Amelia's heart clenched, waiting on the verdict before choosing to beat again.

"Can you start tomorrow night?"

SIMON LEFT QUICKLY after that. He did repeat how lovely it was to meet her, but his dimpled smile seemed troubled. What was surprising, however, was that he didn't leave by the front entrance of the building. No, he disappeared behind a medieval-looking door, tucked away in a shadowy corner behind a magazine rack. Apparently, he had living quarters in the basement, that lucky, lucky librarian. He never had to leave, and Amelia doubted *his* rooms smelled like fish.

Once he left, Rosalinda gave Amelia a quick tour of the main floor and a brief lesson on the electronic checkout system, before leading her to the break room—the name of which did not do it justice. Amelia could only imagine it had originally been a judge's chambers. There were floor-to-ceiling walnut cabinets, a bay window, and a beautiful stone fireplace. Near the hearth was a desk, a seating area with two chesterfield armchairs, and a wooden stand with a black rotary telephone on its top. Some modern conveniences had been added to the area closest to the door though. A small refrigerator, microwave, and sink had been installed, along with a round table and chairs.

"Now where did I put that . . ." Rosalinda's words trailed away as she gestured for Amelia to sit at the table. She then shuffled over to one of the cabinets to rummage through its drawers.

"Rosalinda?"

"Yes, dear," she said, focused on her search.

"Is everything all right with Simon? He didn't seem convinced about the need for another librarian." Truthfully, Amelia wasn't sure if she wanted the answer to that question, but getting this job felt like a dream, and that meant she should prepare for rude awakenings.

Rosalinda sighed. "Don't you worry about Simon. He is a funny, brilliant, hardworking man, and he is like a son to me. He has also dedicated his life to keeping this library going, but that doesn't mean he always knows what this place needs." She scoffed lightly. "Or what he needs, for that matter."

After another minute or so of searching, Rosalinda shouted, "Aha!" She then gripped something in her fist and turned, hiding it behind her back. "I think you're going to like this."

A fluttering of excitement tickled Amelia's ribs. There had been so many highs and lows tonight, she wasn't sure she could take much more.

When Rosalinda reached the table, she placed the object down on its surface with a *thunk*. "Gorgeous, isn't it?"

A key! A long, hefty key with an ornate bow and wonderfully jagged bit.

Amelia reached her fingertips toward it. "It's precious." She then curled her hand into a fist and grimaced. "Did that sound too *Gollum*?"

Rosalinda laughed. "Not in this library."

Amelia picked up the key with reverence. It was so satisfyingly heavy.

"The original iron locks of the building were solidly made, so there has never been a need to replace them. Be careful not to lose it though. I'm not sure where we could have another one made."

Amelia gripped the cool iron in her fist, the key's ends sticking out either side. *Never.* Never would she lose it. Just then the library let out a groan from somewhere deep within the walls, and Amelia clutched the key to her chest like it might be snatched away.

Rosalinda chuckled. "Don't worry. You'll get used to the library's quirks soon enough."

"Quirks?"

"Given the building's age, flickering lights, drafts, creaks, and groans are to be expected." She glanced around the walls. "I also tend to believe that old buildings have personalities. This one in particular."

Amelia frowned in question.

"Well, you likely already know that the building was once a courthouse."

Amelia didn't answer, but, of course, she never would have come to this interview so unprepared.

"Now, I realize how this may sound, but I've worked at this library since I was a young girl, and I believe after so many years of witnessing people at their most destitute, it has learned to care about those who step into the shelter of its walls."

"Care?" Amelia replied far more dryly than she intended.

"I would go so far as to say that it wanted to transform itself into something more welcoming, and when Simon's family bought the building and filled it with so much love, it blossomed and became all that it is today. It does so much for so many."

Simon's family owned the building? She had come unprepared after all!

"I believe this place *feels* for people," Rosalinda said fondly. "It enjoys helping."

Amelia forced a smile. It was a lovely thought, but *ridiculous.*

"Would you listen to me prattling on? Simon thinks I'm being ridiculous."

They were made for each other!

Please stop.

Rational Amelia was right again. What was the matter with her tonight?

"He says a building is just a building, but deep down he knows better. He's as connected to the library as I am, if not more so." Rosalinda walked past her toward the door. "Let's not worry about all that tonight though."

Worry? Why would she be worried?

"I will give you a more thorough tour tomorrow," Rosalinda continued, "but we should get you to try out the key before you go."

Amelia rose to her feet, her mind still sorting through all that she had learned. Out of everything she could have landed on, though, it was the building's quirks that she kept coming back to.

Flickering lights? Drafts? Creaks and groans?

Of course, all those things could be because the building was old—*or had a personality?*—but there was another explanation.

Amelia followed Rosalinda back to the main hub of the library, a sinking feeling swirling in the pit of her stomach. While her boss continued her path to the front door, Amelia jerked to a stop in the main reading room. Something had changed in the few minutes that they had been gone. It felt different. Instead of being overcome with joy, happiness, and a sense of utter belonging, Amelia felt very much on edge . . . like the second-floor mezzanine had suddenly come alive and was now hovering over her with the outstretched wings of some terrifying bird of prey.

Don't look. Keep on walking. Remember the rules.

Yes, that was sound advice. Rules were rules for a reason, and whenever Amelia had broken the rules in the past, it had never ended well. Then again, being prepared was also important.

Don't do it!

Amelia flicked her eyes up to the mezzanine.

For a fraction of a second, she registered a familiar, eerie glow emanating from a spot by the railing. It was fine. Expected really. She was a little surprised that she hadn't spotted it earlier, but . . .

Amelia stiffened before some strange sense made her turn her head. *There!* On the other wing of the second floor. Another glow. *Two?*

Stay calm.

That was certainly one more than expected, but perfectly manageable.

Amelia was directing her gaze back to the foyer in search of Rosalinda when she caught yet another glowing form hiding in the stacks. A shiver ran up the back of her neck. This time the eerie light felt darker, more ominous.

Three?!

Amelia snapped her gaze forward and hurried into the foyer.

"There you are," Rosalinda said. "I thought I lost you. Is everything all right?"

Amelia forced a smile. "Yes, everything is wonderful."

And it was.

Or at least as wonderful as it could be given the library was haunted by a trio of *ghosts*.

Yes, ghosts.

The word, nay, the reality she had been avoiding all night was finally out. It had been foolish to try to banish it from her thoughts. As futile as trying to banish *them* from her life. Because try as she might to ignore them, they were always there. Ready to ruin everything.

Ghosts. Ghosts. Ghosts.

Suddenly Amelia was in a very bad mood.

4

"But it's no use going back to yesterday,
because I was a different person then."
—Lewis Carroll, *Alice's Adventures in Wonderland*

AMELIA PUSHED HER APARTMENT DOOR CLOSED against the blustery night wind, then slumped against it, inhaling the fishy scent of home. She was shivering, her muscles ached, and she was completely exhausted from all the spent adrenaline, but thankfully, the walk home had rallied her spirits, and she was once again the happiest she had ever been.

Or at least she thought she was. It was hard to tell. A lot had happened.

Given the stormy weather, the apartment was feeling particularly cold and damp, so Amelia left her jacket on as she walked the few steps over to the kitchenette. Ever since Rosalinda had mentioned tea, she had been yearning for a cup. She opened the cupboard by the fridge, being careful not to pull off the loose knob, and grabbed her only mug.

The loft apartment certainly wasn't much to look at. Its bare white walls and aged appliances were far from inspiring, and then there was the slow drip coming from the ceiling. Her landlord had promised to fix it immediately, but until *immediately* arrived, he had offered her a bucket. Amelia wasn't bothered though. She was used to sparse accommodations. Growing up in the foster system had ensured that.

Amelia clicked on the kettle, and for a moment, its blue glow reminded her of the *three* ghosts she had spotted in the library. In her experience, spirits stuck on the mortal plane were mainly solitary beings. There were exceptions, of course, like the couple with the ghost lanterns who strolled nightly on the boardwalk, but those cases were few and far between. And she had never seen three in one building. A veritable infestation. It was aggravating, but also fine. She simply had to follow the rules, and all would be well. Really, why was she even thinking about ghosts? She had so many other things to think about, like the library, Rosalinda . . .

Simon.

Amelia shook her head and placed a pouch of chamomile tea into her mug before pouring the freshly boiled water over top. Remembering how she reacted to meeting her fellow librarian triggered another faint blush. Admittedly, she had read hundreds, if not thousands, of romance novels, so perhaps she had been primed to get swept up in a moment of *fantasy*, but she knew the difference between fact and fiction. They likely had nothing in common . . . aside from being librarians and sharing an appreciation for tortoiseshell-rimmed glasses.

And in fairness, she had very little real-world experience with romance, dating, or men in general, compared to other women her age, so it wasn't surprising Simon had made her nervous. Next time she'd be better prepared. There was too much at stake for her not to be. The only hope she had of keeping this job was if she could behave normally, and, unfortunately, that meant keeping *living* people at a safe distance.

Stupid ghosts.

Amelia clutched her mug to her chest. For as long as she could remember, she had been able to see spirits—although it had taken most of her early years to figure out what they were and that other people couldn't see them. It wasn't easy, considering she had to do it all on her own. Amelia had been placed in care as a baby, so she never knew her parents, nor what had happened to them. Her social worker had offered on more than one occasion to share the information in her file, but Amelia had always declined. She didn't see how knowing the details of her abandonment would help anything. None of the explanations could be good.

One might assume, given the tender age Amelia entered care, that she would have been adopted outright, but, tragically, she hadn't behaved like most babies. Colic was the reason given, but she suspected there was more to it. This wasn't self-pity. It was experience. Before Amelia grew wise to her situation, her ghostseeing ability had scared many away. It turned out, small children talking with people others couldn't see was disconcerting. As was, say, jumping violently at spirits unexpectedly sticking their heads through walls. Apparently, even staring quietly at a ghost materializing in an empty corner of a room made one *creepy*. It had all been very confusing.

It was books that saved her, of course. One in particular. After years of living in a baffling morass of constant uncertainty, fate intervened when Amelia's kindergarten teacher, Miss Beckers, treated the class to a reading of *Five Little Ghosts*. As the pages turned, realization finally, mercifully settled into place.

Ghosts. She was seeing ghosts.

It was a monumental epiphany, and from that point onward, Amelia learned everything she could about spirits. In the years that followed, she read countless articles, chapters, and books, tracking down all the most authoritative texts on the topic. Well, all except one. *The Ghostseer's Handbook*. The holy grail of reference manuals. Many sources referred to it, but Amelia had never been able to track down a copy. Eventually she had come to suspect it didn't actually exist. It was just an imaginary reservoir of information those in the know pretended to have seen to add validity to their claims.

Regardless, after that fateful turning point, books became the center of Amelia's life, and the public library her sanctuary. It was the one place that offered her real help in figuring out how to live in a world that did not understand her. It was also the only place that allowed her to be herself. There was no expectation to behave like other rambunctious children. So naturally she spent as much time there as she could. In fact, it was in her small neighborhood library that she had come up with the rules. The idea came while flipping through a children's encyclopedia. In it was a picture of the Tōshō-gū shrine featuring the Three Wise Monkeys. *See no evil. Hear no evil. Speak no evil.* In that moment, the answer to so many of her problems became clear. Do not engage with ghosts, period.

Once she had the rules, life became substantially easier, but it still wasn't enough. Spirits often behaved in unexpected ways and showed up in unexpected places, so controlling her reactions wasn't always possible. Despite her best efforts, other children always found her strange, and eventually she concluded keeping to herself was the best option for everyone. So, in the group home, she usually ate alone, and when the other children were watching TV and playing video games, she read. When she turned eleven, she asked the manager and owner of the large Victorian house they lived in, Mr. Adani, if her bed could be moved to the attic. He was horrified by the idea, but after some discussion with her case worker, her request was finally granted, and everyone was much happier.

Once she had finished high school and aged out of the system, Mr. Adani allowed her to continue to live in the attic as she attended university. He cited her unobtrusive nature as the deciding factor, but Amelia often sensed that others felt sorry for her. Not just because she was an orphan but because she was so different from everyone else. They didn't trust in her ability to make her way in the world.

Amelia couldn't help but wonder if Rosalinda was one of those people.

Look at her.

She probably wanted Simon to see how impossible it was to turn away such a pathetic creature, what with her windblown hair and tattered tights.

As humiliating as the thought was, Amelia wasn't about to look a gift librarian in the mouth. She was a pathetic creature in some ways—or at the very least *cursed*—but she knew with every fiber of her being she would be an exceptional nighttime librarian. And she wasn't about to let any ghosts ruin that.

A librarian.

It was going to take a while for that reality to sink in.

Amelia dumped the last bit of her tea into the sink and got ready for bed, changing into her new plaid flannel pajamas that she had bought as a luxury just the day before at a cozy shop in town. She then snuggled beneath her quilts.

Soft light flooded through the window above the bed. The clouds had finally parted, revealing a full silver-white moon, and Amelia couldn't help but wonder how many other people were looking at that same moon right that very moment. Normal, everyday people, living their normal, everyday lives. It was a comforting thought. Amelia closed her eyes.

She would be one of those normal people.

Ghosts be damned.

5

"Isn't it nice to think that tomorrow is
a new day with no mistakes in it yet?"
—L. M. Montgomery, *Anne of Green Gables*

A RED-ORANGE SUNSET FILLED THE ENDLESS SKY ON Amelia's walk to the library, setting ablaze the sea's rippling waves and igniting the distant sandstone cliffs with fiery light. There wouldn't be many more evenings like this. Yesterday's storm had signaled what was to come. But for now, the hills were still emerald green, and flocks of geese were still honking noisily overhead as they made their way to warmer climes. A stinging wind bit Amelia's cheeks and brought tears to her eyes as she braved the boardwalk, but it was more invigorating than unpleasant, not unlike the sensation of the million excited bees that had taken up residence in her chest.

It was her first night of work!

Before Amelia knew it, she was once again standing in front of the towering library, the sun's dying glow reflecting off its red brick.

Gratitude, the likes of which she had never experienced before, filled Amelia from tip to tail, but before she could fully luxuriate in it, the bitter wind gusted once more, rustling the dried leaves of the nearby oak tree, drawing her attention to the dead sea captain. Not that she actually looked at him.

"Back again, are ya, lass?" Amelia didn't answer but hurried to climb the front steps. "Haven't learned your lesson?" She pulled open the door, then jumped to the side to make room for a patron seemingly fleeing the building. The small, wide-eyed man, clutching his jacket to his chest, rushed past her, then hurried down the concrete steps. Once he reached the bottom, he shot a nervous look over his shoulder into the library. Amelia peeked inside. No one was there. She realized as an employee of the library she should probably say something, but it was a little unclear what that *something* was. Thankfully, by the time she looked back, the man was already halfway across the parking lot.

"There goes a wise one!" the captain shouted over his pipe. "Run, man! Run!" He laughed heartily, but it quickly dwindled to a sigh.

Amelia watched the man dive into his car before the library's unique scent of books and old wood beckoned her inside.

Really, who was she to judge eccentricities?

After lowering her messenger bag to the floor, Amelia hung her jacket up on the coatrack and then straightened her forest green cable-knit sweater over the tweed pants she really should have worn the day before. She then adjusted her glasses and smoothed the sides of her hair toward the tight, ironclad bun at the nape of her neck. There was no way her curls were getting free tonight. It was possible she had gone overboard on her librarian-themed stylistic choices, but now that she was in fact a librarian, the choices felt legitimate.

Once she had herself sorted, Amelia took a deep breath and walked out from the foyer into the main reading room. Part of her had been expecting to see the same three ghosts hovering in the very same spots she had seen them the night before, but they were gone. That was nice. Maybe, if she was lucky, they had just been passing through and not somehow sending library visitors fleeing from the premises. Another part of Amelia had also been expecting to see Rosalinda seated at the circulation desk, but much to her horror, delight, embarrassment, and possible yearn-ment, Simon was there.

Wait. What if Rosalinda was gone because she and Simon had had a further discussion to their already-had discussion, but this time he had won and now . . .

Was he going to fire her?

"Amelia. Hello."

Amelia couldn't tell if that was a regular *Hello* or a firing one. It sounded formal, but maybe that was a good thing, because if he was going to fire her, wouldn't he go with something more sympathetic like *Hey, you*? Amelia didn't know. People were easier to understand in books.

Simon unnecessarily shuffled a few papers around on the desk. "Did you walk?" He glanced up, his gaze landing ever so briefly on her windburned cheeks.

Hot prickles crawled up Amelia's neck. *Do not blush again. Not again.*

"Has the temperature dropped?"

"Yes, I—yes. Yes, to both."

They stared at each other a moment before looking away. Simon scratched his brow, gaze averted back to the desk. "I was just tidying up. Rosalinda had to leave early."

Amelia nodded because apparently words no longer existed for her.

He then met her eyes with a terribly serious look. "It's probably for the best. I was hoping to talk to you alone."

No! Run, Amelia! Run! He can't fire you if he can't catch you!

That was Hysterical Amelia. She didn't often come out, thankfully. Amelia stayed firmly rooted to the spot, but every muscle she had tensed.

Simon inhaled deeply, readying his words. "I wanted to apologize for yesterday."

"What?" Amelia exclaimed, loud enough to echo. She glanced around the main reading room, expecting admonishing looks for her breach of library etiquette, but it was empty. "I mean, I'm sorry?"

Simon looked down, but she caught the smirk at her near-obscene reaction. "My disagreement with Rosalinda last night didn't have anything to do with you. You seem . . ."

Amelia politely raised her brow, but her entire existence hung on his next choice of words.

He shook his head, dismissing the rest of the sentence. "I am not doing this very well, but at least it's not as bad as my sophisticated entrance last night."

Amelia didn't blink.

"The pencil? The garland?" He chuckled, but when she didn't return his good humor, he pressed on. "Right. Okay. So, Rosalinda and I sometimes have different ideas about how best to run the library." He nodded down at the desk. "And we've been facing some challenges lately. The building is showing its age, and our circulation traffic—which our funding depends on—has been down for some unknown reason." Amelia desperately wanted to ask for more details, but in a stunning move Simon reached his arms up, interlacing his fingers behind his head, and she was rendered speechless. "I've hired an engineering company to look into what's going on with the building. Hopefully it's nothing. I don't have the funds to . . ." He roughly scratched the back of his head, then crossed his arms over his chest. "Challenges aside, I guess the point I'm trying to get at is Rosalinda has her own beliefs when it comes to the library and what may or may not be going on with it."

Given her eavesdropping of their conversation the night before, Amelia suddenly had an idea of where this was headed.

"I don't want you to get the wrong idea. Rosalinda is as sharp as ever, but . . ." He sighed. "I'm just going to say it. She believes the library is sentient. Like really believes it."

Amelia stayed quiet. Given her own peculiarities, silence was probably the safest option. It was funny. She could see ghosts, so it seemed hypocritical to be skeptical of sentient buildings. And yet, she was. Probably because if Rosalinda was picking up anything unusual, it was likely from the spirits Amelia had spotted yesterday. Or maybe other spirits. Ghosts didn't always stay rooted to one place. Maybe the library was some sort of hub for the dead.

What a horrifying thought.

The point was that while full ghostseers such as herself were rare according to her research, that didn't mean humans couldn't pick up on ghostly activity. In fact, sometimes it was impossible not to. Some spirits could interact with the living world in small ways, by, say, knocking over objects or casting unusually long or dark shadows. Normally these instances were easy to dismiss—the old-building explanation was standard—but not everyone was so easily convinced.

Simon rocked back in his chair. "Because Rosalinda believes this so deeply, she has been making some unilateral decisions lately based on what she thinks the library is telling her."

Unilateral decisions like hiring me.

"Given *my* personal skepticism of the supernatural, there has been some conflict."

"Me too," Amelia blurted.

"I'm sorry?"

"I am also skeptical of supernatural things. The most skeptical. Very large . . . skeptic." *Well said, Amelia. Very normal.*

Simon quashed the beginnings of another smirk, then adjusted his glasses before looking back at her. "I hope you won't hold any of this against Rosalinda."

"Never."

The word must have held too much intensity because the corner of his mouth twitched again. "I would completely understand if you wanted to reconsider your decision to work here."

Was he trying to get her to quit? He had mentioned that he didn't have the funding for repairs. Did that also mean he didn't have the funding to hire her? "Never," she replied, *again.* What was wrong with her? "I mean, also, never." That was so much better.

"Right," he replied, slapping the desk. "Now that that's done, I'll get out of your way." He pushed the rolling chair back from the circulation desk and got up.

Get out of my way?

He was leaving? Just like that? He couldn't leave. They still had so much to talk about. And he had to . . . train her! Rosalinda was supposed to show her around, so didn't that mean he needed to give her a tour? Maybe while holding her hand? No, that wasn't right.

"There shouldn't be much for you to do tonight. Just flick off the lights marked *daytime* when you lock up," he said, pointing to a panel of switches. "I'm sure Rosalinda will get you started on some special projects tomorrow, so really, you can leave as soon as we close."

Leave at closing? *No!* This wasn't at all how things were supposed to go. Amelia wanted to stay. She wanted to stay in the library as long as she could. Didn't he realize she only had an empty fish apartment to get back to?

Simon must have read her upset because he added, "You'll be paid for the full time, of course."

Amelia took a determined step forward. "Are you sure there isn't anything I can do?"

"I don't think so." Suddenly he frowned. Amelia followed his gaze to the returns cart, loaded with a small stack of books. "I meant to reshelve those earlier. Most are from the second floor, and Rosalinda doesn't go up there. She has a bad knee. I'll do it now."

"No!" Amelia snapped. Where *was* her library voice? "Please. I'd like to do it."

He stopped, turning his attention fully to her. His eyes were such a unique hazel green. She could study them for hours on end and still find nuances. *Focus, Amelia.*

"I would like to do that. Return the books."

Simon's brow raised. "You would?"

"I've always imagined that there must be something uniquely soothing about putting each book back into its proper space, restoring the library shelves to their fully organized states." So she *was* capable of complete sentences. That was a relief. "Ever since I was little, I've dreamed about what it must be like to wander through the stacks pushing a cart filled with books, tracking numbers on spines, passing all the different fictional lifetimes." And now, she was conversing. That was good. Perhaps her childhood dreams sounded a touch pedantic, but still good. "When you think about it, libraries are such a monumental feat of organization. The genius behind the Dewey decimal system? The division of knowledge categories? The hierarchical structure?" Was she speaking too quickly? And . . .

Dewey decimal system? "Clearly, recent advancements in library technology are incredible, but how I adored those old library cabinets!" What? Where was she headed now? "Each little drawer bursting with a multitude of undiscovered wonders? They were like guides to the universe, each card an escort to a new world." She was rambling. Clearly rambling. And yet she couldn't seem to stop. "And there were so many worlds to explore. Worlds full of adventure, excitement, intrigue"—*That's enough, Amelia*—"mystery, suspense, danger, and of course we can't forget—"

Stop!

"Romance."

As soon as that last word passed her lips, her mouth snapped shut.

Amelia wasn't quite sure how it had happened, but somehow, she had gone from saying far too little to saying far too much. And she also couldn't help but notice, during her unexpected diatribe on the virtues of library organization, that Simon's expression had remained tightly neutral. Likely out of fear.

"So," she concluded, "I would like to return the books."

Now she was done. Completely done. Fully cooked, one might say.

The full heaviness of the library's silence fell upon them. And even though it had been only a few seconds since it began, the silence seemed to be stretching to an eternity, but she clearly couldn't be the one to break it. She had said more than enough.

Amelia dared to meet Simon's gaze once more. His eyes, while attentive and thoughtful behind his tortoiseshell-rimmed glasses, were otherwise unreadable.

Please say something.

"We've kept them," he said. "The cabinets. Most are on the third floor in storage, but I kept one for myself in the basement." He pinned his lips shut. It seemed like he wanted to say more but then thought better of it. Amelia could only imagine what it would be like to have such self-control. After a moment he added, "And you're right about the returning of books. I can't quite explain it, but it is soothing. The world is such a chaotic, unpredictable place, but . . ."

Don't stop. Please, don't stop.

"The library makes sense of it all."

Amelia blinked.

Forget the obstacles. They were meant to be. They could live together in the library forever, reading books, reshelving books, cataloguing books, doing other things that didn't necessarily require books, but—

"You know," Simon said, "if you're not in a hurry to leave when the library closes, I could show you the third floor. I've been working on a collection of rare . . ." Most unexpectedly, Amelia found Simon's voice fading away. She never would have thought it possible her attention could be stolen from him, but something was happening in the far corner of the circulation area. The shadows there were moving, swirling, coming together to form a shape. *Please. Not now.* Amelia tried desperately to pull her gaze away, but the presence forming was so heavy and dark, it was impossible. Suddenly two small circles of light sparked in the gloom. She couldn't tell what they were at first, but then she realized they were eyes! Glowing, bulbous blue eyes. And they were fixated directly on her.

Rule number one: Do not look at them.

"Amelia?"

She jerked her gaze to the ceiling, then side to side, unable to find a safe place to land.

"Is everything—"

"No!" She blinked and snapped her focus back to Simon.

He looked a bit startled.

"I mean, no, not you. I—"

"Please, you don't have to explain." He pushed in his chair. "You probably want to get home."

What had happened? What was he thinking? How had she looked? Bored? Distracted? Horrified?

"Maybe another time." He smiled but avoided all eye contact as he walked around the desk. "I've left my number on the notepad. Just text if you need anything."

No!

She clutched her hands together. He was clearly headed for the door behind the magazine rack. He was leaving for the night.

Don't go!

Suddenly he stopped and smiled at her again over his shoulder. "Good night, Amelia."

She couldn't let him go. Not like this. Not with this crazed Dewey-decimal-system-loving impression of her.

Say something!

"Good night, Simon."

In seconds he was gone.

AS DEVASTATING AS Simon's sudden departure had been, and it had been truly devastating, it was a good reminder. Ghosts always ruined everything, and if she wasn't more careful going forward, they would ruin this too. She couldn't believe she'd reacted that way. Or reacted at all, for that matter.

But at least Simon hadn't given her *the look*.

It was the expression people had been giving Amelia her entire life when she couldn't hide that she'd seen a ghost. It was that unique, easily recognizable, what-is-wrong-with-that-girl look. Once it came to another person's face, any possibility of a normal interaction—forget relationship—was over. They could never quite see her the same way again. Amelia had received the look countless times when she was a child, but not so much anymore. That blue-eyed terror had gotten the best of her because she was overstimulated by all the changes in her life. It wouldn't happen again. That being said, keeping interactions with Simon to a minimum was likely the wisest course of action. She never wanted to see *the look* on his face. And as disappointing as that was, really, she had so much to be grateful for. This was her first shift as a working librarian. That was more than enough.

In the hour the library remained open, only one person came in. Amelia had almost been certain she recognized the middle-aged visitor in the heavy plaid jacket as the owner of the crab shack in town, but, of course, she couldn't be certain without speaking to him. Amelia knew talking to visitors was part of the job, but the mere thought of approaching him and uttering the words *May I help you find something?* had made her palms prickle with sweat. It would have been so much easier if he had come to her. But that hadn't happened. No, after perusing the mystery section for nearly fifteen minutes, twisting his knit hat in his hands with a clear look of confusion on his face, he left. While relieved, Amelia couldn't help but find the situation tragic. Not only had she disappointed herself, but he had left without a book.

Other than the one failed encounter, though, the rest of the evening was everything Amelia hoped it would be. She wasn't entirely sure what to do with herself a good deal of the time, but sitting at the circulation desk was thrilling in and of itself. Better still? The ominously dark, blue-eyed ghost was gone, at least for now. Not that Amelia was letting her guard down. It was certainly annoying not knowing when, where, or if it might pop up again, but such was her life. If she wanted to spend time in the outside world, or at least in this library, she had to get better at ignoring surprise appearances. And if she couldn't, well, there were other options.

Theoretically.

One in particular was tucked away in a packing box on the top shelf of her apartment's only closet. But she wasn't entirely comfortable with going that route. At least not yet. It felt *extreme*, and it came with a real risk of exposure.

No, it wouldn't come to that. Amelia could do this. If the worst that happened was creepy looks from the shadows, then there wasn't a problem.

Second after glorious second ticked by, and before Amelia knew it, the moment she had been waiting for arrived.

Closing time.

Amelia hurried over to the front door and flipped the sign in the window before turning the lock. She then returned to the main reading room and looked around. Nothing. No strange shadows. No creepy glows. Just her and the place she was always meant to be.

Standing in the center of the room, she suddenly felt like all the books on all the shelves were holding their breath waiting for her to greet them. It took everything in her to resist holding her arms out and spinning in a circle like Belle in *Beauty and the Beast*. She had only seen the movie once, on a group outing, but it had made an impression. And why did she have to resist? No one was here. It was just her and the books. Amelia threw her arms out and took half a turn before stumbling over the edge of a carpet. Embarrassment lightly colored her cheeks before she remembered that it didn't matter! No one was around to see it! No one living, at least. And really it was only the living who mattered.

Amelia clutched her hands by her waist and walked sedately back over to the circulation desk. That was enough celebration. She had a job to do. First, she needed to double-check that everything here was in order. She scanned the top of the desk. A metal mesh cup full of pens and pencils. A stapler. Tape. Scissors. All were perfectly arranged exactly as they had been five minutes ago. She couldn't resist touching the singular library stamp resting on an ink pad. It was an enigma. Checkouts were done electronically, so which lucky books got that stamp?

She had so much to learn.

Amelia then faced the book-return cart parked by the desk. It was older and industrial-looking, with its worn rubber corrugated mats and chipped paint on the handles, but all its imperfections only added to its beauty. She had to name it! They were about to become good friends. But what? What was a good name for a library cart? She couldn't think of anything appropriate. Amelia took a breath. *It's okay. Relax. You don't have to do everything the first day.*

She pushed it gently with her fingertips and was delighted to find the wheels squeaked just so. She wrapped her hands around the cool metal handle. "You and I are going to become very good friends . . . Carty."

That was terrible.

"Cartwell?"

Much better.

Amelia backed Cartwell out carefully, turning it in a gentle arc to face the stacks. There were fewer than twenty books to put away, but they were from multiple genres, so she'd get to visit every corner of the library. *Excellent.*

Amelia pushed the cart through the aisles, traveling section to section. Once she had returned the books on the first floor, she took the ramp alongside the curving west stairs to the second and repeated the process. It was a lovely experience but went by far too quickly. When all the books had been safely put to bed, she traveled back down and pushed Cartwell to the nautical-compass inlay in the center of the marble floor and stepped up onto the bottom rail. Possessed by unexpected emotion, she pushed off the floor with her free foot to give herself a spin. As she moved in a slow circle, a smile touched her lips.

She had finally found it. There was a place in the world for her. After years of doubt, she'd finally found a place where—

Suddenly she stumbled off the cart.

Be cool, Amelia.

She had glanced up for only a second, but she knew what she had seen.

The ghosts were back.

All three of them.

6

So many horrid ghosts.
—William Shakespeare, *Henry V*

AMELIA PUSHED CARTWELL TOWARD THE CIRCULATION desk, taking deliberate care to keep a steady, inconspicuous pace. She was just a normal person doing a normal job, not seeing anything unusual. Regardless, she could feel them staring at her.

What was going on here? This was not how ghosts usually behaved. They should be off plotting revenge, or attempting to solve their own murders, or at the very least obsessing about the mistakes they'd made in life, not staring at some poor, everyday living human performing routine tasks. But the way she could feel them looking at her, it was almost as if *they knew.*

No, that was impossible. It wasn't like she walked around with a sign that read *ghostseer* on her back. And she hadn't reacted when she saw them. Not really. She froze for maybe a second? She gave no other sign that—

"She saw us! She totally saw us!"

A young man's voice floated down from the mezzanine.

"Do you really think so?" another voice answered. An older man's this time. "I'm not certain."

"Dude, don't be fooled by that resting librarian face. She saw us yesterday too."

Apparently, she needed to fine-tune her surreptitious glances. And *resting librarian face*? Amelia supposed she should be offended, but . . . she looked like a librarian!

"Braden, manners," the older man chastised.

What?! Since when did ghosts call other ghosts by their names? Yes, Amelia had always tried to avoid spirits, spending most of her free time in her attic room, but she had gone to school and had been forced on group trips to parks, stores, *libraries*. So, of course she had witnessed many, many ghosts. Well, maybe just *many*. And the ones she had witnessed usually exhibited a limited range of behaviors, such as staying in one spot, muttering comments at the living or to themselves, and repeating behaviors, like the couple walking the boardwalk every night. Amelia knew of one ghost back in Charlottetown who had been waiting patiently for the same canceled bus for years. That was normal. What these ghosts were doing was just . . . weird!

Calm, Amelia. Breathe.

Yes. Right. She needed to stay calm and follow the rules. Everything would be fine as long as she didn't look at or listen to them again.

"I'm telling you, professor," the one called Braden said. "This is it. Our way out. She's the one we've been waiting for."

The one they've been waiting for? Either the ghosts could also see her charming resemblance to Belle from *Beauty and the Beast* or . . . they had been waiting for some hapless human to torture for nefarious ghostly purposes!

Easy, Amelia.

Yes, easy. She could handle this. While they did have her outnumbered, they seemed innocuous enough. They didn't look *unmanageable.*

Well, at least two of the three didn't.

In her stolen glimpses, she'd gotten a fairly good look at the bunch. *Braden* appeared to be about twenty, with spiky, frosted-tipped hair and a tiny goatee. He wore ridiculously baggy jeans and an oversize orange shirt with thick white hems. Amelia imagined he died in the late '90s, early 2000s. Everything about him screamed Blink-182 and *Dude, Where's My Car?* Beside him, but farther back from the railing, stood, no, correction—*floated*—an older gentleman with wild white hair. He was wearing a tweed jacket with elbow patches, so even if the younger man hadn't called him *professor*, the professorial vibes were evident.

And then there was the one with the blue eyes.

The newly designated bane of Amelia's existence. The destroyer of romance. The butcher of dreams. The—

Amelia.

While most ghosts appeared much like living humans, simply more transparent and glowy, there were a few with different and, unfortunately, more terrifying auras. These were the ghosts that featured in horror movies. Amelia had only ever seen a spirit like this once before, on a high school trip to France. Amelia almost hadn't gone. She knew traveling with her classmates would be stressful, but she couldn't resist, not when her costs were covered after her teachers arranged for her fees to be paid under the school's charitable funds. She was a very good student. It all had gone so smoothly until they visited the Eiffel Tower. With the help of a pair of binoculars, she had spotted *it* standing atop the iconic structure in an executioner's mask, holding an axe. For just a second, Amelia experienced a historical thrill, wondering if the ghost was that of Charles-Henri

Sanson, the executioner responsible for ending the life of King Louis XVI during the French Revolution, but then, in a very surprising move, the ghost dove toward the crowd in which Amelia had been standing, axe leading the way, shouting, *Vive la république!* Amelia didn't remember much after that, but according to her teacher, she had screamed quite loudly and fainted dead away. She spent the rest of the trip on the bus. The thing Amelia remembered most about that ghost, though, was how dark it felt. This ghost wasn't that bad in terms of evilness, but it did have a disturbing presence with an emotional nuance she couldn't quite put her finger on. Or perhaps it was the ghost's dirty chin-to-ankle dress with the equally dirty bonnet that was putting Amelia off. Really, it looked like someone had just dug her up from a collapsed coal mine. Or a grave. The only part of the spirit that wasn't dirty was her bulging blue eyeballs.

Time to take her leave.

Amelia continued steering Cartwell back in the direction of the circulation desk. Yes, everything was fine. Still perfectly wonderful. The ghosts were simply a minor bump in an otherwise superlative road. And while she couldn't be sure, because she wasn't about to look back, it was possible the ghosts had already given up on trying to get her attention. That's what usually happened when she followed the rules. Amelia exhaled with anticipatory relief, but as the air passed her lips, it swirled into a frosty cloud.

Or not.

Classic ghost trickery. They were trying to out her. Well, she was ready. She'd had a handful of ghosts over the years suspect her abilities and engage in obnoxious behavior to get her attention, but if there was one thing those experiences had taught her, it was that once the game had begun, winning was the only option.

Amelia hummed a little tune, each note releasing a tiny puff of frozen breath. Not that she noticed. *Aren't you cold, Amelia?* one of her many interior voices asked. *Not in the slightest, but thank you for asking, Amelia,* another answered. Rational Amelia was rolling her eyes.

"She's humming," the ghost with the frosted tips, Braden, said somewhere behind her. Somewhere on her level. He'd come down from the second floor.

"Remarkable," the professorial-looking man called out. He sounded like he was still on the second floor. "Such poise."

Despite being perfectly comfortable in the not-at-all-chilly room, Amelia did think it was a good idea to head out. Her instincts were telling her the ante was about to be upped. But she couldn't leave too fast. *No, no, no.* She had to play this just right.

"We know you can see us," Braden called out.

They knew no such thing. And his voice had come from a mere few feet behind her this time.

Steady, Amelia.

"We would like to talk to you, if you would be so kind," the other man shouted from somewhere on the mezzanine.

Absolutely not. Amelia did not talk to ghosts.

She looked around the circulation desk one last time. Again, everything appeared to be in its rightful spot. *Good. Good.* She picked up her messenger bag from the floor and flicked the daytime light switches off as Simon had instructed. The library fell into a drowsy nighttime embrace.

Done.

She headed for the foyer, but the moment she stepped across the threshold, all the lights in the library came back on, flickering violently. Amelia halted her step. Clearly, she had seen that, and they knew she had seen that, but what they did not know was how she was explaining it to herself, if that made sense. Regardless, Amelia knew what to do. She trotted over to a sconce and tapped it with her fingertip. "My, the wind is fierce tonight," she observed in a mumble, a loud enough mumble to carry throughout the library.

The professor ghost barked a distant laugh from the second floor. "Delightful."

Amelia walked with unbothered steps back into the foyer and over to the coatrack. She rested her bag carefully at her feet and then grabbed her jacket off the hook. She pulled it on with quick—but not too quick!—efficient movements.

"Don't worry. I've got this," Braden said.

Amelia tensed, hopefully imperceptibly.

After a loud throat clearing, a low sound filled the room, traveling up and down some heretofore unknown musical scale. *Wooohooooo!*

Amelia's averted eyes rolled of their own accord. *Ridiculous.* Braden was wailing and moaning like something out of *A Christmas Carol.* Next, he'd be rattling ghostly chains. She fastened the buttons of her jacket up to her chin before tightening the belt at her waist.

Woooooohoooooo!

He had gone up an octave. This was embarrassing for everyone.

Amelia retrieved her bag and dropped it over her shoulder before reaching in for the large iron key.

Wooooooooohooooooooo!

Ghost Braden was really ruining this moment for her, but it sounded like he was almost out of . . . whatever it was the halfway dead breathed.

Where was that key? Amelia rummaged around, but she couldn't find—

Her bag fell to the floor, spilling its contents.

Lip balm, pens, her wallet, and a tissue pack slid across the floor along with the key! She collected the items, then pushed up to her feet the very moment Braden started to cough. Just as she had anticipated. In all likelihood, he was probably capable of wailing for an eternity, but living habits must die hard.

"Sorry," he called back to the main reading room.

"Not at all," the professor shouted. "It was a valiant effort."

"I think it's time to call in the big guns," Braden answered.

Big guns? Amelia did not like the sound of that. Not at all.

"Minnie, you're up."

Minnie?!

Amelia felt her heart stumble and trip into a faster beat. There were only three of them, and Braden and the professor had been talking, so that meant . . .

A new ghastly wail rose from what had to be the depths of some distant pit of hell to swirl through the cavernous interior of the library. Amelia snapped her gaze to the front door, but in some strange warp of time and space, it felt like it had stretched back and away from her. Instead of escape being mere feet away, it was miles. Otherworldly moans curled around Amelia like a giant snake as a wave of vertigo rocked her balance. She was going to faint. Just like she had in France. She was going to drop and—

No. Absolutely not!

Amelia tightened her grip on the key. This was her library now. She was not going to be driven from it in a state of terror. She had to do something.

So she did the first thing that came to mind.

She sneezed. Faked a sneeze actually.

Then she did it again. And then again.

In fact, Amelia didn't stop sneezing until all the horrific wailing dropped away into an awkward, questioning sound.

A smug smile stretched across Amelia's face. *That's right, Minnie.*

Your wails mean nothing to me. She then resumed her step, the soles of her shoes slapping happily against the tiled floor. When she had almost made it to the door, Braden's ghostly face suddenly appeared mere inches from her own.

"Dude! Don't leave! We need your help!"

Amelia didn't blink. She had been expecting such a maneuver. *Amateur.* She walked right through him, ignoring the cold squishy sensation roiling through her insides. She opened the door, and a welcome blast of frigid night air washed over her.

"Please! You don't get it!"

Amelia stepped outside and shut the door behind her. She then turned the key in the lock.

"Nice! Real nice!" Braden's voice shouted after her. "But this isn't over. You can't ignore us forever!"

Amelia's smile withered as she trotted down the steps.

A bright moon peered down from the clear, black sky as a bone-chilling wind swirled the fallen leaves over the walkway.

You can't ignore us forever.

Maybe she could. Maybe she couldn't. Either way, she wasn't about to take any chances. Amelia pulled on her gloves, threw her shoulders back, and clicked her way down the path. Mere hours ago, she had been certain it wouldn't come to extreme measures, but it had, and now there was only one thing left to be done.

The ghosts had to go.

7

> Supreme excellence consists in breaking
> the enemy's resistance without fighting.
> —Sun Tzu, *The Art of War*

AMELIA'S SLEEP THAT NIGHT WAS FAR FROM RESTFUL. Even though she had made the decision to take care of the library's ghosts before they caused any lasting damage and had no intention of changing her mind, she tossed and turned until the wee hours of the morning.

When she finally gave up on sleep, she rose to head into the village for supplies. Luckily there was both a hardware store and an apothecary shop catering to tourists in town. Between the two of them she was able to get what she needed. Once that was through, she came back to the fish shop, had lunch, and tried to relax with one of her favorite alien-romance comfort reads. Given all her literary pursuits, some might find it odd that she was an admirer of extraterrestrial love, but those people had clearly never partaken of the genre. After attempting to read the same page at least twenty times, though, she abandoned her efforts and paced the apartment.

The plan was straightforward, but that didn't mean there weren't a million ways it could go wrong. *Theoretically.* She didn't really know, given she'd never attempted this particular form of ghost extraction before. There was also no guarantee what she had in mind would work. Regardless, she had to try. She was proud of the way she had handled herself the night before, but she had been alone when the ghosts launched their full assault. Behaving normally was always more difficult around people, and she couldn't take the risk that they wouldn't try something like that around the non-ghostseers.

Finally, it was time to leave. The day was cold and cloudy, but, thankfully, not wet. As always, the sea accompanied her for the first part of her walk, heaving in moody blue-gray shades, but when she turned into the village, she was greeted by a sidewalk carpeted with damp golden leaves that cushioned her every step. Despite her distaste for all things autumn, Amelia couldn't help but note, the gloom brought out a soft richness to the fading red and yellow hues of the village's remaining foliage, and the spirited colors of the various shops and cafés seemed even more vibrant. It was a gentle beauty to be savored among the island's more spectacular sights.

Late-afternoon shadows stretched across the drive as Amelia walked up to the library, her overstuffed bag hanging heavily on her shoulder. When she neared the top, she glanced about to see if anyone, living or dead, was lurking. Fortunately, while there were a few cars in the small parking lot, no one was outside. That was a nice bit of luck.

Luck that could turn at any time.

Amelia dipped her chin behind her scarf. She had to find cover. She was completely exposed standing out on the library's lawn, and the last thing she wanted was an audience. Any moment, a reader seeking a new dragon wars adventure could pull into the lot and witness what she was doing, or a poetry lover sitting inside by the windows might glance up from a bit of verse and spot her activities. And one of those people might mention her actions in passing to

Rosalinda or Simon, and that would lead to uncomfortable questions for which she did not have the appropriate answers.

Maybe this was a bad idea. She could give it more time. Get a better lay of the land. Observe and—

Stay the course, Amelia.

Right. Now was the time for resolve. Bold action.

Amelia glanced up at the sky as she crept by the parking lot headed for the side of the building. It was getting dark early now. The sharp crescent moon was already hooking clouds over the sea, and soon stars would dot the sky. Amelia lowered her heavy messenger bag to the ground by a series of thick sumac bushes. The last of their leaves rustled in the low wind as she flipped the flap open. Amelia then lifted the small but heavy plastic container filled with the supplies she'd bought earlier in the day from her bag.

Howlite. Salt. Tourmaline.

Everything she needed to make a ghost barrier.

A dog barked in the distance as Amelia hefted the container up to her hip. Originally, she worried she would have to dig a trench around the library, dump the minerals in like seed, and cover it back up again in order to make the barrier, but upon rereading her research notes on the topic, she was delighted to discover that she only had to sprinkle the mixture over the earth in a fairly even line. This particular recipe had been cited in twenty-eight sources, so she felt some confidence in its efficacy. But regardless, the point was that the process was extremely forgiving, which was good, because Amelia didn't have trench-digging time if she wanted to remain unseen.

Heart thumping in her throat, she headed over to the closest corner of the front wall with her plastic container, beads of sweat pricking her brow despite the temperature. She needed to be quick and careful to stay out of sight of anyone beyond the library's windows. Once she reached the shadow of the building, a sudden chill gripped her. Yes, the temperature had dropped, but this cold seemed to be coming from the library itself. She stared momentarily at the brick, then dismissed the sensation. She was imagining things. That's all. She wrapped her scarf around her neck in another loop with her free hand, then removed the lid from her container and dug her gloved hand into the grainy concoction.

Here goes nothing.

Taking slow, even steps, Amelia gently released the minerals from her clenched fist to the ground, but when she turned the corner, she came to a dead stop. For just a second, she thought she saw something running over the east wall. It looked almost like a silver crack cutting a path through the brick from the building's base all the way up to the third floor. But then she blinked, and it was gone. An illusion. The dying light had to be responsible for that.

Amelia continued with the barrier until she reached the building's other side and then carried on to the front of the library. Glancing nervously about, she laid her trail until she reached the stairs that led up to the entrance. She needed to leave a space there for now. Moving past the steps, she resumed her march on the other side. She had almost reached the end when the dreaded but somewhat expected call came from the front door.

"Yoo-hoo! Amelia?"

Amelia whipped around to see Rosalinda peeking over at her.

"What are you doing, dear?"

"Oh, I was just . . ." She looked down at her plastic container. "Fertilizing the library's lawn." That excuse had sounded much better when she had been pacing back at the apartment. "It helps to do it before winter."

Silence followed, and Amelia felt heat stir in her chest. Rosalinda was going to challenge her. At the very least ask her follow-up questions, which would lead to more lies and that would lead to—

"Well, that is so considerate of you."

What?

"Are you almost finished?" Rosalinda tightened her cardigan around her chest and did a cute little shudder. "It's getting cold. You should come in."

Amelia looked down at the plastic bin. "Yes—I, yes."

"Don't be long!"

ONCE AMELIA HAD hung up her coat, Rosalinda wrapped her arm around hers and said, "I'm so glad you're here." The older woman's eyes twinkled with as much enthusiasm as ever, but Amelia couldn't help but think she looked a bit pale.

"I know I'm early, but I'm glad to be here too," she said. "Is everything all right though?"

"Absolutely fine, but I was hoping to ask a favor of you. A friend of mine is in town, and we wanted to have an early dinner, so I was hoping you might cover the last of my shift?"

"Yes." The answer to that question was always yes. Even if working alone a little earlier in the day did make it more likely that she'd have to interact with visitors.

"Wonderful. If that's the case, maybe I'll leave now and have a little rest before I go."

Along with being pale, Rosalinda did also look tired. This was one of those tricky social interactions Amelia didn't know how to handle. She wanted to ask Rosalinda if she was feeling well, but was that too forward? Rude? Did older people get annoyed with being asked about their health? Apparently, all this showed on Amelia's face, because Rosalinda said, "I stayed up too late finishing the last book in the Ice Planet Savage Lover series. Have you read it?"

Twelve times. Amelia had read it twelve times.

Rosalinda continued before she could answer. "I highly recommend it." As they headed back to the circulation desk together, she added, "I'll just go collect my coat from the break room, but . . . where did I leave my purse?"

Amelia followed Rosalinda's searching gaze over the circulation area. "I'm always losing things." Suddenly the older woman snapped her fingers. "Now I remember. Would you be a dear and fetch it for me?"

"I'd be happy to." It was the truth. Amelia felt a little like an eager puppy around Rosalinda. "But where is it?"

"The workroom."

A pang of nervousness pinched Amelia's heart, and by *pang*, she meant *avalanche of crushing anxiety*. Simon worked in the workroom. Amelia wasn't yet prepared for another sudden one-on-one interaction with him. Maybe he was in the basement, though, or—

"Simon is finishing up a restoration project in there," Rosalinda said. *Innocently*. Maybe too innocently. "It's good to see him taking a break from worry. It's a lovely little project. You should ask him about it."

Amelia studied every line and crease of Rosalinda's face. Granted she had never been in this situation before, but suddenly it felt a little like she was being set up.

Rosalinda backed away trilling, "Tell him I said goodbye, would you?"

"Of course," Amelia muttered. "I'd be happy to."

BEFORE SHE REACHED the workroom, Amelia smoothed her hair and straightened her glasses in the reflection of the fire hose case on the wall. She had no intention of starting up any long conversations with Simon, but was it so wrong that she wanted to look her best? At least there wasn't any sign of the ghosts. It was possible that meant they were lying in wait, though, looking to startle her at the most inopportune time. All the more reason to fetch the purse quickly, then go.

The door to the workroom was slightly ajar, so Amelia peeked in. Simon had his forearms resting on the table, his legs reaching back in a runner's stretch. Amelia never could have imagined a librarian looking so *Olympian.*

"Knock-knock," she said, lightly rapping her knuckles on the door. *Knock-knock?* That had been a mortifying choice. Amelia willed her heart to stop beating to avoid any blushing.

"Hello there," he said, straightening. "You're early."

"Yes—I, yes." Eloquent as always. "Sorry to interrupt. I told Rosalinda I'd get her bag. She's leaving."

Simon glanced over to the door. "Is she all right?"

"Yes, fine," Amelia said, folding her hands by her waist in a gesture that likely would have looked more natural a century ago. "She's going out to dinner with a friend."

The tension in his shoulders dropped. "Oh, good."

Silence fell quickly and awkwardly as Amelia stepped in the direction of the purse. "Are you restoring a book?" And that clearly was the most painfully obvious statement she could make. Simon must have thought so too, given the twitch at the corner of his mouth. "I am."

"Very good," she replied.

Very good?

Time to get the purse and go. She clearly wasn't up to this, but on the way to Rosalinda's bag, Amelia couldn't help but crane her head to peek inside the plastic tub Simon had resting on the table. There were pages inside, floating in some sort of liquid. It was fascinating, so fascinating that she hit her hip on the edge of the table, causing a small tidal wave in the tub.

Simon's smile grew. "Would you like to take a look?"

Would she ever?! This wasn't even about Simon. Amelia wouldn't have been able to resist such a tempting offer from anyone. She hurried in closer. "Rosalinda mentioned you were working on something."

"It's an old book of fairy tales," he said, his voice dropping. "Some of the pages have fallen out and the cover needs touch-ups, but overall, it's in good shape."

Amelia glanced up at him. *Oh*, they were standing very close. Probably too close. That's why his voice had dropped. He would have been yelling at her if he kept his previous volume at this murmuring distance. Amelia swallowed hard before saying, "Does it affect the value if you rebind it?"

"Yes, absolutely, but this is a sentimental job," he answered. "The owner wants to give it to her granddaughter for a birthday gift."

"What is the liquid you have the pages soaking in?"

"Just hot water. Sometimes that's all it takes to remove the stains and old glue." He held up a thin scalpel. "Once the residue has softened, I'll be able to scrape off any imperfections." His hands were large, his fingers long, and yet he held the scalpel with a fascinating delicacy. "See the rounded tip? It's less likely to cut the paper than, say, a retractable knife." He looked down into the bin. "Thankfully, the owner didn't use tape to reinforce the pages. People are always doing that, but it's acidic and destroys the integrity of the paper."

Amelia didn't catch any of that. She was too fascinated by the dedication in his voice. She knew he was a man of passions. "You really love doing this, don't you?"

He met her eyes. "I do."

A sudden hesitancy sprang up between them, but then Simon asked, "Would you like to try?"

"Oh no." Amelia backed away with her hands up. "I wouldn't want to ruin it."

"It's not difficult. I'll show you. Here." He offered her the scalpel.

She stepped forward once more and accepted the thin blade, then lowered it toward the bin. "What do I do?"

"You just . . ." Suddenly his hand was over the top of hers, guiding it into the warm water. "Move it like this." He then steered her grip so that the scalpel lightly scraped away a thin string of glue. Amelia couldn't help but tense. His words, his actions were so casual, but for her . . . she couldn't remember the last time someone had touched her hand. "You're a natural."

Simon pulled away, and Amelia felt like she had been left in the cold of a thousand-year-long winter. "How did you learn to restore books?" she asked, scraping at more glue, fighting to keep her voice neutral.

"My dad taught me."

Amelia straightened and glanced back at him.

He gave her a small smile. "I'm sure Rosalinda has already told you my parents died. It's okay."

She nodded. "I'm sorry, Simon. That must have been terrible. It still must be . . ." There was so much more she wanted to say, but as always, words seemed to fail her when emotion was involved.

He crossed his arms over his chest and leaned back against the counter. "They gave me an incredible life. I have to be grateful for that. Growing up here was magical."

Amelia frowned. *Magical* and *childhood* were not words that often went together in her world. She peered into the water at the floating pages from the book of fairy tales. A picture of a castle with a girl chasing a golden ball by a creek stared back at her. "The Frog Prince." Amelia had never liked that one. She couldn't relate to the princess or the prince. Maybe just a story about a frog would have suited her better. She glanced back at Simon. "How so?"

He blinked as though surprised by the question. "Oh, well, we were together all the time. My dad was a lot of fun. On snow days, he'd teach me how to restore books and sort through donated documents, but then we'd toboggan down the ramp by the stairs." Simon smiled and looked in the direction of the west staircase, seemingly viewing the memory he'd been holding on to since youth. "My mom was convinced I'd break my arm. And speaking of my mom, on cold, rainy days like we've been having, she'd make us both tomato soup and grilled cheese sandwiches, and we'd read by the fire on the second floor back when the hearth was still functional." Simon's smile deepened a moment before he looked up at Amelia.

Amelia, who had lost the ability to speak.

"I'm sorry. Did I say something wrong? Is everything—"

"That sounds wonderful," she whispered.

And it did. Like a fairy tale.

He studied her face a moment, then gave her a small smile. "It was. They were good parents, and they loved the library so much."

Amelia nodded. "It's admirable that you've managed to keep it going."

"I couldn't have done it without Rosalinda," he said before inhaling deeply. "It's a labor of love for her. She worked here before my parents took over and has rarely missed a day. It is a special place. Did you know a shipping magnate originally bought it to use for storage?"

Amelia did know that. After being caught off guard the night of her interview, she had done a deep dive into the building's history.

"It sat unused for decades until his great nephew had the idea of turning the family's private library public. When he decided to sell the building, everyone thought it would shut down, but my parents wanted to keep it going despite all the impracticalities. They put everything they had into this place."

"And now it's yours," she replied quietly.

Simon sighed and scratched the corner of his jaw. "It's not as glamorous as it sounds. I feel like a bankrupt aristocrat trying to keep the country estate. Government funding keeps it going, and, believe me, if they wanted to take it over, I would have to consider it. But the interest isn't there despite the historical significance. It would be easier and cheaper to build a new library."

"A new library?" Amelia couldn't hide her disgust.

"I feel the same way. That's why I've been trying to come up with ideas to make the place more profitable while doing book restoring and trading on the side. I'm hoping to one day turn the third floor into a bookstore and rare archive of sorts." He shook his head and looked away. "We've always attracted our fair share of tourists visiting the Green Gables region, but I'm hoping to attract even more, and maybe researchers, if I can ever get things organized up there. At least that was the plan until all the problems with the building began. If there is something wrong structurally speaking—"

"There's not."

He looked at her quizzically.

"I mean, I'm sure it's nothing too serious." And she was sure for the most part. All the creaks, groans, and flickering lights? The ghosts had to be responsible for those. Once they were gone, the building would go back to normal. She was sure of it.

"So, you're an optimist."

Amelia blinked. "Not usually. No."

Simon laughed outright. It was a beautiful sound. "You know, I don't think I've ever met anyone quite like you, Amelia. For the most part, you're quiet, but why do I always feel like what you're not saying could fill one of those old card cabinets with endless stories of adventure, intrigue, and . . ."

Romance.

Those were her words from when she had been prattling on about her love for the Dewey decimal system. He had remembered her words.

"Sorry, I don't know what I'm talking about." He let go of an embarrassed laugh. "Forget I said anything. This time of year always makes me think about my parents. The anniversary of their death wasn't too long ago. And I guess I start rambling. I didn't mean to—"

"No, no, don't apologize," Amelia blurted. "I understand. This time of year is hard for me too." She felt sick as soon as the words left her mouth.

"Really?" He uncrossed his arms and planted his palms on the counter as though settling in for what had somehow, horribly, become her turn to share. "Why is that?"

"Many reasons." Amelia's eyes flicked over Simon's face. He had such a warm, open countenance. It would be so easy to lose herself and tell him . . .

Tell him what, exactly?

Right. She had to stop this. Simon had been so incredibly vulnerable with her, sharing his childhood memories, and all she could do was repay him with dishonesty. If he did eventually find out her secret, this conversation would be one of the many he would replay in his mind, wondering why she had never told him the truth, marveling at how easily she had lied. Amelia laid down the scalpel and moved to pick up the green leather purse sitting on the counter. "I should probably get back to Rosalinda."

"Of course." It was impossible not to hear the disappointment in his voice. "And, again, sorry about all that."

"Please. Don't be." She grabbed the bag and clutched it to her side.

"Maybe next time I'll let you get a word in," he said quickly. "You could tell me about your parents."

"They're gone." Amelia gripped the bag tighter, realizing how blunt that sounded.

"What? Amelia, I'm so sorry. Here I was going on and on. I didn't realize we were . . . the same."

"We're not." Again, blunt. Amelia forced a smile and met his eyes. "No, you see, it's fine. Really. It happened when I was a baby. I know nothing about them. I don't even know if they're alive or . . ." She was handling this terribly. She didn't want to present herself as some Dickensian orphan. She wanted Simon to see her as a normal person, filled with sunshine, good humor, and joy for life.

Perhaps that was too much to hope for. *Normal* would be fine.

"I'm so sorry." His dimple touched the corner of his mouth, but somehow it looked sad. "I didn't mean to pry. I guess I was just awkwardly trying to say thank you for listening."

She looked down at her fingers twisting the purse's handle and nodded.

"You're easy to talk to. People must tell you that all the time."

Amelia forced another smile but hurried for the door without looking back. She couldn't let Simon see how those last words affected her . . .

Because of course no one had ever said anything like that to her. Not even once.

8

"Let the wild rumpus start!"
—Maurice Sendak, *Where the Wild Things Are*

AMELIA SPENT THE FINAL HOURS THE LIBRARY REmained open sitting at the circulation desk. As the minutes ticked by, the lingering sadness from her conversation with Simon slowly abated under the comfort that came from being in the library. Indeed, the longer she sat in the chair, the more comfortable she felt, as though each passing minute somehow more deeply convinced her of her place. The sense of rightness was so strong, in fact, that it allowed Amelia to check out books for not one but two visitors with very little difficulty. The first reader didn't speak to Amelia at all, just passed her the books. Nods got them both through that interaction. During the second, though, the woman asked Amelia if she was new to the library, and she replied yes. Perhaps not the most robust of conversations, but she had done it. With a smile.

Gold star, Amelia.

The rest of the time, the library was completely quiet, except for when a book came sliding through the outside returns slot unexpectedly and Amelia screamed. In fairness, nerves were to be expected.

She had a job to do tonight—a job outside her regular job—and the stakes were high.

At eight o'clock sharp, Amelia walked to the front door, turned the sign to *Closed*, fastened the lock, and marched back into the main reading room. She couldn't help but feel a little like Mrs. Danvers from *Rebecca*. An evilish head housekeeper of an English manor probably wasn't a character most people wanted to emulate, but seeing as she was about to make some unwanted inhabitants feel extremely unwelcome, it seemed appropriate.

Suddenly Braden shimmered into view, blocking her path. "Hey, dude," he said with a smirk, "what's going on?"

Amelia almost stopped her march—*almost*—but instead opted to walk right through him. The cold, somewhat gooey feeling of death seeped through her for the second time in as many days. *Ugh*, that was awful. A truly awful sensation. She picked up her messenger bag resting by the chair, then continued to the nautical compass in the middle of the floor. From the corner of her eye, Amelia spotted the professor ghost on the mezzanine a few feet back from the railing, looking down at her. There was no sign of the creepy ghost, but Amelia suspected she would pop up anytime now.

"You should be flattered," Braden said. "The professor never leaves his chair. At least not until you showed up."

Amelia was not flattered, nor did she care about the professor's behaviors. Any of their behaviors.

"Okay, but seriously though? What's the 411?"

411? When she reached the center of the room, Amelia lowered her bag to the floor then kneeled in front of it. She should have brought her noise-canceling headphones. They really made following rule number two so much easier. It was fine though. This would all be over soon enough. She reached inside her bag.

"What's in the bag?"

Before Amelia could even think about ignoring Braden again, she heard someone hissing icy words beneath their breath. Keeping her face tilted down, she glanced in the direction of the horrible whisper. The dark one in the bonnet was back, hiding behind a rotating wire bookshelf of paperbacks. It was truly a terrifying sight, but thankfully, Amelia wasn't close enough to make out the ghost's actual words. They were probably something like *Die, librarian. Die.* Oh! What if the ghost had been killed by a librarian? Maybe that's why she was haunting the library. Maybe she had been pushed down the stairs! Or hit with a heavy book, like a dictionary! Or—

Focus, Amelia. It's time.

Indeed, it was. Amelia pulled a small tin box free from her bag.

She had purchased it from a most unusual store called the Grubbling in Charlottetown. The old stone building had captured Amelia's eye, but it was the name that drew her inside. She loved archaic words, and she had looked that one up on the spot in her favorite online Middle English dictionary. *Grubbling: (v.) to rummage through pockets and drawers.* It dated back to the 1500s.

The shop was an eclectic assortment of knickknacks and antiques, and the maze of shelves inside was loaded with paintings, jewelry, *and* leather-bound books. For the first time in Amelia's life, though, she hadn't been interested in the books.

No, it was the small tin box without any special markings that had caught Amelia's attention. She couldn't say how or why, but somehow, she knew without knowing what it was.

Not that she believed in such things.

The moment she had picked it up a woman in her late fifties or early sixties with silver corkscrew curls and the most alive eyes Amelia had ever seen appeared at her side and said, *How thrilling! A spirit box. You don't see those every day.*

Amelia couldn't have been more shocked. *A spirit box.* That was exactly what she had suspected it was. She had read all about them but never actually seen one. Not even a photograph. Faded illustrations only.

The woman suddenly held up a sucker in the shape of a maple leaf to Amelia's face. *Lollipop?* When Amelia didn't answer, the woman shrugged and put it in her own mouth, before narrowing her gaze back at the tin. *I've always thought them a bit rude.* She flicked her eyes back up to Amelia. *Spirit boxes. Not lollipops.* The woman inhaled sharply, then smiled. *But you're the ghostseer.*

Amelia's jaw had dropped as the woman twirled what appeared to be a wooden stake in the air before shoving it in a holster strapped to her thigh. *I love your hair, by the way. It's in all the right spots.* She then winked and was gone.

It had been a bizarre experience, but it had also given Amelia the confirmation she'd needed. She purchased the spirit box on the spot and held on to it just in case a situation arose where she might need it.

And now it had.

The sharp corners of the tin dug into Amelia's palms. It was so light. Unsubstantial. Given what it could do, she was always surprised by how flimsy it felt.

"What's in the box?" Suddenly the scent of what Amelia suspected was Axe body spray overwhelmed her senses. Braden had leaned in by her shoulder. "Is that for us?"

Oh yes, it is most definitely for you, but don't worry. You won't feel a thing.

Wait. Amelia rocked back on her heels, resting the box on her lap.

They wouldn't feel anything, right? She wasn't entirely sure. As she understood it, ghosts couldn't feel pain . . . unless they believed they could feel pain? From what she had read, the research was mixed.

Suddenly a deep cold pressed against Amelia's other cheek, and the creepy hiss she'd heard earlier whispered directly into her ear, "*Seeeecrets.*"

Amelia's insides quivered. *Secrets.* So that's what Minnie had been hissing about over by the paperbacks. Somehow that was even worse than *Die, librarian. Die.*

"We should really talk about this, Amelia," the professor called out from the mezzanine. "May I call you Amelia?"

Tsk-tsk. Sneaky ghost trying to trick her into answering. One of them must have overheard her name. Although he didn't sound sneaky, just polite.

"While I am certainly in no position to question your ghostseeing capabilities—"

Amelia jolted. *Ghostseeing?* How did he know the technical term?

"I fear it will not have the intended effect."

And what could he possibly know about its intended effect? Keeping hold of the box with one hand, Amelia closed her messenger bag with her other and pushed it to the side.

"We watched you make the barrier earlier, so I can only assume that the box is some sort of trap?"

Hmm, so the professor was both sneaky and smart. He had solved the mystery with just one clue. Although now that she was thinking about it, she supposed the jump of logic wasn't *that* great.

And yes, the spirit box was indeed a trap: a simple but powerful tool designed to suck in any ghost within a hundred-yard radius. It was exactly what the situation called for, and yet now that her plan was out in the open, the idea of using it felt, if not rude, certainly *awkward.*

"I don't think that box of yours is going to work, so would you please just talk to us?" Braden said, floating up to the enormous chandelier dangling overhead. "I've been haunting this library for months, trying to get someone's attention, and now you're here, but it's like we're dead to you." He snorted at his own joke.

First, no. She would not talk to them. That would be breaking the rules. And second, the joke was on him. That was an admission of guilt. Braden had just confessed that he at least had been actively haunting the library for months, likely driving all sorts of innocent readers away. Suddenly Amelia felt much better about evicting them.

Braden arranged himself in the chandelier's many arms, then threw back his head in despair. "What kind of ghostseer are you anyway?"

Ghostseer! There it was again.

"Like aren't you supposed to be a friend to us spirits?"

What? Where had he heard that? Amelia forced her shoulders down from her ears. She could not let them know they were getting to her.

Now is the time, Amelia. Open the box. They're trying to manipulate you. Goad you into answering them. But if you open that door even a little—

Braden scoffed loudly. "You haven't even asked us how you can help."

He said it almost as though that were her job. That her ability to see ghosts meant she was duty bound to help them. The sheer idea was . . . very uncomfortable. Rational Amelia was right. It was better to end this quick. No talking. She pressed into the edge of the lid with the pad of her thumb.

"I mean, my murderer could be walking the streets this very

moment planning his next kill, and you're doing nothing about it," Braden went on.

Don't answer him, Amelia.

She wouldn't. Of course she wouldn't. But was that true? Was there a murderer roaming the streets of the fishing village, and she was the only living person capable of stopping them?

"I mean, I wasn't murdered, but I could have been."

Truly insufferable.

Open the box, Amelia.

"Help me out here, professor," Braden said with a sigh of frustration. "She's like a brick wall."

The professor cleared his throat. "I'm sure she—I'm sorry, *Amelia*—has very good reasons for her caution."

Yes, she did. Amelia lifted the spirit box and tilted it side to side, pretending she wasn't in fact listening to them, just inspecting the tin. Not that she was fooling anyone. Clearly. And she didn't quite know why she wasn't opening the box. Perhaps it was a simple case of curiosity killing the cat. But as long as she didn't answer them, she couldn't see the harm, and truthfully, it was a unique experience listening to people talk about her and her abilities . . . even if they were dead.

"You see, Amelia," the professor said kindly, "while I am quite content spending my days here in the library, reading in my little nook by the fire—"

Amelia almost asked *What fire?* but then she realized he had to mean the decommissioned fireplace on the second floor. The one Simon had mentioned earlier. It did make for a nice little nook with the matching wingback chairs at its sides.

"Braden, here, would desperately like to leave, but he seems to be stuck."

Stuck? Amelia resisted rolling her eyes. There was quite literally no one stopping him from leaving. Not that she would point that out.

"But we don't have anyone living to help us get to the source of the problem," he posited lightly. "Someone, say, gifted at research?"

Amelia pressed her lips together.

Say. Nothing.

"And Minnie—"

The cold pushing up against Amelia's cheek deepened. Minnie must have moved in closer. Amelia squeezed her eyes shut.

"She could likely benefit from having someone to talk to."

"*Seeeecrets.*"

The word crawled with icy legs over Amelia's skin.

"Braden and I have tried, but we can't get beyond, well, *secrets.* But, again, if there was someone good at research, who could help us look into her past, then perhaps we could help her find peace. Every soul deserves to find peace, don't you think?"

Rational Amelia was right! He was manipulating her. Yes, of course she thought every soul deserved to find peace, but it wasn't her job to make that happen. No, this—what was happening right now—was exactly what she was trying to avoid. This was not how she wanted to spend her days. Or nights! She would not sacrifice her time alive parsing through the pasts of the dead, so they could what? Live *their* best undead lives? They had their chance. Whereas she had spent all her years up until this point living a small, scared existence because of spirits. That was done. It was her turn now.

"Given you're a librarian—"

Amelia nearly gasped. How dare he use that against her! Was he trying to imply she was an unhelpful librarian?

"—and given that you can see us—"

He had no proof of that!

Just open the box, Amelia.

The professor wasn't done speaking though. He had been working himself up to asking her the question they all likely knew he was going to ask for a while now, and Amelia found she couldn't stop listening.

"So, given your unique abilities and your chance arrival at this particular library," he continued cautiously, "maybe *you* could be the one to help us?"

"No!"

The shocking sound of Amelia's own voice echoed over the walls of the library, followed by a horrifying silence.

Oh dear. What had she done?

Amelia glanced about cautiously. She had jumped to her feet without even realizing it, but . . . not one of the ghosts had reacted, so maybe they hadn't heard that? Or maybe she hadn't said it at all? Only shouted it in her mind. Or—

"I told you!" Braden screamed, tumbling from the chandelier. "I told you she could see us!" He rocketed toward the floor until he came to a dead stop hovering in front of her, brilliant victory beaming in his smile. "Damn, I thought you were never going to crack." He crossed his transparent arms over his chest. "It's over now though. We got you! You have to help us."

Suddenly Amelia's horror vanished. Because that was where he was wrong.

Outwardly, she didn't react. She didn't move. She didn't breathe. She didn't blink. She simply held Braden's gaze until the smile faded from his face. Once that had happened, she said in a tone so icy, she gave herself chills, "Let us be clear. I am speaking to you this one time, and this one time only, because there is something you should know."

Braden swallowed, making his ghostly Adam's apple jump in his throat. "What's that?"

Amelia stepped toward him until she was close enough to feel his cold, and somewhat sparkly, aura waft over her.

"I. Don't. Help. Ghosts."

And with those words she flipped open the lid of the spirit box.

9

Ay, now the plot thickens very much upon us.
—George Villiers, Duke of Buckingham,
The Rehearsal

A GREAT GUST OF WIND ROARED THROUGH THE LIbrary, and before Amelia could blink, Braden, Minnie, and the professor stretched into thin, glowing wisps that were immediately sucked in sparkling whirlwinds toward the box. Once they were fully inside, she slammed the lid shut.

It worked.

She couldn't believe it.

But it had worked!

Truthfully, at several points during the encounter, she had felt the tiniest bit guilty about taking this route, but now that it was done . . .

Well, it had to be done, not just for her, but for the library, Rosalinda, Simon, and the ghosts. Of course, once she got them outside, she'd finish the barrier so they couldn't get back in, and then she'd set them free. And yes, they might be angry—maybe give her a hard time when she came to and from work—but she could stomach that if it meant the library was ghost-free. Eventually they'd get bored, surely, and then they could use this opportunity to grow, figure out what it was that was keeping them on this mortal plane, and move on.

Everybody would win.

Clutching the box to her chest, Amelia jogged to the front door. She grasped the handle and wrenched it open before launching herself toward the outside, but instead of diving into the cold night air, she was hit by an invisible force that knocked her from her feet and threw her right back into the library.

When she hit the floor, she rolled like a log all the way back to where she had started, the box tumbling from her hand and breaking into pieces.

Amelia lay spread-eagle staring up at the ceiling through the slits of her eyes, completely, utterly stunned.

Suddenly Braden and Minnie appeared above her, their transparent faces blearing the view of the chandelier.

"You okay?" Braden whispered.

Amelia snapped her eyes shut. That was better. The cool, hard tile of the marble floor felt grounding, almost reassuring against her back. Granted, it hadn't felt that way when she was tumbling over it. At least she hadn't hit her head. *Wait!* Maybe this was all a dream? Maybe she had hit her head on the boardwalk the night of her job interview and everything that had happened since then was just the result of coma-induced imaginings!

"Did she just die?" Braden muttered. "Is she dead?"

No, this wasn't a coma. It was all too *annoying.* Maybe if she just kept her eyes closed, the ghosts would go away.

"I think we of all dead people would know, Braden," the professor called out from a distance. What was he still doing up on the mezzanine? Should he not also be checking on her? Curiosity alone would seem to dictate an up-close look. And what was his obsession with the second floor anyway? Did he—

No. *No!* She didn't want to know!

How could she have let this happen? And why hadn't the spirit box worked? Was it because she tried to use it on three ghosts at once? She had to go back and check her notes. Maybe she had missed that detail. Or maybe she should have done something differently. Or given this scenario more time to play out. Or done anything else but this . . .

But now it was too late. The damage was done.

Amelia blinked her eyes open.

"Hey!" Braden shouted with goofy excitement. "There you are. You all right? Say something."

Amelia shook her head in disbelief. "What . . . is wrong with you?"

In a knee-jerk reaction, she almost slapped a hand over her mouth, but what would be the point? She had broken all three of her rules already. There was no going back. Now she had to face the consequences.

"We're trapped! That's what we've been trying to tell you!" Braden threw his arms wide. "We're prisoners in this old hella-boring library."

"Bite your tongue," Amelia snapped, struggling up to a seated position. She was going to feel her tumble across the marble floor tomorrow, but for now, it didn't seem like any serious damage had been done.

"Bite your tongue?" Braden laughed, then made a face. "How old are you?"

Amelia frowned. "How old am I?" She knew what he was getting at. Given the fact she was raised by books from a variety of genres, time periods, and geographical settings, Amelia knew she didn't exactly speak like most other people her age, but he didn't have to draw attention to it. "How old are *you*? Forty? Forty-five? Fifty? What year did you die?"

Braden gasped like all the undead air had been sucked right out of his lungs. "Ghost years don't count!"

Amelia gave him a skeptical eye roll.

"Damn, I think I liked it better when she wasn't talking," Braden said to Minnie. The bonneted nightmare didn't react, simply held her glowing death stare.

"Children?" the professor ghost called out from above. "I assure you, you're both very young. Perhaps we could shift the conversation to something more productive? It's lovely to hear your voice, Amelia."

Amelia cut Braden a look but then regained her composure. She had lost herself there momentarily, but it wasn't her fault! She was talking to ghosts. Dear God, she was talking to ghosts. She gripped her forehead and took a long, slow breath. "Right. You want me to listen? I'm listening. What is going on here? What have you all done to upset the order of the universe? Why are you trapped?"

"So, you automatically think it's our fault. Nice." Braden didn't exchange looks with Minnie this time because at some point the ghost had relocated. That was disturbing. "We don't know why we're trapped," Braden continued. "We just are. We've all tried to leave. Lots of times. Well, not the professor. He's happy right where he is, but I've tried. I still have lots I want to do with my afterlife! I think Minnie has tried to leave too, but I can't be sure. It's hard to know, what with the *secrets* thing."

Even though Amelia didn't know where Minnie was, she could

still somehow feel the ghost's bulbous blue eyes drilling into her skull.

"That's why your little box didn't work." Braden flung a hand in the direction of the smashed bits of tin scattered across the floor. "You have to help us. I'm going crazy here. This is like my version of hell. Do I look like a library guy to you?"

"No," Amelia said plainly.

He frowned. "You didn't have to answer that quickly."

The professor cleared his throat. "Braden, perhaps I could . . . ?"

Braden held up his hands and floated back and away, giving up the floor. Amelia appreciated the space. The library was suddenly feeling quite claustrophobic.

"If I'm not mistaken, Amelia," the professor called out from above, "you seem to have great affection for the library."

She refrained from answering but did look up to—*give her strength*—acknowledge his existence.

Taking her silence as agreement, he continued. "Given that is the case, you should know the problem goes beyond us simply being trapped. Something is happening to the building, and we suspect it isn't good. Unlike Braden, I have been here for as long as I can remember, and I've never experienced anything like it. Minnie, I assume, has been here even longer, at least a century, and I believe she would say the same. Isn't that right, Minnie?" He directed his gaze to a spot just beyond Amelia's left shoulder. An icy voice that sounded like it was traveling on a stale wind through catacombs suddenly whispered over the back of her neck, "*Seeeecrets*."

Lovely. Amelia stepped away without looking back.

"Yes," the professor continued, "it is a secret in a sense. Or a mystery. But whatever force that is keeping us trapped in the library is also damaging the building." He gave Amelia a look so filled with pleading she had to avert her gaze. "Try as we might, we can't fix the situation by ourselves."

"I see." Amelia tapped her foot lightly on the tile and closed her eyes. "I hate to be blunt." She didn't actually. "But why don't you all just move on to the other side? Like you are supposed to."

"I told you. I'm not ready yet," Braden said.

"I'm afraid I can't," the professor added.

Minnie didn't say anything at all.

Right. They didn't want to move on. Marvelous.

A heavy silence fell over them, making it difficult for Amelia to breathe . . . and that inability to breathe stirred up feelings of panic. Before she knew it, brief hysteric thoughts were piercing her consciousness like shards of glass. This couldn't be happening. Why was she listening to them? The library was fine. They were the problem! This was what happened when you talked to ghosts. They got in your head. Confused everything. Granted, she had never actually talked to any other ghosts, but—

That's enough, Amelia. Go home.

Amelia picked up her messenger bag off the floor and headed for the foyer.

"Where are you going?" Braden shouted after her. "Didn't you hear what he said?"

Do not look at them. Do not listen to them. Do not talk to them.

"You're a ghostseer! You're supposed to help us."

Amelia stilled. *Supposed to help them?* Again, he said it with such authority, like it was understood.

The problem was even if she wanted to help them, she wasn't the ghostseer they thought she was. She wouldn't know where to begin. So why would she risk everything she had so recently gained for a doomed plot?

"You're our only connection to the living world," the professor said. "Even if you don't know what's going on, there have to be people who would help. People you can talk to."

Ha! He wanted her to tell other people? Tell them what? That there were three ghosts—only she could see—trapped in a library who needed a rescue party?

Amelia hiked her bag higher on her shoulder and walked on.

"Be honest," Braden shouted, floating after her. "You know there's something weird going on. Tell me you can't feel it."

Amelia stopped. All she had ever felt from this library was a sense of belonging. Yes, people kept saying something was going on with it. Then there was the terrified expression of that man fleeing the building . . . and the fact that she had been thrown by an invisible force across the floor.

Maybe it was worth trying to sense *something*?

Against all her better judgment, Amelia closed her eyes and felt . . . *nothing*. Well, not nothing. She was aware of the library's presence, its unique scent and feel brushing up against her skin. She could also sense the weight of all the books and hear the murmurings of their stories, but those things were likely just impressions she wanted to feel. Was there anything more?

Amelia pushed beyond her own thoughts.

Hmm. There was something . . . a distant but ominous, cold, dark *something*.

Yes, incredibly, in some extrasensory way, she felt like she was picking up on the approach of an enormous presence. Like she was witnessing the rise of some great Lovecraftian leviathan, not from the depth of the ocean, but from all existence—a terrible beast threatening to destroy not only the library, but every soul within its uncaring grasp.

Amelia's eyelids snapped open. *Ridiculous.* Of course she felt something. It was placebo! She hurried for the door.

"Oooh, don't you even!" Braden shouted. "I know you felt it!"

Amelia gripped the door handle but couldn't seem to find the strength to open it.

"You have to help us."

No, Amelia. Now is the time to regroup. Recommit to the rules.

Behind her, Braden and Minnie floated up to the threshold of the foyer. She didn't have to turn; she could feel them there.

"Please," Braden said, his voice suddenly drained of all vigor. "You're our only hope."

Don't do it!

Amelia pushed the door open and stepped outside. As it slowly closed behind her, she peered over her shoulder to give the ghosts one last look.

"I'll think about it."

AMELIA LAY IN bed underneath her heavy quilt listening to the slow drip of rainwater plunking into the bucket resting in the center of the room. Her landlord still hadn't patched the ceiling.

I'll think about it?

How could she have said that? She had gone into tonight believing she was prepared. But she clearly hadn't been. Not at all. In fairness, though, the library's ghosts hadn't behaved much like ghosts. No, they had behaved like *people.*

And people were something Amelia knew very little about.

In the stillness of the dark apartment, Amelia was subsumed by a sudden sense of loneliness.

What was she going to do? She had no idea how to handle this.

If only she had someone to talk to.

She could try Rosalinda. Amelia felt there was a chance she'd believe her, given her own beliefs about sentient libraries, but then Simon would most likely find out, and she knew he wasn't a believer in supernatural things. She couldn't risk that. And there was no one else. There never had been, and there likely never would be because the truth was there weren't just three rules for ghostseeing. There were four.

Don't tell anyone the truth. Not ever.

Really, that was the most important rule of all because it was the one that kept her safe. It was the one that would allow her to have a life, even if it was a lonely one. So that meant she had to figure this out on her own. And she would! This job, this place, was worth fighting for. While she didn't know exactly what was causing all the library's problems, Amelia couldn't help but think staying the course, finding a way to get the ghosts out of the building, was the best way to set things right. Yes, the professor had been going on and on about talking and researching, but all that could take a really long time. Amelia wanted to end this quickly and definitively. There had to be other ways to banish spirits from a building. And Braden at least didn't appreciate being stuck in the library. So, she'd find a way to get him unstuck. As for the other two, well, she'd deal with them afterward. On the outside.

New hope sizzled, rallying Amelia's dampened spirits. Yes, there had to be another way. Some heretofore undiscovered mechanism to banish ghosts from the premises. Her academic resources might have failed her, but that didn't mean there weren't other, more mundane options. What did the everyday homeowner do in this situation?

Amelia clicked on her lamp and grabbed her phone off her rickety nightstand. Turning to the internet for ghost information was always a risky proposition, but she was a self-appointed expert on the subject matter. Surely, she would be able to separate the wheat from the spectral chaff.

Several hours later, and many dollars poorer, Amelia placed her phone back on the night table. Most of the sites she discovered had been overwhelmingly disappointing, but she had purchased a number of items on credit from one seemingly trustworthy online shop. Likely none of the products would help, but at least she had done something.

Amelia glanced over at the alien-romance novel she'd tried to disappear into earlier that day. Now that she had accomplished something, maybe she would be able to lull herself to sleep with the trials and tribulations of blue-horned love.

Just as she snuggled deep into her quilts, an unexpected *ping* jolted Amelia up to sitting. Given her lack of friends, she didn't often receive texts. Amelia looked over at her phone suspiciously. Hopefully her web surfing hadn't invited in a world of spam. She reached over and tilted the screen.

Simon!

Amelia tossed her book to the side—something she would never normally do—and jumped up to sit with her back resting against the wall. She clutched her phone with both hands.

Hi Amelia, I hope this text doesn't wake you. Is it possible for you to come in early tomorrow? Rosalinda can't make it, and I have some business with an engineering company. Let me know when you get this. Simon.

Without any thought, Amelia texted, Yes. Then clenched her fist in frustration. She was monosyllabic with this man even by text! She needed to add something warmer, friendlier.

Thank you.

Amelia squeezed her eyes shut and shook her head as the phone pinged again.

No, thank you. And sorry for texting after hours.

A second chance!

No apologies necessary. I was reading before bed.

The steady *plunk* of raindrops in the bucket resting on the floor became deafening as Amelia hyperfocused on the three dots in the message window. He was writing her back. That's what the three dots meant, didn't they?

Suddenly they disappeared.

No! She couldn't let him go so easily.

You?

Amelia's grip on her phone turned her knuckles white. What had she done? That wasn't appropriate.

Also reading. Which book?

He'd answered her! They were communicating, chatting like friends. She had to reply. Amelia glanced over at the couple embracing on the cover of her interspecies romance, then texted, War and Peace.

Tolstoy before bed. You're a braver reader than I.

Truthfully, Tolstoy had always given Amelia trouble. At times she found his work long and maybe a touch boring. It was an unusual stance for her to take. She normally loved big books and rarely found classics boring, but—none of that mattered! Simon was making Tolstoy jokes! Amelia smiled, then typed, You?

The Hound of the Baskervilles. Sherlock is always my go-to in the fall.

An excellent choice. Truly. Stormy moors, ancient rock huts, wind and rain raging outside. She should really pick up a copy herself and—

Night Amelia.

No! She'd bungled things again! She should have been typing something, anything, to keep the conversation going, but she'd missed her chance. There was nothing to be done now except, Night.

Amelia's arms fell to her sides. As sad as it might seem, that had been the greatest text exchange of her life. *And* they texted now. She supposed their conversation that day had brought them closer. Better yet, the overwhelming feeling of loneliness she had been holding was gone, and—

Manage your expectations. Simon is not meant for ghostseers like you.

Gripping her quilt, Amelia scooted back underneath the covers.

That seemed a little harsh. She was painfully cognizant of all the obstacles that stood in the way. But everyone needed free time to dream impossible dreams. And was it really so impossible to wonder if one day she and Simon could be something? Even if that something was simply friends? Was it so preposterous to think that maybe if they got to know each other, *really* know each other, trust each other, that she could tell him the truth? That he would be able to believe her because the weight of what he knew to be true about her character would outweigh his disbelief? And then maybe . . .

Stop.

Amelia blinked against the sudden sting in her eyes and clicked off her light.

It had been a long day, and she was no longer in the mood to read.

10

"I shall find out thousands and thousands of things."
—Frances Hodgson Burnett, *The Secret Garden*

WHEN AMELIA ARRIVED AT THE LIBRARY THE FOLlowing morning, the ghosts were waiting for her in the foyer right where she had left them.

Because of course they were.

Well, Braden was in the exact same spot. Minnie, though, was hiding ominously in the shadows of a tall, leafy green plant. The professor, Amelia could only assume, was still on the second floor.

"So?" Braden asked before she had even had the chance to take off her coat.

Amelia cut him a look, then unraveled her scarf at a methodically slow pace. Thankfully, sleep had restored her resolve if not her spirits. She had faced challenges before. This one was no different.

"Did you think about it? Are you going to help us?"

Peeking into the main reading room, she hissed, "We are not talking about this right now."

Braden's eyes widened with cartoonish excitement. "But you're going to help us?"

"I am going to try." She hung her coat up before hefting her bag back up to her shoulder. "But the only way this is going to work is if you guys leave me alone during working hours. I'm not going to be able to help you if I get fired for talking to people no one else can—"

"Amelia?"

Simon!

Where had he come from? It didn't matter. The important thing was now he was standing in the entrance of the foyer, wearing a navy crewneck sweater over his collared white shirt and slacks. It was a stunning ensemble.

Amelia wanted to give him an excuse about what she was doing having a whispered argument with herself by the front door, but when she realized she had nothing beyond *I was just* . . . she went with, "Good morning." It was unfortunate, really, given that she'd spent several hours upon awakening planning out her conversation with him. She had a delightful Sherlock-esque opener ready, but it was gone now too.

Stupid ghosts.

He looked about the room, confused. "Thank you for coming in. It looks like it's going to be another quiet day." Worry touched his brow. Amelia's fingertips tingled with the desire to smooth it away. "I hope you won't be too bored."

All tingling ceased. What did he mean by that? Was he trying to get her to quit again?

He plunged his hands into his pockets. "Hopefully the engineering company will have some answers about what has been going on with the library."

"Really, I'm sure it's nothing serious," Amelia said. "The library seems perfectly fine to me."

Just then the lights flicked on and off. Simon glanced about the room while Amelia glared at Braden chuckling by the switch.

"Amelia?"

"My apologies," she said, turning back to Simon. "I thought I saw something, but it was *nothing.*" Out of the corner of her eye, she caught Braden clutching his nonexistent heart. "And please, don't concern yourself about me. I was actually hoping to get some research done today if you have nothing ready for me to do. The Wi-Fi in my apartment is subpar, to say the least. Is it possible to use the library's computers?"

The now familiar twitch came once again to the corner of his mouth. "Of course. What are you researching? Can I help?"

Amelia's chest caved at the request, making it impossible to breathe, let alone respond. More than anything she wanted to say yes, and yet she had to find the strength and say, "Oh no. The topic isn't all that interesting."

"Do you often research uninteresting topics?" He adjusted his glasses and gave her a charming smile.

"I suppose that depends on one's definition of *uninteresting.*"

"Fair enough." He looked back into the library. "Well, if you need anything, or you change your mind, I'll be in the workroom."

This was death by a thousand cuts. "Thank you, but I'll be fine."

"Right, of course you will," he said, rocking on his feet. Surprisingly, he didn't seem all that eager to leave. "I mean, you're a librarian. You don't need another librarian. It's like they say, you don't want too many librarians in the . . . library."

Was he blushing?

She must have made him uncomfortable. And he was wrong. She did want another librarian! After she had three fewer ghosts.

"Well, good luck with it." He held up his hand, then left.

"Bro," Braden said, floating up to her side as she watched Simon leave, "why didn't you let him help you? And why were you talking like that?"

Amelia frowned. "Like what?"

"Like you're about to correct everyone's grammar."

As terrible as it was, she could see how that might be the case. She was self-aware enough to know that her affectations did get worse when she was nervous. Growing up it had been a form of self-defense. She'd have to work on that. Maybe avoid the use of *subpar.*

Suddenly, Braden leaned in close enough for her to see the individual ghost hairs of his goatee and studied her face. "Ooh, I get it now. You like him."

"What?" She scoffed. "No, I—"

"If it makes you feel any better, I think Librarian Ken likes you too."

Amelia's gaze flashed to Braden's. She must have looked a little intense because he floated back, but she couldn't help her intensity. Hearing someone else, even a ghost, speculate that Simon might like her, was almost more than she could take. It was like a dream come true, except . . .

He doesn't like you, Amelia. How could he? He doesn't know who you really are.

"I didn't let *Simon* help me," Amelia explained, looking away from Braden, "because I'm not telling him anything about you all or your unfortunate presence in the library."

"*Seeeecrets.*"

Amelia jolted badly enough that her faux-leather ballerina flats nearly slipped out from underneath her. She'd forgotten about Minnie, but the ghost still hiding in the plant wasn't wrong.

"Yes," Amelia said, restraightening her sweater, "it is a secret, and

I plan to keep it that way. Now, leave me alone. We'll talk after the library is closed." As she crossed the threshold from the foyer into the main reading room, she muttered, "And my name is not Bro."

FOR FOUR AND a half hours, Amelia searched—she searched every database, catalogue, and archive she could think of. Unfortunately, and perhaps unsurprisingly, *trapped ghosts* didn't yield many results. She then loaded up Cartwell with all the books she could find in the library on spirits in general and pushed the lot back to the circulation area. She wasn't particularly optimistic about discovering anything useful. Given her research over the years, Amelia was already familiar with most of the texts in her selection, certainly the authors, and she couldn't remember reading anything about ghosts being held hostage in a library, but it was possible she might come across something new.

After flipping through the pages of the first ten or so books, though, things started to feel hopeless. She couldn't find any mention of ghosts being stuck in buildings anywhere. The closest she came was an old catalogue card being used as a bookmark. The title listed on its front was *Spectral Irregularities and Other Problems.* The title was vague, but trapped ghosts did seem to fall into that category. Plus, she had never come across this book or this author, and that was intriguing in and of itself. Unfortunately, when she looked for the call number, there wasn't any.

Suddenly the light in the library dimmed and a sheet of rain hit the windows. Amelia put her head down on the circulation desk.

She had forgotten her umbrella again.

A second later, a small clatter sounded by her ear. Amelia whipped her head up and instantly spotted on the desk a steaming teacup covered with painted pink rosebuds nestled snugly in a saucer.

"You looked like you could use a cup," Rosalinda said, appearing just behind Amelia, and quite pleased with her handiwork.

"Thank you so much." Amelia pinched the delicate handle and lifted the cup until she was able to catch the sweet, spicy scent of Earl Grey. After so many frustrations, it was almost enough to move her to tears. "You're not supposed to be here."

"My day ended early, and I had this strange feeling you all might need me." Rosalinda held a tin out to her. "Cookie?"

Ginger snaps. Perfect for dipping in tea. The kindness of it all was too much. Amelia sniffled as she lowered her hand into the tin, and Rosalinda's delicate eyebrows shot up in concern. "Oh no, what's the matter?"

"Nothing," Amelia said brusquely, quickly grabbing a tissue off the desk. "It's just been a long day."

"I can see that," Rosalinda said, surveying all the mini stacks of books littering the circulation area.

Horror surged in Amelia's breast. What had she been thinking leaving all these ghost books lying around? "They're for a friend." She almost supplied a name, but when all she could come up with was Bedelia, she pressed on. "She's a bit of a ghost aficionado."

Lies. Lies. Lies.

"Were you able to find what you—I mean *she*—needs?" Rosalinda asked, still eyeing the collection.

"Not exactly," Amelia answered, trying to hide the dejection from her voice. "There is this one book that might help. I found an old catalogue card for it, but there's no number. It must have been weeded from circulation."

"Do you have the card?"

Amelia passed it to Rosalinda, who lifted her chained glasses from her chest to get a better look. "We still have this one."

"We do? Really?" Amelia felt the tiniest bit presumptuous including herself in the *we*, but Rosalinda didn't seem to mind.

"I wouldn't get too excited just yet." She dropped her glasses back to her chest. "Do you see this marking?"

Amelia stared at the spot Rosalinda indicated on the card. "S. C.?"

"Special collections. This book will be upstairs on the third floor. It's currently not open to the public."

The legendary third floor! The floor Simon had talked about that first night before Minnie had ruined everything. She hadn't allowed herself to think about it since then. It was all too upsetting, but now . . .

Amelia pushed her chair back. "That's wonderful. Would it be okay if I went up and did a quick search?"

"By all means," Rosalinda exclaimed, "but I don't think there will be anything quick about your search."

AFTER HUNTING FOR the door marked *Staff Only* hidden away in the shadows of the second floor, Amelia climbed a thin, dark staircase up to the third level. When she reached the landing, she was greeted with a bouquet of nerves. Suddenly she felt like a trespasser. Would Simon mind her coming up here alone? In their brief conversation, she'd had the impression that this was a special place to him, but then again, Rosalinda had told her to come up.

Amelia gripped the door's old brass knob, glinting dully in the darkness. Speaking of Rosalinda, she'd insisted Amelia finish her tea while she prepared her for what she would find up here, but when Amelia opened the door, she instantly realized that was impossible.

Breathe.

Breathe, yes. It was an innate skill, but heavy, heavy excitement was threatening to crush Amelia's lungs, making it exceedingly difficult. If this library was indeed a universe filled with catalogued worlds, she was now an explorer in thrilling, undiscovered territory.

Thin light stretched from the west-facing Roman arched windows, casting a mysterious, almost dreamlike glow across the wooden floors. Amelia struggled over where to direct her focus first. There was just so much. It was the shelves, though, that dominated the space and held everything together. Amelia had thought of the stacks on the floors below as tall, but these were towering. They were also industrial, but not in a shiny box-store way. They were far too old for that. No, these were more Victorian-factory chic. And they weren't just filled with books—although there were hundreds, if not thousands, of them up here. No, these shelves were also stacked with boxes of all shapes and sizes. And while some were labeled with tags identifying the contents as newspapers, maps, or letters, most were mysterious treasure chests waiting to be opened. It would take a lifetime to go through them all. What Amelia would give to have it be her lifetime.

Tentatively, she walked down the center aisle that split the room into halves, dust motes swirling with each of her steps. For some inexplicable reason, she felt the urge to hold her breath, maybe fearing if she made too loud a noise, it would all disappear. After passing the first two rows, dominated mainly by boxes, Amelia entered the book section.

They were all so deliciously *old.*

Rosalinda had explained that despite all the beautiful chaos, the nonfiction books, at least, were divided by subject area, and Simon had made attempts to alphabetize them by the authors' last names. There were hundred-plus-year-old manuals on gardening, cooking, etiquette, astronomy, and more. The topics were endless, and all offered views into worlds long past, but Amelia couldn't stop to marvel at any of those now. No, she was headed for the far back corner, where she'd find the paranormal section.

It was tragic, really. There were so many subject areas Amelia wanted to lose herself in, but she was stuck focusing on the part of her life she wanted most desperately to forget. It had to be done though. She promised herself that once she had the library's ghost problem sorted, she would have all the time in the world to explore.

When Amelia reached the end of the aisle, she turned left and headed into the shadowed corner. It didn't take long to confirm she was in the right place. Every shelf was packed with books on vampires, werewolves, witches—a great deal on witches—but where were the ghosts?

Amelia scanned the stacks, then planted her hands on her hips. She had to do this systematically. She walked back to the beginning of the shelf and dropped her gaze to the bottom ledge, walking slowly, scanning titles. When she reached the halfway mark, the books changed to zoology, so she headed back again, scanning the titles on the second shelf from the bottom. She then repeated the process for the shelf above and then the shelf above that. Amelia searched on and on, somehow knowing . . .

. . . the ghosts would be at the very top.

Amelia craned her neck, barely able to make out the titles.

How was she supposed to get up there?

As soon as she had formulated the question, she spotted the answer. At the very end of the aisle, past all the zoology books, hidden in the gloom, was an old-fashioned rolling ladder. She ran over in light steps and placed her fingertips on the smooth metal. "Hello," she whispered. "What's your name?"

Don't talk to ladders, Amelia. Cartwell is enough.

Rational Amelia could really be a killjoy at times.

Wrapping her hands around the railing, Amelia gave the ladder an experimental tug. Gears at the top and bottom of the track let out a low whine but resisted moving more than an inch.

"Has no one been taking care of you?" It sounded like it needed oil, but there was no can in sight, leaving brute force as the only option. Amelia moved to the ladder's side and gave it a push. Then another. After a few more failed attempts, the ladder suddenly groaned, its wheels finding traction, allowing Amelia to push it in lurching steps all the way over to the paranormal section.

There.

She then grabbed the handrails and planted her foot on the bottom plank. Hmm, it felt a bit wobbly. She'd have to be careful. Climbing with wary steps, Amelia didn't stop until she reached the utmost platform, her eye level right at the bottom of the top shelf. She needed another step to make this comfortable. If only she were taller . . . and didn't see ghosts. Every wish she'd ever had ended that way.

There were so many books on spirits, but what truly surprised Amelia was that there were so many she had never heard of. *The Encyclopedia of the Dead. Spectral Lexicon. Manual of Manifestation. Ghostscriptium?* But no sign of the book she came up here to . . .

There! *Spectral Irregularities and Other Problems.*

Amelia pulled it free, then leaned against the ladder to flip through the pages.

Her heart sank with every word. This wasn't what she needed at all. The book was a ghost-hunting manual, focused on the difficulties involved in pursuing spirits. The last thing she needed was to find more ghosts! She slid it back on the shelf and eyed the other selections.

Running her fingertips along the spines, she stopped at the very thick *Encyclopedia of the Dead*. It seemed like as good a place as any to start. She pulled it out, then tucked it under her arm. She then gripped the railing with her free hand, readying herself to climb back down, but just as her foot dropped to the first step, she spotted something in the gap left by the encyclopedia. Another book pushed behind all the others.

As her eyes captured the title, chills raced over her arms and up the back of her neck.

It couldn't be.

She'd thought its existence a myth, but there it was, staring her in the face.

The Ghostseer's Handbook.

11

What you seek is seeking you.
—Rumi, attributed

AMELIA STARED INTO THE SHADOWS OF THE TOWERing shelves at the book she'd always hoped to find. The ghostseeing text that had always evaded her. The manual that promised to answer the questions she'd held for so long. The handbook that might finally tell her about *herself*. Suddenly she lost hold of the heavy encyclopedia pinned to her side. It hit the floor with a weighty *thwack*, releasing a cloud of dust into the air. Her fingertips flew to her mouth. "I am so sorry."

Focus, Amelia.

Yes, she would have plenty of time to apologize to the encyclopedia later. Right now, there was only one book that mattered.

How was this possible? Amelia had searched the world over, or at least its databases and catalogues, and had never found evidence of a single copy still in existence. But there it was, tucked far back in the shadows cast by the other books, its gilded cover winking at her in the gloom. She reached through the empty slot, ignoring the delicate tickle of what she suspected were spiderwebs caressing her arm.

Finally, her fingertips brushed the cover, but the shelving was so deep, there was no way she was going to be able to reach it.

Unacceptable. She needed that book.

Amelia's gaze darted side to side, up and down. Maybe she could stack some books on the ladder for extra height. Given the structure's general wobbliness, though, that seemed like a dangerous plan. She needed a tool. Something that would give her the extra inch or two she needed to reach the book. But what?

Her glasses!

Amelia gripped the ladder tightly with her left hand and grabbed one of the tortoiseshell arms of her lenses with her right. She pulled her glasses off her nose and blinked. While the blinking did nothing to restore her sight, she would not be dissuaded now. She reached her hand once again into the hole, turning her head to the side so she could stretch her arm as far as it could go. Now if she could just hook the top of the cover with the curved tip of the arm, she might knock the book toward her.

Amelia swatted her hand.

Missed.

She stretched up on her tiptoes, doing her best to ignore the quavering of the plank beneath her feet, and swatted once more.

Missed again.

Amelia stretched even harder, muscles and sinew straining at the effort. Now she just needed to flick her hand so . . .

Success!

She jerked her arm out and pushed on her glasses before peering up and into the hole. *No!* She had hooked the cover, but it hadn't tipped the book forward. The motion had flipped the cover back, opening the book, splaying the pages like a fan. Now what was she supposed to do? It was even farther away.

This was incredibly frustrating. Amelia stared back into the hole and tilted her head. She was looking for a way to retrieve the text but was soon distracted by the heading on the top of the book's left page.

A Congregation of Ghosts.

Fresh tingles pricked the back of Amelia's arms.

What were the odds?

The Ghostseer's Handbook was the book Amelia had always wanted to find, and a congregation of ghosts was the exact problem she wanted to solve. It was almost as though the library were providing her with the very thing she needed.

Ridiculous.

Though it did suddenly feel like someone or some-*library* was watching her with thrilling anticipation, waiting for her next move.

Absurd.

Amelia squinted at the page, straining to make out the words. Really, if the library were trying to help her, why hadn't it put the book within reaching distance? Or given her longer arms? That second part wasn't right, but the point stood. Besides, she hadn't even read the page yet. Likely, the information contained in the type wouldn't help at all.

There was only one way to find out.

A Congregation of Ghosts

When one thinks of a haunted house, one assumes such a place is haunted by the presence of ghosts. While this certainly can be the case, any parcel of land or manmade structure is capable of taking on psychic energy and, in a sense, becoming haunted.

Oftentimes these locations are the sites of tragedy—fires, battles, plague hospitals, etc. Even the most obtuse of humans can feel the remnants of emotional memories, but ghostseers are often particularly sensitive to such places.

As are ghosts.

These locations are usually only haunted for short periods of time. The bulk of psychic energy is naturally swept up in the flow of the cosmos, leaving few emotional echoes behind, but in rare cases the energy becomes stuck, and the law of attraction comes into effect. The result can be quite dangerous. For example, a building that has experienced great tragedy can attract more tragedy, strengthening the sentiment over time.

Amelia wasn't sure she understood all that entirely, other than to say sad places became sadder? Oh dear, and perhaps scary places became scarier.

The darker emotions, however, are not the only ones to haunt dwellings. Just as one can feel the peril upon entering a haunted house, one may have quite a different reaction entering another structure. There are places that vibrate with happiness and joy. There are also structures that have taken on the role through some cosmically baffling process of comforting those who pass through its doors.

Well, that was a nice thought. It also reminded Amelia of Rosalinda's theory that the library had come to care about people over the decades.

Most unfortunately, it is these structures of comfort that are unwittingly capable of causing the most destruction.

What?! Amelia's brow furrowed. That was much less of a nice thought. How could comforting places be capable of destruction?

While there have been notable examples of ghost lovers dotted throughout history, for the most part, spirits dwelling on the mortal plane are solitary creatures consumed by earthly pain.

Aha! Amelia thought of the ghost couple walking the boardwalk every night. She knew they were the exception rather than the rule. She directed her gaze to the top of the next page.

However, when a building takes on an aura of comfort, more than one spirit may be drawn to its energy. This is unsurprising given these beings have been unable to shed the sorrows of life. In attracting the dead lies the danger. A congregation of ghosts with unresolved earthly issues poses great risk through the development of a rare but powerful phenomenon: a cosmic vortex.

Cosmic vortex? Amelia had already been struggling to follow along, but now she was completely lost.

In the living world, whirlpools occur when a current collides with an obstacle (like a dam or narrow passage) that causes water to rotate and swirl, creating a vortex. Similarly, when a building holds too much psychic energy—in the form of ghosts with unresolved issues—it becomes an obstruction to the flow of the universe itself. Energy then swirls around the structure, trapping the ghosts in place. In the early stages of this phenomenon, the vortex is quite weak. If even one spirit faces its earthly issues and moves on to the next plane, that is usually enough to disrupt the trapped energy.

So, just one ghost needed to move on for all of them to be free? That sounded hopeful.

However, if the spirits remain, refusing to move on, over time the force builds, and this cosmic power grows in strength until the obstruction is destroyed. It is difficult to say what happens to the spirits. Some believe these unfortunate souls are flung to the far corners of the universe, others alternate dimensions. Some believe they are obliterated outright.

Amelia grimaced. While she was no fan of ghosts, obliteration felt extreme.

Likewise, it is difficult to predict how long the process will take. The vortex grows minutely at first, but then exponentially—

That was the end of the page.

Amelia leaned into the railing and chewed her lip. She couldn't say she believed or even understood everything she had read, but it did seem to fit what was going on. So, really, that settled it. Everything had already been settled for her, of course, but now the ghosts would see it too. It was time to go.

A distant noise jerked Amelia back into the moment. She should really go downstairs, but she couldn't! Not until she had *The Ghostseer's Handbook* in her grasp. There was only one option.

Amelia gingerly lifted her foot from the top plank of the ladder and rested it on the edge of the shelf just a few inches above. She then bounced up and grabbed the very top of the unit with her free hand. She was completely off the ladder now, clinging only to the shelving. Feeling the backward pull of gravity made it clear that this was a very bad idea, but, then again, she'd already come this far. Amelia reached her hand into the slot. The edges of the book's pages brushed her fingertips. So close. She stretched even farther, her arm feeling like it might dislocate from her shoulder, but . . . she . . . almost . . . had . . .

"Amelia?!"

Simon!

Startled, Amelia lost her grip on the top of the shelf, but, fortunately, when she reeled back, her foot landed on the top plank of the ladder and she caught the railing. *Safe.* But then, quite suddenly and most unexpectedly, the ladder jerked beneath her.

On its own!

And she was falling.

Down, down, down . . .

Right into Simon's arms.

12

To a luckless me this privilege befell.
Unwilling and unwelcome is my errand,
A bearer of ill news, whom no man loves.
—Sophocles, *Antigone*

CRADLED IN SIMON'S ARMS, AMELIA BLINKED AT THE dust motes swirling frenentically in the air. It seemed the safest thing to focus on.

Please tell me you didn't do that on purpose, Amelia.

That was really too far. Even the thought that she might do such a thing sent a rush of hot prickles up to Amelia's cheeks. And she hadn't! The ladder had moved on its own . . . hadn't it?

"Are you okay?" Simon asked, voice full of concern.

Amelia nodded but didn't dare look up. She could not meet his gaze, not when they were this close. Not when she could smell the faint scent of aftershave on his neck and feel the warmth of his chest. If she looked up, there was no telling what she might do.

"Rosalinda said you had come up here." The feel of his breath by her ear sent shivers racing. "I wanted to warn you about the ladder, and then what did I do? Startle you and—" Simon must have realized he was still holding her, because he released her feet to the floor and then his arm from around the small of her back. It was devastating. "Are you sure you're all right?"

"I'm fine. Really, I should be thanking you for . . ." Catching her and holding her tight? Yes, she was extremely grateful for that.

"Were you able to find what you were looking for? I know it's a bit of a mess up . . ." Simon faltered as his gaze dropped to the floor. *The Encyclopedia of the Dead.* He bent down to retrieve it, a twinge of confusion coming to the shape of his eyes as he passed her the book.

"Oh, this isn't for me," Amelia stammered. "It's for a friend. She's a believer in that kind of nonsense." *Lies. Lies. Lies.*

And Simon knew it. He didn't have to say anything. It was clear.

This was why Amelia hadn't wanted to rush things. It was not the first time she had been in this situation.

It was amazing what people could express without saying anything at all. Like at this very moment, it was plain Simon didn't believe her, but he wasn't upset. He was simply waiting for her to explain. No, correction, his silence was giving her an opportunity to explain—a small break in the conversation to find courage. He was silently expressing that it was okay for her to push past whatever embarrassment she held for what was really going on and tell him the truth. She could be vulnerable because he was promising not to judge, and that was because, in his mind, whatever it was she was holding back, surely, was no big deal. Maybe she did believe in supernatural things despite what she had said in their earlier conversation. Or maybe she simply enjoyed ghost stories and felt silly about it. Whatever it was, it was fine. Something they could smile over. This type of interaction happened all the time. It was how people became friends.

Or at least Amelia imagined it was. She wouldn't know because her secret was no small thing, so she had always been forced to let her lies stand.

As the silence dragged on, it deepened, pushing them apart without ever having moved them at all.

Finally, Simon put on a smile and said, "I should probably let you get back to your research." He had given up. People always did. He turned to leave. "Oh, Rosalinda said to take your time. No one has come in."

Don't go . . .

She couldn't let him walk away like this. They would lose all their progress.

"The weather!"

He looked back at her. "The weather?"

"It hasn't been ideal. I'm sure that's why people aren't coming in."

He nodded, then turned again.

"Wait! I'll come with you."

This time when he looked back, his smile had brightened.

"I'm done here," Amelia said, scurrying toward him, "but I'd love to hear more about how this floor came to be."

He sighed with good humor. "It's a bit overwhelming, isn't it?"

"In the best possible way."

As they headed for the door, Amelia peeked back at the bookshelf where she had last spotted *The Ghostseer's Handbook*.

They'd be seeing each other again very soon.

FOR THE REST of the day, Amelia performed all her regular duties, but the time passed in a blur. She and Simon didn't have much of an opportunity to talk about the third floor because he had another call, but, unbelievably, he wasn't the thing rattling her focus.

Learning that moving on was the only way for the ghosts to free themselves was one thing; having a conversation with them about it was another. Braden still had lots he wanted to do with his afterlife, the professor was happy right where he was, and given that Minnie had been in the library for over a hundred years or so, Amelia didn't think any of them would be in a hurry to move on to whatever came after death. As a result, she suspected this talk might be a touch difficult.

She originally wanted to hold the meeting in the center of the library again, where she had a clear line of sight to the exit, but knowing the professor's preference for the second floor, she whispered to Braden in passing to spread the word that they'd gather in the sitting area by the decommissioned fireplace at closing time.

When she arrived for the meeting, Amelia found the professor seated in a large wingback chair with Braden standing at his side. Minnie, while not readily visible, was likely hovering malevolently somewhere in the shadows. Amelia nodded her greeting and sat in the opposite chair before glancing over to the fireplace. Much to her surprise, it was crackling happily with ghostly blue-green flames. So, spirits could start fires. That was good to know. She put her hand toward it but couldn't detect any warmth.

Braden, unimpressed with her experimentation, cleared his throat and glanced at his watch. He wasn't actually wearing one, but the meaning was clear.

She was late.

As soon as the library had closed, she had locked the door and run upstairs to retrieve *The Ghostseer's Handbook*, but she couldn't find it anywhere. It was gone. Well and truly gone. It had completely disappeared as though some hidden trapdoor had swallowed it whole. But it was fine. Yes, it likely held the answers to all the questions she'd agonized over her entire life, but for now, she had more pressing ghost issues to deal with.

Amelia fidgeted with the sleeve of her sweater. She had no idea how the ghosts were going to react to what she had learned, and Braden wasn't making things any easier with the hopeful yet mildly suspicious looks he was giving her. The suspicion felt unfair, spirit box aside.

"How wonderful," the professor said, opting to be the one to get things started. "All of us here together." No one shared in the sentiment, at least not openly, but he held on to his companionable smile. "So, Amelia, we are all ears. Were you able to find any information for us?"

"Yes, I was. I found a book." She pinched her lips together and nodded. "It's called *The Ghostseer's Handbook*."

"That sounds promising," he said. "And were you able to take anything useful from it? I know young Braden here would love to be on his way."

"Don't worry, professor," Braden said quickly. "I'll visit all the time."

He patted Braden's hand. "I know you will."

"Well," Amelia said, struggling to keep the pitch of her voice under control. It was suddenly sounding a bit squeaky. "There is a way for you to get out of the library." She gestured over at Braden but wasn't quite able to make eye contact. "But . . ."

"But what?" Braden asked, his head cocked to the side.

She was just going to have to say it. "The only way for you to get out of the library is to move on." She swirled her hand like a carpet unrolling across the floor. "To the other side," she added. "Or whatever comes next."

"What? No." Braden folded his arms over his chest. "No way."

"Patience, Braden," the professor said. "I'm sure Amelia has more to tell us."

Amelia flicked her gaze between them. "I'd be more than happy to explain what has happened the best I can, but it won't change the ending."

"No," Braden said, voice rising. "Not happening. I'm not moving on. There's still stuff I want to do."

"You mentioned that." Amelia sighed. "But what could you possibly have to do that's so important that you're willing to defy the natural—"

"I want to travel the world!" Braden shouted. "Well, more of it. I haven't even been to the bottom of the sea yet."

"Right." Amelia nodded her head in agreement but then switched to a side-to-side shake of the head. "Be that as it may, I'm afraid you don't have a choice."

"Don't have a choice!" Braden's eyes bugged. "Dude, what are you—"

"It's Amelia."

"Really?" Braden asked. "You're going to give us a hard time about names? You haven't even bothered to ask what the professor's is."

Amelia blinked. He had a point. "My apologies," she said, turning to the professor. "I don't know your name."

"Oh, that's quite all right." He shrugged happily. "I don't remember it."

"You don't . . . ?" Amelia whipped her gaze back over to Braden.

"Just because he doesn't remember it, doesn't mean you shouldn't have asked." He puffed his chest out. "And Minnie isn't even Minnie's real name."

Amelia scanned the shadows, preparing for a jump scare.

"I just call her that because for the most part, she's as quiet as a mouse."

Amelia frowned. A mouse who fed on people's terror instead of cheese.

"And she seems to like it."

The now familiar "*Seeeecrets*" reached out from the shadows, wrapping itself around Amelia's throat.

Braden shuddered. "See?"

A heavy sigh escaped Amelia. This was exactly what she wanted to avoid. The truth was she did not care to know their names. She didn't want to know about their lives. She didn't want to make friends. With them at least. She desperately wanted living friends. But that would never happen if she spent all her time with the dead.

The professor cleared his throat. "I fear we are getting off track."

"Thank you," Amelia replied. "I agree."

He then adjusted himself in his chair, placing his elbows on the armrests and folding his hands in his lap. "Perhaps you could tell us what you have learned in more detail, so we can better understand."

"Well, apparently—"

"Apparently," Braden mocked.

"*Apparently*," Amelia repeated, "there is a phenomenon called a congregation of ghosts. When multiple ghosts gather in a building, they can become trapped in the confines of the structure."

"What?" Braden snapped. "How does that work?"

Just then the spine-tingling hiss of "*Seeeecrets*" emerged from a new dark spot in between two windows. Amelia jumped, but at least she knew where the bonneted terror was hiding. "Actually, no, Minnie, it's not a secret," Amelia corrected. "From what I could tell, as ghosts, you all don't belong on the living plane, and the combined weight of your unfinished business in the form of energy is basically obstructing the natural cosmic flow of the universe, which is forming a sort of whirlpool or vortex that you all are now stuck in."

Well done, Amelia.

She smiled. That had been a simple but clear explanation of a complicated phenomenon. Well done, indeed.

Braden dropped his chin to his chest. "I didn't get a single word of what you just said."

Amelia's smile withered. "I'm not sure that you need to understand the science behind it, so much as you need to know what to do about it."

The ghosts exchanged confused looks. Well, not Minnie, her bulbous blue eyes simply continued to glare unblinkingly out into the darkness.

"Again, it's really quite simple." Amelia paused, taking yet another thoughtful nod. "You need to move on or . . ." She wasn't quite ready for the *or* part just yet. "Suffice it to say, it's time to let go of your unfinished business and head on into the tunnel, take your leap of faith into the passageway, or light, or whatever you'd like to call it, and see what's on the other side." Amelia thought about adding that just one of them moving on might be enough to free them all, but really, every one of them needed to get on with their *existences.* And, of course, there was the fact that if only one moved on, that still left the library with two.

The ghost fire crackled happily through the heavy silence that had fallen over their group.

Unsurprisingly, Braden was the one to break it. "So, you're saying it's our fault we're trapped."

The professor chuckled nervously. "I don't think that's exactly what she means."

Amelia inhaled stiffly. Sugarcoating the situation wasn't going to help any of them. "No, that is essentially what I mean."

"And why should we believe you?" Braden asked, refolding his arms over his chest.

Amelia's eyes widened with incredulity. "I'm sorry? What exactly are you suggesting?"

"You don't even like ghosts."

The professor pushed himself up in his chair, saying, "Let's all take a moment—"

"And where is this *handbook* of yours?" Braden asked, putting on a bit of a British accent. Was that supposed to be her? She didn't sound British.

Easy, Amelia.

Yes, easy. She needed to keep her composure. She couldn't let them have this effect on her. "Unfortunately, the book has temporarily gone missing, but—"

"Oh sure! '*Missing*,'" Braden said with air quotes. "How convenient."

It wasn't, actually. Not at all. "Just so I'm sure I understand what you're getting at, you think I made all of this up just so you'd move on, and I could have the library all to myself?" As she said the words, Amelia couldn't help but think that was actually quite brilliant.

The professor held up his hands. "Amelia, Braden, no one is—"

"Did you?" Braden yelled.

"No! I never even thought of that until now." Quite honestly, if she had, she might have considered using it, but she had not! "Look, I'm not making this up. And there's more."

Braden scoffed. "More? I don't think I want to hear anything else you have to say."

This was exasperating. Here she had broken her rules to help these ghosts—and yes, help the library, Simon, Rosalinda, and, well, herself—but this was the thanks she got? "Listen. I realize this is not what you wanted to hear, but it seems that your defiance of the natural order has consequences, so perhaps this is the perfect opportunity for you to address the issues that have been holding you back and—"

"Who says we have issues? I don't have issues. I was loving my afterlife," Braden said, patting his chest. "I've stood on the top of Everest, sunbathed in the middle of the desert, and nose-dived into a volcano. Everything was awesome until I got trapped here."

Somehow Amelia doubted that. Something had led Braden to the library's comforting pull, but—she did not care! She was not his afterlife therapist!

"And I know the professor is happy right where he is," Braden went on, "and Minnie—"

"*Seeeecrets.*"

Amelia jerked again. Minnie had moved. She really didn't like it when Minnie moved. It was a little like spotting a spider in the bedroom only to have it disappear while retrieving a tissue. Not knowing where it might be was much worse.

"Okay," Braden conceded, giving the shadows a sideways look. "Minnie may have a little something-something going on."

"You know what?" Amelia offered. "If you want to believe your issues aren't the issue, fine. But I can assure you, your presence on the living plane is."

"So that's it then? That's all you've got. Move on?" Braden shook his head in disbelief. "Didn't your parents teach you anything? Doesn't this run in families? What kind of ghostseer are you?"

"A terrible one!" Amelia shouted. "And my parents abandoned me when I was a baby. Or died. I'm not entirely sure."

Braden hissed some air through his teeth. "My bad."

Amelia inhaled stiffly, clinging to the last of her composure.

"Look, I don't know where you all are getting your information or what it is you think I should be doing, but I never wanted to be a ghostseer, and I don't want to spend my life with the dead. Just because I can see you doesn't mean I want to."

That had sounded harsh. Apparently, Braden felt the same because he mumbled, "Ghosts are people too, you know."

"That's debatable."

Braden gasped so loudly, Amelia thought he might turn himself inside out.

A smallish pang of regret hit. She hadn't meant to say that. It had just come out, but these ghosts needed to face some harsh truths. "All I meant was that we'd have to agree on a definition of what it means to be a *person* before you can make that claim." And now she was making things worse, and yet she couldn't seem to stop. "After all, isn't a large part of being a person living a life? Ghosts exist in a never-ending limbo, so . . ."

Braden reared back. "You. Are. Horrible."

Amelia squinted. This meeting no longer felt productive. "Right, well, I did my best, but you all need to help yourselves now. Maybe you don't have any traumatic secrets holding you back, but—"

"*Seeeecrets.*"

Never in a thousand years would she get used to that. "The point is, this is a ghost problem. Not an Amelia problem. Not a library problem. A ghost problem. And if you don't take care of it, there will be dire consequences."

"Dire consequences?" Braden looked down at the professor. "That's bad, right?" The professor nodded in response. "What kind of dire consequences?"

"Well, I hate to be the bearer of even worse news, but . . ."

Braden looked at her skeptically, but she was telling the truth. This conversation had become tiresome.

"If you choose not to remove your collective obstruction in the cosmic flow of the universe, the universe will remove you."

The professor frowned. "I'm not sure I understand what that means."

"The book wasn't entirely clear," Amelia said. "There was some speculation that you could be flung to the far corners of space, transported to an alternate dimension, or possibly obliterated."

The professor and Braden exchanged another look before staring back at her.

"But don't you see? All that can be avoided." Amelia forced a smile. "All you have to do is move on, like you're supposed to. By the sounds of it, you still have time if the vortex is only in its early stages."

Braden dropped to sit on the arm of the professor's chair but sank all the way through it and then through the floor. A moment later, he popped right back up. "No. No way. I'm not buying it. Again, you're just trying to scare us."

Amelia felt her left eyebrow travel high up her forehead. "Believe me. Don't believe me. I don't care. You are on your own now."

"Fine. I don't care either." Braden shot up right through the ceiling to the third floor.

"Amelia, Braden, please," the professor called out. "Let's talk about this."

Braden's frosted-tipped head poked down through the floor. "No, I'm done."

The professor sighed. "Minnie, do you have any thoughts on the matter?"

Amelia spun around, following the professor's gaze. Minnie was literally inches behind her. *Courage, dear heart.* Perhaps this was an opportunity. Out of all the ghosts, Minnie seemed the least happy with this existence, so maybe she could be the first to move on.

"Minnie," Amelia said, unclenching her jaw, "there must be a part of you that would like to see what comes next, to be free from whatever it is that is holding you back."

The cold, glowing blue stare of the ghost chilled Amelia to the bone, but if she wasn't mistaken, there was something else in those eyes. Perhaps a flicker of interest?

"Is that true?"

Amelia thought she might have seen another considering glimmer, but before she could investigate any further, before she could even blink, a blast of cold, dry air hit Amelia's face. Minnie had exploded—quite literally exploded—into a cloud of dust and spiders.

The entire mess almost instantly evaporated into nothingness, but *dust and spiders*!

Amelia whipped around to face the professor. "Did you . . . ? Did that . . . ? What is the matter with all of you?!"

The professor didn't answer but offered her a very kind smile.

13

It was the best of times, it was the worst of times . . .
—Charles Dickens, *A Tale of Two Cities*

THE FOLLOWING DAYS PASSED IN A CONFUSING BLUR of happiness and melancholic dread.

So much of Amelia's new life was wonderful, the best it had ever been. She loved almost everything about being a librarian, like returning and reshelving books, going through new-release catalogues, sorting through donated diaries, letters, and genealogy documents. Interacting with visitors was still awkward, and she hadn't yet managed to utter the words *May I help you find something?* to anyone, but she felt she was getting closer to doing so every day, and, while it was hard to be sure, it seemed like people didn't find her as strange at work as they did in the outside world. Perhaps a certain level of introversion was expected in the library or at least it was better tolerated. Context was everything.

Then there was teatime.

Every day right before she left, Rosalinda would make them both a cup of tea to sip at the circulation desk. It was normally quiet around the supper hour. They would talk all about their current reads and anything that might have gone on during their days. Amelia had never known anyone like Rosalinda. She was so open and unafraid to talk about things others might find unusual, like a library being a sentient. Better still, Rosalinda never pushed to know more about Amelia's life. Her new boss had to suspect she led a quiet existence, but she spared her the embarrassment of ever having to make anything up. Rosalinda just *accepted* her and all her eccentricities. As Anne of Green Gables might say, in Rosalinda she had found a kindred spirit.

Then there was the flip side of Amelia's new life.

The days were cold and rainy, and the sea grumbled in such a way that even tea and cookies couldn't relieve the gloom. Everyone in the village seemed to feel it too, and the number of visitors to the library dwindled by the day. A few loyal readers battled the elements to search out their next literary adventure, but for the most part, the library was painfully quiet, except for when it was groaning with the wind. Whether those winds were earthly or cosmic, Amelia couldn't be sure.

Then, there was the other issue.

The ghosts.

The ghosts were, well, they were *ghosting* her.

Amelia knew she shouldn't be bothered by it. She should be grateful, in fact. It was just that they seemed to be doing absolutely nothing about the predicament they were in, and that left her feeling a little bit *guilty*. Of course, they were perfectly entitled to make their own decisions. If they were comfortable with potential obliteration, so be it, but Amelia couldn't help but wonder if another ghostseer had walked through the library's door, then maybe that ghostseer would have been able to explain what was happening in a more effective manner. And if that had happened, maybe the ghosts would have trusted the information given and at least one of them would have decided to move on. Amelia suspected that her long-standing distrust—nay, profound dislike—of ghosts had perhaps come through in her explanations. She absolutely believed they were responsible for their own choices, but could they make the best choice if they didn't fully grasp the situation?

Sadly, she suspected the answer to that question was no, which meant, despite all her rules, she felt obligated to try to get through to them one last time.

Amelia wasn't about to call a meeting though. At least not with Braden. She didn't want to get sucked into another argument, and that ghost really knew how to push her buttons. Nor was she in any mood to be terrified, so Minnie was out too. That left the professor. He seemed like the most reasonable of the bunch.

So, on one particularly cold and blustery night, Amelia climbed the stairs to the second floor and approached the professor's nook. He looked so cozy in his wingback chair by the ghost fire, book in his lap. What *was* he reading? Had he memorized entire books in life and now could manifest them in death? Or was he in some sort of dream state where he was just imagining what he was reading? Amelia was truly fascinated, but she needed to stay focused on the job at hand.

"Hello, professor," she said quietly.

He looked up, taking off his reading glasses, which promptly disappeared in his hand. "Amelia, what a lovely surprise."

"May I join you?"

"Please." He gestured to the chair across from him. "I would be delighted. Could I offer you some refreshments? Coffee? Tea? Cocoa?" Suddenly a transparent, stainless steel pitcher appeared on the table, along with some oversize mugs. Amelia's eyes bulged. She knew ghosts could manifest objects, but she'd never seen it done up close like this. He poured some sparkling liquid into a cup before sliding it toward her.

Amelia frowned at the offering. "I don't think I'll be able to drink that."

"Have you ever tried?"

She cocked her head.

"As a ghostseer, I wouldn't be surprised if you could interact with the spirit world and share in our manifestations."

She supposed that was possible, but voluntarily talking to a ghost was hard enough on her sensibilities, let alone sharing a warm beverage. Besides, she'd already had her tea. "Perhaps in a bit. But while we're on the topic, how do all of you know the term *ghostseer*? It's not commonly used. And how did you know I was one? Did I give something away?"

He smiled as he prepared his own cup. "Unfortunately, I don't have a satisfactory answer to your first question other than to say *we just know*? Maybe it is ingrained information revealed only upon death." He frowned. "Or maybe I've simply forgotten. My memory is terrible. It varies, but I rarely hold on to anything for long. As for your other question, Braden swears he caught you looking at us, but really, I think you just have a certain welcoming glow about you."

Amelia frowned. Welcoming glow? Unlikely.

The professor cleared his throat. "So, is this purely a social call or . . . ?"

"No," Amelia said, folding her hands on her lap. "I wanted to talk to you about the *situation* in the library."

The professor settled back into his chair, holding his mug delicately in his hands. "I see."

"I couldn't help but notice that you are all still here."

He nodded.

"If you're waiting for me to do something—save the day, so to speak—you should know I'm not who you think I am. As I tried to explain before, when it comes to helping ghosts, I wouldn't know where to begin. I have spent my life trying to ignore your kind completely." *Your kind* probably wasn't the best choice of words.

Instead of taking offense, the professor peaked his bushy eyebrows in a kindly fashion. "That must have been difficult growing up. Always hiding your experience with the world. And may I take this opportunity to say I was sorry to hear you lost your parents. That also must have been hard."

Once again, Amelia frowned, so deeply this time, her glasses slipped down her nose. Was he empathizing with her? And if so, what for? She could only imagine that he was trying to lure her into finding other ways to help them. "Yes, well," Amelia replied, adjusting her glasses, "I never knew them. I grew up in care, so—"

"Not adopted?" he asked.

"I had colic as a baby, and—" Amelia caught herself. "We're getting off topic."

"I'm sorry. I'm prying. It's been so long since I've met someone new."

Amelia turned her gaze to the window. The inky sea heaved moodily against the cold, dark sky. "The point is, I'm grown now, and while I'm sure it doesn't mean anything to you, becoming a librarian has always been my dream, so—"

"How wonderful!" the professor remarked. The enthusiasm in his voice drew her gaze back over. "Your dream has come true!" He seemed genuinely happy for her, which only made Amelia more uncomfortable.

"Yes, yes it has. There's just one problem."

The professor's eyes widened. "What's that?"

Was he joking? "You."

"Ah." He took a long sip from his mug. "Right. Again, my memory isn't the best."

"I'm not sure if you realize it, but your presence in the library is having a negative effect not just on me but on the patrons at large, and the timing couldn't be worse. The library is experiencing some structural issues, which may be expensive to fix, so keeping its numbers up is essential."

"Really?" The professor looked genuinely surprised. "We're affecting people? I can certainly see how our actions have affected you, but for the most part we are rather well-behaved."

Amelia pulled her skirt over her knees and popped her eyebrows. "It seems you all give off a *vibe* that visitors find disturbing." She didn't know this with any kind of certainty, but it seemed a reasonable supposition.

"Hmm, how fascinating." He raked his fingertips through his unruly white hair with his free hand, but the gesture did nothing to calm its mad-scientist impression.

"Look," Amelia said in her most reasonable tone, "I can't help but think we all want the same thing here."

The professor frowned kindly. "I'm not sure that's true. I believe you want us out of the library, yes?"

Amelia tried not to nod too vigorously.

"And Braden also wants out of the library," the professor continued, "but he does not want to move on. He has his whole undead life ahead of him, so I'm not sure there is a win-win scenario in there for you both." He rubbed his chin thoughtfully. "Now, I'm not opposed to moving on in principle, but I can't."

"Why not?" Amelia asked with unintended petulance.

"I don't remember." He sighed. "You see, I have forgotten everything from my former existence. All I know is that I'm right where I'm supposed to be."

"You don't remember why you're remaining on the mortal plane, but you feel you have to?"

He nodded.

"But"—Amelia shook her head—"isn't that incredibly boring? Frustrating?"

"Oh no," he replied amiably. "I'm quite happy right where I am. Minnie is a different story though." He looked off into the shadows. "I suspect she would like to move on, but whatever happened to her in life has become too damaging over her many years to face now. Unless . . ." His words trailed off as he gazed into the fire.

Unless? This professor had better not be once again implying what she thought he might be implying. "Be that as it may," Amelia said. "You seem to be forgetting one key element here."

He looked back at her with his brow raised.

"The cosmic vortex?" She dipped her chin. "You did hear the part about being flung to the far corners of the universe, correct?"

"Oh yes." The professor shuddered. "That all sounds very cold." Suddenly a ghost blanket appeared over his lap. "But I believe you said we have time?"

"Well, yes . . ." Amelia struggled to find words that would get through to him. "But I don't know how much time."

He nodded over his mug. "That is troubling, isn't it?"

She would have felt better if he sounded more troubled. "So?"

He raised his brow again.

"Aren't you going to do something about it?" She threw her hands up. "Are you just going to let it happen?"

He shrugged. "Again, we're stuck. Unless . . ."

There it was again! Amelia raised her left eyebrow to its highest degree. "Unless what?"

"Unless you would reconsider your position on helping us?" He finished with a smile.

She knew it! That's what all the empathy had been about. "Again, I wouldn't know how to start."

He tilted his head side to side in apparent consideration. "Perhaps you could consult the handbook you were telling us so much about."

"It's gone. Disappeared. I've looked everywhere."

He squinted knowingly. "Never fear. This library is a funny place, but it does have a way of helping people find what they need."

Amelia regarded him skeptically, then muttered, "You're not the first person to tell me that." Suddenly, the professor went very still. "What happened? Are you all right?" He seemed unable to hear her. Amelia waved a hand in his line of sight. "Professor?"

He blinked. "Sorry. For a moment, I thought I remembered something."

"Did it have something to do with the library?"

"I think so, yes. Maybe. But it's all gone now." He pulled his blanket up his lap. "That happens sometimes. Where were we?"

"The funny library," Amelia said dryly.

"Oh yes." He paused to take another sip. "Perhaps the library has its reasons for keeping the book from you."

Amelia's eyes widened with deep offense. The very thought of the library somehow purposely denying her a book after the amount of love she had shown it was . . .

There were no words.

Not unlike Simon's, the corner of the professor's mouth twitched with amusement. "But until that's resolved, maybe there's another way."

Amelia didn't like the sound of that *maybe.*

"Perhaps, you could get to know Braden and Minnie." He said the words lightly, but they were not light words. "I've come to care about them both, and I would love nothing more than to help them, but I also think you might be better equipped than an old fuddy-duddy like me to get them to open up."

Better equipped? Was he serious? What exactly did she have in common with a 2000s-era frat boy and a banshee who haunted her dreams? Nothing. That's what. Really, the question had been rhetorical.

"You never know, you might enjoy it," he said. "You all could even end up friends."

Amelia nearly spit out her cocoa.

"Is it good?" he asked, glancing over at the mug in her hand. *The ghost mug.* She hadn't even realized she'd picked it up. She was drinking ghost cocoa! The second she had the thought, it disappeared, which, admittedly, was too bad.

It *had* been good.

MAKE FRIENDS WITH ghosts.

Amelia lay in bed looking up at the ceiling of her fishy loft. She had been staring at the same water stain for at least an hour, but sleep refused to come. She was far too perturbed by her conversation with the professor. He had no idea what he was asking of her. Making friends was not in her skill set, and making friends with ghosts went literally against everything she had taught herself to believe. Not to mention the fact that it was too dangerous. The more she interacted with ghosts, the more likely it was that she would be caught by the living interacting with ghosts, or *nobody*, from their perspective. And then that would be it. *Poof!* All her hopes for a normal life would be gone.

No. She wasn't going to do it. Absolutely not. Under no circumstances.

The situation would resolve itself one way or another, and besides, she had enough issues of her own without trying to help them figure out theirs.

Of course, if the ghosts were responsible for the library's dwindling numbers, it might have to close, and then what would happen? Guaranteed, her life would be ruined. Simon's too. Actually, who was she kidding? Simon would likely be fine. He would be brokenhearted certainly, but he probably had all sorts of friends, all over the world, who would get him back on his feet. Rare-book dealers. Restorers. Librarians. He would find a new position, somewhere in Europe probably, maybe Oxford. She could easily see him working in a towering Gothic library with some other, much more sophisticated librarian who didn't fall off ladders. They'd get to know each other, share books, wear scarves, and recite poetry in quiet moments. They'd probably have picnics on riverbanks with scones and freshly made lemonade, which would eventually become dinners in their rooms and . . .

No, she refused to follow them back to their rooms.

Amelia, focus.

But did the ghosts care about any of that? No, they didn't. Because ghosts cared only about themselves. And the professor wanted her to make friends.

Suddenly, Amelia's phone pinged, jerking her from her internal rant. She snatched it off her night table with blazing speed and looked at the preview screen.

It was Simon!

Sorry for texting so late. Again. I wanted to let you know there will be workers at the library tomorrow. Be careful coming in.

That was all . . . except there was another ping!

Reading anything good?

Amelia clutched her phone to her chest for just a moment, soaking in the deliciousness of the request, but then she placed it gingerly back on her nightstand.

That was another thing she was not going to do. Of course, she would eventually text him back. In the morning. That would be much more appropriate. But, until things were settled, she couldn't keep letting him in, only to push him away.

She glanced over at her phone.

No, Amelia. Be wise.

Right. It wasn't fair. To either one of them. She pinned her hands between her knees and stared blankly at the far wall of her apartment, but . . . suddenly it felt like the phone was looking at her. It seemed only polite to look back.

Stop it.

She crossed her arms over her chest, pinning her fingertips to her ribs this time.

You know what? Don't listen to her. It's fine. Text him back.

Amelia's eyes widened. What voice was that? It certainly wasn't

Rational Amelia's. *You two work together. You're librarians. It's only natural he'd want to know what you're reading. It's not that deep.*

Oh, and this Amelia used slang! She also made good points.

Amelia snatched her phone off the table. She knew it was a bad idea, but it was just one text.

Thank you for letting me know.

Or two.

And I'm reading Vera.

Amelia's heart pounded in her throat as she waited for his reply. Watching the dots chase one another in their box at the bottom of the screen was almost more than she could take.

By Elizabeth von Arnim?

She pressed her lips together. Was he a fan? Or did he think her old-fashioned and weird? Oh, the agony.

That's the one.

Seconds ticked by.

That might be an even better choice for fall than Sherlock.

14

Go on, prove me wrong. Destroy the
fabric of the universe. See if I care.
—Terry Pratchett, attributed

IT WAS ANOTHER COLD, WET, BLUSTERY DAY.

Amelia trudged along the boardwalk, her umbrella clutched low to her head. The steel-gray sea rumbled with discontent at her side as seagulls wheeled above its waves searching for churned-up morsels. Amelia barely registered any of the Gothic beauty though. For the first time in days, she wasn't headed into work early. No, gray skies and a splitting headache had greeted her upon awakening and lasted through the afternoon. Now she would be lucky to make it in on time.

She and Simon had texted late into the night about novels featuring women trapped in ancestral homes with husbands tormented by the memories of their dead first wives. It had been wonderful, but in the cold light of day, she also knew it had been a mistake. The situation was too unstable. Next, he'd want to talk about books in the library, and that was far too dangerous given where things stood.

Amelia glanced over at a forgotten Halloween ghost floating from a tree branch, twisting in the wind. It appeared she couldn't get away from them even on the outside.

Something had to give.

It was maddening, really. She had quite literally resolved, just the night before, to let the ghosts fend for themselves, but the stakes were too high. Every day they remained in the library was a day that Amelia could lose everything. And yes, they had been quiet lately, but she could only imagine their intrusive behavior would escalate as the situation with the vortex worsened.

And speaking of the vortex, for some strange, inexplicable, *infuriating* reason, Amelia still felt guilty about how all that seemed to be unfolding. She suspected the professor and his cocoa were to blame.

She had to talk to *them.* Again. Tonight.

Maybe now that they'd had some time to think about their choices, she could—not make friends—but reason with Braden and Minnie. She had to try. It was time to end this particularly annoying chapter in an otherwise beautiful book. Maybe then she and Simon could . . .

One step at a time, Amelia.

She didn't want to go into the situation blind, though, so she'd spent some time that day learning what she could about Braden and Minnie online. Luckily her Wi-Fi seemed to be behaving. While she was unable to uncover anything about terrifying ghosts in bonnets in her search, she was able to dig up a fair bit about Braden.

The minute Amelia arrived at the library, Simon and Rosalinda left to go to dinner together, and no one else was around. Even though she normally relished the quiet, the hours that followed dragged under the dread of her planned conversations, and Amelia caught herself wishing for visitors as a distraction. Just before closing, it struck her that this might be her first shift without a single patron, but . . . then she spotted movement in the mystery section.

He was back. The man from the crab shack.

It seemed impossible that he had snuck past her, but there he was perusing the stacks with the same look of frustration and bewilderment he'd had on his last visit. The time had come. Despite the uncomfortable tension gathering in her shoulders and the familiar prickle of sweat on her palms, she welcomed the opportunity. This was her chance to prove her worth. Test her mettle. Demonstrate that she was a librarian.

Amelia rose from her chair, gripped her hands together, then walked around the circulation desk before she could give herself any excuse not to. Despite her determination, though, with every step her nerves grew. Not helping matters was the fact that she hadn't settled on an opening line.

After giving it some thought, she realized *May I help you find anything?* was a touch formal. *Can I help you?* was more colloquial, friendly even, but she wasn't sure she could get the words out. They didn't make sense. Of course she *could* help. Her abilities were not in question.

It didn't matter. She just needed to say something.

The man didn't look over as she approached, so Amelia stopped a few feet away and cleared her throat. "Can I help you?"

"Sorry? What's that now?" he asked, twisting his woolen hat in his hands.

"Can I help you find something?"

The man shook his head. "No, I don't think you can."

Amelia frowned. She never should have given him that opening. "I'm sure you're mistaken. If you'd tell me what it is you're looking for, I'm quite certain I could—"

A snort of laughter came from the DVD rack not too far from where they were standing. *Braden.* Of course he would be the one to witness her struggle. He was eyeing the movies as though he were minding his own business, but that laugh had most definitely been his.

The man used the opportunity afforded by Amelia's distraction to scurry past. "Best be on my way. It's getting slippy out there."

"Wait," she called after him. "If you're looking for a mystery, I could recommend—"

"That's the thing," he said without turning. "I don't know what she wants." He raised his hand. "Thanks though."

She? What? Before Amelia could get any clarification, he was gone.

More muffled laughter burbled over from the movie section. Heat stirred in Amelia's chest, but she quashed it. She refused to be shamed by a ghost wearing jeans three times too large. And she would not be goaded into another argument. She had more control than that. In fact, she had so much control, there was really no reason not to seize this opportunity to talk to Braden. Given the library was once again empty of visitors, now seemed like as good a time as any to get this conversation over with.

Amelia smoothed her hair back and walked over. Braden must have sensed her coming, but he gave no sign of it. Clearly, he wanted to make this as awkward as possible. She had expected nothing less.

"Hello, Braden." Hmm, that also sounded formal. She probably should have gone with *Hey.*

"'Sup."

Or *'Sup.*

"Nice job with that," he said, shooting a look over at the mystery section. "Very natural. Not at all scary librarian."

Scary librarian? Of course, Amelia was aware of the stern, shushing librarian stereotype, but was that the impression she had given? It certainly wasn't what she had intended. Should she have started with an icebreaker? Talked about the weather? Maybe—

Focus, Amelia.

Right. There would be time to hyperanalyze her failed service encounter later. Most likely when she was trying to sleep.

"I was hoping we could talk."

Braden furrowed his brow but kept his focus on the DVDs. "Have you come to say sorry?"

Amelia blinked. She knew very well there were things she could apologize for, but now that he had so smugly pointed that out, she was feeling less inclined, especially considering they were the ones who had started all this. All she wanted was to be left alone and—

Amelia.

Rational Amelia sounded like she had a headache too.

"And what exactly would I be apologizing for?"

"Oh, I don't know," Braden said, wheeling on her. "Maybe you could start with trapping us in a tin box to boot us out of the library?"

"Believe me," she replied, "that option was not my first choice. I was hoping you all would pick up on the very clear hints I was dropping to be left alone, but no, instead you wailed at me like a starving husky. Would you care to apologize for that?"

"Husky? What are you talking about? I don't sound like a husky." Braden turned back to the stand looking incredibly sulky. "You know what? Let's just call it even."

"Good," Amelia said. "Now, perhaps it might be wise if we discussed the other issue."

"*Perhaps it might be wise*," Braden repeated under his breath, again in a British accent, before letting out a heavy sigh of frustration. "All these look so boring. Movies were better when I was alive." He turned back to her. "And there's nothing to discuss. You don't know what you're talking about, and I don't have issues holding me back from going . . . wherever it is ghosts go."

"Everyone has issues. The fact that you say you don't have issues almost certainly confirms it."

He gave her a bored shrug. "I'd love to help you, dude, but there's no there, there."

Amelia's eyelids fluttered shut. *Dude.*

"Truth is I had an awesome childhood with awesome parents." He flicked a guilty-looking gaze over to her when he spoke the word *parents* but then pressed on. "I had a great life."

Amelia studied his face, searching for hints of dishonesty. She couldn't detect any, but there did seem to be something more going on beneath the surface. "Well, I'm glad your life was wonderful, but I saw your obituary. It said you were twenty years old when you died. Aren't you the slightest bit sad that your life was cut so short?"

"Nah," he drawled. "It was epic."

"It said you died in a tragic accident?"

"Snowboarding."

Amelia nodded. "That is—"

"Off a second-story roof. I did this gnarly triple cork right off the edge. I got so much air that I landed in the road and then—POW!" Braden clapped his hands together, but it didn't make any sound. "Snowplow got me. Live fast and die young." He shrugged then stretched out his ghostly limbs before whipping around to glare at her. "Wait a minute. You looked up my obituary?"

"It's still online," she said. "Your parents put it in a number of papers."

Braden's chin dropped. "You stalked me on the web?"

"I wouldn't call it stalking." Amelia frowned. *Wouldn't she?* Certainly not in the sense he meant. "I was just trying to get to know you."

He threw his arms out. "That's not how you do that! Why wouldn't you just ask me?"

"That's what I'm doing now," Amelia said, stiffening her posture, "and look at how well it's going."

Braden huffed a laugh. "Well, you can call off your investigation, Detective McGruff."

Before he could go on, Amelia interrupted. "Detective McGruff?"

He looked at her sideways. "McGruff the Crime Dog?"

"I have never heard of such a dog."

"Oh my God, I really am old." Braden shook his head. "You know what? Forget it. I'm fine. My life was great. I don't have any unresolved issues, and I don't need your help."

AFTER HER CONVERSATION with Braden, the last minutes to closing no longer dragged but slithered by with excruciating slowness. When the time finally came, Amelia went through her usual end-of-day tasks but registered very little of her actions. She was too distracted by what lay ahead. Given her remarkable lack of success with ghost number one, she had considered abandoning her attempt to reach ghost number two entirely, but she knew she couldn't do that. Her to-do list was incomplete, and if she didn't at least try to get through to Minnie, the guilt would haunt her—even after the ghosts were sucked into oblivion. So, once she had finished her duties, she gathered her courage, swallowed hard, and forced herself toward the stairs, whispering *Ghosts can't hurt you* over and over again.

It was the truth.

It was in all the ghost books, at least the ones she'd read, and surely if ghosts could actually hurt people, she would know. It wasn't as though history was rife with examples of people dying under mysterious circumstances—like strong swimmers suddenly going under in creepy lakes or inexplicable fires taking lives under supernaturally revengeful circumstances.

Actually, there were probably quite a few of those.

This line of reasoning wasn't helping.

Amelia stood with her hand on the newel-post at the bottom of the staircase and looked up the curving flight of steps.

Up you go now.

It sounded so simple. And it was. All she had to do was put one foot in front of the other. What could be easier? Amelia inhaled a long, steadying breath, then climbed.

Up, up, up she went, all the while thinking that talking to a ghost on a cold, windy autumn night in a creaking building with flickering lights seemed to be asking for trouble. She felt like a character in a horror movie with a shoddy flashlight investigating a noise in the attic. But really, this needed to be done. When she had asked Minnie about moving on, she was sure there had been a flicker of interest in her eyes, her petrifying bulbous blue eyes. And that was something Amelia needed to follow up on.

When she got to the top, she paused, unable to move forward, at least until she realized if Minnie jump-scared her right now, she'd fall down the stairs.

Amelia pressed on while the building groaned ominously with the wind. "Stop that," she mumbled under her breath. Really, she loved the atmosphere of the library, with its shifting shadows and whistling eaves. There was even something to be said for the cobwebs tucked away in its high corners and the loose planks that creaked just so if stepped upon. But there was a time for such things.

If a book fell right now, it would be the end of her.

After some searching, Amelia spotted Minnie's bonneted silhouette hovering at the end of a dark corridor of shelves staring directly into the books. Given she was only a few inches from the spines, it was unlikely she was scanning the options.

That wasn't at all terrifying.

"Hello, Minnie," Amelia said, entering the stacks. The shelves suddenly felt much closer together than they had just moments ago, and while all the lights were still on, the corridor was inexplicably drowning in darkness.

Minnie didn't answer Amelia's greeting. She was too busy staring into the bookshelf, and, horror of all horrors, she appeared to be holding an equally creepy bonneted porcelain doll, which also happened to be staring into the bookshelf.

Amelia walked toward the ghost, whispering, *I think I can. I think I can. I think I can.* She'd loved *The Little Engine That Could* when she was younger, but that little engine just had to get over a mountain, not walk into a scene from *The Turn of the Screw.*

Once she stood within a few feet, Amelia steeled herself to speak again. "Minnie?"

Nothing. No sound or movement. The spirit looked like a shadowy photograph superimposed over reality.

"I was hoping we could talk."

Silence.

"Regarding the situation with the vortex?"

A foul creeping sensation clawed its way up from Amelia's ankles to her heart. While Minnie's eyes were still focused on the bookshelf, Amelia could see, just around the side of the ghost's bonnet, that her eyes were widening to a horribly unnatural degree. Then Amelia couldn't see much of anything because her vision was obscured by her own cloud of frozen breath.

Carry on, Amelia.

"I thought maybe the other night you were interested in—"

A high-pitched screech ripped through the air, and Amelia felt her own eyes widen. *What was that?!*

Suddenly the porcelain doll's head rotated in a slow quarter turn, revealing its glowing cracked face.

Amelia stepped back, readying herself to run. "Minnie?"

The doll's jaw dropped, and a horrible dusty "*Seeeecrets*" emerged from its porcelain lips.

"Oh no!" Amelia shouted, throwing her hands in the air. "This is where I draw the line. No, thank you!" She spun on her heels and strode for the stairs. "You know what?" she announced to the rest of the library. "I am done! Well and truly done. I mean it this time. Stay? Go? Be obliterated? I don't care. You are on your own."

She had tried. She really had, but some ghosts just didn't want to be helped. Her conscience was clear.

"Amelia? Is that you?" the professor called out.

She froze at the top of the stairs. She didn't have to answer. She could just keep on going.

Suddenly, Braden appeared five or six steps below her with his hands out in front of him. "I know, okay? I know I said we didn't need your help, but, dude—"

"It's Amelia," she snapped.

"Something's happened. And you're going to want to see it."

15

Don't Panic.

—Douglas Adams, *The Hitchhiker's Guide to the Galaxy*

AMELIA FOLLOWED BRADEN TOWARD THE BACK WALL of the second floor, where the two wings of the mezzanine connected, being careful to give the stacks that had last concealed Minnie and her doll a wide berth.

"Over here!" the professor called out. He really didn't have to, though; Amelia could see where they were going. It was impossible to miss the eerie glow coming from the corner of the east wing even if she couldn't see the source. Braden sped on ahead, leaving her behind.

A near-painful tingle ran up the back of Amelia's neck when she approached the aisle between the bookshelves that would reveal whatever it was back there. She also had a horrible suspicion Minnie was following her again, hiding in the shadows, but she wasn't about to check and see.

When Amelia peeked around the final bookshelf, she saw the professor and Braden hovering a few feet back from . . .

What was that?

On the wall, near the far back corner, there was a *patch.* It was the only word Amelia could think of. It was the size and shape of a puddle and rippled with strange silver-gray light. The location almost made it look like someone had hung a cloudy mirror.

Amelia took slow steps to join the ghosts.

"Do you guys feel that?" Braden asked. Not waiting for anyone to answer, he reached out his hand in the direction of the strange phenomenon. At first, Amelia couldn't tell what was happening; then slowly, horribly, his fingers stretched toward the unnatural shape like the tips were being sucked into a hole. For a moment, he seemed mesmerized by his ever-stretching fingers, until he snatched his hand back, cradling it in his other fist.

Amelia looked herself over. Thankfully, no part of her was elongating, but she could feel a strange pull, both cold and somehow empty. She walked closer with tentative steps.

The professor reached for her. "Do you think that's wise?"

Amelia shook her head. Of course it wasn't wise, but given she wasn't stretching like a pulled piece of gum, she could only think the patch had a different effect on ghosts than it did on the living.

As Amelia neared, the cold, empty sensation grew, seeping into her bones. She peered into the . . . what? Portal? Gateway? She was pretty sure this wasn't the tunnel to the other side. If it was, there would be a lot more ghosts roaming the earth given how unwelcoming it felt. As she stared into the unending shifting currents of gray, it felt like something was looking back at her. For a second, she was certain a giant tentacle was about to slash out, snatch her around the waist, and pull her inside.

Despite all her feelings about ghosts, under no circumstances did she want these ones in particular ending up in there.

Amelia reached out her hand.

"What are you doing?" Braden snapped. "Don't touch it!"

He was right. This was a terrible idea, but it felt like her brain had split in half and she had to prove to herself that she was in fact seeing what she thought she was seeing. Amelia poked her fingers into the center of the shape, but instead of pressing through, her fingers bounced against *something* that felt like a trampoline or wet sponge. She snatched her fingers back, leaving the gray currents rippling and swirling in her wake.

She backed away slowly.

"Perhaps we could discuss this at the hearth," the professor said. "I fear I've been away from my spot for too long."

"It's okay," Braden said. "You go. We'll be right there. Take Minnie with you."

Amelia peeked over to watch him leave, and when she did, something else on the wall, farther down, caught her eye.

"Where are you going?" Braden asked.

Amelia couldn't explain it right now, not even to herself, but she was jogging over to the large corkboard screwed into the brick. For a moment, she eyed the poster fastened to it. Yes, this would do nicely. She collected the pushpins in her hand and brought the poster back over. Ever so carefully she placed the glossy paper over the patch, then pressed the pushpins into the cracked grout of the brick—something she would never normally do—until it was firmly in place. Perfect.

Braden observed her warily as she came back to stand beside him once more. "You good?"

"I couldn't focus with that staring at me." Amelia surveyed her work. The poster had a kitten sitting on a book with a rainbow arcing over its head. Underneath it read *Books take you where you want to be.* Much better.

Suddenly the poster began to flap. Then in a lightning-fast

movement, the glowing patch swallowed it whole like a vacuum cleaner sucking up a tissue.

Amelia blinked, then looked at Braden.

"You know what you were saying about this just being a ghost problem?" he asked.

Amelia nodded.

"Somehow, I think it's more than just a ghost problem."

16

> "I like people who make me love them. It saves me so much trouble in making myself love them."
>
> —Lucy Maud Montgomery, *Anne of Green Gables*

THE NEXT TWENTY-FOUR HOURS PASSED IN A SURreal daze. After the interdimensional portal on the wall—at least that was Amelia's best guess for what it might be—ate her kitten poster, she found she wasn't quite up for a chat. She told the ghosts she would see what she could find out and went home. When she arrived, she went through her usual bedtime routine. She made herself a cup of chamomile tea, put on her flannel pajamas, and got into bed with a book. For fifteen minutes she read before realizing the book was upside down.

After a dreamless sleep, she got up the next morning and headed right back to work.

Through all this, she found herself unable to string together a coherent thought about what had happened or what she should do about it.

Why? Well, because an interdimensional portal ate her kitten poster.

Thankfully, though, by the time she arrived back at the library, a single course of action had managed to emerge from the swampy quagmire of her nonexistent thoughts.

She had to find *The Ghostseer's Handbook*.

Braden was right. This wasn't just a ghost problem. That hole ate a part of the living world. What if it grew? What if it started eating books next? The thought was horrifying. Amelia certainly didn't know what to do about the situation, but the handbook—it might have some answers.

Amelia settled into the chair behind the circulation desk. Neither Simon nor Rosalinda mentioned how early she had come in, which was nice because she really didn't have a good answer for that particular question. Glancing at her watch, she realized story time for the nursery school was about to begin. Given everything that was going on, story time was exactly what she needed. Despite its seasonal theme, Amelia found listening to Simon recite *Room on the Broom* by Julia Donaldson was something she hadn't known she was missing in her life. It made everything simpler. The world could make sense again, at least for a little while. She planted her elbows on the surface of the desk and rested her chin on the heels of her palms as she watched the children get settled.

Yes, this was exactly the distraction she needed, except . . .

Was that Minnie?

Amelia straightened as she watched a shadow coalesce behind a woman reading in a chair. Thankfully, in daylight, Minnie wasn't nearly as terrifying as she normally was. In fact, in the bright light of day, the nightmare in a bonnet looked . . . young, maybe only twenty, twenty-five, and the bulging appearance of her eyes was much less startling. It seemed to have more to do with the dirt covering her face than anything else. It was actually a touch heartbreaking. From what Amelia had read, while ghosts usually manifested looking much as they did at their time of death, they could control their appearance, so she was choosing to look that way.

It's not your concern, Amelia. Focus on the library.

True, and yet she couldn't take her eyes from the ghost who had now fully materialized behind the woman in the chair. What was she doing? Why was she stalking that woman? They couldn't possibly know each other. Maybe she was a descendant of her family line? Amelia watched her for another minute or so. Minnie didn't appear to be doing anything other than lurking, but the woman in the chair did wrap her sweater more tightly around her shoulders.

Amelia dragged her gaze back to story time.

Shockingly, instead of pulling out *Room on the Broom* as he had for all the reading groups in the past few days, Simon brought out a new book. *The Berenstain Bears and the Spooky Old Tree.* Amelia sighed contentedly. She had loved the Berenstain Bears as a child. The idea of living in a cozy treehouse with all its carved-out rooms, quilts on the beds, stockpiles of berries and nuts, surrounded by a family full of love? *Magnificent.* In fact, the thought was still very much appealing as an adult. She couldn't help but wonder if Simon felt the same way.

"I know that look."

Amelia jumped, then smiled up at Rosalinda, who was standing by her shoulder. She was as stealthy as Minnie. But much cuter in her cardigan and pearls.

"What look?" Amelia asked lightly. "What do you mean?"

Rosalinda smiled knowingly. "Agony, isn't it? All the uncertainty. The not knowing what other people"—she glanced over to Simon—"are thinking."

An exhale dropped Amelia's shoulders.

"The way he looks at you," Rosalinda went on, "it reminds me a little of . . ."

"Reminds you of what?" Amelia asked far too desperately.

Rosalinda laughed, but there was a certain melancholic wistfulness to it. "Oh, of a love from long ago that didn't work out. I'll tell you about it sometime, but for now, let's stay on topic." She popped her eyebrows adorably. "I have to know. Is there something maybe beginning between you and Simon? He's being coy."

Coy? What did that mean? Good coy or bad coy? "Nothing," Amelia said. "I mean there's a lot Simon doesn't know about me."

"Well, of course," Rosalinda answered. "You've only just met."

"True," Amelia replied with a slow nod, "but . . ." She shrugged and looked down at the desk.

Rosalinda laid her hand on her shoulder. "Whatever it is, I'm sure it's not as bad as it seems."

Oh no, being a ghostseer was worse. Much worse.

Amelia glanced over to the reading carpet. Simon was doing a wonderful job of making spooky faces while he read. The kids were enthralled. She then turned back to Rosalinda offering her a small smile, but she suspected it looked sad. The older woman responded with a soft *tsk*. "Now you listen to me. I will always be the first to shout Simon's virtues from the rooftops. But I'd do the same for you. We also may not have known each other that long, but, well, just this morning, before I even got out of bed, I realized something." The older woman paused dramatically. "How lucky am I to have Amelia Bates in my life?"

For a second, time stopped, but then Amelia laughed awkwardly and shook her head. Rosalinda was just being Rosalinda, and yet, Amelia wanted to say something in return. Something that expressed *her* regard for her coworker, but she hadn't the faintest clue what. All her words felt wrong.

"Amelia?" Rosalinda prodded gently. "Are you all right?"

She forced a smile. "Yes, thank you." Before Rosalinda could respond, she added, "Could I ask you something though?"

The older woman's expression lit with far too much hope and enthusiasm. "About Simon? I know I'm interfering, but my instincts are telling me—"

"No. Sorry." Amelia cleared her throat to loosen some of its tightness. "About the library."

Rosalinda sighed with resignation. "Well, that is another one of my favorite topics. And you know you can ask me anything."

"You mentioned once that you believed the library had a personality of its own." Amelia peeked up at her.

"Oh yes." Rosalinda nodded sagely.

"Do you ever feel like it's"—Amelia couldn't quite believe she was about to ask this—"playing tricks on you? Maybe hiding things?"

"All the time." Rosalinda gazed about the grand room. "But it usually has its reasons."

"Yes, well, I'm not saying I necessarily believe in such things, but if I did . . ." She just had to say it. "How do you get the library to do something?" Amelia thought for sure Rosalinda would question that further, ask her what she meant, but instead she replied, "I'm not sure it's possible to *make* the library do anything."

Amelia tapped the desk with a pencil. Of course not.

"Buuuut . . ." Rosalinda continued, drawing out the word at an intentional, tantalizing speed. "You could try asking it nicely."

Asking it nicely?

Amelia's skepticism must have shown, because Rosalinda added, "I do have one other trick for those occasions when I'm looking for something and I just can't seem to find what I need."

"Yes?"

"Well, after I've asked very nicely for the library's help," Rosalinda leaned in close and whispered, "I close my eyes really tight." She squinted her entire face adorably. "I wait ten seconds and then"—her eyes popped open—"ta-da!"

"Does that work?"

"Not usually," she said, "but it's fun to try."

AFTER CLOSING, AMELIA arranged a few returned books neatly on Cartwell and pushed her way through the stacks. She had spotted all the ghosts that day: Minnie, of course, at story time; the professor in his usual spot by the fireplace; Braden lying limply in the chandelier, looking as though the unending boredom of being trapped in the library might kill him—or kill him again, as the case might be. Yet not one of them pushed her to discuss all that had happened the night before. It was possible they were respecting her boundaries, but there were other explanations. Maybe they had given up on trying to get her to help altogether. She wasn't sure how she felt about that, which was disturbing in and of itself.

Amelia guided Cartwell through the maze of bookshelves, but for the first time in her history of employment, she found it impossible to enjoy the journey. She tried to keep her focus on the magic that came with wandering through all the literary worlds, but her gaze kept trailing up to the corner of the east mezzanine with the eerie silver glow. She had been sure to keep an eye on the spot throughout the day, just in case it made any sudden movements, but the strange phenomenon looked just as it had the night before. She also noted that not one of the library's visitors seemed to observe the patch outright, but not a one ventured over to that side of the second floor either.

The presence of the cosmic curiosity was certainly distracting.

If only her kitten poster had held.

Three remaining books waited patiently on Cartwell's trays to be reshelved. Two were reference, the other a space opera. Normally Amelia would have looked at each one, taking a moment to wonder about the person who had picked it up, pondering whether they had found what they needed, questioning if this was a book she might want to read—the answer was usually yes—but she couldn't. Here she was surrounded by thousands of books, and all she could think about was one.

"Why are you doing this?" she muttered under her breath, glancing about her surroundings. "I was under the impression you wanted my help."

The library didn't answer.

Pulling Cartwell to a stop, Amelia picked up the space opera. The cover depicted a woman in an astronaut suit floating in a starless black sky. The idea of an interstellar escape read was tempting . . . until she remembered the patch and the fact that the ghosts might be flung to the far corners of the universe. *Back on the shelf you go.* Amelia pushed on to the end of the aisle before wheeling right, headed for the reference section.

"I'm not sure what kind of game you're playing," she whispered, again to the library, which was really just stone, wood, and other inanimate materials. "But time is likely of the essence."

She picked up one of the remaining books, *Ethics in Travel*, and fitted it back in place, wondering briefly how densely populated the rest of the world was with ghosts. Were there cultural differences when it came to spirits hanging around to bother the living? And if so, why had she never investigated that before? A move might be in order.

Amelia pushed the cart a few more steps and picked up the

remaining hardcover. *The Ultimate Guide to Wedding Planning.* She had no thoughts on that, or at least none that she wanted to explore.

"Do you even know where the handbook is?" she asked suddenly. "Or are you torturing me for no reason?"

The library stayed mum.

A small voice in her head suggested she do as Rosalinda recommended and ask the library *nicely*, but she wasn't feeling all that nice. Once again, she was trying to help, and all she seemed to be getting in return was pushback.

"Seriously," she said, with a foot stamp, "what do you want from me? Should I close my eyes and count to ten?" Amelia gripped the handle of the cart and squeezed her lids shut. "Okay, I'll play your ridiculous game. One . . . two . . . three . . ." Absurdly, she went all the way to ten, then snapped her eyes open.

Nothing.

"To think I believed we had something special." Amelia shoved the cart forward and heard a book slap against one of the trays.

What was that?

She must have missed one. Amelia craned her head to look down at Cartwell's lower shelf. Before she even saw the blue cloth cover with gold embossed letters, she knew what she would find.

The Ghostseer's Handbook.

"You have got to be kidding me," she murmured. She looked side to side for confirmation she was in fact seeing what she thought she was seeing, but no one was around. She then looked up at the ceiling, searching for any possible way the book could have fallen through the third floor down to the bottom tray of her cart, but there was none.

Amelia snatched up the book and clutched it to her chest. "You're not getting away this time." She jogged in light steps back toward the circulation desk. *Wait!* She forgot Cartwell. She almost went back for her abandoned colleague but then realized it was too big of a risk. The library might impossibly steal the book back any second.

After running around the circulation desk, Amelia placed the handbook on its surface, taking care to keep her palm on it at all times. She then sat in the rolling chair, her heart pounding in her throat. In an ideal scenario, she would devour the entire text in one sitting, but it was a thick little beast, so that strategy seemed dangerous. What if something horrible happened, like she fell asleep? No, she couldn't take the chance.

Amelia flipped frantically for several minutes until she found the page entitled *A Congregation of Ghosts.*

Now where was she?

Some believe these unfortunate souls are flung to the far corners of the universe, others alternate dimensions. Some believe they are simply obliterated. Likewise, it is difficult to predict how long the process will take. The vortex grows minutely at first, but then exponentially—

That was where she had stopped.

—building in power until it reaches a tipping point of destruction.

Tipping point of destruction?! For what? For whom? And that was the end of that sentence?! That was where the library had decided to leave her hanging?

Rosalinda was wrong. Not about the library being sentient, but about it being a *helpful* building, because, really, that would have been useful information to have had before she'd spoken to the ghosts the first time.

Even at the earliest stages, these spectrally inhabited buildings may show signs of instability through small cracks, creaks, and groans, all easily dismissed as earthly phenomena. The first conclusive sign of a cosmic vortex, however, is the inability for spirits to leave the confines of the structure. This initial period can last weeks, occasionally months, but eventually the cosmic storm gains power, resulting in more evident warning signs that the point of no return is near.

Point of no return? What? Turning the book over, Amelia studied the cover. Who was this author? Surely, they were being dramatic. She flipped through the book's front matter. No author or publication information. Of course not. She wasn't that surprised. She'd never been able to find those details before.

These signs include glowing soft spots on walls, strange interior winds, and tremors that grow in frequency and strength. At first these phenomena are only sensed by those able to see past the veil, but eventually the barrier to the living world is fully breached. When the maelstrom reaches its full force, complete destruction is inevitable. While localized, the devastation wreaked is akin to a tornado over the site of an earthquake.

Amelia looked up, her shoulders sinking from her ears.

No, it couldn't be. The library would be . . . destroyed?

Once the patches and winds have appeared, it becomes exceedingly difficult for a spirit to move on to the other side on their own. Not only is it more challenging for the passageway to the other side to open amid the vortex's power, the fear of obliteration is often not conducive to transcendent healing.

Now that she was reading it, Amelia could see how that might be the case. Again, these would have been useful insights to have had *before.*

This is where a ghostseer can help. Using their natural compassion and understanding for those stuck on the living plane, a ghostseer can guide a spirit to face the circumstances holding them back.

Without fully realizing it, Amelia crumpled a stray book club flyer in her fist. Suddenly she felt uncomfortable with where this book seemed to be headed.

When a spirit willingly confronts the truth of their life, the passageway to the other side often opens without any dedicated effort, even when stymied by a vortex. But for spirits who are unable or unwilling to face their circumstances, aid is necessary. In order to help these spirits find peace, a ghostseer must be willing to bear witness to the most intimate parts of their souls, to hold their fears, sorrows, and pain. Indeed, it is a ghostseer's gifted duty to show those who have passed love for the parts of themselves that have never experienced acceptance before. When such a connection has been made, the corridor to what lies beyond cannot help but appear.

"We're doomed," Amelia whispered.

It was the truth because there was no way she was doing that. She couldn't do that! She didn't know how to bear witness to the most intimate parts of a spirit's soul. The thought alone made her a bit sick.

> *The situation becomes more complicated, however, when a full maelstrom has been reached. Sending a single spirit on to the other side will likely not be enough to prevent the ensuing destruction. In these cases—*

Suddenly Amelia was plunged into darkness, every light in the library extinguished.

"No!" She yelled it. She couldn't help herself. "Seriously?"

"Amelia, are you all right?" the professor called out from the second floor.

"No, I'm not all right!" Unfortunately, in her moment of pure indignation, she realized her hands were off the book. *No.No.No.NO!* She patted the desk, feeling the shapes of pens, sticky notes, a staple remover—which flipped on its side and bit her finger—but no book! She yelled again, not in words this time, but in pure aggravation.

The lights snapped back on.

Amelia blinked, then looked down at the desk. The book was gone. Just gone.

"Why?" she shouted. "Why do you keep doing this? Do you not want to be saved?"

Braden materialized in front of her, wearing boxer shorts and a Hooters T-shirt. "Um, some of us are trying to sleep." He scratched the back of his head. "Who are you yelling at?"

"The library!" she snapped. "And why are you trying to sleep? You don't need to sleep!"

"Why are you yelling at the library?" he asked, rubbing his eyes. "It's not alive."

Amelia threw her arms up in the air. "Tell that to this one! And technically you're not alive either, but I'm yelling at you, aren't I?"

"Damn, bro."

Suddenly Minnie rippled into view beside Braden. He shuddered at her presence but then leaned toward her and whispered, "You're just in time. Library Girl is losing it."

A volcano's worth of frustration readied to erupt in Amelia's chest. "My name is not Library Girl. It's not bro. And it's not dude. It's—"

"Amelia?"

Simon!

17

I lie to myself all the time. But I never believe me.

—S. E. Hinton, *The Outsiders*

SIMON STOOD BEFORE HER IN PLAID PAJAMA PANTS and a white T-shirt. It was shocking. She was used to seeing him dressed for work, but now he was so casual, so adorably rumpled, it was too much, especially after being so cruelly played with by the library. Also, the pajama pants were the same plaid print she wore. Her sensibilities couldn't handle it. She didn't know if she should laugh or cry.

"Are you okay?" he asked. "I thought I heard a scream after the lights went out."

Amelia swallowed down the bubbling hysteria. "I'm fine."

"Are you sure? You sounded upset."

"No, not upset. Embarrassed maybe. I'm . . . afraid of the dark." It was all she could think of, and depending on how much he had heard, it made absolutely no sense.

"Really?" He sounded genuinely surprised, and why wouldn't he be? Grown adults did not normally require night-lights. "I'm so sorry. I thought I fixed the breaker the other day. But"—he sighed—"you know the library."

Oh, at one time, yes, she believed she did, but now Amelia was starting to think she didn't know it at all.

He frowned, then looked about the room. "I could have sworn I heard you talking to someone."

"I was." Amelia looked around too, as though someone other than a ghost might appear. "On the phone!" She picked up her mobile from the desk. "When the lights went out, I got scared—"

Don't repeat yourself, Amelia. It makes it sound like you're lying.

She was lying! Rational Amelia was not helping.

"—so I called a friend. He calls me pet names sometimes, but I'm not a fan of that." The blush was coming. There was no stopping it now. "It's a sensitivity of mine."

Amelia fully expected to see the look she had been dreading take root in Simon's features, the one that communicated that once again he knew she was lying or, worse yet, how strange he now realized she was. But it didn't come. Instead, he glanced at her phone and looked . . . disappointed?

"Oh snap! The boy is jealous!" Braden barked. "Of me! That's hilarious."

Any thrill of happiness that Amelia might have experienced at the thought of Simon's jealousy died before it could be born. Incredibly, she had forgotten, for just a moment, Braden was there. For a mere second, it had felt like she and Simon were alone, but in her life, she could never truly count on being alone with someone, could she? Amelia smoothed her hair in a self-soothing gesture. Why did everything have to be so impossible?

"Would you like me to stay while you finish up?" Simon hiked his pajama pants up his waist and Amelia temporarily blanked out. Once she had a hold of herself, she muttered something about it not being necessary.

"Well, in that case, if everything's okay . . . ?"

And there it was. The pause. The invitation for her to explain, to share, to tell him the mystery friend on the phone meant nothing to her. But she couldn't do any of those things. It was too dangerous. Lies multiplied like viruses.

"Yes. Perfectly okay."

He smiled, but his disappointment was plain. "I'll leave you to it."

Don't go . . .

But she couldn't think of a reason to make him stay, not with the ghosts staring at her.

"Good night, Simon," she called after him.

As he disappeared behind the door that led to the basement, she sank back down into her chair. *Again.* Again, she had pushed him away without an explanation that made sense.

Braden and Minnie were still hovering a few feet from the desk, almost looking like they felt sorry for her. That was the last thing she needed. "Could you two please . . ."

"Braden? Minnie?" the professor called out. "I think Amelia would like some time alone."

She closed her eyes and nodded. When she opened them again, the ghosts were gone.

"Why are you doing this to me?" she whispered, glancing around the library. "Do you enjoy watching me embarrass myself? Are you bored too? Is that it?"

Amelia grabbed a pencil she had knocked from the canister and dropped it back in the tin. What was happening? Had she really just read that the library would be destroyed if the cosmic vortex turned into a maelstrom? Yes, yes, she had read that. As twisted as the library's sense of humor seemed to be, she still desperately wanted to save it for everybody's sake. And that meant getting at least one of those ghosts to move on before things literally spun out of control.

But why? Why her? Why did she have to be the one to fix this?

Asking that was about as useful as asking why she had to be a ghostseer. She just was, and fixing this situation was up to her. If she was going to do this, though, she had to do it her way. It was extremely unlikely she was going to be able to form that deep, empathetic connection the book had described to get the ghosts to move on. She didn't have those kinds of skills. Nor, by the sounds of it, did she have the time. And the ghosts had made it very clear they weren't interested in exploring the moving-on option even under the threat of obliteration. But the book had also said when ghosts were confronted with the secret truths of their lives, the passageway naturally opened. That was something she could work with. If she found out the ghosts' secrets, she could confront them with the truth, and they'd have to move on. It was for their own good. The only problem was, even with her stellar research techniques, she wasn't going to get very far unless she had more information. And to get that information, she did have to get to know the ghosts at least a little bit better. Find out about their lives. Maybe get them to trust her without telling them why. That didn't sound very nice. But, again, it was for their own good. For everybody's good!

Amelia threw her head back over the chair and swiveled side to side.

"I don't know what you were thinking choosing me for this job," Amelia said to the library. "I don't have the first clue about how to make connections with people, living or dead."

Suddenly a book tipped over from the counter onto the desk. A book Amelia could have sworn wasn't there a minute ago, but this time it wasn't *The Ghostseer's Handbook*. She jolted up in her seat, flipped the hardback over, and read the title.

How to Win Friends and Influence People.

Amelia dropped her forehead onto the desk with a *thunk*.

18

You can make more friends in two months
by becoming interested in other people
than you can in two years by trying to
get other people interested in you.
—Dale Carnegie, *How to
Win Friends and Influence People*

FOR THE FIRST TIME IN DAYS, WHEN SHE GOT BACK to her apartment, Amelia spent most of the night reading in bed. Initially, she had been annoyed by the library's *helpful* book recommendation, but then she realized she didn't have any choice but to take it. And she didn't bring just the one book home. She brought a whole stack. Given that reading was her go-to coping mechanism for most of life's trials and tribulations, it surprised her that she hadn't studied this particular subject area before.

It turned out that getting close to people wasn't so much about being seen as a good person or even a normal person. It was about getting to know other people. Perhaps this shouldn't have been a startling revelation, but it was. Amelia's focus was usually on her own deficiencies and abnormalities—which was yet another deficiency if not an abnormality. She hadn't ever truly considered she should be diligently working on putting the focus on other people, but now that she was giving the idea proper consideration, it didn't seem that difficult. After all, she watched Rosalinda do it all the time. She seemed to know everybody who came into the library, and she was always asking about their lives. Amelia could do that. In theory.

Speaking of Rosalinda, she texted Amelia around noon the following day to see if she was available to come in early. Once again, Amelia was more than happy to oblige. No questions asked. There was actually a small part of her that wanted to be at work for the busier part of the day so she could practice her new techniques.

When she arrived, Rosalinda had already left and Simon was busy with a small group of preschoolers dressed in smocks sitting around the children's table. He looked ridiculously adorable stuffed into one of the tiny chairs, brushing a little boy's palm with paint. Amelia took her seat behind the circulation desk. As a rule, she didn't approve of paint in the library, but Simon seemed to have things under control—and the little boy was in hysterics at the paintbrush tickling his fingers. The only negative was that a couple of the mothers were looking like they might swoon, which seemed tremendously inappropriate.

"Dude, just make your move already."

Amelia jolted, sending her wheeled chair wobbling. She then cut a look at Braden, who was hovering over her shoulder. "I have no idea what you're talking about," she mumbled.

"It's so obvious you like him."

She really had to be more careful about the way she looked at Simon when other people were around.

"Hey, I get it," Braden said, looking over at the children's area. "He's all handsome and broody, like Dylan from *90210*. Actually, who are we kidding? He's definitely a Brandon. Maybe even a David."

"Dylan? David?" Amelia whispered. "What?"

"I'm not that old! Did you grow up under a rock?" Braden shouted. "My point is, I'm pretty sure he likes you too, so what's the problem?"

"First, Simon is not broody. He has a lot on his mind," Amelia whispered. It was true. Simon was naturally good-humored and kind. Even when he was worried, he always took the time to ask visitors about their days and inquire about their families. Just like Rosalinda. He always had a smile ready, and he truly listened to what people had to say. He—

Braden snapped his ghost fingers in front of her face. "You still there?"

"Second," Amelia said, catching herself, "you wouldn't understand."

"Try me."

Amelia swallowed hard. She was not about to explain to Braden all the reasons why she couldn't pursue a relationship with Simon. She needed to find out more about his issues, not the other way around. Given that was the case, she should probably stop arguing with him and adopt a friendlier tone. She scratched her nose and mumbled behind her hand, "I wasn't looking at Simon. I was looking at Minnie." It wasn't completely a lie. Amelia had spotted Minnie stalking yet another reader. "Have you noticed she's always hovering over people. What do you think she's doing?"

Braden dropped his chin. "You're kidding me, right?"

Amelia met his gaze before realizing it probably looked like she was staring at nothing to the other people in the library. *What?* she mouthed.

"She's reading. She's bored out of her mind locked up in this place. Just like I am." Braden sighed and shook his head. "From what I've seen she's mainly into romance, especially those historical ones with the big fancy English houses and the women always wearing those toga dresses."

Toga dresses? Wait, did he mean . . . ?

Amelia glanced back to the woman Minnie was leaning over and peered at the cover of the paperback she was holding. For the love of Jane Austen, Minnie was a Regency romance reader! How could that possibly be? That didn't line up at all with her love of spiders. But now that Braden had put her behavior into context, Minnie did appear to be staring intently at the open book. *Oh!* And now she was looking at the woman like she couldn't understand what was taking her so long to turn the page. Never in a million years would Amelia have guessed that would be the case. But now, maybe it was something she could use . . . after she started phase one of her plan with Braden.

"Follow me," she whispered. "I want to show you something, but we have to be quick."

"Show me what? Are you going to trap me in a box again? Don't get me wrong, that was a wild ride, but—"

"No, I have a surprise for you. I think you'll like it."

AMELIA LED BRADEN up the stairs to the third floor. She didn't like leaving the desk unattended, but with Simon keeping everyone so engaged with craft time, it meant she could sneak away without being noticed, and, besides, outside the scheduled playgroups, they weren't getting many visitors at all.

Amelia opened the door to the third floor and directed Braden over to a large storage room. She had discovered it on one of her many searches for *The Ghostseer's Handbook*. Once inside, Braden looked around at all the boxes, bits of old furniture, and outdated AV equipment before turning his confused gaze back to her. Amelia lifted a large cardboard box resting on the floor and placed it on an old study table. She then opened the top, stepped back, and gestured for him to have a look.

Braden floated to the table, then right through the wood to get a closer look at the contents of the box. "No way."

"I heard your complaints about modern-day movies, so I thought you might want to see these." The box was filled with old DVDs set for donation, all from the '90s and early 2000s.

"I don't believe this." For a moment, it almost looked like he would cry happy tears, but then his expression abruptly turned sad. "But . . ."

Amelia pointed over at the TV resting on the top shelf of a wheeled cart, a DVD/VHS player underneath. "If you'd like, I could pop in one of these *films* for you." She had taken a brief look at the titles. None seemed to fall within her range of interest, but she suspected Braden might feel otherwise.

"You would do that?" he asked. "For me?"

Amelia almost reacted with offense, but given all that had transpired and her ulterior motives, really, it was a fair question. "Yes, I would. I know you're bored stuck here and—" Suddenly the cold feeling of death grabbed Amelia, pinning her arms to her sides. Braden was hugging her. "I could kiss you."

"No thank you," Amelia mumbled.

Braden let her go and whirled back to the movies. "I don't know where to start!"

"Maybe just pick a couple for tonight."

"But there are so many I want to see!" Braden shifted the DVDs around in the box.

"You're very good at that," Amelia said. Truthfully, she'd never seen a ghost so adept at interacting with the living world. He was pushing the cases around with ease, and his hug, while cold and disconcerting, had also felt quite solid.

"I work out," he replied in what Amelia was guessing was an Arnold Schwarzenegger imitation before lifting a pile of DVDs out from the box. It was a remarkable sight, until his already transparent form faded in and out and the plastic cases tumbled to the tabletop.

Amelia stepped in closer. "What happened? Is that normal?"

"Yeah," he drawled, scratching his head around his frosted tips, "as strong as I am, I can't manifest my form while using *all* my strength. Those DVDs are like two hundred pounds in ghost weight."

"I'm sure." Amelia dropped her gaze to study his selection.

"Now, don't you go judging me, bro."

She rolled her eyes up to his. "Amelia."

He flung his hands out to the pile. "These here are all classics."

Technically that might be true.

"Hey, but before we dive in—"

We? The word stood out starkly, but Amelia knew he probably hadn't meant it. In the group home, the other kids had never asked her to join them for movie night, and she had never minded. *Much.*

"—I gotta ask," Braden said in an uncharacteristically timid tone. "Remember how you were yelling at the library last night?"

"Yes, Braden," Amelia answered dryly. "I do."

"It made me think like maybe you found something out? Or were about to? Something that could help us?"

Amelia chewed her lower lip, then shook her head. "Not really. Just more of the same. That's why I was frustrated."

Out of all the lies she had told in the past weeks, that one had to be the worst. She took no joy in her deception but held any guilt at bay. It was a necessary evil. In order to save the ghosts and the library, she had to gain their trust quickly and find out as much as she could about their lives. If they knew the library itself was in danger, they'd question her motives and shut down. She had to handle this carefully.

Amelia folded up the box and put it back on the floor. She then gathered up the DVDs into a tidy pile. "I'll come back up at closing," she said, walking the collection over to the AV stand. "And—

"There you are," a voice called out.

The DVDs slipped in her hands, but she managed to hold on to the lot by pinning them against her chest as she whipped her gaze over to Simon peeking around the side of the door. How was he always startling her like this? Did he practice moving like a cat?

"Sorry," he said. "I didn't mean to scare you. I was just going to grab some lunch in town. I'd be happy to pick up something for you."

Amelia swallowed. "I . . ."

"Say something," Braden whispered.

"I'm fine," she stammered, "but I'll be right down to watch the desk."

Braden leaned in so they were shoulder to shoulder. "Now smile."

Amelia felt the corners of her mouth stretch to the sides.

"Not like that!" He tried to swat her with the back of his hand, but it went right through her elbow. He must be tired. But, apparently, her efforts were enough to encourage Simon. He walked in the room. "Did you find some old movies?"

"No."

Simon looked at the DVDs she had pinned to her chest. Braden did too.

"I mean, yes."

"Why are you so red?" Braden asked.

She was red?! She hadn't even felt the blush come that time.

"Rosalinda said I could take some DVDs before they're donated." Sweat tickled her forehead. "I don't have cable or, as I believe I mentioned once, good internet at my apartment and . . ." She was giving too much detail again. Sure sign of a lie.

Simon bent slightly and scrutinized the covers.

"Let's see . . . *Scream. Point Break. Harold & Kumar Go to White Castle*, and *American Pie*." His smile broadened as he met her gaze.

"I'm told they're classics," Amelia replied, making Braden chuckle.

"Absolutely. I guess I just wasn't expecting . . ." Simon squinted, and somehow the magnificent crease by the corner of his mouth appeared, making Amelia's heart stop. "You are always surprising me."

"I knew it!" Braden squealed like a twelve-year-old girl. "I told you he liked you!"

Amelia did her best to block him out. "That's me. Surprising." She cocked her head to the door. "We should probably . . ."

"Oh yes." Simon held his smile, but the crease was gone. She had shut him down. Again.

Soon he'll stop trying completely.

Amelia didn't know if that voice had come from Rational Amelia or not, but it spoke the truth.

Simon left the room, and Amelia moved to follow, DVDs still pinned to her chest.

"Hey!" Braden shouted. "Where are you going with those?"

Amelia hissed under her breath, "I'm supposed to be taking them home, remember?"

"Damn, I already forgot your cover story." His eyes widened. "It must be hard having a secret identity."

He had no idea. "I'll come back at closing," she whispered. "Don't worry. I . . . got you."

TRUE TO HER word, once the library was closed, Amelia set Braden up with *Point Break* in the storage room. She was apprehensive about Simon coming upstairs and seeing the TV playing a movie all by itself, but the odds were against that happening. Simon almost never left the basement after his shift, and even if tonight was the exception and he made it all the way up to the third floor, he'd likely come up with his own ridiculously implausible excuse for what he saw. People usually did.

Once Braden was settled, Amelia went back downstairs and completed her closing routine. She then pulled out a small, specially curated collection of books she intended to use later on before clicking off the library's daytime lights and closing the front door with enough force for Simon hopefully to hear it in the basement. Finally, she headed back upstairs.

Bursts of gunfire greeted Amelia from the storage room when she arrived on the third floor, so she steered herself to the stacks to explore. Given her lack of sleep and the dim lighting, though, it was difficult to focus on any of the titles. After about ten minutes or so of aimless wandering, she found herself headed to join Braden. Judging by the raucous soundtrack and occasional fits of yelling, she reasoned that it might be the very thing she needed to stay awake. When she had almost reached the door, her steps came to a halt. Again, despite his earlier *we*, Braden likely didn't want her company. From his perspective, and maybe her own, she was a bit of a party pooper.

"Why are you hovering? Get in here!" he shouted. "This is the best part."

An unexpected prickly cool wave surged up from Amelia's shoulders to her scalp. He was inviting her to movie night after all. She entered the room and looked around for a place to sit. Luckily, there was an old leather beanbag chair, a relic from the '70s, in the corner, so Amelia settled into that, while Braden floated cross-legged in front of the TV.

It didn't take Amelia long to pick up the plot, and while extreme sports and bank robbery were not among her usual interests, the complex bromance drew her in. As the movie went on, she found herself remarkably engrossed.

When the credits rolled, Braden asked, "So? What did you think?"

"It was . . . an adequate film."

"Adequate film?!" he shouted. "That was awesome!"

Amelia smothered the smile threatening to commandeer her lips. "*Adequate* is all you're getting from me." She tried to push herself to her feet, but given the depth of the beanbag chair, that was more difficult than she'd anticipated. Eventually she was forced to make an undignified roll out of it onto her hands and knees.

"You know what you need?" Braden asked.

"Do tell." Amelia stood up. "I love it when boys inform me of what I need."

"You do?" he asked, genuinely excited.

She blinked at him. "No." Apparently more had changed in the last twenty or so years than she'd realized.

He shrugged it off. "You need to go skydiving."

A surprised chuckle escaped her.

"I'm serious," he said. "You'd appreciate life more if you tasted death."

"Hmm, I see." Amelia walked over to the TV. "Which one do you want next?"

"*Scream*." He looked down at his lap. "I wish I could manifest food and stuff the way the professor can. Popcorn would be awesome right now."

Amelia placed the DVD in the tray, then cued it up to play before heading for the door.

"Wait. Where are you going?" Braden called after her. "You're not going to watch?"

She rubbed her eyes. "I have business to attend to downstairs. Besides, I don't love horror movies."

"Why not?"

She arched her left eyebrow. "Because I'm already living one."

Braden frowned in confusion, then barked a laugh. "I get it. Because of us, right? Good one."

"I'll check on you before I go," Amelia said, unable to stop the corner of her mouth from curving.

"Okay, but it's your loss," he shouted after her. "This movie rocks."

Once outside the room, Amelia looked down at her watch.

Midnight. That should be late enough.

Of course, she hadn't been serious about her life being a horror movie, but given what she was about to do, she couldn't help but think of the aptness of Chaucer's observation that many a true word had been spoken in jest.

Amelia walked purposefully toward the door that led to the stairs. Now that she had made inroads with Braden, it was time to tackle the bonneted fright show that was Minnie.

Suddenly a loud scream tore through the shelves of the special collections floor.

Amelia froze, her hand gripping the doorknob.

"I'm okay!" Braden called out. "Don't worry. I'm okay."

This time Amelia allowed herself to smile fully.

Ridiculous ghost.

19

"I declare after all there is no enjoyment like reading!"

—Jane Austen, *Pride and Prejudice*

THE DARKNESS OF THE THIN STAIRWELL CONSUMED Amelia as she stole down the steps, each plank creaking beneath her feet. When she stepped out onto the second floor, she spotted the professor reading a manifested book by the green-blue flames of his ghost fire. He looked quite cozy. Truthfully, Amelia wanted to be that cozy. Perhaps she could change her plans and work on the professor tonight. They could get to know each other better. Maybe have some cocoa. Maybe—

You're going downstairs.

Rational Amelia was such a shrew.

As she headed down the curving staircase to the first floor, her heart took up an uncomfortably fast rhythm. Who needed skydiving? All she had to do was creep around a very old library at night to scare herself silly.

Not that the library was the problem.

There is nothing to be afraid of.

Probably.

She's just a twenty-something-year-old woman.

A hundred-and-twenty-something-year-old woman who breathed terror into the hearts of the living.

You are doing this, Amelia.

Yes, yes, she was. She didn't need to remind herself of all the reasons why, especially not the one sleeping in his T-shirt and flannel pajama pants somewhere down on the floor beneath her.

Amelia crept to the circulation desk and picked up the books she had selected earlier before tiptoeing over to the children's area. She smoothed the back of her skirt flat against her legs and settled into Simon's reading chair. It was quite comfortable. Hopefully, Minnie wouldn't be offended that she had taken the only adult seating by the story-time rug. If insulted, there was no telling what she might do—like send her doll after her. Amelia could clearly see that little porcelain nightmare chasing her through the stacks, dirty pinafore and pantaloons flying, knife raised in the air. How she got a knife there was no telling, but—

Focus, Amelia.

Right. She opened the first book's cover and cleared her throat. Then in the firmest speaking voice she was capable of, considering the circumstances, she announced, "*Pride and Prejudice.*" She dared a glance up, scanning the shadows. None of them moved. She couldn't decide if she was grateful for that or not.

"'It is a truth universally acknowledged, that a single man in possession of a good fortune must be in want of a wife.'" Amelia looked up once more, then continued to read the entire first page of the book. It was a beautifully reproduced 1894 illustrated edition, so before she turned to the next page, she rotated the book around and held it up in the air just like she'd seen Simon do so many times. As she moved the book in a slow arc in front of her, she caught sight of something that made her throat tighten. It was hard to be sure in the dim light, but it looked as though a shadow was reaching out across the floor from the bottom of one of the bookshelves.

That was terrifying.

Amelia continued to read, her fingers trembling. With her eyes glued to the page, she couldn't see anything or anyone. Nevertheless, it wasn't long before a subtle, yet distinct, cold twined around her ankles, sending shivers racing up her spine.

Steady, Amelia. Steady.

Amelia carried on, word after word, until the story finally managed to break through her fear and calm some of her nerves. When she reached the next illustration, though, they all came zinging back. Inhaling deeply, she turned the book around again and directed her gaze to where she had last seen the shadow.

Shivering spines, Minnie, still in her bonnet, was creeping her way toward the alphabet carpet . . .

. . . on her hands and knees.

It took everything in Amelia not to whimper or run—every muscle fiber was fully twitched and ready to go—and she would have, had it not been for one thing. Minnie had stopped mid-creep to look up at the illustration. She was following the story.

With a quavering exhale, Amelia turned the book back around and resumed reading, glancing up a minute later to catch Minnie sitting in front of her. A strange, near impossible transition of emotion shifted through Amelia's being. She had gone from pure terror to something else. A feeling she couldn't quite name, but it wasn't unpleasant.

Over an hour passed, but Minnie gave the book her rapt attention, studying each picture closely. It was remarkably satisfying to have such an attentive listener. As the pages turned, though, each taking some adrenaline, Amelia found herself struggling to keep her eyes open. And despite the fact that they had now made significant progress bonding over Regency romance, she did not want to fall asleep in front of Minnie. Jane Austen lover the ghost might be, but that was no guarantee she didn't devour people's souls while they slept. Stifling a yawn Amelia said, "I'm afraid we'll have to end it there."

Minnie straightened, her eyes bulging more than usual.

"Oh no, don't do that." Amelia held the book to her chest like a shield. "Don't get upset. I'll read more tomorrow."

Minnie jutted a single finger up in the air.

"I'm sorry. I don't . . ." Amelia squinted and cocked her head. "Are you asking for one more chapter?"

The ghost nodded vigorously.

"Very well, but after that it's off to bed. Do we agree?"

The ghost nodded again.

Amelia resumed reading, and sure enough, the second she finished the chapter, Minnie exploded into a cloud of tiny wriggling spiders that quickly evaporated to dust.

ONCE AMELIA HAD returned the books to the desk, she dragged herself back up to the third floor. Braden was so engaged in the movie he was watching that he didn't even turn as she approached. Apparently, he had found the strength to put one of the DVDs in by himself. Amelia snuggled into the beanbag chair and closed her eyes. She just needed a moment's rest before she went home. Instantly, the world began to drift away, then . . .

A blanket dropped over her.

"Thank you," she mumbled.

"No problem, dude. Sleep tight. Don't let the—" Braden burst out laughing. "This movie kills me every time. And I'm already dead!"

Amelia rolled her eyes beneath her lids but fell asleep smiling.

20

"'We cannot tell the precise moment when friendship is formed. As in filling a vessel drop by drop, there is at last a drop which makes it run over.'"
—Ray Bradbury, *Fahrenheit 451*

DAWN'S FIRST BRIGHT RAYS REACHED ACROSS THE third floor, forcing Amelia to blink her eyes open. After a moment of confusion at the lack of fish smell, she remembered she was in the storage room. Despite having slumbered curled up in a beanbag chair, she had slept fairly well. It was very cozy, and the blanket Braden had fetched her was nice and warm, but the hours had been too few.

Speaking of the blanket, though . . .

She hadn't fully registered it the night before, but that had been very kind of Braden. A niggling of guilt wormed its way into her thoughts. Things were changing with the ghosts. There was no denying that. She wouldn't go so far as to say she liked them, but shockingly, maybe she did. Just a little. A minuscule amount. Negligible, really. At times, Braden could be funny, and the professor sweet, and Minnie, well, she didn't give her nightmares the way she used to, so that was something.

You are on a dangerous path, Amelia.

Didn't she know it. Getting close to anybody at this stage was risky. She had a library and three ghosts to save. By any means necessary.

After sneaking her way downstairs and then outside, Amelia headed to the fish shop and went straight to bed. After a prolonged nap, she got up again, and spent several hours engulfed in some research books she had borrowed from the third floor. As the day grew long, she left for work. Despite her fatigue, she was happy to go. Every minute she was away from the library was a minute she longed to be back. In fact, life would be so much easier if she could sleep there all the time. Like Simon. Not in the basement of course, but maybe there was an attic she could call her own?

"Thar she be. Back for more, lass?"

Amelia clutched her coat against the cold autumn wind as she scurried over the cobblestone path. Once again, the sea captain was smoking his pipe by the old oak tree on the library's front lawn.

"Best not go in there."

And once again he was spouting dire warnings nobody wanted to hear.

Amelia rushed past.

"Something bad's been churned up in those walls. Something . . ."

His voice faded as Amelia trotted up the front steps. *Yes. Yes.* She'd heard it all before. That first night she'd visited the library, she'd dismissed the spirit's cautions, but she'd come to realize he was likely picking up on the cosmic vortex. Not that she was about to discuss it with him. No, she had enough ghosts to worry about.

Mired in her usual troublesome thoughts, Amelia went inside, removed her coat, and headed for the circulation desk without really registering her surroundings . . . until she saw the package on the desk.

The library received packages all the time, so that wasn't the issue. No, what stopped her in her tracks was who it was addressed to.

Amelia Bates.

For a moment, she couldn't imagine what it might be, but then it hit her. The ghost supplies she had purchased from her reckless night of online shopping! She had used the library as her location because her fish-shop apartment hadn't shown up as a legitimate address.

That night felt like a lifetime ago. She'd been so desperate to get rid of the ghosts back then, the *how* of it all hadn't been important. Amelia grabbed a letter opener from the desk drawer and sliced through the tape. She had no intention of using the items anymore, not unless the ghosts wanted her to, but she was still curious.

Before lifting the top flaps of the cardboard box, Amelia furtively glanced around the great room. No one was there. Not even Simon or Rosalinda. That was odd, but it did give her the opportunity to examine her purchases in private. She removed the packing from the top and pulled out the items one by one. As expected, it was all *junk*. First there was a small transistor radio. It was supposed to influence ghost frequencies, but Amelia was pretty sure it was just a radio. After that came an old steel desktop fan, which, while aesthetically pleasing, was also likely just a fan. And finally, there were a couple of flasks with cork tops. Amelia couldn't even remember what those were supposed to do.

Well, that had been a waste of money.

Amelia repacked the items and placed the box under the desk just as Rosalinda appeared from the foyer in a thick wrap sweater and knitted hat with appliqué leaves. "Hello there!" she called out.

Amelia straightened up to her feet. "Well, hello to you. I was starting to wonder if I was the only one in today."

"Simon should be here somewhere," Rosalinda replied, taking off her hat. "He wants to tell us about his latest meeting with the engineering company. But don't worry, I brought cookies."

Amelia hadn't been worried, but now she was. "Is it bad news?"

"I guess we'll have to wait and see." The older woman smiled grimly, then scanned the top of the desk.

"Are you looking for something?"

Rosalinda patted a spot just beneath her left collarbone. "I seem to have misplaced my brooch." She shook her head. "I'm always losing something, aren't I?"

"I'll be sure to keep an eye out for it." Amelia made a mental note to ask the ghosts if they'd seen it.

"You're such a dear," Rosalinda replied, before turning to look around the room. "Any visitors about?"

"I don't think so."

Rosalinda sighed. "Well, I have a few things to take care of, and I know Simon's busy, but maybe we could meet back here in an hour or so?"

"Of course," Amelia said. "I actually have something to do myself."

"Perfect." Rosalinda headed for the break room. "I'll let Simon know."

For once, Amelia hadn't lied, but she did make sure to wait until Rosalinda was gone before she pulled out her phone and headed over to the printer.

The time had come to tackle ghost number three.

Given the professor's difficulty recalling why he was still here, Amelia had done some cursory research into improving memory. Unfortunately, most of the advice she had come across hadn't seemed useful. Brain-teasing puzzles like crosswords and word searches could possibly help, but it was unlikely the professor could use a pencil or turn more than a page or two from nonmanifested books. For obvious reasons, medications, exercise, and diet modifications were also out, but she had come across another avenue of possibility that was potentially promising. So after printing off a few pages, Amelia headed upstairs.

She found the professor in his usual chair, ghost newspaper resting on his lap, steaming mug gripped by his chest, face turned to the window. Following his gaze, Amelia realized she had never truly taken the time to appreciate the expansive view from this vantage point. At least not at this time of day. For once there was no rain or clouds, and the sun had just begun to set, bathing the distant beaches trailing down the coastline in golden light. Small groupings of birds swooped and danced against the infinite sky as the glittering sea tossed sparkling light with every ripple.

She would never tire of the island's sunsets. Each one was a gift.

Surprisingly, though, the sea wasn't the only thing sparkling. The professor himself, from his manifested shoes to his untamed white hair, glittered prettily in the warm late-day glow. Amelia had never seen a ghost look so . . . ethereal.

She was tempted not to disturb him, but, as the old maxim went, *needs must.*

"Hello, professor," she said, stepping around the side of his chair.

A broad smile instantly warmed his face. "Amelia, what a wonderful surprise. Would you care to join me?"

"I would." She took the seat across from him. While it was risky talking to the professor during opening hours, she did have a clear line of sight to the stairs and was ready to spring up should anyone appear. "I've brought something that I . . ." Amelia trailed off with a frown. *Wanted to try on you* sounded callous. *I thought might help your memory?* Even that felt presumptuous.

"A Rorschach test!" the professor said, looking at the papers in her hand.

"Yes." Amelia glanced down at the first sheet of ink blots she had printed off. Perhaps it wasn't the most valid form of psychological assessment, but it seemed like a place to start. "I was hoping that maybe . . ." She trailed off again. Guilt about tricking the professor into helping the library was muddying her thoughts. But she wasn't tricking him, at least not entirely.

The professor gestured at her with his mug. "You were hoping that those amorphous blobs might tap into my unconscious memory," he said with excitement. "What a brilliant idea."

Amelia kept her gaze on the papers. *Brilliant.* She didn't hate her idea being called that. "So, you're open to trying?"

"Absolutely," he said. "If I can finally resolve what is holding me back, or maybe simply remember what it is, perhaps I can move on. I've discussed it with the others, and, well, we were wondering if maybe removing the weight of one ghost alone could stop the vortex. If that ghost were me, then Braden and Minnie could do as they please with their afterlives. Do you think that's possible?"

Amelia stiffened. That was quite a good guess given she had opted not to share that particular bit of information back when, above all else, she wanted the library to be ghost-free. "I'd say that's definitely a possibility."

The professor smiled. "Well then, let's get started."

Despite their shared enthusiasm, it soon became clear that the inkblots were useless. It wasn't because the professor was resistant in any way. No, he was quite agreeable. It was more that he saw the same thing in every print.

A butterfly.

Amelia had to admit, many of the blots did in fact look like butterflies—or tentacled alien monsters—but it wasn't exactly a useful observation, unless, of course, the professor was a professor of lepidopterology. She made a mental note to follow up on that. Perhaps she could look up all the butterfly experts who had died in the last hundred years or so. The thought was only mildly daunting.

"I'm sorry to have wasted your time, Amelia."

"No, I knew it was a long shot. It was good of you to try." Amelia gathered the papers on her lap.

"I suppose you have to get back to work now?"

"I suppose." Amelia looked around. Not a soul had come in, as far as she could tell. "I have a meeting in a little while, but—"

"Ah! Wonderful. The sun is just about to fully set. You should really see it from here."

"Oh, I . . ." Amelia was fully intending to politely decline the offer, but when she glanced out the window, the sun, now fiery red, melting into the distant horizon, caught her in its majestic hold. With the presence of the portal on the east wall, somehow it felt all the more comforting. "I suppose I could stay for a moment or two."

Unfortunately, as soon as the words had left her mouth, regret bloomed. Amelia sat back stiffly against her chair, folding her hands in her lap. Coming to the professor with a planned activity was one thing, but this was different. What was she supposed to do? What were the expectations of her in this scenario? Should she comment on the beauty of the sunset? Use the opportunity to ask the professor questions about himself? Provide facts on the nature of celestial patterns? If only she had brought her notes on making friends.

"I should have mentioned," the professor said, stealing her attention away from her thoughts. "My preference has always been to watch the sunset in silence." His apologetic grin was guileless, but his eyes held a kind understanding for her that was impossible to mistake. "Does that sound all right to you?"

Amelia's shoulders dropped, and a smile found her lips. "That sounds lovely to me."

IT WAS LOVELY.

Perfectly lovely, but before Amelia knew it, the sun had set, and it was time to join up with Rosalinda and Simon for their meeting. She bade the professor farewell and headed downstairs. As she walked toward the circulation desk something, or rather someone, caught her eye.

There was a visitor in the library after all. The suspected owner of the crab shack.

He had returned.

21

Call me Ishmael.
—Herman Melville, *Moby-Dick*

THE MAN STOOD ONCE AGAIN IN THE MYSTERY SECtion, sporting the same plaid jacket and holding the same woolen cap. He was also wearing the same perplexed look of frustration on his face.

Another chance.

Truthfully, Amelia's last encounter with the man had been haunting her. She had replayed her actions over and over, but she still wasn't sure how she should have handled the situation. And, truthfully, she had been doing so much better when it came to interacting with visitors—and that was high praise coming from her. Still, she was not one to give up easily. She would get this man help whether he liked it or not.

Hmm, that did sound a touch scary librarian.

Amelia fast-walked stiffly the rest of the way over to the circulation desk.

"Oh, there you are. Thank goodness," Rosalinda said at her approach. "Simon will be up any minute, and I can't find my glasses now." She patted the front of her sweater, then looked up. "They're on my head, aren't they?" Before she could answer, Rosalinda smiled and brought them down to her chest before fully catching Amelia's expression. "What's wrong? What's happened? Is it the library?"

"No, it's that man," Amelia hissed, pointing her index finger, shielded by her chest, over to the mystery section.

Rosalinda placed her hands cautiously on the circulation desk and peered over. "What man?" She rose to her feet. "I don't see—"

"Don't look!"

Rosalinda froze.

"We don't want to spook him."

"No, of course not," she replied, barely moving her lips. Amelia truly appreciated how willing this woman was to join an escapade.

"Just glance over. Quickly."

Rosalinda flicked her gaze to the stacks. Once she spotted the man, her shoulders dropped. "That's just Wayne. He runs the crab shack in the village."

She knew it! She knew she had recognized him. Amelia hurried around the desk and led Rosalinda farther back into the circulation area, out of view. "Have you noticed how frequently he comes in?"

Rosalinda frowned, deepening her wrinkles adorably. "I don't think I—"

"Often. At least weekly," Amelia said. "But he never takes anything out."

"Really?" Rosalinda cocked her head back in the direction of the stacks. "I hadn't noticed. Maybe—"

Amelia gripped Rosalinda's hand. "*And* he's refusing all offers of help." Well, likely only hers, but that was neither here nor there. "Don't you think that's odd?"

"That's just Wayne. He's always been a shy one. Stubborn too. He'd walk in circles before admitting he was lost." Suddenly, Rosalinda's brow furrowed in thought.

"What? What are you thinking?"

"It's just that Wayne has never been a big visitor to the library, but his wife is a different story. I heard she hasn't been well. I wonder if he is looking for something for her?"

A wife? The mysterious *she*!

"I'll go ask if I can help." Rosalinda pulled her sweater in tight to her body, but before her feet managed a step, she added, "Unless you'd like to."

Amelia made a face. "I'm not sure that's the best idea. I failed miserably the last time I approached him."

"Miserably? Really?"

Amelia nodded quite seriously.

"I'm sure it wasn't that bad. You're so good with people."

Amelia let out a hearty "*Ha!*" then slapped her hand over her mouth.

Rosalinda squeezed her elbow. "Stop. You are. The only person you have to prove it to is yourself."

"I see. How do I do that?"

Rosalinda frowned. "Do what?"

"Prove it to myself?"

"Well, I didn't mean you actually had to prove it. Really, Wayne is just—"

"My Moby Dick." The words had come unbidden, but they rang true.

"I'm sorry?" Rosalinda looked mildly perturbed. She was likely recalling how things ended for Ahab, but that would not deter Amelia. She certainly didn't want to be overbearing, but Wayne kept coming back! Clearly, he wanted something. "I will handle this."

Rosalinda studied her face before her eyes lit with excitement.

"Yes, you will." She gripped Amelia's other elbow. "He won't make it easy, but if anyone can help him, you can."

Amelia nodded sharply, then strode out from behind the circulation desk, headed directly for the mystery area.

A moment later she headed straight back.

Rosalinda's eyes widened at her approach. "What happened?"

"He wasn't there." Amelia frowned. "I think he left while we were talking."

Rosalinda grimaced. "Oh."

"Yes."

"Next time, then."

"Next time."

Suddenly a new voice entered the mix. "What next time?"

Both Amelia and Rosalinda jolted at Simon's appearance.

He laughed. "I'm sorry. What did I just stumble upon?"

"Nothing," Amelia blurted before Rosalinda could reply. She really didn't want to explain her struggles to adequately help library patrons, certainly not to him.

Simon looked to Rosalinda, but she shrugged blithely giving him a tight-lipped smile.

"Right." The corner of his mouth twitched. "Well, in that case, let's get this meeting started."

ROSALINDA MADE THEM each a cup of tea, which was wonderful, and set out a tin with fresh cookies on the small table just behind the circulation desk. The three of them needed to stay out in the open for the rare visitors who came in.

Amelia couldn't help but feel there was a certain rightness to them sitting together. It was as though everything was exactly as it should be . . . except for the look on Simon's face. All his previous good humor had drained away, leaving only worry behind.

"So, I had a call with the engineering company," he began, tapping a pencil absentmindedly against a blank notepad. "While they weren't able to definitively find the source of the problem, they do have an idea about what might be going on."

"Is it that bad?" Rosalinda asked.

He nodded tightly. "They think it might be a foundation problem."

Amelia didn't know a lot about architecture or structural engineering, but she did know that a foundation problem sounded serious.

"They want to start digging trenches around the building, starting at the east wall, to get a better look."

"Why there?" Amelia asked, fearing she already knew the answer.

Simon glanced up in the direction of the patch without seeming to register the glow. "The structural irregularities are focused in that wall."

Rosalinda squeezed Simon's hand. "Will it be expensive to fix?"

"Most likely, yes. But something needs to be done. It would be irresponsible . . ." He collapsed back in his chair, struggling to find the right words. "To simply hope for the best."

Amelia suddenly felt like the library itself was spinning off into space. This was bad. Incredibly bad. She couldn't let Simon go ahead with the engineering company's plans when the ghosts and cosmic whirlpool were likely responsible for all the library's woes, but he would never believe what she had to say. Not now. It was still too soon. "Is that the only option? When is all this happening?"

"They are doing a consult with another company," he said with a sigh, "but we're looking at a week from now. Maybe two."

"A week!" Amelia shouted. A solitary woman looked over from the stacks—and Braden from the second floor. "A week?" she repeated at a much more appropriate volume.

"I'm afraid so. Apparently, the building is *vibrating* at a low level. They've never seen anything like it. Soon it could be too dangerous for people to be inside."

A heavy silence fell over them before Simon pushed himself to his feet. "I wish I had better news. I'll give you both some time to process. I have to . . ." He sighed again, then retreated in the direction of the basement, looking heartbroken.

Amelia's eyes darted side to side, searching for answers that didn't exist.

"Oh, don't look so sad. I know how you feel about the library," Rosalinda said gently, "but I also know the library is going to be okay."

Amelia snapped her gaze up. "How could you possibly know that?" She didn't mean for it to come out so curtly. Thankfully, Rosalinda didn't seem to mind. "The library's working on it."

"The library," Amelia said, dropping her chin. "The same library that is vibrating and may be close to imminent collapse?"

Rosalinda's eyes sparkled. "You'd be amazed by what this library can do."

Amelia attempted a smile, but it held no optimism. She already knew the library was working on it—*probably*—but so far, its plan seemed entirely contingent on her ability to get the ghosts to move on. While she had made some inroads with the three, unsurprisingly, she was nowhere near the soul-baring level required to open the passageway to the other side, and she was no further along in discovering what issues might be holding them back.

She had to do more. Push harder. But . . . she needed help!

Revealing her secret wasn't an option, but that didn't mean she couldn't ask questions. One had been niggling at her for a while now, but she had been hesitant to ask either Rosalinda or Simon because she didn't want anyone living to associate her with, well, the dead. But now was the time for bold action.

"Rosalinda?"

"Yes, dear?"

"I know your thoughts on the library being sentient, having its own personality, so to speak, but . . ." Amelia frowned. What she was about to say felt very dangerous. "Have you ever heard anything about the library being haunted?"

22

"All we can know is that we know nothing."
—Leo Tolstoy, *War and Peace*

OUTSIDE A SUDDEN WIND GUSTED AND SMALL WHISTLING cries from unseen cracks and crevices swirled around them. Amelia had meant for the question to be light and conversational, but everything about Rosalinda's demeanor shifted to something quite serious. "Have you seen one?"

"A ghost? Oh, I . . ." Amelia should have anticipated the question and had a lie at the ready, but she hadn't—that was often the trouble with sudden, bold action—so she opted to answer Rosalinda's question with one of her own. "Have you?"

"No." Rosalinda glanced out the nearest window. Darkness had fallen quickly. "But if I had to guess, the library must have its fair share of ghosts. All old buildings have them, don't you think?"

Yet another question Amelia did not want to answer. "But are there any stories that have stuck around over the years?"

Rosalinda nodded, then paused to nibble a cookie. "I suppose the most popular one is about a young lady doomed to wander these floors for an eternity. It is said she wears a bonnet and a long dirty dress."

A young lady? Bonnet? Long dirty dress? Perhaps Amelia should have found the courage to pursue this line of questioning sooner. "Who says this?"

"Oh people, but they're all long gone." Rosalinda chuckled. "These were stories I heard as a child."

"Is there a particular tale behind this young woman?" Amelia prodded. "How she came to haunt the library, perhaps?"

"Oh yes." The older woman's eyes widened with dark interest. "Legend has it she killed her family, and she haunts the library as punishment. Remember, these walls once housed jail cells." Rosalinda took in the frown that had come over Amelia's face. "Horrible. I know."

It was horrible, yes, but it also couldn't be right. Obviously, there was something terrible in Minnie's past, and she could be terrifying at times, but murder her family? That wasn't possible. They had read *Pride and Prejudice* together!

"Now, I personally have never felt any malevolent presences here, but sometimes . . ." Rosalinda trailed off with a mysterious look.

"Sometimes what?" Amelia asked.

"Sometimes when the library is closed, strange things happen. I'll catch a shadow twisting in an unnatural way or hear a creak that makes me think I'm not alone . . . and, of course, I'm not."

Amelia tensed. "You're not?" Why was she getting scared? She knew there were ghosts in the library. Hearing it from another person's perspective, though, made it seem much creepier.

Rosalinda shrugged cutely. "No one is ever alone in a library"—she waved her hand out at the shelves—"not with all these lives to be shared."

"Right," Amelia said, unable to keep the disappointment from her voice. "Of course." For a moment there she'd thought Rosalinda was going to confess that she too could see ghosts, not just pick up on strange shadows and creaks.

"Whatever the case may be," Rosalinda said, suddenly looking wistful, "if there are spirits here, I'd like to think they're happy."

PRECIOUS DAYS PASSED with Amelia following the same routine. From the moment she woke up, all the way through to the end of the day, she snuck in research, tracking down books and using every database she could think of to find information on the ghosts, especially Minnie, but there was nothing. She couldn't dig up a single account of an islander killing her family. It was hard not to conclude that the stories Rosalinda had heard as a child were likely just that: stories. Maybe someone had somehow witnessed Minnie in all her terrifying glory and made up a dark tale to go along with what they had seen. It was the only thing that made sense. If Minnie were a murderer, it would have been in every newspaper. Just look at the infamy of Lizzie Borden. Children jump-roped to rhymes about her. Of course, it was possible that Minnie had killed her family and gotten away with it, so it never made the papers, but Amelia didn't want to believe that.

Whatever the case, she was no closer to helping Minnie move on.

The same could be said for Braden. They had formed a connection. There was no doubt about that. Every night was movie night now, and given Braden's natural enthusiasm for, well, everything, the experience was usually somewhat amusing. Unfortunately, anytime Amelia brought up anything personal, his mood turned and he immediately shut down. He had no issues. He was bored but fine. The funny thing was the more Braden told her he was fine, the less Amelia believed him. But every time she pushed, it only caused tension.

As for the professor, she had tried a few more exercises to dig into his hidden memories, but they weren't able to get much beyond the surface. Moreover, as far as Amelia could tell, there wasn't a single butterfly scholar dead or—actually just dead—who looked anything like him.

And to make matters imminently worse, the library's problems seemed to be intensifying. The lights flickered at least three or four times a day, while the walls and floors groaned constantly. Then there was the patch on the second floor. It had grown from the size of a small puddle to that of a kiddie pool: a cold eternal kiddie pool threatening to drown them in oblivion.

They were all on edge. The ghosts weren't talking about it, but it was clear they knew the situation was becoming dire. She suspected they could feel it in their intangible bones, just like she could feel it . . . in her head.

Amelia had woken that morning with a throbbing headache, and it only grew worse the closer she got to the library.

When she arrived at the top of the drive, she noted there wasn't a single car parked in the lot. That wasn't all that surprising, given the dwindling number of visitors, and the fact that there were no reading groups or classroom visits scheduled for the day, but somehow it felt ominous.

The ill-omened feeling only deepened when she went inside.

Walking with instinctively quiet steps, Amelia entered the main reading room. It was as still as a ghost town, except all the ghosts had fled. She tucked her bag underneath the desk before checking for Simon and Rosalinda. They were also nowhere to be found. For a moment, she felt like she had entered some old *Twilight Zone* episode, where she was the only person left on earth—and that eerie feeling was not helped by the extra-eerie feeling coming from the second floor. The thought made her skin crawl, but she knew she had to go check on what was going on up there.

Amelia climbed the steps, then walked toward the back end of the mezzanine. She could have taken the staircase on the east side—it certainly would have been the quicker route to get to the patch—but she wanted to check in on the professor and maybe get a look at what was going on from a distance before she committed to any particular course of action.

Thankfully, the professor was safe and sound in his chair by his ghost fire, asleep with a newspaper resting on his chest. She tiptoed past and then journeyed over to the other side. Cutting a path in front of the bookshelves, Amelia didn't stop walking until she came to the last aisle. She peeked down its length. What she saw there dropped her heart to the earth's fiery core.

The gray swirling patch now stretched from the floor to just over her head. She could walk right into it if she wanted to.

Amelia couldn't say how long she stayed staring into the nothingness, but at some point, nudged by some inexplicable compulsion, she stepped closer. This was a bad idea. Terrible. But once again, she was mesmerized by the uncanny spectacle playing out on the brick wall. It was like staring into the heart of the universe, both awe-inspiring and frightful.

Amelia stopped when she reached the end of the shelves. The patch was almost within touching distance. Its limitless, uncaring cold pulled at her as a strange sound tickled her ear.

Pages . . . flapping in the wind.

Suddenly an object whizzed by Amelia's left ear right into the swirling silver-gray mists. It had flown by so quickly she barely had time to register what it was.

A book!

So, posters weren't enough after all. It was officially eating the books!

Anger erupted in Amelia's chest. Unfeeling universe or not, this was an outrage. She glanced around the shelves. There weren't many empty spaces, so maybe that was the first one?

She had to do something.

She looked about frantically until her gaze landed on a metal cabinet filled with island maps and newspapers. It was decently sized, but not so much that she wouldn't be able to push it over the patch. It was only a temporary fix. She knew that, but she couldn't just leave some big, gaping hole to oblivion hanging around snacking on literature.

Amelia ran back up the aisle she had first come down, turned, then raced down the next one over. She didn't want to get too close to the patch. Not anymore. If it could inhale books, people couldn't be that far behind. She positioned herself on the far side of the cabinet and gave it a tentative push. It was much heavier than she'd imagined. She planted her hands more firmly against the cool metal and stepped back so she could really lean into it. She pushed again with a grunt, but it only moved a fraction of an inch.

Come on, Amelia. Put your back into it.

She supposed Rational Amelia was trying to be encouraging, but she came across as judgmental—as was often the case.

Amelia pressed into the cabinet with her shoulder, and it moved another few inches. She was going to get it! It might take everything she had, but she would cover the hole. She pushed against the cabinet again, digging her feet in. This time, though, it moved much too quickly, and she tumbled forward, falling to the floor. Lying flat on her belly, Amelia craned her head, then peeked to the side. The patch was only a few feet away, and . . .

It felt like it was reaching for her.

With an almost curious touch, its grasping tendrils of cold began to wind around her wrists, torso, and neck. This had been a terrible, horrible, no good, very bad idea. Forget the cabinet. All she wanted to do now was get away.

Keeping her eye on the swirling silver-gray mists, Amelia pushed herself to her hands and knees and shuffled back toward the nearest bookshelf. She knew if she could just break free from this one area, it would be fine.

And it would have been . . . if an enormous book hadn't been somersaulting midair down the aisle headed directly for her.

Right before it hit, Amelia spotted the title. *War and Peace.*

Somehow, she had always known Tolstoy would be the end of her.

23

This wasn't just plain terrible, this was fancy terrible. This was terrible with raisins in it.
—Dorothy Parker, attributed

THE CLASSIC MONSTROSITY HIT AMELIA IN THE SHOULder, sending her reeling to the floor. The instant her back hit she began to slide.

No.No.No.NO!

Amelia scrambled against the wood planks, trying to scream, but her lungs couldn't catch any air. The patch was sucking the wind from them. Then, before she could even fully register the horror of what was happening, her right foot dipped into the unearthly mists. She didn't have to look. The sensation was like nothing she had ever felt before, both violently cold and somehow icky. Amelia flung her arms forward and grasped the only thing available to her, the foot of a bookshelf.

For a half second, relief surged through her veins, but it was quickly replaced by the terror of a new sensation.

What in the name of Sir Isaac Newton? *Was she stretching?!*

It was one thing for Braden's fingers to stretch. He was a manifestation! But she was flesh and bone. This had to be breaking all the laws of physics. This—

"Dude!" a voice shouted. "What are you doing?!"

Amelia blinked up, her eyes watering from the cosmic winds. Braden and Minnie were staring at her with horror. Yes, even Minnie looked terrified by her situation. Amelia opened her mouth, but couldn't manage more than a whispered "Help."

"*Okay,okay,okay,*" Braden said, sounding more panicked than she would have liked. "Hang on. We're coming."

"No!" Amelia croaked. They would be sucked in. "Find . . . a rope."

The ghosts exchanged frightened looks before Braden yelled, "A rope? There's no time for that!" He dropped to his knees and army crawled toward her. Minnie dropped down behind him, copying his movements.

"It's not as bad on the floor," he shouted.

Maybe if your foot wasn't already halfway to another galaxy! *And* there went her shoe. Lost in the outskirts of space. Gone where no shoe had ever gone—

"Hey!" Braden snapped. "Stay with us. Give me your hand." He grunted, reaching his own toward her.

Amelia shook her head violently because the hand he wanted her to give him was also the hand she had wrapped around the leg of the bookshelf. Her one anchor to this planet. The only thing stopping her from being sucked into the vortex.

"It's all good." Braden's fingers wrapped around her wrist. "I got you." Surprisingly, his grip felt secure, as secure as a real live boy's. "Now let go."

Amelia shook her head again.

"We'll pull you back."

Minnie peeked up from where she was kneeling on the backs of Braden's legs and nodded.

They were insane. That thought must have shown in her hysterical glare because Braden said, "It's the only way. You can't hold on forever."

It was true. Her hand was already starting to ache, but . . . she couldn't! Mainly because every time she thought about releasing her grip, she imagined snapping like an elastic band into the void.

"You have to trust us. We're your only hope."

Amelia met Braden's eyes and then Minnie's before squeezing her own shut.

It's the only way, Amelia.

She flexed her fingers open. For a sickening moment she jerked back, but Braden's grip held. "Nice! You did it! Now, we're just going to back up."

"My foot is stuck," Amelia choked out between gasping breaths.

Braden nodded. "Don't freak out. Just dig in with your other foot and push yourself toward me." Minnie nodded with what almost looked like encouragement.

Amelia dug her toes into the floor and inched forward. It was working! Except . . . while her body was moving forward, her other foot was still firmly in the patch. "Braden?! Is my leg stretching? Like your fingers did?"

He looked around her. His eyes widened; then he snapped his gaze back to her. "No."

"You're lying! Minnie?"

The instant Amelia said her name, the ghost girl went into her signature daze.

"Forget your foot," Braden said. "Just a little more and you'll pop right out. Everything will be fine."

Forget her foot? "You don't know that! I don't want an extra-long leg, Braden."

"Breathe. You got this."

He sounded very confident, but his body was starting to fade in and out the way it had when he had been lifting the DVDs. She weighed more than four movies! The shock was enough to return her to the moment.

"Okay, on the count of three," Braden said calmly. "One, two, three. Heave!"

Amelia felt the tug on her wrist, but the vortex still had its grip on her ankle. "Help!" she suddenly screamed. Forget her secret. She needed a live human's help even if it meant being exposed. "Help me!"

"What in the heavens?" The professor appeared behind Minnie.

Another ghost. Wonderful. She was going to die. They were all going to die.

The white-haired ghost looked stunned but then dipped to the floor to grab Minnie's ankles.

It wasn't going to work. Braden was getting fainter, and he was the strongest of the lot. She was going into the vortex, and they were all going in with her. Amelia knew she would be bad at helping ghosts, but she had no idea that she'd be this spectacularly bad.

"It's no use," she yelled. "You have to—"

"We're not giving up," the professor shouted. "Neither are you."

With renewed force, Braden retightened his grip on her wrist and pulled back up onto his knees. He then looked at her leg. "Does that hurt?"

"No! Why?"

Braden blinked. "No reason. Everyone heave!"

At first it felt like nothing was happening, but then the hold on her ankle reached its maximum force and released with an earsplitting *pop*!

Braden tumbled back into Minnie and the professor, yanking Amelia with him. They all landed in a strange cold tangle. Given the ghosts' lack of tangibility, it felt a little like a ball pit of death that somehow smelled like Axe body spray and . . . smoke? Which one of them smelled like smoke? Amelia rolled onto her back and gave the air another sniff before she remembered—*my leg!* She snapped her head up. Her leg was fine. Perfectly proportioned. She dropped her head down again, her skull thumping against the wood.

Suddenly Braden shot up into the air and pumped his fist. "Boo-yah! That was awesome!"

Amelia exchanged looks with the professor and Minnie.

"That was like riding a wave with a great white on your tail! Or shredding down a mountain, avalanche at your back!"

Neither of those things sounded good.

"I feel so . . ." Suddenly Braden's excitement dropped away. "Alive."

Amelia wanted to say something. Ask Braden what he was thinking. But she couldn't. Not now. Not with Simon standing at the end of the aisle staring at her lying starfished on the floor.

"Amelia? Are you okay?" he asked. His brow was furrowed with concern and bewilderment, but there was also the beginning of something else in his expression. "I thought I heard someone calling for help."

She tipped her head up. "Yes." *And* she was back to monosyllables. At least they never failed her.

He cocked his head. "What are you doing?"

"I was . . ." What? What could she possibly be doing that would make any sense?

"Adjusting your back," the professor whispered.

"My back! I was adjusting it." She tagged on a forced smile at the end.

"Oh," Simon replied with a confused blink. "Do you have back problems?"

"No."

That had just come out.

"So, you hurt it just now?"

"No."

She'd done it again! Why couldn't she have just said yes? Then this brutal interrogation would be over. "I was trying to move the cabinet with the maps."

"The cabinet . . . ?" Simon looked over at the metal cupboard. "Why?"

Amelia propped herself up on her elbows. "I thought it might get more use if people could see it when they were in this aisle."

Simon scrutinized her face before looking over to the cabinet and then down the corridor between the bookshelves. The ghosts followed his gaze. "I see what you mean."

"Really? He bought that?" Braden asked. "Are we sure this guy graduated library school?" He laughed, then held up his hand to Minnie for a high five, but she had returned to her trance state. His fingers crumpled and his hand dropped to his side.

"Why didn't you ask me for help?" Simon said, overlapping the exchange between the ghosts. "I'll move it now."

"No!" Amelia suspected she had surpassed the number of times one could say no in a conversation before things became awkward a long time ago, and yet they kept on coming. "I wouldn't want you to get hurt too."

Simon reached his hand down to her. "Do you think you can

stand?" Amelia swallowed hard, putting her hand in his, ignoring the knowing look Braden was giving her. "Careful," he said, helping her up. Once she had her footing, he released her, and walked past.

"Simon, wait!"

He looked over his shoulder at her, confused. Actually, no, there was definitely more than confusion playing out on his face. There was hurt too, and for the first time Amelia thought there might also be frustration. As much as he was playing along, he also knew she was lying. She couldn't blame him of course. She also couldn't tell him the truth. Most of all, though, she couldn't just let him walk up to the portal! "Do you feel that?"

He hesitated. A strange look came over his face as he reached his hand out toward the swirling patch. Amelia almost shouted for him to stop, but before she could, he placed his hand directly on it. "I thought I felt a draft for a moment. Is that what you meant?"

She wrapped her arms around her waist and nodded.

He smiled sadly at the wall. "Poor old library is going through a lot." Then he moved to the side of the cabinet and pushed it over the portal. "Is that good?"

"Perfect." Amelia could still see the silvery-gray glow around the cabinet's edges, but it was fully blocked. For now.

"Can I help with anything else?" The faint hopefulness in his voice nearly broke her heart.

"No, thank you."

Simon nodded, and left without so much as a goodbye.

Braden leaned toward her and whispered, "You gotta know that display of muscles was all for you."

Amelia sighed. No, she did not know that.

In fact, the only thing she knew for certain was that this day had damaged more than just the library.

24

If you tell the truth, you don't have
to remember anything.
—Mark Twain, attributed

AFTER THE RESCUE AT THE PORTAL, THE NEXT FEW days passed in a tired blur. Simon was as friendly as ever, at least superficially, but Amelia knew things had changed. He had stopped asking questions and pulling threads, even when there were no threads to pull, and Amelia didn't think it was because he was busy. In some ways it was a relief, but mainly it just left her sad.

The whole situation was making Amelia sad.

The ghosts could tell things were different too. She'd kept her normal routine of watching movies with Braden and reading to Minnie, but the experience was often ruined by the sickening sense that they were wasting time. No one said anything, but it was clear they all felt it. Everyone's spirits were dampening.

So much had changed.

After her tangle with the portal, all the ghosts had asked Amelia if she was okay at one point or another—well, Minnie had only said *Secrets*, but Amelia thought she detected an inflection at the end. Either way, it wasn't a question she knew how to answer. A great deal had been thrown at her in the past few weeks, but as one might expect, the portal's attempting to swallow her whole had made her see things differently. She could have died . . . except she hadn't, because the ghosts had saved her life.

The ghosts had saved her life.

It was not a scenario she could have ever imagined happening. The Amelia she was before she started working at the library would have found it inconceivable. Back then, ghosts were a nuisance at best and the bane of her existence at worst.

But now . . .

Unfortunately, her *feelings* for the ghosts changed nothing—aside from making her feel worse about everything. She didn't have to enjoy the fact that she was lying to them—or at least not telling them that the cosmic maelstrom would not only sweep them away but also destroy the library—but it was too late to change tactics. If they found out the truth now, it would look like she had been manipulating them with movies and books so that she could find a way to force them to move on and have the library all to herself. And it would look that way because that was the truth. That was the plan she had devised.

But now was not the time to have a crisis about existential matters.

She had a job to do.

So, the following day, armed with some new techniques to try on the professor, Amelia battled the wind and rain to reach the library half an hour before it opened. Rosalinda had plans, so Amelia had offered to work the entire day. Normally the prospect would have been both thrilling and daunting, but given how likely it was that there would be no visitors, it was neither. Amelia ducked in the front door quietly, not wanting to alert Simon, and headed directly upstairs.

The professor smiled as she approached. "Amelia," he said kindly. "I wasn't expecting to see you this time of day. How lovely of you to stop by. How are you doing?"

She dropped into the chair that she now considered her own. "Fine. Thank you." For a moment, she felt the warmth of the ghost fire, but as soon as she noted the sensation, it disappeared. "I know I've been keeping to myself a bit, but . . ." She glanced at the papers fastened to the clipboard on her lap. "I thought we could try something new. If you're game."

"Always. What did you have in mind?"

"Word association," Amelia replied. "You're familiar with the concept?"

The professor pyramided his fingertips by his chest. "I am."

"Essentially, I'll give you a word, then you reply with the first thing that pops into your mind. What do you say?"

"I say that sounds delightful." There was something about his demeanor that made Amelia think he wasn't all that convinced it would produce any useful insights, but once again, they were running out of time, and Amelia was running out of ideas.

They spent the next half hour engaging in one-word back-and-forth conversations, with unfortunately very few surprises. Amelia would say *Rain.* He would say *Umbrella.* Amelia, *Beach.* The professor, *Sand.*

Eventually, they reached the final list of words. "Do you need a break before we begin this last set?" Amelia asked.

"Hit me," he replied with an excited gleam in his eye. After the first few rounds, he'd adopted a competitive verve, as though the lists were a game he might win. He *was* very quick with his answers.

Amelia picked up her pen to tick off the words, then inhaled deeply to indicate she was about to begin. "Green."

"Grass."

"Cigar."

"Churchill."

"Reliable."

"Amelia."

She dropped the clipboard to her lap and gave him a questioning look.

"From my limited observations from the second floor, you are always on time, if not early. You never forget to provide entertainment for Braden and Minnie, and you always come prepared for our sessions, so it seems very much to me like you are someone who can be counted on."

Those were all complimentary things for him to say, so it was funny that they made her feel inadequate.

"I . . . thank you." She cleared her throat. "Shall we continue?"

The professor waved out his hand with invitation. "Please."

"Haunt."

"Library."

"Beautiful."

"Butterfly."

Amelia glanced up from the list, and he winked. "Professor, are you sure you're not a lepidopterist?" She had already shared her theory with him.

"No, I don't think so, but I do have a deep love for butterflies. Their preciousness and fragility are a metaphor for life itself. It's all so fleeting, and yet so deeply beautiful."

Amelia glanced out the window toward the sea, rumpled and steely in the day's tempestuous wind. The professor wasn't wrong, and the sentiment was lovely, but it was also looking like, once again, her efforts to dig into his memories would fail. "Just a few more."

He nodded.

"Popcorn."

"Movie." Then with a smile, he added, "Braden."

"Paper."

"Pen."

"Sun."

"Moon."

"Car."

"Stop."

Amelia's pen froze, hovering above the page. *Bus stop* or *truck stop* might have made sense, but *car* and *stop*? She dropped her gaze to the next word but looked back up before she said it to take note of the professor's reaction. "Goodbye."

For the first time, the professor hesitated before answering. "No."

Amelia laid her pen down on the clipboard.

He frowned, then looked away, softly repeating, "No."

"Professor?" she prodded.

"I haven't remembered anything. It's just . . . a feeling." He shook his head, and a melancholic sadness shaped his features. "Perhaps that is enough for today."

Amelia gripped the sides of the clipboard. *Now?* They were so close. They both knew it. As sweet as this man was, she had to—

Man, not ghost.

What was happening to her? She closed her eyes.

Hold the line, Amelia. Whatever it takes.

Rational Amelia was right, of course, and yet she replied, "Certainly. Another time."

AMELIA WENT BACK downstairs and proceeded to go through the ridiculous pantomime of pretending she had just arrived. She didn't want to make up yet another lie for Simon about what she had been doing upstairs, because even if she said something banal like *Research* or *Tracking down a book*, that would lead to more questions. *What are you researching? Which book?* And the lies would just go on and on. Or worse yet, he might not ask anything at all.

It was easier just to sneak around, but it was all so *tiresome*.

And, as it turned out, unnecessary.

Seconds after she came back in, she received a text from Simon letting her know he was downstairs making some phone calls.

Thus, Amelia sat at the circulation desk all alone.

There wasn't much to do, so she picked up the book on island history that had come in for her by interlibrary loan. She had been hoping to find some reference to a girl in a bonnet with a tragic past, but she wasn't overly optimistic. In the recesses of her mind, she was mulling what had happened with the professor, but the interaction had left her feeling so tender that she needed space to give it proper consideration. The words *car* and *stop* kept coming to mind though.

With sustained effort, Amelia eventually lost herself in the history of the island, reading late into the day. The book began with the Mi'kmaq Nation—when the island was called Epekwitk—then moved to the earliest French settlers and then the British. It was a brutal existence back then, lives filled with violence and a constant threat of starvation. None of the information was new to her, but somehow it resonated differently. Just like the professor had said, life was precious and so very fragile. Even with all her many struggles, there were millions of people living and dead who had endured so much more than she ever had or likely ever would. And they would continue to do so. Maybe for the sight of a butterfly.

Eventually she slammed the book shut. As fascinating as it had been, it didn't have any of the answers she needed.

"Amelia?"

Simon!

"Hello . . . there," she stammered. "What are you doing up here?" That was wrong. She was doing social interaction wrong again. And why was she so nervous? Reading a book on island history wasn't something she needed to lie about. Apparently, guilt was now her default setting.

"I wanted to check in. It must have been a long day up here." He was uncomfortable. She could see it in the way he was adjusting his glasses and in his almost apologetic grimace for interrupting her. Once again, she had made him uncomfortable. "I haven't asked. How is your back doing?"

"It's much better," she replied. This was terrible. They were so awkward around each other now. "Thank you. I must have just temporarily pinched a nerve."

"Good. Good." He rocked on his heels, hands in his pockets. He looked so handsome in the sleepy nighttime light . . . and tired and worried.

Amelia thought back to the first time she had set foot in the library. She had been so swept away by the sight of him. The way she'd imagined he was some character out of a romance novel felt like a memory from a different lifetime. Now that she knew Simon, she realized he was so much more than that surface impression. He *was* smart and dedicated. She had been right about that. But he was also so very kind, the type of person who wanted to do what was best for everyone even when he didn't know what that was and even when he had the weight of the world on his shoulders.

More than anything, she wanted to carry some of that weight for him. She wanted to be someone he could share his worries and fears with. She wanted to make him feel understood. He deserved that. Even if nothing romantic ever transpired between them, she wanted to be his *friend.*

It really seemed like he could use one.

"You okay?" Simon asked gently. "You looked lost in space for a moment there."

Amelia flashed back to her foot being stuck in the portal. "Let's hope not," she whispered. "I mean, I'm fine. Just thinking."

"There's not much else to do around here." Suddenly, his eyes narrowed in on something underneath the desk.

Amelia gripped the armrests of her chair and froze. *What? What now?*

He leaned in to get a better look.

"Is it a mouse?" she whispered.

It seemed a little ridiculous to be afraid of a mouse, given she had survived Minnie's porcelain doll, but Amelia really didn't like mice, especially ones by her feet that might run up her legs.

"No, not a mouse," he said, coming around beside her. He bent to his knees before leaning to reach underneath. Dear God! What was happening? Amelia thought her close encounter with the possible intergalactic wormhole upstairs had been the most extreme experience she could have, physiologically speaking, but Simon's shoulder resting inches from her thigh, well, it was possible she might die. Happy. Die happy.

A moment later, Simon leaned back and got to his feet with a cardboard box in his hands.

Amelia frowned. It took her a second to place it, but . . . that wasn't just any box.

It was her box. The one with all the ghost-trapping equipment.

25

Forthwith all hell broke loose and roar'd around.
—John Milton, *Paradise Lost*

THE LIBRARY GROANED LOWLY AS SIMON RESTED the package on the corner of the circulation desk. "I've been waiting for something from a bookdealer friend of mine." He pried open the cardboard flaps. "It's—" His expression morphed into confusion. He stared at the contents, then flipped the cardboard down to read the label. "I'm so sorry." His gaze jumped to hers. "It has your name on it."

Think, Amelia. Think like you've never thought before! "Right! Yes," she said with a chuckle. "I ordered it online. I was thinking it might be fun to have one of those escape rooms in the library. For kids. So, I ordered a mystery box to get some ideas."

"A mystery box?" he asked.

"I'm sure you've heard of them. You look at the evidence, then figure out the mystery?" She chuckled again, but it sounded a tiny bit hysterical. "I believe I was scammed though. It's all junk."

Simon gifted her with his beautiful side-dimple smile. Oh, how she had missed seeing it on his face. "That is such a great idea. The library certainly has the mysterious atmosphere for it."

Seeing him so pleased was enough to ignite a flicker of joy in Amelia's heart, but . . .

Lies. Lies. Lies.

He looked back into the box. "Let's see what we've got here."

Amelia almost reached out to stop him but then remembered it was fine. It really *was* all junk.

"Is this a transistor radio?" he asked, looking completely, adorably bemused. "It looks like it's from the fifties."

The radio had been her most expensive purchase, but she doubted it was an authentic antique. And, again, it also wasn't supposed to be a radio, or at least not *just* a radio. It was meant to do something along the lines of breaking up ectoplasmic molecules. Not to the point of obliteration or anything like that, it was just supposed to make it impossible for ghosts to exist comfortably in the living realm. Now that it wasn't two in the morning, she couldn't help but think it all sounded like something out of *Ghostbusters.* Braden had her watch that one a few nights ago. She should really look into the company's return policy.

Simon ran the pad of his thumb over the volume dial and clicked it on. It didn't make a peep.

"It probably doesn't have a battery," Amelia said with a shrug.

He held it up to his ear. "It almost feels like it's vibrating."

"Really?"

"Let me just . . ." Simon adjusted the dial, changing the frequency and—

Suddenly a loud zap came from the break room, quickly followed by a shout.

"WHAT . . . IS . . . HAPPENING?!"

Amelia jolted in her chair, sending the wheels spinning and forcing her to grip the desk for balance.

Simon reached for her. "What? What happened?"

"Sorry." Amelia forced a smile—even though Braden was still yelling. "I lost my balance there for a second. These wheely chairs are tricky." Wheely chairs?

Simon returned her smile. "Happens to me all the time." He then turned his attention back to the radio, and Amelia slid her gaze over to the break room.

Oh dear.

Yes, the shouting had definitely come from Braden. He was making his way out of the room best he could. Maybe not all her purchases had been junk, after all. It did look a bit like his ectoplasmic molecules were breaking up—kind of like an old TV screen that couldn't quite catch a signal.

"Make it stop!" he shouted in a garbled voice.

Amelia cringed. "Does it hurt?"

Simon looked at her.

She tore her attention from Braden. "I mean, can you hear anything?"

"No, I . . ." Once again, Simon held the small box up to his ear while Braden shouted, "Of course it hurts!" Amelia almost reached for the radio, but then he added, "Actually, it doesn't, but it's weird! Tell him to stop!"

Well, she couldn't exactly do that, but . . .

Amelia held out her hand. "Let me try. My hearing's quite good." Simon passed her the radio. She held it up to her ear, surreptitiously spinning the dial. Unfortunately, she turned it up instead of down.

"S-t-o-p!" Braden yelled in a very strange, staticky voice.

She rolled the dial the other way until it clicked off. Solid-ish once again, Braden dropped to the floor and then right down through to the basement. Oh, he was going to be mad. She could tell by the filthy look he gave her on the way out.

"Let's see what else we've got in here," Simon said, rummaging around.

Oh no . . .

As he investigated the contents of the box, Amelia caught Minnie creeping closer to the circulation area, moving shadow to shadow, curiosity beaming in her glowing blue eyes. Amelia could understand the curiosity, but what was she thinking?! Had this ghost no sense of self-preservation? Amelia planted her chin on her palm, smiling her interest at Simon while shooing Minnie away with her other hand.

Simon picked up one of the flasks with a corked top.

At least that didn't look too dangerous.

He pinched the cork with his thumb and forefinger and pulled it out with a little *pop*!

Suddenly a cold whoosh rushed through the library—one that Simon didn't seem to notice, but Minnie certainly did, given she was suddenly caught in some sort of miniature tornado that was lengthening her out into a mere ribbon of a girl. Once she was fully stretched, the top part of her shot up into the air, only to dive right back down into the flask. It was a spirit box! No, bottle! A spirit bottle!

For the most surreal of seconds, Amelia found this all to be quite fascinating. She hadn't really believed there was a whole world out there with ghost contraptions! And that had to mean there were other ghostseers too. Maybe a lot of them. Ghostseers she could—

Focus, Amelia!

Right, this was terrible.

Within moments, Minnie was squashed into the small bottle, her alarmed blue, blue eyes pressed up against the glass.

Simon pressed the cork back into the mouth of the flask and set it down. "Just a bottle, I guess."

Amelia met Minnie's panicked gaze and mouthed, *Hang on.*

"It looks like there's one last item." Simon reached into the box and pulled out the vintage table fan. "This is nice." He turned it in his hands to view it from all angles. "We have to plug it in."

Amelia nodded, but when he turned away, she swiped the flask from the counter and pulled off the cork. Minnie shot out materializing on the other side of the desk. It was then Amelia received her second filthy look of the evening . . . before Minnie exploded into her cloud of spiders.

Amelia turned back to Simon as he bent over to plug the fan into an outlet close to the floor. He straightened up again, reached for the switch, and said, "Fingers crossed."

"Fingers crossed," Amelia replied weakly.

He flipped the switch. A soft whirring sound filled the air.

"It works!"

Amelia smiled at him, then glanced nervously around the room. Everything appeared to be fine. It was a very weak current.

Then she heard it.

Or him! It was the professor. He was making various *Whoa* sounds like he was balancing on a tightrope. Amelia glanced up to the second floor. The good news was that he wasn't falling down. The bad news was that he was floating up. All the way up until he reached the top frame of the tallest window, which he splatted against, a little like a bug on a windshield.

"Amelia," Simon said, stealing her attention back, "if you're not planning to use any of this stuff—"

"Not me," she spluttered. "I have no use for it."

"Would you mind if I took this fan? I'd pay you for it, of course." He clicked it off, and Amelia caught the professor floating back down to the second floor. "It would look great in my . . ."

Amelia couldn't focus on the rest of what Simon was saying because Braden was back, and yes, he definitely was mad. "No! He cannot have the fan! That librarian is a gangster!"

Amelia dragged her gaze back to Simon. "Believe it or not," he continued, "it can get pretty hot in the basement in the summer."

"Of course you can have it," she said.

"What?! No!" Braden shouted. Minnie even chimed in with her signature *Secrets,* but somehow this time it sounded more like a four-letter word.

"But do me a favor?" Amelia added.

Simon raised his brow.

"Maybe get the wiring checked before you use it again. Who knows how old it is? We wouldn't want the library to burn down."

Simon blinked at it. "Good idea."

"No, not good idea!" Braden shouted.

"You should go find a spot for it right now." Amelia gave Simon a big, eager smile. "See how it looks in your place."

Familiar disappointment touched his features. "Right. I'll do that." He walked a few steps, then turned. "Thanks, Amelia."

She smiled. "Of course."

Once he was gone, her smile withered. Even though she was staring at the top of the circulation desk, Amelia could feel the ghosts glaring at her. All three of them.

Eventually, Braden said, "Seriously?" His voice wasn't quite a yell, but it wasn't quite normal speaking volume either.

"Let me explain," Amelia began.

"Sure. Explain. I'd love to know why you have a box of ghost-torturing devices." Now he was shouting.

"They're not . . ." Amelia closed her eyes and took a breath. "I bought these a long time ago. When I first started working here. I didn't know what they'd do."

"Oh, that explains everything," he said, nodding far too vigorously. "But if you didn't know what they could do, why did you buy them? Are you decorating your apartment, like Simon?"

He had her there. She was lying again. Without even realizing it.

"Braden," the professor called out, "give her a chance."

Amelia glanced up at him, nodding her thanks. "Okay, yes. I knew what they were supposed to do, but once they arrived, I put them away." She could hear the pleading in her own voice. "I was never going to use them." That was mostly true. They didn't need to know that she had first assumed they were junk and a waste of time.

"Right," Braden said. "But when lover boy there started using them—"

"His name is Simon," Amelia snapped. "Not Lover Boy."

"But when *Lover Boy* there started using them," Braden said even louder, "you sure took your sweet time getting him to stop, and then you let him leave with one of them!" He flung a hand out in the direction of the door that led to the basement.

"What was I supposed to do?! I can't risk exposing who I am! If I told Simon the truth, he would fire me, and then—*then!*" Amelia said with a violent poke in the air. "I wouldn't be able to help you, would I?"

"Sure." Braden rolled his jaw angrily. "More like he'd stop being into you."

Amelia blinked, stunned. "That's not . . . There is nothing between us."

"And what about the library?"

The library . . . ? *Uh-oh.*

"I've been thinking. It's pretty obvious that whatever is happening around here isn't just affecting us. And we all know how much you care about the library, but you're not talking about it. Seems a little weird, doesn't it?"

Minnie nodded in agreement. The professor just looked pained.

Apparently, unbeknownst to her, this argument had been simmering for a while now. Well, there was no point in trying to cover it up anymore. "Fine. It doesn't change your situation in any way, but yes, the cosmic maelstrom is also affecting the library." Amelia inhaled deeply, trying to steady herself. "If it reaches its tipping point, the building will also be destroyed."

Braden put his hands on his hips and nodded down at the floor. "So, all the games you've been playing with the professor, all the reading you've been doing with Minnie, all the movies we've watched together . . . that was never about us. You were just trying to save the library."

"No. I mean"—Amelia squeezed her eyes shut—"perhaps in the beginning, but—"

"Stop. I don't want to hear any more of your lies." He crossed his arms over his chest. "It's all you do. Even when you're not actually lying, you still kind of are, always hiding behind your big, fancy words and buttoned-up sweaters."

Amelia almost corrected him on that last one, until she realized she might in fact be proving his point.

"Nobody ever gets to see the real you. Except, I finally thought we were getting somewhere." He pointed at her. "And I saw you laughing at *American Pie* behind your book. Don't even try to deny it."

She stayed silent. There might have been one or two parts that had shocked her into—

"But then you go and do this." He shook his head. "After everything, we still aren't real to you, are we?"

"No, that's not true. I—"

"Like seriously, what's your damage?"

What's your damage? Where to begin? Amelia huffed a small laugh.

"I'm sorry. Is that funny?"

No, not at all.

This was exactly the type of thing she'd wanted to avoid. They had a crisis on their hands, and instead of focusing on that, they were arguing . . . about all the mistakes she'd made.

"Look, we all get that you're the ghostseer, and you're the one who is supposed to be helping us, but the truth is you need us too. Can't you see that?" Braden waited a moment for her to answer. When she didn't, he threw his hands in the air and floated back into the gloom of the library. "Forget it. There's no point. With you, it's always two steps forward and eight billion steps back."

As he disappeared into the shadows, Amelia looked to Minnie, but she had crossed her arms over her chest and was already following Braden. She glanced up at the professor next, but after giving her a sad smile, he turned his back too.

And just like that, she was all alone.

26

There is a way to be good again.
—Khaled Hosseini, *The Kite Runner*

AMELIA HEADED TO WORK THE FOLLOWING DAY with every expectation that things would be back to normal.

The night before, she'd tried to keep their usual routine. Once the library had closed, she had gone up to the storage room to put in a movie for Braden, but the third floor was as quiet as a ghost mouse. When she headed back downstairs, she stopped off at the second floor to check in with the professor, but he was dozing again, and it didn't feel right to wake him given what he'd been through. After that, she went all the way back downstairs, sat in her chair by the reading rug, and picked up right where she and Minnie had left off in their next read, *Sense and Sensibility*. But if Minnie was around anywhere listening, she gave no sign of it, and Amelia discovered the experience was a lot less fun without her.

So, she had gone home.

Thankfully, though, after a night filled with uncomfortable dreams, the morning sun lifted her spirits. Yes, the ghosts were mad. And yes, they had some reason to be, but they also needed her to help solve their collective predicament. So, justified in their anger or not, everyone needed to push past this little hiccup. Surely, they'd already come to the same conclusion.

Amelia's optimism held until she stepped inside the library . . . where things did not feel at all *normal*. The building's atmosphere as of late often felt *empty*, but this emptiness came across as purposeful, leading Amelia to conclude almost instantly that her status as persona non grata was being extended another day. The irony was not lost upon her.

Quiet as it was, though, as Amelia undid the buttons of her coat, the familiar prickly sensation of being watched crept up the back of her neck. She dropped her coat off her shoulders, then snapped her gaze over to the towering plant, fully expecting to spot Minnie there . . . but she wasn't. Either she never had been or she was quicker than Amelia had given her credit for.

Smoothing back her hair, she took another surreptitious glance around. Not a ghost to be seen, but the prickling feeling wasn't going away. *Ugh*. She was in no mood for games. She knew she had done wrong, but would it kill the ghosts to be a little more understanding? No, it would not. Literally.

Amelia sighed and picked up her bag. "Braden?" she called out quietly. "Could we talk about this?" She waited, but when no answer came in return, she murmured, "Minnie?"

Nothing.

It was fine. Amelia was used to being alone.

And she had work to do.

She walked through the foyer to discover the circulation desk empty once again. Tucking her bag by the chair, Amelia spotted a book with a sticky note bearing her name affixed to its cover. It was another interlibrary loan on local history, but she wasn't interested in taking any more shots in the dark today. No, she was going to try a new angle. Ever since her tangle with the patch—when the ghosts had saved her life—Amelia had been turning something over in her mind. She was sure she had smelled smoke during the rescue. What if all the dirt on Minnie wasn't dirt at all? What if it was soot? She had to search the archives for fires. Maybe she had been looking for the wrong thing all along.

Once settled in the chair behind the circulation desk, she rolled over to the computer, taking one last glance around the library. Empty. Even the die-hard readers were staying away now. She couldn't blame them. For so long, Amelia felt nothing but love from this place, but it was impossible to ignore the cold, empty dread that now filled its walls. Somehow everything felt dimmer too. Gray.

Focus, Amelia.

Yes, she needed to focus. There was still time. If she could find out what had happened to Minnie, then maybe everything would be—

"Simon, no. Don't do it."

Amelia's fingers froze above the keyboard. That had been Rosalinda's voice. She rolled back her chair and turned in the direction of the workroom.

"It's only for a few days. A few weeks at most."

"No, I'm not upset about the library having to close. It's all the digging into the library. I have a bad feeling about it." That was definitely Rosalinda. Amelia was suddenly on her feet. She had been telling herself that her previous eavesdropping had been a one-time thing, but the tone in Rosalinda's voice was so unlike her. She sounded almost desperate.

"The truth is I have a bad feeling too." There was exasperation in Simon's tone, which was equally uncharacteristic. "But doing nothing is not the answer. And they're digging *around* the library, not into it. It's the only way to get a look at the foundation."

Amelia tiptoed toward them.

"But does it have to be tomorrow?" Rosalinda pleaded. "There's still time."

Tomorrow?

Simon sighed with frustration. "Time for what?"

"I'm not sure exactly," Rosalinda said, "but I know Amelia is working on something."

"Amelia?" He sounded completely bewildered now. "What could Amelia possibly be working on that would affect the library?"

"I'm not entirely sure about that either and it's not my place to speculate, but maybe you could talk to her about it?"

A long pause followed. "Amelia doesn't talk to me. Not really."

That was it. Even if everything worked out with the ghosts and the library, Simon was never going to trust her or even want to get to know her better. Not after all the damage she had done.

"Oh, Simon," Rosalinda said, sounding heartbroken for him. "I know how much you care for her. And if ever there was a better suited—"

"Please, don't. It's fine. I'm fine. Amelia has made her feelings clear, and the last thing I want to do is make her uncomfortable. She's good for the library. I don't think there's anyone as passionate about books." They both chuckled, and Amelia couldn't help but smile.

"And she really cares about people." His voice had turned thoughtful. "Did you know she dropped off the new Stephen King book to Margaret Withers last week? To her house, I mean."

Amelia shook her head. That really wasn't a bother. Margaret's arthritis had been acting up, but she was a big fan, and the book had just come in. Besides, it was on the way to the fish shop.

"I did," Rosalinda answered. "It was pouring that night."

It was pouring every night.

"She also helped Sam Frontenac fill out his health-card renewal form on the library computers not too long ago," Rosalinda added. "Spent over half an hour with him. Sam is so easily frustrated by anything electronic, but she hung in there until it was done."

Amelia scoffed lightly. Sam Frontenac had every reason to be frustrated. Those forms were infuriating.

"Oh, and you should have seen her helping Chelsea Rivas the other day." Rosalinda giggled. "Chelsea was trying to track down books seven and eight in the Ice Planet series, but she was so embarrassed about it that she could barely get the words out. Once she realized Amelia was a fan, though, she walked out proudly with a whole stack."

"Amelia likes the Savage Lover series?"

"She does."

And her secret was out. No matter. Amelia straightened and jutted her chin. It was just like she told Chelsea: If it was wrong to read about blue-horned love, then she didn't want to be right.

"Well, you knew. That very first night she interviewed, you knew," Simon said. "Remember how you told me to look at Amelia, *really* look at her?"

"I dared you to tell me that she didn't belong."

Amelia wrapped an arm around her waist.

She . . . *belonged*? That's what Rosalinda had said?

"I couldn't do it. You were right. And life is certainly more interesting with her around. I would never want to be the one responsible for separating her from the library," he continued. "If there still is a library in the future."

"But Simon—"

"I promise you. I'm fine." He laughed. "If anything, these past few weeks have shown me that maybe there is more to life than books and this place. Who knows? I might even sign up for one of those dating apps you always used to pester me about."

WHAT?!

Amelia jolted and somehow knocked a book from the counter. She slapped her hands over her mouth.

Simon let out a noisy exhale. "Let's not talk about this anymore." Amelia's shoulders dropped. They must not have heard. "I don't want to upset you. You shouldn't even be here. I told you that you didn't have to come in today. You need to rest more."

"I'm fine," Rosalinda replied. "Don't you worry about me." Silence followed, and Amelia was sure Rosalinda had given Simon a hug. "And I'll go home, but I want you to think about what I said. Give it a little more time before you call in all those workers with their machines. Amelia is a remarkable young woman. She might surprise you."

Simon's voice dropped. "She already does. All the time." Amelia heard footsteps coming in her direction. She hurried back deep into the circulation area and hid behind a cabinet.

"Come on now. Let's go."

"Don't be silly," Rosalinda said. "You don't have to drive me."

"I want to."

"But the library . . ." she protested.

Simon huffed. "Amelia has a key, and I really don't think anyone will be in today. And, hey, we can stop for butter tarts," he suggested, brightening his tone, "the ones from the Seaside Café?"

"Oh, all right, then," Rosalinda muttered before tagging on, "You're a good boy, Simon."

ROSALINDA AND SIMON walked right by the circulation desk without seeing Amelia. When she heard the front door lock, she came out from her hiding spot and sat back in her chair.

As wonderful as it had been to hear all the lovely things Simon and Rosalinda had to say about her, she couldn't enjoy it.

Everything was such a mess.

The ghosts weren't talking to her, the library was falling apart, and Simon thought she didn't care about him. She couldn't even comfort herself with the thought that he cared about her, because how could he when he didn't really know who she was?

For what had to be the millionth time in her life, Amelia wished she had someone to talk to. But there was no one.

Except . . .

She glanced up to the second floor.

Yes, the professor had turned his back on her last night along with the others, but he didn't seem like the type to hold a grudge, and he was always so sweet and empathetic and kind. Surely, he wouldn't turn her away.

Not if she apologized.

Amelia had been avoiding that particular option. The word alone made her feel uncomfortable, *vulnerable*, but she had to make things right with the ghosts, and, if that's what it took, well, she'd do it, or at least she'd try.

Amelia's heart pounded as she climbed the stairs, then treaded over to the nook by the fireplace. The professor wasn't asleep. He was clearly reading a ghost newspaper. But normally he would have looked over by now, smiled, and given her a warm greeting. So, instead of taking her chair, Amelia stood a few feet back and clasped her hands by her waist. "Hello, professor."

He folded his newspaper and placed it on his lap, where it promptly disappeared. "Amelia."

"Can I join you?"

He waved his hand out. Neither spoke as she took her seat, and they sat in awkward silence for a good minute or so. Amelia had been hoping he might offer her some ghost cocoa, but that didn't happen. Not that she deserved cocoa. She stared down at her fingers twisting in her lap. "I wanted to apologize for yesterday."

When he didn't answer, she peeked up at him. His expression was still neutral. It was a terribly unpleasant look on him.

"I'm sorry."

He still didn't answer.

Amelia's experience with apologizing was limited, but judging by his lack of reaction, she was guessing that she needed to elaborate.

"I haven't handled much of anything very well since I got here." Amelia was tempted to launch into a series of explanations that stemmed from her childhood, but now didn't seem like the time. "I'd like to do better though. For all our sakes. Also"—she inhaled deeply—"Braden was right about pretty much everything, but especially the part about my needing you, all of you. Since coming to the library, you three have opened my mind up in ways I never thought possible. You're also the only people who know who I really am. I recognize that it was wrong of me to lie. You deserved better, and for that I am truly sorry."

The professor held his unreadable gaze another agonizing moment, but then his expression cracked into a huge smile. "Very good, Amelia."

The transition was startling. "What?"

"That apology was very well done."

"Really?"

"Yes, it was honest, and you didn't get wrapped up in excuses or needless explanations. You accepted responsibility and expressed a desire to change!" His eyes widened with enthusiastic appreciation. "Bravo."

Amelia looked down at her fingers, warmed by the compliment. *Bravo.* She certainly hadn't been expecting that. A moment later she peeked back up. "Thank you, but . . ."

The professor raised his brow.

"Do you think Braden and Minnie will feel the same?"

His animated expression crumpled.

"Right." Amelia sank back into the chair. "That's actually why I came up here. Aside from apologizing, that is. I wanted your advice about how to move forward."

"Well, I may have one or two thoughts," he said, pyramiding his fingertips by his chest. "I'd be happy to share them, for what they're worth."

"Please."

"Well, to begin, I wouldn't worry too much about Braden and Minnie. While they may be a touch more difficult to win over, I have every reason to believe they'll get there in the end." He gazed at her knowingly, then added, "But can I make an observation?"

"Of course."

"This all has been very hard for you, hasn't it?"

She blinked. "What all?"

"Getting to know us. Letting us in."

Amelia hadn't been expecting him to say that, but he certainly wasn't wrong.

“From what you have told me, and, frankly, from what I have witnessed, being a ghostseer has not made your life easy. The gymnastics you do existing in a world with both the living and the dead must be exhausting.”

Amelia’s breath caught. Her life *was* exhausting. So very exhausting.

“And please correct me if I’m wrong,” he went on, “but I would also imagine that growing up in care hasn’t made it easy for you to get close to people, and yet I still see you trying, despite how terribly unsafe it must feel.” He held her in his gaze a moment. “Forgive me if this sounds too patronizing, but I’m very proud of you, Amelia.”

I’m proud of you?

The professor’s earlier *bravo* had been surprising, but this? Amelia couldn’t have been more shocked if he had suddenly come back to life.

He smiled gently. “Judging by the look on your face, I’ve overstepped.”

Amelia resisted the urge to touch her cheek. How did she look? Horrified most likely.

“It’s just you have taken so many personal risks for us. That’s no small thing. It should be acknowledged.”

Amelia swallowed against the sudden tightness gripping her throat. “Well, thank you, but really, I haven’t taken that many risks. At best, I consider myself a bare minimum ghostseer.”

He chuckled. “I would say a reluctant one, but don’t you see how that makes all that you’ve done even more meaningful? I know how important this place is to you, but you were willing to risk your position here to get to know us, to see how you could help.”

Amelia made a considering noise in lieu of an answer.

"We were all a little hard on you last night, and for that I am sorry."

Now he was apologizing to *her*? Amelia twisted her fingers more tightly together. No. This was . . . no. This would not do. "It's fine. Really." She could see the professor was about to argue, so she added, "But speaking of the library . . ." She told him all that she had overheard about the building having to close. When she was through, she added, "I'll be back as soon as I can though. I think I'm close to finding something out about Minnie. Maybe it will help not only her, but you, Braden, and the library."

"Just us and the library?"

Amelia looked up at him, confused, but then she shook her head and turned away. *Unbelievable.* Apparently asking the professor for his advice had opened a floodgate she hadn't realized existed. One or two thoughts indeed. "You're talking about Simon."

"By all accounts, he seems like a good person."

Amelia arched an eyebrow. "By all accounts?"

"Given my limited mobility and ever fleeting memory, Braden and Minnie have drawn firmer conclusions, but if their reports are to be believed, it sounds like he cares for you too."

Amelia bounced her knee. This was ridiculous. She had come to apologize, and now she was on the verge of tears. Actually, those two things probably did go together quite frequently. "Maybe in a different life, under different circumstances, there could be something between us. But . . ." She closed her eyes. "All I have ever done is lie to him."

"You believe he deserves to know the truth."

Amelia's eyes snapped back open. "He loves this library. He has devoted his life to it, and he is about to spend who knows how much money trying to save it, and for what? I don't think an engineering company can stop a cosmic maelstrom."

The professor regarded her carefully as the ghost fire crackled beside them.

"But that wasn't the truth you were talking about." Amelia stared out the window to the sea. "You're asking if I think he deserves to know the truth about me." The professor remained silent, waiting for her to go on. "Yes. Simon deserves to know that . . . I am a ghost-seer." Amelia stiffened. That was the first time she had said those four words aloud. She half expected the declaration to bring the library crumbling down around her, but time merely ticked on.

"Do you not trust him enough to share the truth?"

"What?" Amelia straightened in her chair, which was difficult; it was very plush. "No, it's not that. Simon is a good person, and incredibly kind. Even in the very likely scenario that he didn't believe me, he would never be cruel."

"Perhaps, then, you're afraid if he knew the truth, he wouldn't be able to look at you the same way?"

Amelia's chin dropped. How did he know that? How did he know about *the look*? The dreaded look people had always given her when the truth was close to coming out. "Were you a mind reader in your living life?"

The professor put a hand on his belly and laughed outright. When he was through, he smiled but then gave her a contemplative look. "Could I offer another observation? One that I've picked up over the years?"

Amelia arched an eyebrow. "Only if you can tell me where, when, and under what circumstances you picked it up."

His eyes twinkled. "I cannot."

That was unfortunate. It might have solved everything. She flopped her hands over the armrests of her chair. "Go ahead."

"All of us need connection—even introverted nighttime librarians—but in order for that to happen, we have to be vulnerable. We need to trust."

Amelia frowned. "Who says I'm introverted?"

The professor's eyebrows popped up in surprise, and they both laughed.

"Trusting people is not easy for me," Amelia continued once they were through. "I think it's in my DNA. Centuries of history have taught us ghostseers to keep our guards up."

The professor tapped his knee. "I'm not talking about trusting other people though. I'm talking about trusting yourself. If you were to tell Simon the truth, and he did look at you differently, what would happen?"

Amelia imagined seeing *the look* on Simon's face, seeing that unique mix of confusion, fear, and disgust in his eyes—the look she had seen throughout her life when she hadn't been able to guard her reactions quickly enough or come up with a good enough lie to convince others her reality was the same as theirs. The look that said she was not normal. To see that on Simon's face would be . . .

"I couldn't handle that."

"Really?" the professor prodded. "Would you go mad? Drop dead? Explode into a cloud of spiders?"

The corner of Amelia's mouth twitched, which was funny because she was once again blinking away tears. "No, but my heart might break."

"Ah," he said, gazing over at the fire. "I can't help but think when it comes to forming real, deep connections, when it comes to *love*, that the risk is worth the reward." He looked back at her. "You?"

27

We read to know we're not alone.
—William Nicholson, *Shadowlands*

THROUGHOUT THE REST OF THE EVENING, THE LIbrary creaked and groaned like a ship being tossed over a stormy sea. It was painful to hear. It also matched how Amelia was feeling. She was going to have to be very careful about asking the professor for advice going forward. She had gotten much more than she had bargained for.

I'm very proud of you, Amelia.

What a thing to say.

When Simon returned, he talked to her briefly about closing the following day, and Amelia pretended to be surprised, but it was hard to say if he bought it. Her heart wasn't into putting on a performance, and Simon didn't linger.

At closing, she went up to the third floor to see if Braden wanted her to put on a movie before she left, but once again, he was nowhere to be found. Amelia then made her way slowly back down to the first floor, committing to memory the feel of her hand running along the banister's smooth edges.

How? How was she supposed to go?

It will only be for a few days.

Not even Rational Amelia sounded like she believed it.

Instead of heading over to the circulation desk, Amelia stood on the nautical compass in the center of the marble floor just like she had the night of her interview. It was time she and the library worked a few things out.

"Hello," she said with a small wave. "It's Amelia. You probably already knew that." Her face suddenly burned. That was a first. She was blushing for a library. "I was hoping we could have a talk. A real talk. I'm not going to pretend anymore that you're not there. You are very much alive, and, truthfully, I have always known that. There are stranger things in heaven and earth—" Now was not the time to hide behind the words of others. "I need your help."

A strange hush fell over the room.

"I don't want to seem ungrateful," Amelia said, glancing about the great cavernous space. "You have helped me so much already, but"—she wagged a finger in the air—"you also haven't always made it easy. Is that for your own amusement? Are you trying to teach me some kind of lesson? Because if that's the case, I'm not sure I've figured out what that is, and we're running out of time. All of us."

Amelia turned to face another wall. "I love working here, being here. This place . . . no, *you* are incredibly special. You have an amazing gift for making people feel welcome. You comfort them and offer escape when their lives are difficult. You show them how impossible circumstances can be made better, and you remind us of what an incredible gift it is to be alive in this marvelous world. I'm not sure if there is any other place that can do all that. And I don't want it to end." She shook her head. "But I also don't know what to do. I've made a lot of mistakes and wasted a lot of time. I know that.

But I'm ready now. I'll do whatever it takes." It wasn't until she said the words that she realized how deeply she meant them. "I need help though. *The Ghostseer's Handbook.* I think it might have the answers we need to save you. To save us all, but I can't find it. And I have an inkling that you are the only one who can get it for me." Amelia paused. "So, what do you think?"

The hushed silence that had fallen over the library thickened, making it almost difficult to breathe.

"Would you like me to close my eyes again?" Amelia squeezed her lids shut and counted to ten, but when she opened them, nothing had changed. Her shoulders dropped. "Right." She walked over to the circulation area and reached underneath the desk to grab her messenger bag. "I'll give you some time to think about it." When Amelia came back around the desk to leave, a shadow caught her eye.

Minnie was sitting cross-legged on the children's carpet.

She wanted story time!

Amelia dropped her bag and hurried toward her, then threw her hands up in the air when she remembered she had forgotten the book. She rushed back over to the circulation desk, nearly flipping herself over the counter to grab *Sense and Sensibility* before trotting back to the story-time rug. She sat in her chair, carefully arranging her skirt before daring to glance up. Minnie looked the way she always did, with her blue eyes glowing in the darkness of her dirty bonnet. At one point, the sight would have struck terror in Amelia's heart, but now it warmed her all the way through. Minnie's hidden features did make it hard to tell if she was still mad though. Amelia opened the front cover of the book, then paused. It didn't really matter if Minnie was angry or not. She still owed her an apology—and maybe then the flashbacks of her ghostly form being squashed into that flask would go away.

The problem was every time Amelia tried to talk to Minnie about anything other than books during story time, she would spontaneously combust into creepy crawlies . . . but that was no excuse not to try.

"Minnie?"

The ghost's eyes widened with alarm.

"Please don't go." Amelia jutted her hand up. "I promise we'll get to the book, but I want you to know that I'm sorry."

For a moment, it seemed like Minnie had retreated into her signature trance state, but then in a move that nearly knocked Amelia off her chair, she shook her head side to side.

"No?"

This time Minnie nodded.

"I'm confused," Amelia said. "You don't accept my apology? That's okay. I—"

The ghost shook her head more vigorously.

Amelia struggled to decipher Minnie's expression hidden in the shadows. "You don't want my apology?"

When Minnie opened her mouth, Amelia fully expected to hear *Secrets* come out, but instead, the ghost whispered in a creaking voice, "No sorry for . . ." She placed a hand on her chest. "Minnie."

"What? Yes, sorry for Minnie. I didn't handle what happened last night particularly well, and you do deserve an apology."

"NO!"

Minnie's unearthly shout echoed through the building, and Amelia froze, hand at her throat.

"Bad," the ghost whispered, patting her chest again.

More than anything, Amelia wanted to argue, but she didn't know what it was Minnie had been carrying this past century, and she didn't want to minimize her pain or the guilt she clearly believed was justified. So, instead of quarreling, she asked, "Minnie, would you like to move on? If you could?"

Long seconds passed before she nodded almost imperceptibly.

"To do that, I think you'd have to let go," Amelia murmured. "You'd have to forgive yourself."

The ghost turned her gaze to the floor, her bonnet shielding her face. She then shook her head in a small motion.

Amelia sighed. "Minnie, I don't know what you think of me as a person, but believe me when I say this is about more than just the library for me. I don't know what happened in your life, but I believe whatever it is holding you back, you've likely paid the price for it many times over by now. I want to help you." She blinked, surprised by the emotion the words brought up. "I just wish I knew how."

Minnie looked up and pointed at the book.

"You want me to read?" Amelia asked, holding it up. "That will help?"

The ghost nodded.

It wasn't much, but that was something Amelia could do.

28

And this mess is so big
And so deep and so tall,
We can not pick it up.
There is no way at all!
—Dr. Seuss, *The Cat in the Hat*

THE SOUND OF RAIN TAPPING AGAINST WINDOWS reached Amelia through her dreams. She curled her blanket in closer to her chin, refusing to open her eyes. She was so tired . . . but the rain sounded heavy. Did she empty the bucket before she went to bed? Her landlord wouldn't be happy if it overflowed and water dripped down to the fish shop below, but then again, if that happened, her landlord only had himself to . . .

"Amelia?"

Simon?

Was she dreaming about Simon? That was nice. She liked Simon dreams, except . . . why didn't her apartment smell like fish? And why was she sitting up? Amelia rubbed her mouth and peeked at the book pinned to her chest. *Sense and Sensibility*. Where was she? What time was it? She blinked her eyes all the way open. *Uh-oh.* She hadn't been dreaming about Simon. He was standing right in front of her, looking as wondrous as ever, but also not happy.

Amelia glanced around and everything came back. She had read far more to Minnie than she had intended to. Probably because she was putting off what she knew had to come next—leaving the library—and then she must have fallen asleep.

She struggled to pull off the blanket and sit up. The blanket . . . Braden must have fetched it for her. At least he didn't completely hate her. *One problem at a time, Amelia.* "Simon, good morning." Was it morning? She looked over to the window. No, still dark. "I was just—"

He closed his eyes. "Please. Don't." His chest heaved, and he released a heavy sigh. "Whatever explanation it is you're thinking up . . . just don't."

Amelia studied his expression, trying to figure out where this was headed. Pinned lips. Frown. Hurt in his eyes. Clearly, no place good.

"I would like to say a few things." He held up his hands. "First, if I ever made you feel uncomfortable, I am sincerely sorry. We work together and—"

"Uncomfortable?" Amelia frowned. "No, Simon, you have never made me feel uncomfortable." Nervous maybe. Weak in the knees. Alive in a way she never thought possible, but not uncomfortable.

"I never should have texted you late at night. Or asked what you were reading. If I overstepped—"

"Please stop." Amelia put the blanket on the chair and rose to her feet. "I realize we haven't known each other for very long, but I think of us as—"

"Friends?" His eyes searched hers. "Was that what you were going to say? I'd certainly like to be, but—" He cut himself off, scratching the side of his head roughly. "Look, I know something is going on with you. I'd have to be an idiot not to see that. And I also have the sense that you need help with whatever it is you're trying to do." He placed a hand on his chest. "I want to help you, but if you don't tell me what's going on, there's not much I can do."

"What do you mean?" She shrugged. "Nothing is going on. I'm worried about the library, of course, but I'm fine."

He nodded down at the floor. "Amelia, you've been sneaking up to the special collections floor every chance you get, ordering local history books like they're going out of style—which they're really not—you're always jumpy and nervous, like you've been caught doing some illicit library business, and it seems like you have the weight of the world on your shoulders, but you won't let anyone share in the load."

Amelia's chest tightened. She had thought the exact same thing about him. "Simon, I'm not . . ." She had no clue how she wanted to finish that sentence. "Nothing is going on."

"At first, I thought maybe you were researching your own genealogy, and that's why you didn't want to let anyone know what you were doing, but . . . it's two in the morning, and you're asleep at the reading rug with a book on your chest. A book I'm pretty sure you've already read." He looked nervous to say the next part. "And I heard you talking to someone earlier. It's not the first time."

Heat touched Amelia's cheeks. "I was just—"

"Don't say on the phone." He closed his eyes. "Because it's over on the desk."

Tell him, Amelia. It's time.

She knew that was true. It was well past time, and this was clearly the moment, but the way he was looking at her, with so much care and concern, it was nice to be looked at that way. This was the before time, the time before she said the words that would change everything. And as painful as this place was, she was afraid what came after the truth would hurt even more. "Really," she choked out. "Everything is fine. I just lost track of time."

Simon nodded, stuffed his hands into his pockets, and turned his back.

"Wait!"

His shoulders tensed.

Amelia curled her fingers into fists. "There is an explanation for this, for all of it, one I should have told you a long time ago, but—"

A deafening groan rumbled through the library, followed by a quick series of cracks. Simon closed the distance between them in a second and put his arm around her shoulders, as though ready to shield her if the roof caved in. "We have to go." His gaze jumped around the great room like he had never seen it before.

As they stumbled toward the foyer, the bookshelves shook, sending texts crashing to the floor. This was bad. So very bad. They should be running. There was no time to lose. But Amelia's feet weren't working the way they were supposed to because . . .

She couldn't leave!

Terrifying thoughts rushed forward. Was this the tipping point? It couldn't be. Not yet! Amelia looked back to the mezzanine. The professor, Minnie, and Braden were all hovering behind the railing.

Amelia resisted Simon's pull. "Wait! I can't—"

Suddenly Simon was in front of her, gripping her shoulders and ducking to meet her eyes. "Amelia, I know you love the library. Believe me, I know what it is to love this place." He shook his head helplessly. "But we have to go. Now."

"He's right!" Braden shouted, Minnie nodding beside him. "You did your best. It's okay. Go!"

A loud screech of twisting metal came from the second floor, followed by new eerie light. Amelia didn't have to guess what had happened. The patch had swallowed the metal cabinet. It would swallow everything soon.

Simon looked up, but only for a second. As they passed the circulation desk, he dropped his grip on her shoulder to grab her bag buried beneath the pile of books, then half guided, half carried her, pinned against his side, toward the foyer.

This couldn't be happening. Not like this! Amelia craned her neck to look back at the ghosts.

They hadn't moved, only now the professor had his hand raised in goodbye.

29

"It is nothing to die; it is dreadful not to live."

—Victor Hugo, *Les Misérables*

SIMON TALKED TO AMELIA THE ENTIRE DRIVE BACK to the fish shop. His voice was calm and reassuring, but Amelia could barely nod in return let alone decipher what he was saying. He didn't seem to register her lack of response though. She wasn't the only one who was in shock.

When they arrived, he walked her toward the door that led to her apartment. Cold raindrops fell steadily, but neither hurried their pace. "I don't want to go," he said, "but I have to get back to meet the police." Thankfully, by the time they'd gotten to his car, the library had stopped shaking, but Simon had still called. Things were only going to get worse. "I knew this day might come, but I still can't believe it's actually happening."

Despite her stupor, Amelia could feel the pain radiating off him. She almost reached for his hand, but . . . didn't.

"Are you going to be all right?" he asked. "Is there someone I can call?"

Amelia shook her head. "I'm fine." That had to be the biggest of all the lies she had told him.

"Are you sure?"

She nodded.

"Okay, I'd better . . ." He looked back at his car.

"Go," she said, forcing a smile. "And thank you."

She watched him drive away, then stood staring in the direction of the library. The ghosts would be okay. They had to be. The building hadn't come down. Maybe one of them could—

Amelia squeezed her eyes shut and shook her head. Every instinct she possessed was telling her to go back, but to do what? Be there when the building came tumbling down? In some ways she imagined that would feel better than being here alone, not knowing what was happening.

Standing in the rain wasn't helping anyone, though, so Amelia dragged herself up the stairs to her apartment. Her lassitude felt so very wrong. She should be running, screaming, doing *something*, not giving up. After pushing her way inside, Amelia closed the door quietly behind her and leaned on it for support. Was that what she was doing? Giving up?

The room felt so small.

And empty.

She dropped her bag from her shoulder, spilling its contents across the floor, then stepped over the mess, not bothering to pick up any of it. None of that mattered. Not in the face of what had happened. She had failed them. And Braden was wrong. She hadn't done her best. She had fought helping them every step of the way. She could make all the excuses in the world, but she knew the truth. She was a selfish coward, and now . . .

She didn't want to think about what could be happening now.

A drop of rainwater fell into the bucket in the middle of the floor as Amelia sat on the edge of the bed.

Just a drop in the bucket.

All life's moments were like that, weren't they? Except so many of her drops were exactly the same. She had spent so much of her life not living. What had been the point? She had truly believed that all she needed to be happy was to be a librarian, but now . . .

Amelia looked around the room. How was she supposed to do this? Sit here doing nothing? If someone or something could tell her which mountain to move, she'd do it. She just needed somewhere to start.

A tiny flashing glint of gold caught Amelia's eye from the floor. In the low light of the apartment, it was hard to be certain, but . . .

She dove off the bed toward her messenger bag, scattering all the miscellaneous junk on the way. Sitting on her knees, she lifted the clipboard she had used for all the professor's memory exercises, and underneath was . . .

The Ghostseer's Handbook.

Amelia clutched it to her chest. The library had granted her request after all. "Thank you," she whispered. "I do believe in you. I do. I do. I do."

She then flipped the cover open and read like she had never read before.

AN HOUR OR so later, as the first rays of dawn touched the sky, Amelia was back outside the building that felt more like a home to her than any other ever had. She'd maneuvered around the hazard tape that had been put up in the short time since she and Simon had left and jogged up the drive. The parking lot was deserted. Even Simon's car was gone. Of course it was. It wasn't safe for him to live, work, or sleep in the library anymore. Here Amelia had been thinking the library was her everything, but Simon had greater claim.

When she reached the cobblestone pathway that led to the front steps, Amelia caught a familiar spicy scent in the air. She followed it back to the sea captain and his pipe by the old oak tree. It had been days since he had bothered trying to speak to her, so when she stopped in front of him and said hello, perhaps it shouldn't have been a surprise that he reeled back all the way through the tree.

A moment later, he peeked around its trunk wide-eyed beneath his cap.

Amelia held up a hand, half in apology, half in greeting. "I'm sorry. I didn't mean to startle you."

"Lass," he whispered, "you can see me?"

Amelia clutched her coat tight to her body against the frigid morning air. "Yes, I can."

"All this time?"

"I . . . yes." She owed him more of an explanation, but now was not the time. "Look, hopefully we can talk again later, but you need to go. Find another tree to lean against while you smoke your pipe. It isn't safe here."

"Why's that now?" he asked, still looking like he had been the one who had seen a ghost.

"You were right. There is something wrong with the library."

"Aye," he said sagely. "What be the problem?"

She really didn't want to get into all the details, but he was a sailor, so she said, "There's a maelstrom surrounding the building. A cosmic maelstrom."

His brow raised. "A storm from the heavens?"

"Aye." Amelia blinked. She really needed to get more sleep.

"There is a good chance it will destroy the library, and if it does, it may take you with it. So, if I were you . . ."

He straightened, flipped up the collar of his overcoat, and yanked down his cap. "I'll be on my way, then." Before Amelia could turn, though, he added, "Many thanks, lass, and my apologies for my fright. It's been eons since I've been spoken to. A hundred years at least."

Suddenly Amelia couldn't move.

Now was not the time for this. She couldn't even begin to process it properly, but . . . *a hundred years*? And she had just walked past him over and over and over again.

"Well," she said, struggling to find her voice, "whenever you see me, be sure to say hello. And I'll be sure to do the same."

He gave her a big smile, one missing a few teeth, to which Amelia smiled back before resuming her walk to the door.

"Lass! Wait!" he called after her. "If there be a maelstrom, why might you be headed straight for it?"

Amelia stopped, feet planted on the bottom step of the library's front stairs, hand gripping the railing. It was a good question. One she would have struggled to answer even a few days ago, but now . . .

"I have no choice." She glanced back at the sailor. "There are people I care about inside."

30

For small creatures such as we the vastness
is bearable only through love.
—Carl Sagan, *Contact*

AMELIA TURNED HER BELOVED IRON KEY IN THE LIbrary's front lock, and the door swung inward with a loud creak. Fathomless dread filled her core as she crossed the threshold. This didn't feel at all like her library anymore. It didn't even feel of this world. Remarkably the lights were still on, but the luminescence they gave was weak, bled out by the eerie silver-gray glow coming from the patch.

"Hello?"

Nobody answered in the whistling winds.

Please let them be okay.

Amelia walked toward the main reading room, her heart rate picking up with every step. Fallen books lay strewn across the floor, along with the knocked-over chairs and table from the children's area. She headed toward the west stairs, wanting to see the patch on the east side from a distance. There was no telling how dangerous it was now. Gripping the banister, she climbed the first few steps, then turned. What she saw made everything else drop away.

The patch now covered the entire east wall of the second floor, and its awful light was so brutally cold and bright her eyes instantly watered. Some of the stacks around it had been knocked over, stripped of all texts, while other bookcases were simply gone.

Please . . .

Amelia dragged her gaze over the great room, searching every space between the stacks, every corner, every shadow, but there wasn't a soul to be found.

She couldn't give up. No matter what it took. She'd search every square inch—

Suddenly Amelia screamed.

It appeared searching every square inch of the library would be unnecessary, for when she turned to climb the remaining stairs, Minnie's face was a hair's breadth from her own.

Amelia clutched her chest. "You nearly scared me to death!"

It was hard to be sure, but it almost looked like a smile touched the ghost's mouth.

"Amelia? Is that you?" the professor called out from the floor above. "What are you doing here? It isn't safe."

Relief spurred Amelia the rest of the way up the stairs, Minnie in tow. Once she'd made it to the top, she ran to the professor's chair by the hearth. She blinked at the decommissioned fireplace. There were no blue-green flames today.

"I haven't been able to keep it going," the professor said, following her gaze. "The wind keeps blowing out the flames."

Even though Amelia had heard the wind when she stepped inside, she hadn't fully registered the cold current swirling around them, but now she realized just how strong it was and how ominous it felt.

The professor shook his head. "Amelia, listen to me. It's good of you to come, but you know you can't stay. Our fates may be sealed, but—"

"We're not giving up. There's still time." She dug into her messenger bag and pulled out *The Ghostseer's Handbook*.

"You found it." The professor's eyes widened with wonder. "I thought it had disappeared."

"It had, but then it reappeared!" Amelia hopped with excitement, before she remembered she was not a hopper.

"Well, what does it say? Is there another way for us to stop this?"

There was. Possibly. She had also learned that Rosalinda was right to fear the construction equipment the engineering company planned to use to dig around the foundation. The building was extremely fragile and the power of the maelstrom explosive. The slightest touch could bring it all down. "I'll tell you everything, but . . ." She looked around. "Where is Braden? We should all be together when I explain."

The professor and Minnie exchanged looks, before he said, "Braden is having a little trouble processing the situation. Truthfully, we all are."

Amelia pinned the book to her chest. "I understand. Don't worry. I'll talk to him."

The professor and Minnie exchanged another look, a more *awkward* one this time.

It took Amelia a second to figure out what they were getting at, but she got there in the end. *Well, drat.* "Still mad?"

Neither answered.

She had been hoping after the blanket, they were good, but she should have known it wouldn't be that easy. "Where is he?"

AMELIA CLIMBED THE stairs up to the special collections floor. When she got there, she peeked into the storage room, but no Braden.

She then walked down the center aisle of the towering industrial shelves, checking each corridor. When she reached the end, she shot a brief look to the left toward the paranormal section, but it was empty. She then looked right, and, by the far corner, near the wall, she spotted Braden lying on his back, hovering just inches above the floor. His fingers were interlaced behind his head, and he was looking through the window up at the sky.

"Am I interrupting?" Amelia called out as she walked toward him.

Braden glanced over but then stared back out through the window.

The silent treatment. Wonderful. Although, given the sheer number of times she had purposefully ignored ghosts, she supposed turnabout was fair play. "What are you doing?"

He didn't make eye contact. "Just pondering the meaning of death. Which is what you're going to be if you don't get out of this library. Dead."

It really was very kind of him to drive the point home. "Can I join you?"

He shrugged.

Amelia sat on the floor, then hugged her knees to her chest before looking out the window. Even though the sun was coming up, she could still see stars in the sky. The view had to be spectacular up here at night. Given all that was going on, she could understand why Braden had chosen this spot. Hopefully, it was also a good place to finish her apology tour. "I came up here to bring you downstairs so we can all talk. I found out some information about the maelstrom that might help." She inhaled sharply. "But first I want to apologize."

Braden didn't react.

Amelia hugged her knees in tighter. "You were right. In the beginning, I *was* trying to get to know you so that I could help save the library, but so much has changed since then. You have to know that."

Braden rolled his head to meet her eyes, then sighed. "I know. It's fine."

What? That had been easy. Even easier than it had been with the professor. Amelia supposed she was relieved, but Braden looked so dejected that it was hard to take it as a win.

"I've been giving you a hard time from the start," he said. "Being a ghostseer must suck. I can see why you wanted to have nothing to do with us."

Amelia waited for the *but*, the argument, the accusations of wrongdoing on her part, but he said nothing more. This was awful. Where had his fight gone? "No, Braden, the way I treated you was wrong. I should have recognized sooner that—"

"Ghosts are people too?" He gave her a sad smile.

Amelia looked back out the window. "I've wasted so much time. If only I had really tried to help from the start, told everyone the truth, then maybe we wouldn't be in this situation."

"You can't take all the blame. It's our unresolved issues that got us trapped here in the first place."

They fell into silence, watching the stars fade into the lightening sky. A moment later he said, "Hey, can I ask you something?"

"Of course."

"What do you think happens when we die? I mean, really die, like move on to whatever comes next?"

Amelia jerked her gaze over once more to look at him fully, but Braden kept his focus on the sky. The question had jarred her and not just because she hadn't been expecting it. It was that she hadn't expected it from him. And even though his tone was light, she could tell the words hadn't come from an easy place. "Honestly, I don't know. I suppose I've thought about different possibilities."

He peeked over at her. "Which ones?"

"Reincarnation. I like the idea of second-chance lifetimes."

He huffed a laugh. "You mean, you want a chance at being normal."

At one time that would have been true.

"I want to learn from my mistakes. Be a better person."

Amelia fully expected Braden to jump all over that confession, make fun of her, but instead he replied, "That's cool," then let out a noisy breath. "And there's so much of the world to see. You can't do it all in one lifetime."

"And perhaps not just this world," Amelia ventured. "Maybe we could be reincarnated on another planet as another life form."

"What?!" Braden yelled, sitting up. "That would be awesome. I would love that." He made a mind-blown expression with his hands before reclining again.

"What about you?" Amelia asked. "What do you believe?"

"I don't know. I was raised to believe in heaven, and, I mean, that sounds nice, I guess."

"But?"

"I think I would be bored." He frowned. "There is another option, though—or maybe just this idea—that I seriously like."

Amelia raised an eyebrow.

"I like to think that we're all connected. Like the universe is some great Myspace page, and we're all on it, so even if we lose touch for a lifetime or two, we can still find each other again. No one is ever lost."

Amelia smiled. "That's really nice. I like that. Not that I've ever been on social media."

Braden chuckled. "I'm shocked."

Amelia would have thrown a book at him . . . but that would have meant throwing a book at him.

"Hey, bro—" Braden started before finishing with "—melia."

"Bro-melia?"

"I'm trying, okay?" He leaned on his elbow. "I gotta know. How did things go with Librarian Ken? And don't try to tell me there's nothing happening between you two, because nobody is buying that. You've got this whole Ross-and-Rachel, will-they-won't-they thing going on."

"I have no clue what you're referring to."

"*Friends*?"

She shook her head.

Braden rolled his eyes. "It's a TV show. You should watch it sometime. The characters are just like you two, except you're both Ross."

Amelia planted her chin on her knees. "I think that ship has sailed. I've lied to him. Numerous times. More than I can count."

"So, tell him the truth."

Amelia picked at a loose piece of fluff stuck between the floorboards. "It's not that easy."

"Look," he said, "as your friend, I feel like—" Suddenly he cut himself off. "What? What happened? What's wrong?"

Amelia realized he must have caught the shocked expression on her face. "Nothing. I just . . . friends?"

"You don't think we're friends?" Braden's eyebrows peaked in a sad triangle.

"No. I mean, yes. We're friends." Amelia turned her gaze back to the floor. "Actually, you're probably my best friend." An awful moment of silence passed. "I've never had a best friend before, so I don't really know what it's like, and we haven't known each other that long, but—"

"Yeah, same."

"What?" Amelia snapped her gaze up. "I'm your best friend?"

"Yup."

A novel sensation warmed her, a strange but solid happiness she couldn't ever remember experiencing.

Braden shrugged. "I mean all my other best friends are probably dead, so . . ."

"No, no," Amelia replied lightly. "They're all likely middle-aged and married with kids."

Braden's eyes widened. "Why? Why do you always have to do that?"

She snorted softly and shook her head. "I don't know."

Braden laughed in return, then said, "Middle-aged and married. I'd rather be dead." He sighed. Then before she could say anything, he groaned with frustration. "You know what? Forget all that for a second. I have to tell you something." Somehow even more color drained from his face. "You know how you just said you wished you hadn't wasted so much time? That maybe we wouldn't be in this mess if you'd just faced stuff sooner?"

She nodded.

"Yeah, well, ever since you told us about the monster whirlpool threatening to take us out, I've been doing a lot of thinking about what might be holding me back. Maybe if I had faced my stuff sooner . . ." He shook his head hurriedly like he wanted to get everything out and over with as quickly as possible. "When I first died, I think I felt guilty about what my death did to my parents. Nobody should have to go through that kind of pain. But they're okay now. I've got nieces and nephews, and I know my moms and pops believe we'll see each other again, so that's not it."

"What do you think it is, then?"

"I think . . ." He glanced up at the ceiling. "I'm scared. I'm too scared to move on. Me. Mr. Skydiving and White Water Rafting. I'm scared." He released a shuddering sigh and looked back over at her. "Do you know how to resolve that issue?"

Amelia studied his face, searching for some clue of what she could say that might help. Philosophers far better than she had tackled the issue of existential dread, but she knew Braden wouldn't appreciate hearing any of their thoughts right now, and, truthfully, she didn't have any answers of her own. She was scared too. Amelia shook her head.

Braden nodded, and the sad smile she'd seen earlier returned.

Just then another unearthly groan shook the library, louder and more powerful than any of the ones before. As books and boxes tumbled from the shelves, they looked around the walls, searching for the first signs of collapse, and when their eyes met again, Braden whispered, "We're in real trouble, aren't we?"

31

"I'm not afraid of storms,
for I'm learning how to sail my ship."
—Louisa May Alcott, *Little Women*

AMELIA AND THE THREE GHOSTS GATHERED AROUND the cold hearth nestled in the west wing of the second floor. As the bitter winds swirled around them, it was difficult not to draw comparisons to their first meeting. They were all in the same spots. Amelia was seated across from the professor, while Braden hovered by the side of his chair. Minnie was still hiding in the gloom, but she had chosen a patch of darkness closer to the fireplace, so that was something. That first meeting had been so warm and cozy, despite all their animosities, or maybe just hers, but now, they were surrounded by cold, stony shadows.

"So, Amelia," the professor said in his gentle way, "you mentioned you have found something that could help us?"

A small bolt of anxiety struck Amelia's heart. Hopefully she hadn't oversold what she had learned. "Well, it's not so much that I've found something new that can stop the vortex." She placed her palm on *The Ghostseer's Handbook* resting on her lap. "It's more that the book confirms there's still hope. It's not too late to save you from it."

"That sounds promising." The professor smiled, but it wasn't his most convincing effort. "The speculation that if one of us moves on, that might be enough to stop the vortex, does that still hold?" He looked at Braden and Minnie, then raised his brow in question.

"We may be past that point. It's hard to be certain."

His brow dropped.

"I'm guessing the cosmic vortex has gone from a whirlpool to a full maelstrom," Amelia continued. She was no expert, but there wasn't much doubt. "And from what I've read, that means the building is quite fragile now. The slightest touch could leave us sitting on rubble." Well, Amelia would likely be under the rubble, not sitting on top of it, and there was no telling where the ghosts would be—*but* her thoughts were rambling, likely because she wasn't particularly anxious to get to the next part. "Regardless, the vortex's power has likely grown to such an extent that one ghost crossing over to the other side would not be enough. You see, opening the passageway requires cosmic energy, energy that is hard to sustain under the force of the storm's massive power, so—"

"So what?" Braden asked, his voice taking on a hysterical edge. "What does any of that mean?"

Amelia nodded. "Maybe I should read the passage, and then we can discuss." She picked up the book before Braden could complain about it being story time. "'A cosmic whirlpool is easy enough to stop. In most cases, all that is required is that a single spirit travel to what comes next, and the force of the vortex will no longer hold.' That's the stage I'm fairly certain we've missed." She quickly flipped the pages. "Here we are. 'As the storm grows in strength, reaching the level of a maelstrom, the only way to stop the destruction is for most or *all* the spirits within the dwelling to resolve their earthly issues and move on to the other side.'" Amelia looked up. "Two might work. But likely you will all have to go."

The low, unearthly winds swirling through the library whistled eerily as a tense silence fell over them.

"I know. It's not the news you wanted to hear," Amelia said. It also wasn't the news she wanted to give them, but they had to see the alternative was too terrible even to fathom. Moving on had to be better than leaving their fates up to the maelstrom. And there was more. It was possible that even if all three of them were able and ready to go, it might not work. In that scenario there was one last option, but it had even lower odds of success, and Amelia didn't want to discourage them any more than she already had . . . although they did seem to be taking the news calmly. Or at least they were until Braden started screaming. "What?! There's no way we can all move on! You know that!"

"Braden," the professor said, "let's not panic."

"Not panic?! I am totally freaking out! Which ironically happens to be the reason why I can't move on!" He looked at Amelia as though asking if he had used *ironically* correctly. She'd allow it. "You can't go either, professor. You have whatever it is holding you here, and—"

"Actually, I may have news on that front." The professor suddenly looked thoughtful. "I can't explain it, but I feel like whatever it is I have been waiting for is about to come to fruition."

Chills raced up Amelia's arms. "Really?" He gave her a small smile although she wouldn't have characterized it as a happy one.

"What?! What does that even mean?" Braden shouted. "Have you been waiting to save us? Is that what's been holding you back? Because that would be great. But we really need to nail down the timeline." Amelia couldn't help but note that ever since Braden had owned up to his fears, he was much more willing to articulate them. *Loudly.* "And what about Minnie? Any progress on that front?"

Amelia met the glowing blue eyes of the ghost hiding in the shadows. "Yes, I think so. Minnie told me she wants to move on, and that's enough to keep me going."

"Keep you going?! What?"

"I'm going to find something to help her," Amelia said calmly. "Maybe if she opens the portal, everything else will fall into place. We have to hope for the best."

Braden stopped yelling and searched her eyes, probably looking for the certainty he didn't feel.

"I know it's not the ideal solution," she said. "But it's all we've got. Now, given there isn't a moment to lose, I'm going to go upstairs and do some more research, and—"

"And what are we supposed to do?" Braden asked, throwing his hands helplessly in the air.

The first thought that popped into Amelia's head was *Don't get sucked into the portal*, but that probably wouldn't help. "I don't know," she answered quietly. "Maybe just be together."

AMELIA SURVEYED THE special collections floor. Somewhere within this room, buried in one of the many boxes, was the information she was looking for. She was sure of it. Over the past weeks, she had gone through all the books, online resources, microfilm, and microfiche she could find, but here was an untouched mother lode of material. Many of these boxes of newspapers, diaries, and letters had likely gone untouched for years, but today all that would change.

There was an impossible amount to go through, and there wasn't much time, so Amelia rolled up her sleeves and swirled her hair into a severe bun. As daunting as the task might be, she *was* going to find out what had happened to Minnie even if it—well, hopefully it wouldn't kill her.

Amelia went through boxes, scanning each and every page of local village newspapers. It seemed like the best place to start. If Minnie had been in a fire, it would have been reported.

Beams of sunlight stretched and slid across the floor, marking the passing hours. The only times Amelia stopped reading were when she needed a quick washroom break or a refill of tea. Spotting the tin of oatmeal-raisin cookies on the counter of the break room was the one thing that derailed her momentarily from her mission. Memories of the past weeks filled her mind. What she'd give to have another normal afternoon teatime with Rosalinda.

The only way they'd have that chance, though, was if the library was still standing.

Eyes burning, Amelia turned fragile pages late into the night. While she hadn't counted, she must have gone through at least forty or fifty boxes, but she had at least two or three times that to go. Thankfully, the library didn't experience any more major earthquakes, and the wind was much less intense on the third floor, but the wood planks rumbled at regular intervals beneath her feet, and the air itself felt dangerous.

At what had to be two or three in the morning, Amelia could no longer hold herself up, not even to sit, but she still wasn't ready to stop, so she grabbed yet another old newspaper and curled up on her side in the beanbag chair. She couldn't help but think how the Amelia she was weeks ago never would have handled an archival newspaper this way. Things had certainly changed. Her eyelids drooped as her gaze trailed over the words.

In a slow blink, Amelia caught the word *Family* in a headline. Her eyelids lowered, but she forced them back up. Family what?

Tragedy. Her eyes closed again. She had read about so many family tragedies that day. Smallpox . . . pneumonia . . . diphtheria . . .

Fire.

Yes, that's what she was looking for, wasn't it? And there it was right on the front page. *Family. Tragedy. Fire.* But before she could read another word, her mind rolled back into the darkness, and all the words disappeared.

AMELIA WOKE WITH a jolt and sat up, blinking against the sunlight. After pushing away the hair that had escaped from her bun and adjusting her glasses, she looked down at the newspaper lying on her lap. The disorientation of sleep still had her in its clutches. What time was it? What happened? Where did she leave off?

And what was that noise?

It was a loud but distant rumbling. Amelia tensed, worried it was the library again, but it had come from outside. That must have been what had woken her up. She flipped over to hands and knees to push herself up to investigate, but before she got her feet beneath her, she spotted the headline of the newspaper she had been reading.

HORRIFIC TRAGEDY: FAMILY LOST IN MIDNIGHT BLAZE NEAR SUMMERSIDE

Amelia snatched up the paper. While the headline had been the thing to catch her attention, it was the picture underneath that made her world go sideways. It was a family photograph, and right in the center was Minnie.

As Amelia scanned the article, her hand rose to cover her mouth.

No. Oh no . . .

This was terrible. Minnie's secret was so much worse than she had thought. Amelia lowered the paper to her side. And what was she supposed to do with this information? She wanted to help Minnie, to free her from the pain that was holding her back, but talking to her about this . . . Amelia couldn't see how reliving any of it would make things better.

A loud beeping noise forced her from her stupor. She turned her head to the window, not registering what the noise was until—

Trucks!

Amelia jumped to her feet, ran over to the window, and gripped its frame.

There were trucks everywhere. Multiple pickups, a dumpster truck, but it was the flatbed transporting the backhoes that stopped her heart. They were going to dig up the foundation! Amelia gripped the newspaper in her fist and raced for the stairs.

"Hey!" Braden shouted when she burst onto the second floor. "What's wrong? What's happening?"

There was no time to explain. Amelia sprinted down the ramp beside the stairs, blasting past a *No Running* sign.

"Amelia?" the professor called after her.

When she reached the bottom, she darted past the circulation desk, and tore through the foyer. She grabbed the iron handle of the front door and flung it open, shouting, "Stop!"

Nobody stopped. The backhoes kept on rumbling into place while workers in hard hats carried sawhorses and cones to positions around the library. Not a single person had heard her, except . . .

Simon.

He was standing on the lawn only a few feet back from the steps. The surprise of seeing her in the library froze him in a half turn. His mouth moved, but it took a second for him to speak any words. "Amelia? What are you doing here?" His voice was quiet with disbelief, but then he strode toward her and added with more force. "You can't be in there. It's not safe."

"Stop!" Amelia said, jutting her hands out, the newspaper still gripped in her fist. "Please, Simon. Just tell them to stop."

He looked around at the workers. "I can't. This has to be done. If you're worried about the contents of the library, believe me, I am too, but they've told me there's no reason to think the building will imminently collapse. That's why I called all this in." He looked around, bewildered. "I'm trying to avoid a catastrophe. You have to leave."

Amelia groaned, bouncing on the spot. "You don't understand. If that equipment, if one of those diggers so much as touches the building—not even the building—maybe even the energy around the building, it could trigger a force so massive—" She could tell by the look on his face that he wasn't following anything she was saying. "Simon, I know how this looks, but I can't go. Not yet. I need more time."

"More time?" He stepped toward her, and she backed up a step, halting him in his tracks. "More time for what?"

This was it. She had thought the time to tell him had come before, and maybe it had, maybe there were dozens of moments before this one that she should have told him the truth. If she had, maybe all this could have been avoided. But she couldn't go back, and now she was out of options.

"What are you talking about, Amelia? You can't—"

"I see ghosts."

And just like that, it was done. Three words. Three small words were all it took.

Confusion froze Simon to the spot, and Amelia glanced back

into the library. Braden and Minnie were at the mouth of the foyer, their expressions mirroring Simon's shock. It wasn't only shock though. They also looked sad for her. Amelia couldn't quite believe it. Despite all the danger they were facing, they were sad for her.

They didn't need to be though. Her secret didn't matter anymore, not really.

"Please, Simon, just make them stop. And I'll tell you everything."

32

"There's such a lot of different Annes in me."
—L. M. Montgomery, *Anne of Green Gables*

DREAD GRIPPED AMELIA'S HEART AS SHE STUDIED Simon's face. It was coming. He was going to give her *the look*. The beginnings of it were already there, but he was struggling. The confusion, disbelief, and betrayal were right beneath the surface, but for the moment he was torn, holding on to all the things he thought he knew about her—the things he still wanted to believe were true. Grapple as he might, though, he couldn't unhear her words.

Suddenly he turned and threw his hands up in the air, waving them in a big X.

A man in a hard hat came over, and they exchanged a few words before he spoke into the walkie-talkie pinned to his vest. As he walked away, Amelia could hear him say, "It's your money, man. See you tomorrow." Then as if by magic, all the large trucks fell silent, replaced by the sound of distant waves crashing on the shore.

Simon trotted back over but stopped before he reached the steps. He planted his hands on his hips and looked up at her. "Amelia, if this is some sort of . . ." The words fell away. He knew her better than that. At least she hoped so. "Tell me."

Amelia did. The words came haltingly at first, but it didn't take long for everything to come tumbling out. As the workers packed up, she told him about being a ghostseer. The rules she had come up with as a child and had always lived by. She told him about discovering the library was haunted the very first day and about trying to exorcise the ghosts. Then she told him about the professor, Braden, and Minnie and the cosmic maelstrom threatening to rip them away and destroy the library. She told him if the workers started digging, the entire building could collapse. Then she told him about *The Ghostseer's Handbook* and how there was still a chance to stop all of it, but that they were stuck, and now that she knew the truth about Minnie . . .

She looked down at the newspaper in her hand. "She wants to move on, so she was our best hope, but what she went through was so terrible, and I don't know how to make it any better for her."

Simon listened to it all silently, holding himself deathly still.

"I am so sorry," she said. "Being me, having this ability, it's . . ." Amelia held herself tight against the emotions threatening to take her over. "I have always been alone. It's how my life has always been, so I don't know how to trust people. And it's like I have all these voices in my head." Her eyes widened. "Not actual voices. The ghostseeing is enough. But I never know what the right thing to do is." That was the truth. "I don't know how to keep myself safe and still let people in. And I don't know how to connect without lying." She closed her eyes. "All I ever wanted was to have a normal life. At least that's what I thought. But now . . ." She looked back into the library. "I know this is difficult to believe, but you have to trust me when I say there are people in there. You can't see them, but . . . they're the only ones who have ever really seen me." She gripped the newspaper more tightly. "I can't leave."

Simon's expression remained closed, unreadable. He wasn't ready to give her anything. She could see that, and she knew it wasn't fair to expect more. Which made it terribly surprising when he held out his hand and walked toward her.

Amelia stepped back again.

Simon stopped, hurt coming to his eyes, but his hand was still out. "Let me see the paper."

Amelia clutched it to her chest but took small steps out from the entryway of the library toward the top of the stairs. As she did, the wind nearly tripled in strength. The blustery weather out here was worse than what was going on inside. With strands of hair whipping over her face, she held the paper out to him.

Once Simon had it firmly in his grip, he stepped back and read the article silently, hiding all reaction. When he finally looked up, he asked, "What do you expect me to do here? What am I supposed to say?"

"Nothing. You don't have to say anything. But I need more time. I'm going to talk to Minnie," she said, looking at the paper, "or, I guess, Charlotte. If I can get her to forgive herself for what happened, then maybe the passageway to the other side will open. Braden is afraid, which is really kind of mind-blowing if you knew him, but I think he's getting closer to accepting what's happening. And the professor, he thinks he'll soon be ready to move on, so . . ." Once again, Amelia could hear herself as she was speaking. And once again, she knew how it sounded.

Simon stared at her, then looked down and kicked a rock off the path. "I can't let you do this. It's too dangerous."

"Simon, you know the library better than anyone. You grew up here. You can't tell me you've never felt this place," she said, looking up at the building, "was more than just a warehouse for books."

Almost unwilling, his eyes darted over the brick, and his face softened with both pain and love. Finally, his gaze settled back on her. "Amelia, I may not believe in all the same things you and Rosalinda do, but I love this place. It's all I have left of my parents, and it gives so much to people. It's my home. If it goes . . ."

He'd be heartbroken. Devastated. Why had she said that? She was doing this all wrong. "You're right. So right. I don't think you realize how many people you've helped by keeping this place going. How much you've helped me. I want to save it, Simon. Please just let me try. I know I have no right to ask you to trust me. Not when I've lied to you about everything, but—"

"You're asking me to put aside everything I know to be true."

"No," she said quietly. "I'm asking you for more time."

Suddenly Simon's phone buzzed. As he pulled it from his pocket and looked at the screen, worry replaced the frustration on his face. "I have to take this." He turned away, answering the call in a low voice. After a few minutes, he looked over to her again. "It's Rosalinda." He dropped the newspaper in front of the bottom step. "She needs me." He was already backing away. "Amelia, let's go together. We'll come back when—"

"No. I'm sorry, but I can't go."

"Please, Amelia, I don't want to leave you here alone."

"That's the thing." She shrugged lightly. "I'm not alone."

33

"Faithless is he that says farewell
when the road darkens . . ."
—J. R. R. Tolkien, *The Fellowship of the Ring*

MUCH OF AMELIA'S HEART LEFT WITH SIMON AS HE drove away.

He knew everything now, and he had given her the best reaction she could have possibly hoped for, yet somehow it still hurt. She knew he had to have a million questions, and the longer they went unanswered, the more likely it was he'd come to his senses and realize all that she had told him was quite literally unbelievable.

A sudden boom shook the library's windows, like a cannon firing from the east wing. In its wake the air itself felt *different*, like another threshold had been crossed. She needed to get back inside.

Amelia looked down at the newspaper Simon had left in front of the steps, its pages flapping in the wind. She frowned. When she'd first felt it, she'd thought the wind out here was natural, but . . . she surveyed the library's front lawn. The grass was still, and not a fallen leaf was rustling over the ground. There was no wind outside.

Uh-oh.

It was the cosmic winds. They weren't just swirling inside but around the building now. The newspaper! She had to get it before it was lost or destroyed. The instant Amelia stepped closer to the top stair, though, she was blasted with what felt like a hurricane-force gale.

How? When had this happened? The wind hadn't been this strong a minute ago. Had that boom set this force free? Amelia understood the concept of exponential growth, but this was incredible. Masses of hair whipping violently around her face, she was forced to strip off her glasses and shove them down her sweater before they were lost. For a second, she thought she heard Braden shout her name, but the wind, roaring like a runaway freight train, made it impossible to be sure.

Lifting her hand to block the blasting current, Amelia peered almost blindly down the library steps. She was worried the newspaper would already be gone, or ripped to shreds, but it was still there or at least some flapping grayish blob was. The current of the maelstrom had to be tightly wrapped around the building, the paper just on the fringe. Hopefully, inside, it was calmer closer to the eye of the storm. Maybe. She didn't know! She was an arts major! All Amelia knew with any certainty was that she had to get the paper.

Gripping the railing with both hands, Amelia pulled herself closer to the first step, her shoulders straining with the effort. She then slid her foot to the edge and dropped her heel over the lip, heaving herself forward again. Then, bending at the knees to make herself smaller against the tearing force of the wind, she managed to get her other foot down the step. One down . . .

Taking a moment to catch some air, she sat crunched in a ball by the iron railing. For a brief manic second, she wondered what would happen if she were to let go. Would she spin around the library like an insect caught in a vacuum cleaner, or would she be flung through the portal into space? Neither of those options seemed appealing.

Using all her strength, Amelia wedged her heels against the

front end of the step and freed one hand to grab the next rung down before lowering herself again. *Wonderful.* The wind was even stronger here. She could barely breathe at all now, with the currents snatching the barest sips of air. She repeated the movement again, and thankfully the force lessened. From that point, with each step down, the wind eased until Amelia rolled onto the grass . . . and the gale was gone.

"Secrets?"

She peeked up at the library's front door, looking through the tiny dots pricking her vision. Braden and Minnie had forced their way closer to the threshold. Amelia jutted a thumb into the air, but how was it she could possibly hear Minnie's voice? This space maelstrom was really rattling her already shaky understanding of physics.

Grabbing the newspaper, Amelia rolled onto her knees. She spun the thick pages into a tight cylinder and shoved it down the collar of her sweater to join her glasses, before tucking her hem tightly into her pants. She then got up to her feet, took a couple of deep breaths, and steeled herself to make the journey back inside.

"Wait!" Braden shouted. "Are you sure? If you come back in, you may not get out again."

He wasn't wrong. The power of the wind had grown so quickly. Going inside now seemed reckless at best, deadly at worst.

Without answering, Amelia gripped the railing once more and heaved herself up the first step.

THE TRIP BACK into the library was even more perilous than the way out had been. At one point, Amelia's feet left the ground as she hugged the railing, but she was able to hook her foot around a rung and pull herself down.

Once she reached the landing, she crawled to the door and crossed the threshold, and Braden and Minnie pulled her the rest of the way through. Amelia lay flat on her back as the ghosts stared down at her.

This felt familiar.

"You good?" Braden asked.

"That was . . ." Amelia shook her head. "Awesome."

"Really?" Braden yelled, a crazy look of excitement coming over his face.

"No."

Minnie hissed something that sounded almost like a laugh as Amelia struggled to her feet.

Braden shook his head. "You want to explain to us what you were thinking going out there like that?"

Amelia couldn't help but wonder how many times Braden had been on the receiving end of that particular question. "I had to tell Simon to keep all that equipment from the building."

"We heard that, and we heard you tell him about us." Braden grimaced and scratched his nose, which seemed unlikely to actually be itchy. "How did he react?"

"He stopped the workers. That's all that matters."

Braden and Minnie exchanged a look.

"Everything's fine," Amelia said tightly. "We have far bigger issues to worry about."

"Wait. Wait. Wait," Braden said. "But why did you go all the way out there after he left? What did you stuff down your sweater?"

"I didn't *stuff* anything down my sweater," Amelia said.

Minnie and Braden stared at the newspaper-shaped roll at her chest before he said, "It's as natural as breathing, isn't it?"

Lying? Yes, it really was. "Look, I need you both to trust me on this one. I will tell you everything, but I have to talk to the professor first. It involves people and their emotions so—"

"'Nough said." Braden smiled, and Minnie gave her a single nod.

"What? That's it?" Amelia asked. "You're simply going to trust me?"

"People and emotions aren't really your thing, so . . ." Braden trailed off but glanced at Minnie with concern. He must have realized the newspaper had to do with her.

"Right, then." Amelia walked around them toward the stairs. If she had known explaining to people you weren't going to tell them the truth was an alternative to lying, she might have tried that a long time ago.

Instead of finding the professor sitting in his chair by the fireplace, Amelia caught him pacing the floor. When he spotted her, his shoulders slumped with relief. "Thank heavens."

She waved a little hello.

"I heard shouting down below—although it's impossible not to shout with these winds." He gave the air a filthy look, which was adorable on him. "Are you all right?"

She shrugged. That really felt like too much of a question for her to answer at the current time.

"Come sit," he said, heading for his chair. "Tell me everything."

Amelia dropped into her seat across from him. "Essentially, I told Simon the truth and he's giving us more time. I need to talk to you about something more important though." The professor looked concerned, but thankfully he didn't argue. Amelia pulled the newspaper free from her sweater. "I found out something about Minnie, but I don't know what to do about it."

Leaning over the coffee table, she flattened the newspaper in front of him, holding down the sides against the wind. The professor's glasses appeared on top of his head, and he guided them down onto his nose before directing his focus to the front page. Amelia watched the heartbreak play out as his eyes moved over the text. When he was through, he whispered, "That poor, poor child." He then leaned back, lifting his glasses once again to his forehead, where they disappeared.

"Somehow, I thought if I found out Minnie's secret, everything would fall into place, but this?" Amelia met the professor's eye. "I don't see how bringing this up will help. But if we do nothing . . ."

The professor glanced back down at the paper. "The article mentioned that her father survived. Do you think there might be something in that?"

"Something like what?"

He shook his head.

It seemed like an incredible long shot given what had happened, but now that the professor had suggested the possibility, Amelia couldn't ignore it. "I'll look into it. Now that I have dates and names, it should be easier to research. We're running out of time though."

"I feel that too. I'm not sure the library will make it through another night."

"What if I spend the day researching, but when the sun goes down . . ."

"We can talk to her together," the professor finished.

"Thank you."

"No, Amelia. We should be thanking you."

She didn't know if that was true, but with the end of their world looming, now wasn't the time to argue. "How are you doing, professor?"

He exhaled heavily and interlaced his fingers by his chest. "I wish I could explain the power that holds me here. The thought of something happening to you all is unbearable, and yet, I know I am right where I'm supposed to be. It's infuriating."

Amelia's heart tightened with affection. He didn't look infuriated. Disheartened, perhaps. "Professor, I want you to know I did some research on fatal car accidents in the area. The whole island actually."

He nodded. "I imagined that you would."

"I couldn't find anything that seemed to fit." Amelia had gone through every account she could find in the last fifty years, but none of the victims seemed to match the professor's age or description. "I'm very sorry."

"No, I am grateful for your efforts, and while I can't explain it, I do believe my time is near." He gave Amelia a small worried smile, which she returned before getting to her feet.

"Before you go, I would like you to promise me something."

Amelia waited. She knew what was coming.

"Promise me you'll leave," he said. "If it looks like things are hopeless, promise me you'll go."

What was with these ghosts? Did they not remember saving her from the portal? But then again, if things were hopeless . . .

Amelia gave the professor a single nod.

He didn't need to know that it might already be too late.

34

"To love at all is to be vulnerable."
—C. S. Lewis, *The Four Loves*

IF THE PLANKS OF THE OLD WOOD FLOORS HADN'T been shaking beneath her . . .

If the cold cosmic winds hadn't been wailing through the crevices in the brick . . .

If the building's structure itself hadn't been cracking under the force of catastrophic threat . . .

If none of these things had been true, Amelia would have been quite happy sitting cross-legged on the special collections floor, two soaring shelves on either side, boxes in every direction, a mug of tea in her hand.

But, of course, all that was true, and the thought that it all could be gone before another sunrise was more than she could comprehend. And that was without even considering the ghosts.

Amelia had thought her search for information on Minnie's family would be easier now that she had more details, but the library's computers were no longer connected to the outside world, so she had once again turned to the haphazard collection of articles, letters, and diaries. Again, normally, she would have loved hunting through the documents, but nothing was normal about this situation.

Closing the cover of a leather-bound journal, Amelia gently rested the back of her head against the exposed brick of the library's west wall, listening to the unexpected laughter filtering through the stacks. She rolled her head in the direction of the storage room. Minnie and Braden were watching a movie together, and their laughter was a lovely sound even if Minnie's was more of a hiss. Amelia placed the journal and her tea on the floor and lifted a stack of letters from the open box nearest to her hip. As she did, a carving in the brick caught her eye.

Simon.

Amelia placed the stack of envelopes back down and swiveled gently to touch the letters with her fingertips. The moment she brushed the worn grooves, the library seemed to shiver.

"You care about him too, don't you?" she whispered. "I've been thinking, is that why you kept *The Ghostseer's Handbook* from me? Did you want to make sure that things didn't happen too quickly? That Simon and I would . . ." Amelia couldn't follow that sentence all the way through. The uncertainty hurt too much. "That I'd get to a place where I cared too much to leave?" Amelia glanced about the room. "If that's the case, you needn't have worried. I never would have gone." She placed her palm fully on the brick. "The moment we met, I was yours."

Of course, if the library had just given her *The Ghostseer's Handbook* to keep up front, she might have had more time to save them all, but now wasn't the time to quibble.

Amelia dropped her hand, and Braden shimmered into view just feet from where she was sitting. "Do you want me to come back?"

He jutted his thumbs to the side. "'Cause it sounded like you were professing your love to the library."

"That was a private conversation." Assuming Braden needed her to put in a fresh DVD, she rolled onto her knees to get to her feet but then froze momentarily when she saw the expression on his face. Again, ghosts chose how to manifest, consciously or not, and Braden's face looked *different*. "What happened? What is wrong with you?"

"Nothing." He sniffed sharply and rubbed his nose. "I'm fine. What are you talking about?"

"Have you been crying?"

He scoffed. "No."

Amelia looked toward the storage room, catching a glimpse at the DVD menu. *Titanic*. "Ah, I see, but I thought I heard laughter a moment ago."

"I didn't know the ship went down!" he shouted. "I mean I guess I knew it went down, but Minnie found the whole thing pretty funny."

Amelia blinked. "Right. Well, maybe that movie wasn't the best choice, considering . . ."

"Nah, it's fine. It helped actually." He inhaled deeply, puffing his chest. "It reminded me that we all gotta go sometime, so . . ."

"Go?" Amelia tried to meet his eyes, but he was avoiding her gaze. "You mean, you're ready to go, go? Move on? You're not afraid?"

He dug his pinkie fingernail into the back of his mouth like he was trying to free something from his teeth. Given that he hadn't actually eaten anything—in decades—Amelia suspected he was playing it cool. "Yeah, no, still terrified. But I've been giving it a lot of thought, and it's time." Despite the deeply perturbed look on his face, he nodded sagely. "I don't want the professor to be forced to leave if he doesn't have to. And while I don't think I've found enough peace to open the light myself, I figured with your help, Minnie might get there. And if she does, I'll piggyback my way in." He shrugged. "Maybe the two of us will be enough to shut this vortex thing down."

Amelia studied Braden's face. This was a big shift for him, but the way he said *the two of us*, it almost made it sound like—

Suddenly she gasped. "Do you have *feelings* for Minnie?"

"Would you keep your voice down?" he hissed, eyes darting back over to the storage room. Amelia pinched her lips shut. "There's just something about her, you know?"

Amelia couldn't argue with that.

"It's like she's terrifying, but in a cool way. And those eyes! When they're not all glowing and bulging, they're kind of beautiful."

Again, not wrong.

"I mean, why not give it a shot, right?" Braden shrugged. "I've been thinking about it, and you were right about the library drawing us ghosts in with its caring vibes or whatever. I mean, before I ended up here, I had been alone for a pretty long time. It's no way to live." He gave Amelia a look that suggested he thought she might feel the same way. "And who says you can't find love in the afterlife?"

Certainly not her. She was no expert on finding love, living or dead. And yet, there was something about this conversation Amelia didn't like, and it wasn't the idea of Braden and Minnie growing closer. It was something else entirely. "Well, you don't have to decide right now," she stammered. "About moving on, that is. Maybe there's another way." Why was she arguing? Moving on was clearly the best decision he could make.

"Nope, don't try to change my mind." He sliced his hands in the air between them. "I'm sure."

Amelia wrapped her arms around her waist. "Are you really, really sure though?" What was she doing? Why was she putting doubt in his mind when this was clearly the only option.

"Hell ya. It's better than getting lost in the stars, and . . ." He let the thought trail away as he rubbed his hands over his face.

"What?"

"I don't know." He flung his arms out to his sides. "It's all the stupid talks we've been having. They've really got me thinking about my parents. I wasn't lying when I said they're doing well. Last time I checked, they were . . ." Suddenly he sounded choked up. ". . . teaching the little rug rats how to water-ski. Just like they did me. But they aren't getting any younger. If they pass and there's a chance I can greet them on the other side, I want that." He shook his head. "No way I'm breaking their hearts again."

Amelia's shoulders dropped. She could hardly argue with that.

"Plus, if we go together to the other side, I bet Minnie will hold my hand, and once we touch, she'll know—"

"I'm sorry," Amelia said sharply. "I'm going to stop you there. Why don't we let Minnie decide what she knows?"

Braden rolled his eyes. "Duh. It's just that it will be so epic, no one would be able to resist." He looked off into the distance. "Our love story will begin the moment our lives end."

Amelia rolled her eyes in return even though that did sound a tiny bit romantic.

"Speaking of Minnie, how is the research going?" he asked, lowering his voice. "You found something out earlier, didn't you? That's why you wanted to talk to the professor alone."

"I did, but it's not good." She glanced over to the storage room. "Now I'm trying to find something more that will maybe make it better for her, but I haven't gotten very far. I'm not sure such a thing even exists."

"Do you want me to help with the research?" he asked, suddenly looking pained.

"That's sweet of you," Amelia replied, "but somehow I think we would both hate that."

He nodded, scratching his goatee. "I know I would."

"No, you both should do your best to enjoy the moment." As if on cue, the floor rumbled, shaking the bookshelves.

"Awesome." Braden floated toward the storage room. "*Jurassic Park* is next."

"You know," Amelia called after him, "Minnie really enjoys being read to."

Braden stopped abruptly, his back still turned, hovering between the shelves.

"And you are certainly strong enough to turn pages. I've never seen a stronger ghost," Amelia said. "So perhaps I could get you *Northanger Abbey*?"

Braden turned slowly, revealing a deeply unimpressed look on his face.

"Before you say no—"

"Get it," he said. "Quick. And don't think I don't know what you just did there."

Amelia rushed past him.

"The things I do for epic love."

35

Was I deceived, or did a sable cloud /
Turn forth her silver lining on the night?
—John Milton, *Comus*

THE REST OF THE DAY PASSED BOTH TOO SLOWLY AND far too quickly. Amelia was able to learn a few more tidbits on Minnie in some genealogy documents and found another photograph of her family in a book, but nothing significant enough to change the situation.

The building's groans grew throughout the day, and when the sun dropped low in the sky, Amelia knew they couldn't wait any longer. It still felt cruel to confront Minnie with what she had learned, but it was the only option, and as painful as it might be, the ghost deserved a chance to survive this night.

They all did.

Once Amelia had readied herself to go downstairs, she walked to the windows on the west wall to take one last look at the view from the third floor. It was so incredibly serene outside, with the lighthouse blinking down the shore and the waves gently lapping the dark sands. It was a world apart from what they were experiencing. In the distance she spotted the glittering silhouettes of the ghost couple walking along the boardwalk—always wearing cloaks, always holding lanterns, always looking so in love. That made her smile. No matter what happened tonight, at least they were a constant. She'd forgotten to tell Braden about them. There was love in the afterlife.

After a few minutes, Amelia headed downstairs and gathered with the ghosts around the fireplace. She had found an old flashlight earlier, so they weren't completely lost in the unearthly glow coming from the portal, but the atmosphere was far from comforting. The maelstrom's currents were much worse now, which forced them to push the chairs and a small bookcase into a tight circle to provide some shelter from the wind. The professor had given up his wingback armchair for Minnie so that Amelia could get close.

If the ghost knew what was happening, she gave no sign of it.

Amelia had tucked the newspaper beside the seat cushion, along with *The Ghostseer's Handbook*, but she had no plans to show the article to Minnie unless she asked to see it. It was too upsetting. She did, however, have a book clutched to her chest that she hoped might be helpful.

"Minnie," Amelia began, "I don't know how much you remember about your life or what got you here, but I found out some information." She had thought about using Minnie's given name, Charlotte, but that seemed like an abrupt way to start. It was hard to tell if it made any kind of difference though; the ghost had returned once again to her trance state.

"We don't have to talk about it if you don't want to," she continued. "But I found a photo of you and your family. Would you like to see it?"

Suddenly Minnie snapped to attention, then looked at the book in Amelia's hands. After a moment of indecision, she nodded vigorously.

Amelia opened the hardback to the marked page and laid it on the armrest between them, gripping it at the top edge with the heel of her palm to keep the pages flat in the wind. It was a grainy black-and-white shot with Minnie's family seated behind a harvest table in a rustic-looking kitchen. It was the same one that had been in the newspaper but without the jarring headline. There were seven people in the photograph—five children, including Minnie, and her parents. There was also an adorable spotted dog lying on the dirt floor.

"Of course, it's impossible to tell by a photo," Amelia said, "but your family looks wonderful." They did. Even though it was a posed shot, they had an openness about them, a level of familiarity and connection that Amelia had never experienced but had always wanted.

Minnie nodded, sending sparkling sooty tears streaming down her cheeks. When she looked back up at Amelia, she held a big, joyful smile, but it crumpled almost instantly into an expression of heart-wrenching sorrow.

"I know," Amelia whispered. "I know what happened to them and you." She felt her own eyes fill with tears. "I am so sorry." Minnie put her hand on her chest the way she had the last night Amelia had read to her, then pointed at the kerosene lantern resting on the kitchen table in the photo.

"That's your secret, isn't it? The lantern?"

She nodded. "Minnie . . . bad."

The article had said it appeared as though the lantern had been knocked over in the night and given the positioning of the bodies, they concluded that Charlotte was responsible.

Braden and the professor exchanged glances from where they stood on either side of her. It looked like Braden wanted to reach out, perhaps touch her shoulder, but wasn't sure if he should.

Suddenly Minnie made movements as though she were sewing, before pressing her palms together and holding her fingers to her cheek. She then pointed at the kitchen table.

"You fell asleep?" Amelia asked.

Minnie nodded, then stuck out her arm in a jerk.

"That's how the lantern fell."

Minnie touched the photograph once more, her fingertip resting on the teenaged girl seated beside her. "Ruth," she rasped.

"Your younger sister?"

Minnie nodded and moved her finger over the boys' faces. "William. John." She closed her eyes a moment and shuddered before moving her finger again. "Mama. Papa." Then she trailed her touch over to the youngest child, who couldn't have been more than three or four. "Hattie. Baby Hattie." Minnie gave Amelia a look so piercing, so forged with pain, that it left her gutted. "Charlotte . . . bad."

Amelia reached for the ghost's hands, but her fingers went right through. "No, not bad. It was an accident. You're human."

Minnie shook her head and patted her chest again. "No. Ghost."

Those two words shook Amelia harder than any of the maelstrom's cosmic booms. "I'm so sorry, Minnie. So very sorry." And she was, for so many things. For expressing doubt that the ghosts were anything but human. For not seeing Minnie's pain sooner because she was so wrapped up in her own concerns. For waiting so long to help because she couldn't see what a gift it was to be let into these spirits' lives. But mainly Amelia was sorry that Minnie ever had to live through the way her life ended. It was brutal and unfair, and she didn't deserve it. Not at all. No one did.

Amelia opened her eyes just in time to see Minnie reaching out to touch her cheek, to touch the tear Amelia hadn't realized she'd let fall.

"For Minnie?" Her blue eyes rounded with confusion.

Amelia nodded. "For Minnie."

The ghost jerked her hand back, and spiders filled the air.

AMELIA HAD FAILED.

Minnie disappeared to wherever it was she went when she combusted in despair, and with her went their last, best hope. Before she could think of what to do about it, though, the professor floated in close and said in a voice near shouting, "You have to go, Amelia. There isn't much time left."

On cue another earsplitting blast shook the cavernous room, this time sending dust and chunks of plaster raining down. Even more eerie light filled the library, but not just from the patch on the east wing. New silvery-gray spots were popping up on every wall while glowing cracks traced over the brick like thunderbolts.

"It may be too late for that," she answered.

"You have to try," he pleaded.

"We all have to try," Braden shouted, louder than was needed. He angled his gaze up to the ceiling. "Do you hear that, universe? Open the tunnel! I'm ready to go!"

If the universe was listening, it didn't give any sign of it, but something—or rather someone—*was* trying to communicate. Amelia jolted at the buzz of her phone. Its sudden demand for attention was startling given she'd forgotten things like phones existed. She was even surprised it had a signal. She glanced at the screen. *Simon.* He was video calling her. Amelia answered but left her camera off. He didn't need to see any of this.

"Amelia?!" His face came into focus on her screen. His hair was messy and his eyes bloodshot. It looked like it had been years since he'd slept. "Are you there?"

The line was filled with static. She knew the connection wouldn't hold for long. "I'm here."

"What's going on?" he shouted. "I'm outside . . . library but can't get . . . crazy wind!"

"Simon, I'm so sorry. Things have gotten worse. The library . . ." How could she possibly explain what was happening? She was in the thick of the cosmic storm yet still had trouble believing it was real.

"Forget . . . library," he shouted. "Right now . . . care about . . . you!"

"I care about you too. And I am so sorry. I—"

"Really?" Amelia heard Braden's disembodied voice shouting at her before he manifested inches from her face. "Now?! You two are doing this now?"

Amelia met his glare full on. "Yes."

Braden threw his hands in the air. "Sure! Take your time! Talk it out!"

That's exactly what she was going to do, for as long as she could. "Simon, I'm coming to the door." Amelia ran down the stairs, holding her phone in view. She didn't want to lose sight of him now.

"I had . . . talk with Rosalinda," Simon yelled through static. "And I still don't know . . . ghosts, but . . . doesn't matter." His eyes darted over the screen. "Please. Just come outside."

Amelia peered out the front windows. She couldn't be sure, but she thought she could see his shadowy outline on the lawn. "Simon, you need to go. I don't want you to get hurt, and I can't make it to the door." It was true. The winds wouldn't let her past the circulation desk now.

"What . . . you mean?" he shouted. "Why? Turn your camera on."

"I can't. You don't want to see this. It's—"

"Amelia, please."

For once she did as he asked. They looked at each other for a moment through the glitching screen before she flipped the camera and moved her phone in a slow circle. The maelstrom's currents now had books, papers, and other miscellanea spinning around the inner walls while the cracks in the brick pulsated with otherworldly light. Simon grunted as though he'd been punched. "You have to get out of there. Come to the front door. I'll get . . . somehow."

"Simon, listen to me," Amelia said, peering back into the phone. "I am so sorry to put you through any of this, but my only way out now is if I can help the people trapped inside."

"I found something . . . help." He pulled the camera from his face. "I'm texting you . . . picture. Just—"

Suddenly, the screen froze, then went dark. "Simon?"

He was gone.

Amelia stared blankly at her phone, cold winds rushing around her.

"What happened?" Braden appeared at her side. "Did I hear that right? Did he say he found something?"

Amelia shook her head and poked at her phone, trying to get Simon back, but every attempt failed before she could get a connection. "He said he was texting me a picture, but I think the storm is killing the signal."

"Well, that's great! Just great!" Braden shadowboxed with the sky before shouting, "Now what are we going to do? It's game over, man! Game—"

Braden cut himself off when the *ping* sounded in Amelia's hand. Startled, she fumbled her phone, dropping it to the floor. When she bent to retrieve it, it slid away from her fingers.

"It's the vortex!" Braden shouted. "It's sucking it into the portal!"

Amelia dove across the floor, sliding on her stomach to grab the phone. Braden slid in beside her as she scrambled to pick it up. A second later she opened the text.

It was impossible to say what she was expecting to see, but . . . it wasn't this.

"What is that?" Braden asked. "Some kind of sick joke?"

Amelia studied the picture more closely, then zoomed in. She shook her head. Oh no, it wasn't a joke. Not at all. Simon had done what Amelia had come to believe was impossible. That great big, beautiful, brilliant librarian had found the unknown piece of information she had been searching for but hadn't been able to find.

The one thing that could change everything.

36

The butterfly counts not months
but moments, and has time enough.
—Rabindranath Tagore, "On Time"

GETTING BACK UP THE STAIRS WAS AN EVEN GREATER battle than retrieving the newspaper had been. The winds were closing in on them, and while it was still safe within the eye of the vortex, that inner space was shrinking rapidly. The professor met her when she reached the second floor, looking utterly heartbroken to see her still in the library. "What happened?" he shouted. "Did you try to escape?"

Amelia shook her head. She wanted to explain, but there was no time. "Where's Minnie? Has she come back?"

The professor looked over to the nearest bookshelf, and the spirit tentatively floated out from the stacks, wisps of her form stripping away in the wind. She glanced up at Amelia with anguish and guilt pooling in her eyes.

"Minnie, I know it isn't fair to ask this of you, but can I show you one last thing?" Amelia shouted as gently as she could. The winds were so incredibly loud now. "Just one more photograph. It has to do with your father."

The ghost turned her bonneted head, shielding her expression.

"I know it's hard, but . . . please."

An agonizing moment passed, but then the ghost struggled toward her. It had to be taking most of her energy just to manifest in the cosmic storm. Amelia held out her phone.

The picture glowed dully in the unnatural light, and Minnie frowned as she took in the image of the gravestone.

CHARLOTTE WINIFRED ARSENAULT
1898–1918
BELOVED DAUGHTER

The ghost's eyes were glued to the screen, but her expression was stone.

"I know you blame yourself," Amelia yelled, "but your father had this made for you. He survived the fire, and he knew, Minnie. It was clear it was you who knocked over the lantern. But . . ." Amelia pointed to the words *beloved daughter.* "That's how he wanted you remembered."

Minnie briefly met Amelia's eyes, then snapped her gaze back to the photo, studying it as though it might disappear.

"You have been punishing yourself all these years for what happened, but I don't believe it's what your family would want."

Indecision weighed heavily in the ghost's eyes.

"If the situation were different, if one of your siblings had accidently caused the fire, would you want them to punish themselves the way you have?" Amelia asked. "Would you want them to feel what you've felt all these many years?"

Pain flashed in Minnie's eyes. She stroked the image of her tombstone lightly with her fingertips then returned her hand to her chest. Amelia was afraid that she might once again say *Minnie bad,* but instead, she looked up and smiled. It was a fragile, scared-looking thing, but very real. "Beloved?"

Amelia nodded quickly, and before she could say anything more, the spirit whispered in her dry, creaking voice, "Charlotte . . . go now."

The instant the words passed her lips, an explosion of golden light blasted through the library, forcing Amelia to shield her eyes against its sudden brilliance. Blinking, she turned, searching for the source.

A swirling ball hovered beneath the chandelier in the middle of the library, throbbing like a golden heart.

"You did it!" Braden screamed. "Minnie! You opened the passageway!" Suddenly he jumped over the mezzanine railing, flailing his arms and legs in the air as though swimming until he reached the glittering orb-shaped tunnel. Without a moment's hesitation, he stuck his hand inside the small opening. "It feels like a hot tub full of sparkles!"

A wave of pure joy swept Amelia through, but it didn't last long. As beautiful as the light was, there was something wrong with it. Its energy was faltering. One second the hollow sphere was as brilliant as the sun, but the next it would quaver and dim, like it might blink out.

"Keep going, Minnie!" Braden shouted. "Make it bigger!"

The ghost shook her head helplessly.

"It's not big enough!" He shoved his arm in up to his shoulder and grunted. "I swear to you, universe. No more issues. Just let me in. This boy is ready to dip."

Instead of heeding Braden's plea, the swirling circular entranceway grew smaller, and he jerked his arm out.

Amelia had been afraid of this. "It's not you," she shouted, her voice cracking with the effort. "The book said this might happen. The storm is too strong. You two don't have enough strength to open it by yourselves."

"What about the three of us?" They turned to look at the professor, standing by his chair. He appeared terribly grim but also resolved.

"No way, man," Braden screamed. "You can't. Your thing hasn't happened yet!"

Another earsplitting explosion rocked the library.

"I will not let your energy be destroyed," the professor yelled back, his white hair swirling with the wind. "Whatever it is keeping me here, it wouldn't want me to stay. Not like this." He sounded determined, but when he glanced back at his chair, his expression was one of pure devastation.

His words must have meant something to the universe, though, because a bright flash jerked Amelia's gaze back over to the swirling golden light. It was growing, enough for Braden to stick his head in. "Guys, you got to see this! It's amazing!" The sphere then shrank again around his shoulders, and he popped back out. "No!" Braden looked at her. "Amelia! What do we do?"

He was asking her.

He expected her to know what to do. They all did.

Amelia gripped her hands together, unable to move, unable to speak. The book had warned her that even if the three were ready to go, it still might not be enough, and that left only one other option. One that made Amelia sick to think about because it really did mean everything was up to her. She had to try, but—

Suddenly, through the roaring winds, Amelia heard something impossible, so impossible it pushed all other thoughts aside.

A voice.

It was faint in the howling maelstrom, and yet there was no mistaking it.

"Yoo-hoo!"

A peculiar look came to the professor's face, and he stepped toward his chair.

"Um, guys?" Braden shouted, peering down at the first floor from where he was hovering by the chandelier. "Someone's here."

"Hello?" the voice called out again.

No, please . . .

The familiar tone and tenor triggered all the warm feelings it normally did, but underneath, dismay was taking hold of Amelia's heart. She fought her way to the railing of the mezzanine, telling herself she was wrong. Mistaken. There was no way she could be hearing what she thought she was hearing. Again, it was impossible . . .

She gripped the smooth wood of the banister and looked down.

. . . unless Rosalinda was a ghost.

37

Death cannot stop true love.
All it can do is delay it for a while.
—William Goldman, *The Princess Bride*

THE COSMIC WINDS RAGED AT AMELIA AS SHE FORCED her way down the stairs, ignoring the questions of the ghosts calling after her. When she reached the bottom, Rosalinda, wearing her wrap sweater and fall-themed hat, turned and greeted her with a smile. She had never looked more beautiful with her new ethereal glow. Not even death could take away the twinkle in her eye.

"There you are," she said. "Somehow I knew I'd find you here."

"No," Amelia snapped. "Absolutely not." She realized she sounded like a child but couldn't seem to stop herself from saying the words. "I refuse to accept this."

"I know it's hard," Rosalinda said gently, "but—"

"Did you know this was going to happen? All the times you couldn't come in? Or wanted to go home early? Were those all lies?" Now was not the time for accusations, but somehow it felt safer to be angry than to let in the pain this would ultimately bring. "Why didn't you tell me?"

Rosalinda gave her a gentle smile. "I was being very selfish, I'm afraid. I wanted us to get to know each other without my dying getting in the way."

Amelia's shoulders dropped, and in the blink of an eye, Rosalinda vanished, then reappeared in front of her. "Oh," she said with a wobbly laugh. "Would you look at what I can do?"

Amelia would have smiled, but she didn't think she'd ever be able to remember how.

Rosalinda reached out and touched her cheek. "I am so sorry. This is the hardest part about dying. Hurting the ones you leave behind." She suddenly looked both serious and sad. "I want you to know, he stayed with me until the very end."

Simon.

Amelia looked to the front windows, but there was no seeing through the storm anymore.

For a moment, Rosalinda's features contracted with pain, letting some of her own devastation show, but she caught herself quickly and forced a smile. "He's been so worried about, well, *everything* these past few weeks, but I tried to tell him you had everything under control. At least when it came to the library, that is."

A laugh that sounded a lot like a cry escaped Amelia's lips. She then threw up her hands at the unearthly nightmare unfolding around them.

Rosalinda glanced about. "This poor old place has been put through something else, hasn't it?" Her gaze settled on Amelia. "And you've been working so hard to make things better, haven't you?"

"I've been trying," Amelia stammered, "but as you can see, I haven't been doing a very good job."

"I don't know," she replied with a considering nod. "It's still standing." Rosalinda then inhaled deeply, and let go of a contented sigh. "I always hoped I'd come back here before moving on."

"Um, guys?" Braden shouted, hovering twenty feet above them. "I hate to interrupt, but this ball thingy is getting smaller again." He looked at Rosalinda. "You don't have any unfinished business, do you? Because that could be a problem."

Rosalinda smiled. "No. No unfinished business. Except—"

"Except?!" Braden groaned and threw his head back. "Every time I think we're not going to die, it always turns out we're going to die!"

"It's more of a hope I've been holding on to." Rosalinda touched a sparkling piece of jewelry pinned to her sweater, its glittering edges visible around her fingertips.

"Your brooch," Amelia said. "You found it."

Rosalinda nodded, then dropped her hand.

The jeweled pin was an exquisite gold filigree piece in the shape of a . . . *butterfly*.

"Who . . ." Amelia struggled against the sudden tightness in her throat. "Who gave that to you?"

"Albie, my first and only love," she said sweetly. "We never did get around to talking about him, did we? That's my fault. It still hurts. Even after all these years." Rosalinda glanced down at the bit of jewelry. "Back when we were dating, he would come here once he was through with his patients and wait for me to finish my shift. I suppose a part of me hoped he might be waiting for me now."

"Patients?" Amelia whispered, a knot of tangled questions unraveling in her mind.

"Oh yes, Albie was a brilliant doctor. Young, but so far ahead of his time in compassion and empathy." Rosalinda's eyes suddenly widened. "What's wrong, dear? What is it?" A smirk touched the corner of her mouth. "You look like you've seen a ghost."

Amelia shook her head, pushing the question away. "He, Albie, was a psychiatrist, wasn't he?"

"How did you know?"

Because now it was the only profession that made any sense. How could she not have seen it before? Colossal emotions warred in Amelia's chest, crowding out the ability for her to breathe, for her heart to beat. "But . . . you said it didn't work out."

"It didn't." The older woman pinched her lips together and shook her head grimly. "He died."

"Rosalinda!"

"I'm sorry I didn't tell you that either." She grimaced sweetly and twisted her fingers together. "Again, I wanted you to get to know me without all the sorrow. I consider myself to be a lot of fun, you know."

Amelia nodded tightly, ignoring the sting in her eyes. "The most fun." She took a moment to collect herself before asking, "Did he die in a car accident?"

"Of sorts. We were walking across an intersection when the car hit us. The driver had spilled his coffee. Took his eyes from the road." Rosalinda looked away and her body trembled. "My knee was shattered, but Albie hit his head. The doctors said even if he did regain consciousness, he wouldn't be able to function. Or remember anything. Not even me."

They were right. He hadn't been able to remember.

"I stayed with him round the clock, talking to him, reading, hoping he might wake up, but it wasn't meant to be," she said, finishing with a long sigh. "And now, well, he's not here either, so I suppose that also wasn't meant to be."

"No, you're wrong. I mean it is. I mean . . ." Amelia looked up to the second floor. "He's waiting for you, Rosalinda. He's been waiting for you all this time."

Before Amelia had the chance to explain any further, the ghost was gone. She reappeared a second later a quarter of the way up the steps, then in a blink, halfway. Up the staircase she went, battling the winds to keep her form together. Amelia struggled after her. When she reached the second floor, Rosalinda was already at the professor's chair. He'd gone back to it to sit, to wait, just like he had always done. Rosalinda placed her hands on either side of the wingback, then leaned to peek around. The professor shot up, whirling about so quickly, his form blurred. Confusion dropped to raw emotion as he took her in. Slowly, he reached his hand out, and she grasped it in her own, bringing it to her chest.

"Rosalinda," he said, voice breaking. "It's you."

"I'm surprised you recognized me. I've gotten so old." A surprised laugh escaped her. "But so have you." She freed up a hand to stroke his white tufts of hair. "I didn't know ghosts could age, but then again, you always said you wanted us to grow old together."

Ghostly tears sparkled in the professor's eyes. "I did, didn't I?" He glanced down at the brooch pinned to her coat. His eyes widened briefly, and he gave Amelia a smile before turning back to Rosalinda, cupping her cheek with his free hand. "How could I have forgotten?"

"What do you mean? You didn't forget," she said. "You're here."

He laughed. "I know, but I didn't know why. I just knew I couldn't leave."

"You've waited for me all this time, not knowing?" Distress strained Rosalinda's voice. "That must have been—"

"I have been perfectly happy waiting right here." A look of amazement spread across his face. "For you. You are my reason why."

"Hey!" Braden shouted. "Sorry, professor, but we got a problem." Amelia tore her gaze from the reunited pair over to Braden, who was pointing at the passageway. It was barely the size of a baseball now.

They were almost out of time.

There was only one more thing left to do. Amelia just wished it didn't feel like she would fail before she had even begun. "There may be another way to open it," she shouted. Braden looked back at her, confused. "Or open it more. I may be able to open it more." Amelia could feel them all looking at her now. Given how many lies she had told over the past weeks, she wouldn't have thought confessing to one more omitted bit of information would be all that difficult, but it was.

The ghosts exchanged looks before Minnie whispered, "*Seeeecrets.*"

"What did you do now?!" Braden shouted.

"I didn't do anything!" The winds swirled and howled in the awkward silence that followed. "The handbook said this might happen, and if it did, I might be able to help."

"You can open the tunnel?" Braden yelled.

"No, I can't open the tunnel, but I might be able to help it grow. In theory."

"But you're not even dead yet!"

Amelia really could have done without that *yet.* "No, but I am a ghostseer. For the most part. I guess we're about to find out how much of one."

Braden's eyes bugged. "Why didn't you tell us this before?!"

The professor and Rosalinda moved to stand side by side, wrapping their arms together.

"I only just found out." Amelia threw her hands up. "The book said it's a natural ability, but I don't know what that means. I didn't want to get your hopes up."

"Do it!" Braden shouted, jumping all the way from the small tunnel to being within inches of her face. "Do it right now."

She shook her head and backed up a little. "Did you not hear everything I just told you?"

"But you're ready now," he said. "We've grown. You've grown. So, just do it. Like the commercial says."

"Commercial?"

"Nike?!" he yelled. "I am not that old!"

Amelia held up her hands. "I'll try." She closed her eyes, which didn't really help that much. Or at all. She then tried to channel her natural abilities, but absolutely nothing about this felt natural. "Anything?"

"No!" Braden shouted. "Try harder!"

"Braden," the professor chided. "I'm not sure that's helping."

Amelia redoubled her efforts. *Open.Open.Open.* "Now?"

"No," Braden moaned. "If anything, it's smaller."

Amelia snapped her eyes open. It was smaller. In fact, it was almost gone. "See? I don't know how to do it."

"Do you still have the book?" the professor called out against the winds. "Maybe you could read us the passage, and we can see if there's something you missed."

They quite literally had nothing left to lose. Amelia raced over to the chair and reached for *The Ghostseer's Handbook* from where she had stuffed it down beside the cushion. As she did, a floorboard cracked ominously beneath her feet. Thankfully, though, for once the book was right where she had left it. She wrenched it out. "So, again, it explains how the vortex becomes a maelstrom," she spluttered, wrestling with the book's pages, "and then how every ghost within the dwelling must resolve their earthly issues in order to stop it."

"Check," Braden said. "Done. Get to the you part!"

Amelia slapped the book open with her palm when she got to the passage she needed. "It talks about the ghosts having to move on and . . . here! 'If this does not occur,'" she read through her tangled masses of hair, "'and the maelstrom reaches its full power, even the combined intention of the spirits will not be enough to fully open the passageway to the other side and restore balance. There is only one theorized way to do so. The ghostseer, armed with the pure intention of guiding the spirits onward in their journey, must channel the power of the genuine, unique connections formed with each one and . . .'" She slowed her words as a new realization formed in her mind. "'. . . and use the power of those combined connections to help grow the passageway to the other side.'" Amelia closed the book and clutched it to her chest.

She hadn't seen it before, or perhaps she just hadn't realized the significance of the passage, but suddenly she knew exactly what was wrong.

"So, if I understand," the professor shouted, "you can channel our combined intentions to move on and focus that power to help the passageway grow?"

"Yes," she whispered. It sounded so simple. Unfortunately, it was anything but.

The ghosts looked at one another, seemingly confused by her reaction, before the professor continued. "Amelia, what's wrong? You have already done what the passage has suggested. You have formed genuine connections with each of us."

She nodded; then she shook her head again. "But I didn't do the other part."

"What other part?" Braden asked.

"My intention . . ." A deep, almost painful blush came to her cheeks. "My intention isn't pure."

"What?!" Braden looked ready to tear his hair out. "I don't understand. Are you telling me you want to get buried under a building?"

"Of course not," she snapped.

"Then what?"

"The problem is . . ." Amelia paused, clutching the book even tighter. "My intention to help you get to the other side isn't pure . . . because I don't want you to go."

Minnie, the professor, and Rosalinda didn't react beyond exchanging looks, but Braden's jaw dropped to the point of ridiculousness.

"I know. I know! This was not something I ever expected to happen," Amelia yelled. "If you recall, when I first arrived at this library, I wanted nothing more than for all of you to move on. I never wanted to speak to any of you, let alone . . ." Amelia gritted her teeth. "Let alone come to care. But I have." She looked around at them. "And now, how am I supposed to happily send you on your way, knowing what it means?"

Braden gave her a sideways look. "What does it mean?"

"It means . . ." Amelia blinked against the sting in her eyes. "You'll leave and I'll be alone."

Winds swirled and raged around them. Nobody spoke or moved until Braden finally said, "Dude, that is really sweet, but GET OVER IT!"

Minnie put a hand on his shoulder, her glowing blue eyes sad.

"Believe me, I don't want this," Amelia shouted. "Not at all. I never wanted to be a ghostseer, and never in a hundred thousand years did I believe we'd end up friends."

"A hundred thousand? Really?" Braden popped his eyebrows. "Wow."

"But here we are. And I don't want you to go. How do I purify that?"

"I don't think you can." The professor glanced down at Rosalinda, worry etched into the lines of his ghostly face. "Love doesn't work that way."

Braden looked like he was about to start yelling again, but then his shoulders dropped. "I mean, I'd probably feel the same. I do feel the same. I don't want to say goodbye. Everything's just been happening so fast, but . . . I'll miss you." He looked from Amelia to the professor. "You too, man." He then glanced over to Minnie. "I guess we'll never know what could have been." Her blue eyes bulged more than they ever had before.

The struggling golden sphere blinked and quavered against the onslaught of the maelstrom. It was so small now. Any second it would blink out.

Amelia closed her eyes. This couldn't be happening. The entire situation was ludicrously unfair. The book made it seem as though it was the most natural thing in the world to form unique, genuine connections with ghosts and then not be bothered in the slightest by losing them. If she survived this night, she would use all her powers as a librarian to track down the author of *The Ghostseer's Handbook*, or any living descendants that author might have, and she would—well, likely she'd do little more than write a sternly worded letter, but it would be incredibly stern! And she was not a terrible person! Yes, she selfishly didn't want the ghosts to go, but she knew that Minnie deserved to be reunited with her family. And she wanted that more. She also knew that if there was a way Braden could greet his parents on the other side, then she very much wanted that for him. And the professor, Rosalinda, the idea of them being reunited, just to be torn away again? Never. She would always choose their happiness. A hot rush of indignation raced through her veins. What power of the universe could possibly have come up with this ridiculous rule? It was infuriating!

"Amelia?" the professor prodded gently.

"No!" She snapped open her eyes, making him jerk back. "I will find a way to get you to the other side. Even if I have to rip the universe apart with my bare hands, I will find a way!"

Braden opened his mouth, but Amelia cut him off before he could speak. "And don't tell me it's okay or that I've done my best, because I assure you I am just getting started."

Rosalinda clapped her hands excitedly. "You could do it too. Rip the universe apart. I know you could."

Again, she loved how Rosalinda was always so ready to get on board.

"Okay, go team," Braden said. "But—"

"No, you thought I was a scary librarian before. Well, let me assure you—"

"Amelia!" Minnie shouted. "Look!"

Shock at hearing the ghost call her by name crushed Amelia's tirade. She blinked then realized Minnie was pointing at something. Amelia followed her translucent outstretched finger back into the center of the library.

Braden huffed a laugh. "Booyah."

38

"We'll be friends forever, won't we,
Pooh?" "Even longer," said Pooh.
—A. A. Milne, *The House at Pooh Corner*

THE PATCH ON THE OPPOSITE WING HADN'T SHRUNK in size, nor had it stopped emitting its unnerving light, but the golden glow from the passageway—now huge and stable in its form—seemed to create a bubble around them, shielding them from the wind and wrapping them up in warmth, reassurance, and love. It didn't give any indication of what might be waiting on the other side, if anything at all, but it emitted a deep sense of calm and surety and rightness. Everything small fell away, and they were left with the wondrousness of existence.

"I think you solved your intention problems, Amelia," the professor murmured.

"Clarified, not purified," she whispered. "That was the key. Word choice is important." If she ever did find the author of *The Ghostseer's Handbook*, she'd be sure to suggest a rewrite.

"I don't know what you guys are talking about, but . . ." Braden drifted back through the railings to hover in front of the brilliant circle of light now filling almost all the open air at the library's core. "I didn't know it would be like this." He seemed unable to pull his gaze from the tunnel beaming around him like he was floating in front of the sun. "I feel like I could stay here forever just taking it in, but . . ." He turned to face them. "That's not how this works, is it?"

Amelia gripped her hands together. No, it wasn't.

Minnie came to her side and slipped her arm around hers. The ghost's touch was cold and nowhere near as substantial as Braden's, but it was very real. The professor and Rosalinda then came to her other side.

"We couldn't have done this without you," Braden said, floating to join them. "You know that, right? You did this."

They all moved to envelop her in a hug, but Amelia flapped her hands in the air, inadvertently swiping into a few of their forms. "Stop. No. This next part is going to be exceedingly difficult, and I'd like to do it without weeping." Yes, Minnie had gotten a tear out of her earlier, but that was far too risky now.

"Amelia," the professor said gently, "crying is a perfectly natural—"

"Without weeping!"

Braden cleared his throat. "Don't take it personal, professor. She's super uncomfortable with crying. Calls other people out for it too."

Amelia cut him a look, then swallowed hard. "What I mean to say is, you are all very important to me, so I would like to give you each a proper goodbye in the time we have left." She suspected there would be plenty of time for weeping later. "And to do that I need to keep my composure."

Just then the building shuddered and let out another series of cracks. The golden light of the portal dimmed momentarily, then surged, almost like the beginning of a power outage.

Rosalinda and the professor floated out in front of the group clasping hands, silently volunteering to go first. "I hope you don't mind if I do a little weeping," Rosalinda said, dabbing her eyes with the corner of a shimmering tissue.

Of course she didn't. Rosalinda was a lovely, dainty weeper, something others, such as herself, could only aspire to be.

Amelia took a steadying breath. She wasn't entirely sure how to do this, but speaking the truth seemed like an appropriate place to start. "Rosalinda, despite you keeping your impending death from me, I am beyond grateful for the time we were able to spend with one another. Afternoon teatime—" Amelia's voice caught. Her traitorous vocal cords had a mind of their own. "Afternoon teatime with you has been the most rewarding ritual of my life. You have shown me what it is to be welcomed into another's company and to be nurtured. Perhaps that is something people take for granted, but I couldn't be more grateful. In you I have found a bosom friend . . . a kindred spirit that . . ." Amelia looked to the floor, unable to continue.

Rosalinda floated in close and lightly touched her cheek. The sensation was that of sparkling butterfly kisses. "Oh my sweet girl, how lucky am I to have had you in my life?"

The professor floated in close to join her. "I want you to know, Amelia, that not only have you turned out to be a wonderful ghost-seer, but you've always been a magnificent human being. I am very—"

Amelia jutted up her hand. "Please, professor, not again. I am tiptoeing on a high wire of emotion here and—"

"Proud of you," he finished. "I'm sorry. I had to say it."

Amelia's eyes filled with tears, but she refused to let them fall. There were things she still had to say. "Professor, no one has ever worked so hard to see me, and you did that when I didn't want to see you at all. Your advice and guidance have been invaluable to me, but it's the—" Again, she was losing her words to sentiment! All these feelings were infuriating. She gripped her hands together more tightly. "It is the kindness you have shown me that I will always carry."

The professor gave her a beaming smile and wiped a tear from the corner of his eye. "Thank you, Amelia. Very much." He then looked around the group. "I'm not sure how to express what you all mean to me. I wish we had more time." He gave Minnie and Braden hugs, and when they embraced, their glowing auras beamed brighter, but then the library shuddered again, sending more plaster raining down.

The professor gave them each one last smile, then turned back to Rosalinda. In a sparkling wave he manifested as a young man wearing a black suit. "May I escort you to the dance?" He bowed slightly and offered her his arm.

Rosalinda's eyes twinkled, and in a matching ripple, a shimmering party dress fell over her younger form as her hair unraveled into long waves. "I'd be honored." She wrapped her arm through his and together they glided, floating on air, right into the passageway. A brief flash of golden light enveloped them, and they were gone.

Gone.

"Well, they made that look easy, didn't they?"

Amelia looked over to Braden. Despite his flippant tone, he looked nervous bouncing on the balls of his feet, which weren't even connected to the floor. The same could not be said of Minnie though. She was staring rapt into the passageway, her eyes filled with longing.

"Minnie?" Amelia said.

The ghost dragged her gaze from the brilliant opening.

"I hope you are able to be with your family again."

She smiled, but it dropped as she looked down at what she was wearing. A sudden swirling current of air formed were she stood, climbing quickly from her tiny laced boots all the way up to her bonneted head, lifting the soot she had been carrying with her since death. The dark particles floated up and away, disappearing into the ether and leaving behind a cream dress with a simple pattern of blue flowers that picked up the color of her truly beautiful eyes.

"Damn, girl," Braden whispered. "You are one hottie pioneer."

Minnie smiled shyly before floating in closer to where they stood.

"I would like you to know that I will never forget you," Amelia said. "Every time I read Jane Austen, I'll—" *Again!* There was so much she wanted to say, but her emotions kept choking her up. It was probably best to stick to the key points, lest she get nothing out at all. "What I want to say is, it has been my honor to know you."

"Goodbye . . ." The rasp had left Minnie's voice, and the word had a lovely full sound. "Friend."

Friend. Well, that was even lovelier. Amelia felt the creases of her eyelids dampen.

The spirit then floated toward the spiraling golden light but jerked to a stop when Braden shouted, "Yo, don't you be going in there without me. I need someone to hold my hand." As soon as the words left his mouth, he jolted. "I mean, obviously, you don't have to wait for me, or hold my hand, but if you wanted to, I'd want that too, so . . . yeah, just putting it out there." He glanced at Amelia and gave her a double thumbs-up.

Minnie looked to the portal but then nodded.

"Cool. Wait right there." Braden shook out his limbs, then tilted his head side to side like he was preparing for a race. "Okay, so I'm ready for my speech. Let me guess. Just like the Scarecrow, you're going to miss me most of all."

Amelia arched an eyebrow. "Are you referring to *The Wizard of Oz*?"

"You do watch movies!"

"It was originally a book."

He chuckled. "Of course it was." He sighed, then cocked his head, peering up at her from beneath his brow. "I gotta ask. You going to be okay?"

"What do you mean? I'll be fine. The library's standing. I don't know if Simon will let me keep my job, but—"

"That's not what I meant." He captured her gaze. "I mean losing us."

Amelia sniffed sharply and shook her head.

"You know you can't live alone on librarian island for the rest of your life, right? You have to let people in. Like, *breathing* people."

While librarian island did sound appealing, she supposed there was some truth to his words. "I will try. And thank you, Braden. For everything." She wanted to say more, but before she could form the words, her face crumpled in what she was sure was a most unattractive expression.

"It's okay, friend," he said, squeezing her elbow. "I know."

Amelia pressed her fingers to her lips and nodded.

"Now that's enough speeches. We'll all be weeping soon." A smirk touched the corner of his mouth as he floated toward the portal. "You know, I meant it when I said I'll miss you."

She fought to give him a smile.

"But we'll find each other again. You can count on it." He pounded the side of his fist on his chest, right above his heart, then pointed at her. "Amelia."

The golden light from the passageway pulsed as Braden swung his hand over to Minnie. "Let's bounce."

The two clasped hands and entered the tunnel. Another brilliant flash of light erupted through the library, but this time the explosion was so powerful it tore through the force of the maelstrom, disrupting the flow and killing the winds. Blinded by the powerful glare, Amelia squeezed her eyes shut as all the books and furniture crashed to the floor. When she blinked her eyes open again, she was greeted with darkness. The passageway to the other side was gone, along with the glowing cracks running over the walls and the patch on the east wall that had been haunting them for weeks.

Them. There was no *them* anymore.

Amelia had always thought she understood loneliness better than most people, but she had only ever been lonely for things she had never known. Now, for the first time in her life, she was lonely for what she had lost. It was its own terrible pain, like she was being hollowed out of all that she had unknowingly come to rely on to make her whole.

Sickening panic fluttered in her chest. She couldn't go back to the life she had led before. She couldn't bear it. Except—

The sound of pounding footfalls spun Amelia on her heel to face the landing of the staircase.

Simon.

"Amelia?" Gripping the newel-post, he searched the gloom. When he found her, his shoulders sagged. He walked a few steps, then jogged to close the distance between them before looking around at the devastation wreaked on the second floor. "Is it over? Are they . . . ?"

"Gone. It's over."

He nodded.

"The photo you sent," she murmured, "it made all the difference. I know taking me at my word must have been difficult. I don't know how to thank you."

"Please don't." He inhaled a choppy breath. "That was Rosalinda. I told her everything before . . ." He trailed off, unable to finish. Amelia knew of course what he was trying to say, and it killed her to see him struggle. "I want you to know I told her everything. I told her about you being here and what you'd said about what was happening." His eyes filled with guilt. "I'm sorry if . . ."

"No, it's fine," she answered gently.

"I also told her I wasn't sure I could believe in ghosts, and do you know what she said to me?"

Amelia shook her head.

"She said, forget about believing in ghosts, Simon. Do you believe in her?" He laughed sadly and dropped his gaze to the floor.

Amelia touched his arm. "I never expected you to simply believe everything I told you."

"But I do." He looked up to meet her eyes. "Rosalinda was right. From the very beginning she was right. I believe you, Amelia."

"Don't," she said, stepping back. "You don't have to say that. So much has happened. I know you have questions. Take some time to—"

He reached out, fingertips grazing her wrist. "I believe you."

There would be time to go over those three words again and again, a million times, until they finally became part of her understanding of herself, of him, of what they might have together, but that would have to wait. Because right now, he was obviously trying to make things better for her, and as much as her own heart was breaking, his was breaking too. She also knew he was working himself up to tell her about Rosalinda, and if that was one thing she could spare him . . .

"Simon?"

He raised his brow wearily.

"I am so sorry about Rosalinda. She was the loveliest woman I have ever known."

Amelia watched the understanding light in his eyes. "She came here?"

She nodded.

Amelia didn't know what kind of response to expect, or what to say or do next, but when his breath hitched, without any thought at all, she wrapped her arms around his waist and laid her head on his chest, finally allowing her own tears to fall.

They held each other in the dim moonlight streaming through the windows of the second floor, and as terribly deep as the pain was, together, it was a little less lonely.

39

For auld lang syne, my dear, for auld lang syne,
We'll tak' a cup o' kindness yet, for auld lang syne.
—Robert Burns, "Auld Lang Syne"

SNOW FELL IN LARGE FLAKES, COVERING THE LIbrary's lawns in a soft white quilt. Amelia wrapped her arms over her chest, warming herself against the chill pressing up against the windows. It had been a beautiful, bright sunrise, filled with pink and orange clouds, but then the squall had moved in. As lovely as the snow was, Amelia hoped it would stop soon. Today was too important for the weather to interfere.

Simon came to her side and passed her a mug of coffee. She smiled up at him with thanks, and he nodded in return. They had many silent understandings between them now, quiet rhythms that seemed to sooth and comfort them both.

"We're ready, aren't we?" Amelia whispered, not wanting to disturb the cozy quiet of the morning.

"We're ready." Simon took a sip from his mug, watching the snow fall. "I'm glad we were able to make levees."

Amelia was too. It seemed fitting to reopen the library on New Year's Day, the island's day of traditional receptions. They had refreshments to serve and crafts planned for the kids, but more important than any of that, today was the day visitors could sign out books again. Amelia could almost feel the building thrumming with excitement.

They had worked nonstop over the last weeks to get the library ready to reopen, not that they were anywhere near finished. Once the engineering company had given the structure the all clear, they'd set to cleaning and doing the most necessary repairs. Much of the furniture had to be mended, along with several of the shelves, and they still hadn't replaced all the books, but acquiring new ones wasn't exactly a chore, and they had some funds to do it. Rosalinda had left Simon everything she owned, and while not a fortune, it was enough to help the library stay on its feet.

Plus, there was a new source of income. Amelia's rent. It turned out the library's attic was perfectly suitable for an apartment. The floorboards creaked and the beams were exposed, but it didn't smell like fish and there was a view of the sea, so really it was everything Amelia could have ever asked for. And even if she didn't end up using it as a place to sleep forever—if, say, she found another, less solitary location to lay her head—it would still make a lovely office. Virginia Woolf was right about the importance of having a room of one's own.

So much had changed in Amelia's life. Aside from the library filling her days, she had done the impossible and embraced her gift as a ghostseer. The rules were now a thing of the past, and she was making a point to engage with every ghost who crossed her path. She had discovered subtle techniques for interacting in public—eye contact, the occasional wink, and subtle hand gestures went a long way. Once she had removed the anxiety that had come with trying not to ever react, she found it much easier to act *normally*.

It didn't always go smoothly, some ghosts really were terrible, but overall, it was worth it. She had even said hello to the ghost lovers who walked the boardwalk. They had responded with as much shock as the sea captain, perhaps even more. Nobody said anything, but they all remembered the *pumpkin-haired fish wench* comment. As for the sea captain, well, Amelia hadn't been able to find out just yet what was holding him on the living plane, but she had every hope that one day they'd get there.

Then there was Simon.

They were taking things very slowly. He had suggested they get to know each other all over again, and now that they were starting from an honest place, well, it felt quite promising. It also became apparent that they did in fact have more shared interests than just books and tortoiseshell-rimmed glasses, although, really, those two commonalities might have been enough.

Given all that had happened, though, the days were still hard for them both, so every step they took forward was a small, careful one. Thanks to the professor, Amelia had learned a great deal about herself, and she'd realized there were things about her past that needed addressing. She was even starting therapy. Before, she never would have considered such a thing. She would have thought it too dangerous, but now she wondered how much of that was an excuse. After all, she was very experienced at holding back information.

Simon was supportive of the endeavor. So much so that Amelia was considering asking for his help tracking down information about her parents. One step at a time though. One step at a time.

Despite their caution, there was something so safe between them, a rightness of fit that couldn't be denied. Maybe it wasn't possible for Amelia to be happy on librarian island all by herself, but she was starting to believe she could be very happy on that island with Simon.

And just because they were moving slowly that didn't mean they weren't moving forward at all. They spent most of their days together working and their evenings playing games, going for walks, watching movies, and reading. They had even spent Christmas together. Simon taught her the basics of cooking a Christmas dinner and shared a lot of his childhood memories. After that, he surprised her with a rare edition of *A Christmas Carol*, and they read to each other by the fire in his basement apartment. When they got to Jacob Marley's haunting of Scrooge, Amelia couldn't help but smile.

As wonderful as Christmas had been, though, New Year's Eve was a letdown. They had been working so hard to get the library ready that they'd missed midnight completely. Amelia wondered if it had been a subconscious choice. They had both suffered tremendous losses in the past year.

"You're thinking about them, aren't you?" Simon asked, bringing her back to the morning.

Amelia nodded.

He gifted her with one of his beautiful side-creased dimpled smiles that never failed to take her breath away. "I was thinking, tonight, instead of playing games or reading, maybe we could tell stories."

Amelia gifted *him* with a frown. "Stories? What kind of stories? Personal stories?"

"Hear me out," he said, his smile deepening. "I'll tell you stories about Rosalinda, and you could tell me more about the professor, Braden, and Minnie. Or we could tell the whole story, starting at the beginning, from the first night you came to the library. The story of us."

Amelia blinked.

"All of us. We could call it *Amelia Bates Saves the Library*."

"That's a terrible title," she muttered.

Simon chuckled. "It was just a thought. I realize it might be hard, maybe too hard. It's just . . . it's a new year, and I don't want them to be forgotten."

Amelia reached over to squeeze his hand. "It's a lovely idea."

"You think so?"

She nodded. For once, she wasn't lying. She didn't want them to be forgotten either . . . and the dueling POVs could prove fascinating.

"So," he said, rocking on his feet, "is it time?"

Amelia nodded. "Let's open the door."

WITHIN THE FIRST hour, the library had filled with visitors. People wanted to see all that had been done to the building, of course, but mostly they wanted to pay their respects to Rosalinda. Amelia hadn't realized how much she'd missed having people in the library, or really, just people in general. As the day drew to a close, it felt like the entire village had passed through the doors, but there were still one or two people she was hoping to see.

"Amelia!" a voice squealed. "I'm so glad I made it before you closed!"

And there was one of them.

Amelia smiled at the young woman racing toward her with ruddy cheeks and a winter hat with a pom-pom on top. "Chelsea, hello. I'm glad you came in. Did you enjoy the rest of the Ice Planet series?"

"Did I enjoy it? Are you kidding me?" She whipped off her hat, and the static from the dry air sent her hair floating upward. "I devoured it, but now I don't know what to do with myself. Everything just seems so blah."

Amelia pinched her lips together and nodded. A classic book hangover. There was only one cure for that. "Never fear. I thought you'd possibly come in, so I put aside a couple of books you might like. They're on the hold shelf with your name on them."

"Yay! That's awesome. You're so good at . . ."

Chelsea's words trailed away as Amelia spotted a man coming through the foyer. A man wearing a plaid jacket and knit hat.

And there was number two.

A few people greeted him, but he gave only reticent nods in return.

"Hey, what happened? You okay?"

Amelia snapped her attention back to Chelsea. "Yes, certainly. I just saw . . ." My great white whale. "Never mind. I'm sorry, what were you saying?"

"I was asking if you were on social media?"

"Yes, I—yes." The truth was Amelia had joined several platforms. It was a ridiculous thing to do. She knew that. But that hadn't stopped her, and surprisingly, it wasn't as bad as she'd thought. Evidently, there were lots of other people in the world who loved libraries as much as she did. Or at least they claimed to. Some of them took good pictures.

"You have to start posting book recommendations," Chelsea continued. "I'd follow you."

Amelia tried to formulate an answer, but her attention was drawn back to the mystery section. Once again, Wayne was looking frustrated and uncomfortable . . . but Amelia was ready this time. "Chelsea, I am so sorry," she said, backing away, "but would you excuse me for just a moment? There is someone who needs my help."

"Sure, I'll go find the books," she said, "but before I forget, what's your handle?"

"I, oh . . ." This was a touch embarrassing. "It's scary underscore librarian exclamation mark." She then scurried off to the stacks on the opposite side of the room. On her way, she passed Simon, who mouthed the words *Good luck*. He knew all about her quest. Much like Rosalinda, he had been mildly concerned about her Ahab comparison, but, overall, he was supportive.

As Amelia approached the stacks, Wayne turned, noting her hurried approach with widened eyes. Before he could speak, Amelia said, "Come with me."

"Oh no, I'm all right. I just—"

"I said, come with me." Amelia waved a hand for him to follow her over to the circulation desk. Thankfully, he acquiesced without further protest. She wouldn't have wanted to get stern.

Once they arrived, Amelia folded her hands by her waist and began her carefully prepared speech. "Wayne, you don't know me, but my name is Amelia Bates, and I am one of the librarians here. I realize this is highly irregular, but I promise I will only take a moment of your time. You don't have to say anything at all, simply hear me out, and when I'm through, you will be free to go. I will never disturb you again." Of course he was free to go now, but Amelia didn't think that was something that needed to be pointed out. She also didn't think she needed to wait for him to answer. "So, it hasn't escaped my notice that you have visited the library several times over the past few months. I also noticed that on each of those visits you have spent your time in the mystery section, particularly focused on the Agatha Christie selections, if I'm not mistaken." It was obvious by where he always stood and by his slightly dipped sight line focused on the third shelf from the bottom. "And yet, despite these multiple visits, you have never signed out a single book. It made me think that you, or perhaps a loved one of yours, has read all the ones we have, but you were living in hope that some other unread selection would be returned and—"

"How did you know that?" he spluttered.

Amelia frowned. She thought she had just explained how she knew that.

"My wife, she loves Agatha Christie. There's two she really wants to read, but they're never here."

Aha! Now they were getting somewhere.

"At first, I thought someone had checked them out, but now I'm thinking you don't have them, though, so . . ." He shrugged.

"So that is when you speak to a librarian," she answered plainly. "I will get you those two titles, but in the meantime . . ." Amelia stepped to the side, revealing Cartwell loaded with a collection of mystery novels. "I have gathered some texts that might serve as adequate replacements."

Wayne blinked, still looking mildly alarmed, so Amelia persisted.

"On the top rack," she said, waving her hand out, "we have Dorothy L. Sayers, John Dickson Carr, and Ngaio Marsh. These are for mystery readers who enjoy the puzzle above all else. On the next shelf," she said, dropping her hand a level, "we have Elizabeth George and M. C. Beaton. These stories are crafted for readers who are most interested in the cozy village atmosphere. Now some may dismiss these books as fluff, but those people are fools." Amelia wagged her finger in the air. "There is absolutely no shame in choosing charm over brutality. In murder and in life. That being said, if you think your wife *would* prefer something darker, psychologically speaking, we have Ruth Rendell, Patricia Highsmith, and P. D. James." Amelia gestured to the books alongside the cozies. "P. D. James is a personal favorite of mine. I do appreciate her voice. Oh! And I almost forgot Anthony Horowitz. His modern Sherlock Holmes tales are very well received. Finally, it is possible your wife wants to stay strictly in the golden age, and if that is the case"—Amelia gestured to the lowest shelf—"Margery Allingham, Josephine Tey, and Georgette Heyer are all solid choices." She folded her hands back at her waist and eyed the selection, suddenly feeling a bit unsure. "Of course this is just the beginning. There are more modern authors. I could always . . ." She looked back at Wayne. ". . . find more."

The owner of the crab shack stood completely immobile, hat gripped in his hands. Sweat prickled Amelia's palms. She'd overwhelmed him. Gone too far. She'd meant to be helpful, but—

"How many can I take out?"

Amelia straightened. "Oh, well, our policy is ten, but there are exceptions."

"You see, my wife's been sick, been put on lots of bed rest. It's been real hard on her. She loves books, but reading gives her headaches now, so I was thinking maybe I could read to her to cheer her up. I wanted it to be a surprise, but then I get here and there's all these books." He shook his head. "I didn't want to pick the wrong one and remind her she couldn't come herself, so I'd always end up leaving. But something about this place kept drawing me back in. I'm still not sure what she's looking for, but—" He smiled at Amelia. "There has to be something here she'll like, right?"

Amelia looked back at the books. "Take as many as you like. Take them all."

He laughed. "I'm not sure I can get them all out to the truck."

"We'll use Cartwell," Amelia blurted, catching Simon smiling at her from the children's section. "I mean the cart. We'll take the cart. Just let me get my boots."

As she turned for the foyer, Wayne said, "Before you dart off, I wanted to say . . ." Two faint red patches colored his cheeks. "I'm sorry about Rosalinda. I always liked her."

Amelia smiled, breathing in the sudden swell of emotion. "Thank you."

"No, thank you for all this, eh?" Wayne glanced over at the cart. "Really, thank you."

Before Amelia answered, she suddenly remembered all the many lies she had told in this library. There were too many to count. Too many to remember, even. Knowing that was the case, it felt good to know her next words would be among the truest she'd ever spoken.

"I'm so happy I could help."

Acknowledgments

My deepest thanks to my agent, Natalie Lakosil, as always, for her expertise and unwavering support. To my editor, Mary Baker, I am so grateful for your sharp eye, kindness, and care for these characters and their world. Appreciation also to the Berkley team who helped bring this book into readers' hands, including Stephanie Felty, Elisha Katz, and Kim-Salina I. I greatly value your encouragement and dedicated work. Next, to Vikki Chu, cover artist and designer, vast praise for your beautiful work and for capturing the spirit of this story. And lastly, my eternal gratitude to my copyeditor, Alicia Lea, who was confronted with a quotation at the start of every chapter and ensured they were all, in fact, real. Which was fortunate, because a few were not.

To my husband and three kids, thank you for your patience, encouragement, and love. I couldn't do any of it without you.

Finally, to librarians everywhere, thank you for safeguarding stories, welcoming readers, and keeping magic alive. *The Haunted Librarian* was written with you in mind.

KEEP READING FOR AN EXCERPT
FROM AURALEE WALLACE'S

The Late-Night Witches

AVAILABLE NOW!

A MAN STAGGERED DOWN THE SIDEWALK, HIS FEET swallowed by a swirling blanket of sea fog. At times he veered dangerously toward the curb, but just before he would teeter over its edge, he'd lurch back to shamble over the damp grass of his neighbors' lawns. Each plodding step seemed destined to be his last, but he lumbered on, his unfocused eyes and sickly pale cheeks gleaming under the streetlamps, his jaw hanging loosely like a corpse's.

Cassie Beckett put down the yellow highlighter she had been using to mark up the family calendar as he approached. She tilted her chin to the black cat seated primly on the top edge of her wicker chair. "He doesn't look so good, does he?"

The cat didn't reply.

"Hey, Gary," she called out from the porch. "How's the training going?"

The man stopped his forward momentum but continued to step on the spot. He pulled up the pants of his gray sweatsuit and took a sip from his water bottle. "Made it two K yesterday."

Cassie smiled. "Nice."

"Is it okay if I leave this here?" He shook his bottle. "It's empty and I don't want it weighing me down."

"Be my guest."

Gary was training for a half-marathon. He claimed he ran at

night because of work, but that didn't make much sense given that he was an accountant. Cassie suspected he was embarrassed about the shape he was in, but he didn't have to be. Not with her. She admired him for trying something new.

"Thanks." He plunked the plastic container on her mailbox as an infant's cry pealed out from an open window down the street.

Cassie smiled and looked over to the house with the cranberry door, its brass knocker winking in the dark. Every neighborhood had its secret nightlife, and hers was no exception. As though on cue, a man with a baby strapped to his chest emerged from the house. The piercing cries faded away as he walked down his driveway with careful, bouncing steps. When he reached the street, he turned around and walked back toward the house, making sure to keep a steady rhythm.

"Poor guy." Gary pushed up the Rocky-inspired headband that had slipped down his forehead. "Rumor has it the baby is his sister's. She wasn't ready to be a mother, so he stepped up."

Not much stayed secret in the Burrow. The neighborhood wasn't much more than a street in an old suburb of Charlottetown, Prince Edward Island, and nobody could remember how it had gotten its name, but it was quaint with its old homes and tall trees, and Cassie couldn't imagine calling any other place home.

Their newest neighbor had only moved in a month or so ago, and Cassie hadn't had the chance to introduce herself. Granted, she hadn't gone out of her way to either. He was intimidatingly handsome. He had the glasses and bashful air of an English teacher or librarian, but the build of a quarterback. His hair was honey brown and always messy—that was probably because of the baby—but she hadn't seen his eyes up close. If she had to guess, they were hazel. She thought he might have a dimple too, but—all this was ridiculous because Cassie was technically married, even if it didn't feel too much like it these days.

Gary must have caught her look because he chuckled and said, "Yeah, he's a good-looking guy. You'd have to be dead not to notice."

Cassie smiled, hoping the darkness hid the burn coming to her cheeks. "What's his name again?"

"Ben. He's a history professor. Some sort of expert on island lore."

A history professor. She knew she'd been on the right track.

Gary cleared his throat and hiked his pants again. "Anyway, got to get back at it. The longer I stop, the harder it is to get going again."

That observation rang true for Cassie on many levels. "Good luck. And don't forget to take breaks."

He waved and pushed on.

Cassie scratched her cat's chin. "He'll be fine, right?"

She purred.

Janet was right. Gary was an adult. He could take care of himself. Besides, she had enough on her plate. Cassie looked down at the calendar on the old cast-iron coffee table. *Crap.* All of October was yellow. Every square had something. Doctor appointments. Dentist appointments. Hockey games. Basketball tryouts. It was never-ending. She scanned the to-do list running down the column at the side. She was also volunteering for two field trips, which meant she needed to trade shifts at work, and she had to get her daughter skates before her class started its weekly trip to the rink. *Oh God*, and the twins needed Halloween costumes! If only she could cut holes in sheets like moms used to do in the old days. Those women knew how to live.

The jack-o'-lantern sitting on the top step of the porch drew Cassie's eye. At least that was done, and she hadn't had to lift a finger.

It had been the strangest thing. The pumpkin had shown up that morning, its carved face peering into her front door. Someone had obviously spent time on it. Its triangle eyes—peaks pointed in—had been cut to a devilish angle, and its mouth with its two long fangs looked ready to tear through steel. There had obviously been some sort of mistake, but she had no clue what to do about it.

Cassie stared into the dark hollows of the jack-o'-lantern's eyes. While its sudden appearance was somewhat convenient, it was too creepy for her liking. It almost felt like it was challenging her.

"You want to go, Creepy?" she muttered, then looked back at her packed calendar. Who was she kidding? She didn't have time to duel with jack-o'-lanterns. Not with this schedule.

Cassie leaned back in her chair. Being out on the porch of her century-old home always brought her peace. The wood planks were wobbly, and the sage-green paint was peeling, but she had fixed it up with hanging plants, rugs, blankets, and lanterns, and over time it had become her favorite part of the house. It was the perfect spot to watch the moon rise and soak in the night air. Not that she'd have a whole lot of time for that this month. She put her feet on the table, pushing the calendar an inch or two away with the toe of her boot. It was fine. She could do this. As long as she didn't get sick or require more than six hours of sleep—something she didn't seem capable of anyway—it was fine.

Janet nuzzled Cassie's ear as she pulled her mug of herbal tea close to her chest, inhaling its sweet grassy scent. She'd been having some insomnia lately. Stress, probably. She did her best to keep everyone on track, but ever since her husband, Matt, had left for his second tour with Doctors Without Borders—leaving her with their fifteen-year-old daughter and eight-year-old twin boys—it always felt like she wasn't doing enough. Or doing it right. Or doing it the way everyone expected her to. Other moms made it look so easy. At least the ones on social media did.

But ongoing stress aside, something more was going on with her. She'd had this strange, tense feeling lately that there was something she was supposed to be doing. Something aside from all the other things she was supposed to be doing. It was like there was an undercurrent of electricity constantly pricking at her skin, prodding her to do . . . *something.*

It was probably the change in weather. Those first gusts of cold wind always made her restless.

Cassie shifted her tea to her other hand and dug her fingers into her jeans pocket as she watched the heavy fog swirl. She slipped out her coin, a relic from childhood, and flipped it mindlessly between her fingers, feeling the familiar grooves of the engraved sun and moon on either side.

The day had been brilliant and pleasantly cool. The kind of fall day that made a person want to walk around under a canopy of red and gold leaves, wearing a scarf and drinking pumpkin-spiced coffee. Not that Cassie had done any of that. She had spent the day at work discussing circular saws with chainsaw attachments and the intricate workings of septic bed treatments. But it was still nice getting in and out of the van. As soon as the sun had set, though, tendrils of cold mist reached in from the harbor, flooding the neighborhood in a gloomy haze. It had a strange murkiness to it. At times, instead of reflecting the light from the streetlamps, it swallowed it, darkening all it touched. And it moved in peculiar ways too. One minute she could see all the way down the street, but the next, the world beyond her front steps disappeared. For all she knew, someone could be in that cold mist right now staring at her. The thought sent an icy shiver up the skin on the back of her neck, even though she knew there was nothing in the fog. Janet would know if there were.

A low growl rumbled by her ear. Cassie jolted, spilling her tea. "What the heck, cat?" She said it quietly though. Janet did sometimes growl at absolutely nothing—or ghosts, she couldn't be sure—but there were other times when her feline friend picked up on real creatures going bump in the night. Cassie held her breath to listen and heard a grunt come from up the street. Her shoulders dropped. She knew that grunt. And she should have seen this coming.

It was Thursday. Karaoke night.

Cassie slipped her coin back into her pocket and swatted at the drops of tea on her cable-knit sweater, but her hand fell away when the willowy silhouette of a woman emerged from the fog. She was swaying, not unlike Gary, but that wasn't what had Cassie concerned. She was also dragging something. Its metal tip scraped noisily along the pavement.

A baseball bat.

Janet jumped down from the chair and up onto the porch railing in a fluid motion. She gathered herself up into a tight perched position. Cassie considered throwing her granny square afghan over her head, but it was too late. The woman had already spotted her. "Hey you!" she shouted as though it wasn't the middle of the night. "Just the person I wanted to see!"

Eliza, Cassie's sister and in most ways her first child, was stunning. Her hair was long, black, and straight—as opposed to Cassie's sandy waves that lived in a messy bun—and her eyes were large and dramatically dark. That being said, she looked a little rough tonight. The black tank dress wasn't too bad—it showed off her sister's slender arms and the bangles clustered at her wrists—but the work boots on her feet and the flannel shirt tied around her waist looked wrong. So did the scraped knee glaring angrily through her torn black tights.

"Go away," Cassie said tiredly. "I don't want what you're selling."

"Is that any way to welcome your sister home?"

Cassie pointed down the street. "You live that way."

Eliza ambled halfway up the lawn before suddenly pitching forward in giant, awkward steps. When she caught herself, she frowned at the football lying innocently in the grass, then kicked it over to the property next door. One of her oversize boots tumbled after it.

"No. Go get that. Mrs. MacDonald is going to flip out." Cassie didn't talk to her neighbor all that much, but when they did speak, it was almost always about property lines. Mrs. MacDonald was big on property lines. She probably didn't want the chaos of Cassie's life spilling into hers.

"No time for that," Eliza said. "You're going to want to hear about what I've been up to. I promise it has a happy ending."

Cassie did want to hear about what her sister had been up to—in the way she wanted to know about an outbreak of lice in the boys' classroom—but she also didn't want to encourage whatever this was. Besides, she didn't need to ask Eliza where she had been. She knew the answer to that. And she didn't have to ask her who she was with. Cassie knew that too. She certainly wasn't going to ask her sister how much she'd had to drink. She didn't want to know the answer to that. And she definitely wasn't going to ask her—

"Why do you have a bat?" *Frick.*

"Great question. Wait. Why are you out here at—" Eliza looked at her wrist, making her bracelets jangle. She didn't wear a watch. "Why are you out here?"

"Couldn't sleep." Cassie looked pointedly at the bat. "Now you."

Her sister groaned. "It's a long story."

"One you seemed eager to tell me a moment ago."

"Yeah." Eliza sighed. "But now that I've had time to think it over, I've realized I don't come out particularly well in it." She trailed off, distracted by the cat pinning her with a judgmental gaze. "You know what, Janet?" She challenged the cat with a glare, but couldn't finish the thought.

"Eliza. Focus."

"It was self-defense."

"Against?"

"A 2009 Ford F-150."

Cassie pressed her fingers against her eyelids. "No. Absolutely not. I want no part of this." Destruction of property was not on her calendar. "Wait, was it parked or moving?" What was wrong with her? Why was she still asking questions?

"Parked. Definitely parked. But . . ." Eliza trailed off again, her eyes tracking a late moth fluttering up to the streetlamp.

Cassie snapped her fingers in the air. "Okay, start from the beginning." She suspected she already knew the end.

"You want me to start from the beginning? I can tell you the whole story with one word." She struggled to untie the flannel shirt fixed around her waist, then threw it to the ground. "It was Tommy. The asshat."

"Hey!" Cassie shot a look up in the direction of her boys' window.

"Oh shit." Eliza slapped her hand over her mouth. "Sorry."

"You know what? Don't start from the beginning. Just tell me one thing. Tell me you did not commit a Carrie Underwood on his truck."

Eliza opened her mouth then shut it again before squinting and chewing her thumbnail. Cassie imagined she was mulling her strategy. A moment passed and Eliza flung her hand away. "Of course I committed a Carrie Underwood on his truck! Well, half an Underwood. Have you ever tried to beat up a truck? It's harder than it looks. I may have dislocated my shoulder."

Thoughts of damage, insurance, and possible legal action swirled through Cassie's mind.

"Do not give me that look," Eliza snapped. "You would have done the same thing."

That was incredibly doubtful.

"He cheated." She threw her hands wide. "Tommy cheated. Now you know." Eliza stamped on the flannel shirt on the wet grass, then kicked her remaining boot off into the hedge. It was clear who those belonged to.

Even though Cassie had known where the story was headed, it was still a shock. Or maybe just a disappointment. Tommy seemed like a nice guy. The best out of all the men Eliza had dated. Then again, they had only known each other for three and a half weeks. "Who was he with?"

"I don't know. She snuck out the back of the bar. Besides, does it really matter? I wasn't dating the rando chick. I was dating the lying, cheating ass—" She cut herself off and smiled. "Close one." She looked up at the boys' room and mimed turning a key over her lips. "Anyway, he was acting all confused like he didn't know what happened, so I left, and that's when I saw the bat just lying there in his truck bed. I mean . . ." She scoffed and held her hands out.

Cassie pinched her lips together and nodded. *What else could she have done?*

"Hey, you have a pumpkin," Eliza said, her voice instantly changing tone. "It's too early for a pumpkin. You're going to have a pumpkin puddle." She stumbled up to the jack-o'-lantern and grabbed the ropy stem, tossing the top off to the side. She reached in for the candle. “And have you met my nephews?” She climbed the steps and dropped the candle, wick down, into Cassie’s tea. “You’re welcome.” She blinked. “So, where was I?”

Cassie’s mouth opened, but all she could do was shake her head.

“Oh yeah, so after the truck, I may have taken a short forest nap behind the bar, and I think Tommy came out.” She winked and slumped against the porch railing. “See? Happy ending. Just like I told you.”

“How is that a happy ending?”

“Because he didn’t kill me! He couldn’t have missed what I did to his truck.”

Cassie rubbed her forehead.

“I know what you’re thinking—*Eliza screwed up again*—but I was really starting to like him, Cass.” Her voice cracked in a way that made Cassie’s own throat tighten. “He may not be the brightest bulb in the book, but he was super sweet and made me laugh, and sometimes he could be surprisingly deep, almost poetic.”

Brightest bulb in the book?

Cassie pushed herself to her feet. She knew she should send Eliza home. She had to stop cleaning up her messes, but tonight didn’t seem like the night. “Come on.” She held out an arm draped in the blanket. “Let’s go inside and get some sleep before the cops come looking for you.”

Eliza pushed herself off the railing. “Tommy wouldn’t call the cops.” Suddenly her eyes grew wide. “You don’t think he’d call the cops?” She ducked underneath Cassie’s outstretched arm.

“We’ll figure everything out tomorrow. You’re sleeping on the couch though.”

“The couch,” Eliza whined. “Your bed is much more comfortable. I promise I won’t steal the covers.”

She couldn't promise that. She always stole the covers. But Cassie was too tired to fight. Besides, it did remind her of when they were young, and Eliza would climb into her bed after a bad dream. They only had each other back in those days.

Cassie ushered Eliza to the door, calling out, "Come on, Janet." She tossed a look over her shoulder. Janet had risen to all fours on the railing. Her back was arched, and a ridge of fur had risen along her spine. A high-pitched yelp tore through the night. Janet jumped a foot into the air, landed on the porch, and tore past Cassie, claws scrabbling against the wood planks.

What the . . . ?

Cassie suddenly noticed her hands were tingling. It was a peculiar sensation, almost like a warning somehow. "Eliza," she whispered, "did you hear that?"

Her sister leaned against the doorframe and closed her eyes.

That was probably a no. Cassie shook her shoulder. "You go ahead. Wait for me at the bottom of the stairs. I'm right behind you."

Cassie shuffled back out to the edge of the porch. She peered in the direction the sound had come from, but the fog made it impossible to see more than a few feet. She waited. It must have been a fox. Or a raccoon. Or a fox fighting a raccoon. Whatever it had been, it sounded like some poor creature had met its end. As Cassie stared into the swirling mist, the thought of being watched by someone or something hidden in the fog returned. She retreated in slow steps, catching sight of the jack-o'-lantern still staring at her. "What are you looking at, Creepy?"

The jack-o'-lantern held its fanged smile.

Cassie slowly reached back for the door to push it open wider. It was ridiculous, but suddenly she didn't want to turn her back to the grinning pumpkin.

Stupid gourd. He should have been a pie.

"Watch yourself," she said, tossing it one last look. "Or I'm going to light you up." As she turned and stepped inside, a hot gust of air whooshed behind her, and a fiery glow reflected off the outer wall of the house. She whipped back around. The jack-o'-lantern eyes were still black pits, and the candle was still in the mug.

"I'm losing it." Cassie pressed her perfectly normal, non-tingling hand to her forehead. "I'm absolutely losing it."

After spending her formative years reading *Grimms' Fairy Tales* and stirring up potions in the creek behind her house, **Auralee Wallace** knew she would grow up to be a witch. When that didn't work out, she decided becoming a writer was the next best thing. Now Auralee is the author of multiple novels, including the Otter Lake mystery series and the Evenfall Witches B&B mysteries. She lives in Ottawa with her husband, three kids, two cats, and one dog.

VISIT AURALEE WALLACE ONLINE

AuraleeWallace.com

AuraleeWallace.Author